THE MURALIST

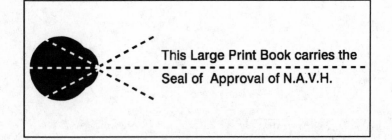

This Large Print Book carries the
Seal of Approval of N.A.V.H.

THE MURALIST

B. A. SHAPIRO

THORNDIKE PRESS
A part of Gale, Cengage Learning

GALE
CENGAGE Learning·

Farmington Hills, Mich • San Francisco • New York • Waterville, Maine
Meriden, Conn • Mason, Ohio • Chicago

GALE
CENGAGE Learning®

LIBRARY OF CONGRESS CATALOGING-IN-PUBLICATION DATA

Shapiro, Barbara A., 1951-
    The muralist / B. A. Shapiro. — Large print edition.
      pages cm. — (Thorndike Press large print basic)
    ISBN 978-1-4104-8408-6 (hardback) — ISBN 1-4104-8408-4 (hardcover)
    1. Artists—New York (State)—New York—20th century—Fiction. 2. Missing
persons—Fiction. 3. New York (N.Y.)—Social life and customs—20th
century—Fiction. 4. Large type books. I. Title.
    PS3569.H3385M87 2015b
    813'.54—dc23   2015035700

Published in 2015 by arrangement with Algonquin Books of Chapel
Hill, a division of Workman Publishing

Printed in the United States of America
1 2 3 4 5 6 7 19 18 17 16 15

For Emma and Charlotte,
the wonders of my world

Eleanor's failure to force her husband to admit more refugees remained her deepest regret at the end of her life.

— Doris Kearns Goodwin, *No Ordinary Time*

The Muralist is a novel in which fictional characters mingle with historical figures. All incidents and dialogue are products of the author's imagination and are not to be construed as real. Minor alterations in the timing and placement of persons and events were made as the story dictated, the details of which can be found in the Author's Note at the end of the book. In all other respects, any resemblance to persons living or dead is entirely coincidental.

1
Danielle, 2015

It was there when I arrived that morning, sitting to the right of my desk, ostensibly no different from the other half-dozen cartons on the floor, flaps bent back, paintings haphazardly poking out. As soon as I saw it, I ripped off my gloves, dropped to my knees, and pawed through the contents. I didn't realize I wasn't breathing until my chest began to ache and little black dots jumped around the edges of my vision.

I stood, hung up my coat and scarf, reminded myself that this needed time, thoughtful research, judgments deduced from fact not desire. But I did know my Abstract Expressionists. Their early paintings as well as their more famous later ones. Jackson Pollock before his drips, Mark Rothko before color block, when Lee Krasner and Willem de Kooning worked representationally. And there was a stirring of recognition, a sense of knowing this was no ordinary cardboard box, no ordinary find.

There were over a dozen paintings, not particularly large, three by four feet was the biggest, small for the Abstract Expressionists, even the early works. One by one, I propped them against the walls and across my desk, put a couple on top of a pile of art books. I inhaled the musty aroma of dust and aged paint, wondered where they had been all these years, who had touched them, loved them, forgotten them.

Rumor had it that this carton was the proverbial box in the attic, uncovered by a bereaved family and full of priceless masterpieces. These rumors are all too common around here and rarely pan out, but the odds were actually better than usual that this was the real deal. In the early 1940s, the WPA/FAP, the art division of the Works Progress Administration, one of Roosevelt's New Deal employment programs, was canceled without notice; the artists were unceremoniously dismissed, all the work they'd previously submitted disposed of.

Hundreds of these pieces were sold at four cents a pound to junkmen while the rest ended up on the sidewalk, some grabbed by art lovers and dealers, most left for trash. This was the possible origin story for these paintings, with the added prospect that some might be early works by the Abstract Expressionists, many of whom were employed by the WPA way before they became who they became.

Even an auction house like ours, with one of the most illustrious names in the business, routinely accepts art brought in by laypersons, in this case the Farrell family of Blue Bell, Pennsylvania. Our fear of missing the Big One is almost as great as our fear of authenticating one that isn't big at all. We try to get people to email photographs, but this request is often ignored, and these mostly valueless pieces are shunted off to cataloguers (i.e., me and my wary band of late-twenty-somethings with undergraduate art degrees from classy colleges and no real marketable skills). Researching these wayward children and logging them into the database is how we make our so-called livings.

Most of the paintings in front of me weren't signed, which wasn't surprising, as the WPA's main concern was with the art and not the artist. I didn't recognize the signatures on the few that had them but some of the unsigned . . . Was it possible? Could that be one of Rothko's geometric cityscapes? A Krasner still life? Another looked similar to de Kooning's early figurative drawings. And two reeked of Pollock's over-the-top symbolism.

My interest in art, and in the Abstract Expressionists, stems from my grandfather's stories about my mysterious great-aunt Alizée — although when I enrolled in art school I'd pictured myself in a studio, not a cubicle. According to family legend, Alizée worked for the WPA and hung out in New York City with all the up-and-coming artists of the day. Grand-père claimed they were her friends, lovers even, and that she had a significant influence on their work. A point my mother declares is unverified speculation. Aunt Alizée disappeared under shadowy circumstances in 1940, so she isn't telling.

I visualized her two paintings, the only ones in existence as far as anyone knew: the colors, the brushstrokes, the brash energy. Grand-mère had given them to me because I was the artist in the family, and they overwhelmed the scant wall space of my tiny studio apartment, dwarfed the furniture. One was a beguiling and slightly disturbing abstraction, a shape-shifting ode to lily pads or clouds or fish, which I called *Lily Pads* because it sounded better than *Clouds* or *Fish.* The other, *Turned,* was in-your-face unavoidable, neither abstract nor realistic,

14

something else completely, a smash to the solar plexus.

Unfortunately, in opposition to the gut reaction I'd felt for Pollock, Rothko, and Krasner, I saw nothing in any of the paintings that bore a resemblance to my aunt's work. Over its lifetime, the WPA/FAP had employed hundreds, if not thousands, of artists who created hundreds of thousands of paintings and sculptures, so the chance that any of these were made by my aunt was more than slim. As was the chance the carton contained any WPA paintings at all. Still.

"Hey," my friend Nguyen interrupted my thoughts. His first name was Tony, but no one ever called him that. "Can I see what you've got here? Seems like the least you can do after I finagled it for you." He was an aspiring lifer at Christie's, an associate specialist, two-going-on-three pay grades above me, and had always wanted to work for an auction house. He played the kowtowing lifer's game with a wry selfawareness that amused us both. I was in it mostly for the inadequate benefits and piddling semi-monthly check.

I stepped into the hallway so he could slide into the cubicle. He was, after all, the one who'd alerted me to the box's possibilities and then sent it my way.

He pointed to the maybe-Rothko. "His New York City series? Has his sense of alienation."

"So does a lot of art from that period," I argued for argument's sake.

"True." His eyes scanned the rest. "Anything that might be your aunt's?" We had lunch together at least once a week, and there were few secrets between us.

I shook my head. "My mother claims there aren't any more."

"How does she know?"

"That's what I said."

"If your aunt could disappear, why couldn't her paintings?"

"The assumption's that she was too crazy to paint any more. Remember? That whole mental institution thing."

He waved me off. "You sound like your mother."

"Ouch," I cried. "Anything but that."

He turned toward the space where a door would be if I had one. "If any of these turn out to be real," he said as he walked down the hallway, "you've got a hell of a lot of work to do, girl."

Nguyen was right. It's much easier to research a painting that proves to be worthless than one that might be valuable. The actual decision wouldn't be mine, that was for someone with a PhD and reams of experience authenticating art. I was only responsible for the preliminary forensics, but months of hard labor lay in front of me before I passed on the canvases. Everything from dating the age of each one to determining the chemical composition of the paint and the degree of rust on the nails holding the frames together. All of which would be redone after me, and then redone again. There are a lot of unscrupulous people around and too many galleries and auction houses had recently been caught with their pants down.

I flipped over the maybe-Rothko to check the backside of the canvas. To my semitrained eye, it looked to be anywhere from fifty to a hundred years old, which would be about right. As I was returning the painting to my desk, an odd ridge on the back caught my eye. I wiped away what was probably seventy-five years of dust with a cloth I kept around for just this purpose.

It wasn't a ridge. It was a vellum envelope. I grabbed my tweezers and carefully pulled it off. Inside the envelope was another painting, roughly a two-foot-square canvas. I checked the backs of all the other paintings. Under heavy layers of dust, I found two more vellum envelopes, each enclosing another two-foot-square canvas. When I turned over the paintings to which the envelopes were attached, facing me were the maybe-Rothko, the maybe-Krasner, and one of the maybe-Pollocks.

I took the three square canvases into the hallway where the light was better. I knelt, ignoring the sharp blast of pain as my knees hit the thinly carpeted concrete. The three appeared to be the work of a single artist; all had a deep red undertone and contained images of abstracted flora and fauna, two had pieces of newsprint pasted to parts of the canvas. But the styles were quite different: one was more surrealistic, one more cubist, and the third an unusual combination of techniques. All were stunning.

As I stared at them, I was rocked by a wave of vertigo. I pressed my hand to the wall to steady myself. Then my brain caught up with my physical reaction, and I understood where the dizziness and trepidation came from. I told myself I was mistaken, that it couldn't be true. But the colors, the brushstrokes, the energy, the mix of styles . . . The paintings looked like my aunt's work. Could these squares be the creation of the enigmatic heroine of my

18

childhood? Not possible and yet possible still.

Alizée, so charismatic, headstrong, and talented. Disappeared into pre–World War II New York City at almost the same time the rest of her family disappeared into Europe. Just as lost, just as gone, but with no bombs, no concentration camps, no lists of the dead, no explanation. The stoic silence of my Holocaust-surviving grandparents shrouded what little might have been known until the carton showed up in my office, lifted the veil, and let me inside.

2
ALIZÉE, 1939

Alizée painted at a makeshift desk, an overturned shipping crate with one side sawed off to accommodate her legs. According to the label, it once held uniforms for butchers; she hadn't known butchers wore uniforms. She worked in a warehouse that jutted into the Hudson River where eight different mural projects were being created side by side, and armies of artists clutching charcoal or brushes or marble pestles bustled through the yawning space.

Two years ago, she'd returned to the States after seven years in France. Seven more than she would have chosen, but she'd learned early on that the vagaries of fate had far more power than she did. She was nineteen at the time and had been living for that moment, had done battle with her family, her friends, even her art teachers, to realize it.

Nevertheless, at the first sight of Lady

Liberty, she was swamped by a wrenching sadness and that odd sense of floating above her own head. From afar, she watched the shadows darken the space around her as she stood on the ship's deck, searching for people bustling with energy and opportunity, the ones she remembered and the ones she knew weren't there anymore.

Obviously, the country was in the midst of a depression, and she'd thought she was prepared for this. But the mute shipyards bounded by weathered warehouses, their wide doors swung open to reveal their lack of wares, unsettled her. It was well into the morning of a working day, yet grimy men, newsboy hats cocked, sat on posts along empty piers, smoking cigarettes and watching the boat's arrival with no interest whatsoever.

This was where the memories lived, and that would be difficult, but it was, she somehow knew, the only place her real life could begin. And she was right. Now, although the empty warehouses and grimy men were still perched on the New York City docks, she'd beaten back most of the sadness and moved on.

"Looks swell." Lee leaned over her shoulder and squinted at the tiny four-by-six-inch canvas she was painting. "If you like wooden patriotism."

"My favorite," Alizée said dryly. Although she got a kick out of making fun of the stiff, overly enthusiastic style imposed by the WPA, she wasn't about to complain about receiving a paycheck to produce art. Even if other artists actually designed the works she was painting, it was a hell of a good gig.

Lee squatted, looked more closely at the small panels. She'd taken over directing the mural from a boy who'd gone to fight Franco in the Spanish Civil War, receiving the unacknowledged and unpaid promotion because she'd worked for the WPA longer than any of the other assistants. She was ostensibly Alizée's boss, although neither of them thought of it that way; they'd been friends long before this particular project. Lee frowned at the six four-by-six-foot pastel studies Alizée was miniaturizing, the original WPA-approved drawings for the mural.

Alizée didn't like the frown. "What?" she demanded in mock dismay, then lit a cigarette. "Now you want to change it after I've worked my butt off for a week?"

It would take time to redo her efforts, but that was all it was: An effort. A job. Her own paintings were her real work. And those were very different from these: less tangible, more multidimensional, more in the process of becoming something else. When she worked on the mural, she was outside it; it was separate from her. With her own canvases, there was no space in between.

"Something queer about it." Lee cocked her head to the side. She was far from beautiful, but there was a voluptuousness about her, both in body and temperament, that made men forget all about her plain face. Lee claimed she didn't like going to parties with Alizée because, as she put it, "Alizée captures the room," which was ridiculous. Lee garnered attention, particularly male attention, everywhere she went.

Alizée walked up to the original drawings, thought for a moment, then rubbed her palm vigorously along the left legs of three shipbuilders shouldering a large slab of wood until the original lines of the sketch were indistinct. Then she started refashioning their calves. "Better?"

Lee nodded and pointed to the men's shirts. "A little more blue mixed in with the gray, I think."

"Jumble Shop?" Alizée asked.

"Sure." Lee sat back down at her desk, which was next to Alizée's.

After work, they often went up to the West Village for a beer dosed with arguments about the future of art, the meaning of art, the political in art, the abstract in art, just about anything in or of art. It reminded Alizée of the Dôme café in Paris, but without all the depressed faces and gloomy war talk.

A Frenchman might complain that the artists who flowed in and out of the Shop in paint-splattered waves drank too much, debated too boorishly, laughed too loudly, and didn't look beyond the streets of New York for either their art or politics, but he would also be forced to admit that they knew how to have fun. To Alizée, it was as if each person at the Shop was years younger than his or her European counterpart.

She loved the levity, the lightness, but more than that, she reveled in the shared certainty that being able to make art was the most amazing gift anyone could receive. Granted, it was tough for everyone these days, particularly tough for artists, and particularly, particularly tough for female artists. But just last week, her usually critical teacher, Hans Hofmann, proclaimed that one of her paintings was so good he would never have believed it was painted by a girl. He'd meant it as the highest compliment, and she'd taken it as such.

She had the mural job, which was no little thing, and she was happy, proud, of that, although it was difficult to get the galleries to show anything painted by a girl, especially if the paintings were abstract. But if she was going to spend her days working representationally, she damn well wasn't going to do the same on her own time just to please some pigheaded gallery owner. So she went to the Shop to drink and gripe with her like-minded comrades.

Lee leaned toward Alizée's desk, her eyes shining wickedly. "Forgot to tell you Bill and Jack said they can't make it to the Shop until a bit later, but Mark said he'd be there around five, so let's leave here on the early side."

Alizée shrugged.

Lee grinned. "He's such a wonderful, sweet bear of a man."

Alizée picked up a piece of pastel and bent over her work, shielding her face with her hair.

"Oh those soft, sensuous lips . . ." Lee whispered in her ear.

Alizée shook her off with an awkward laugh. She wasn't about to discuss Mark. With Lee or with anyone else. There was nothing to discuss. Would never be.

She turned back to her mock-up: a miniature of the six-panel mural to be hung on the walls of a high-school dining hall in

Washington, DC. Last week, she'd constructed a three-sided box, one-twelfth the size of the actual dining room with cutouts for the windows and doors. This week, she was using pastels to color in the six panels, at one-twelfth their size, and would hang them on the tiny walls exactly as they would be at the high school. This was the final step before the actual painting on canvas would begin. When the panels were complete, they would be shipped to DC and pasted on the walls.

It felt like playing instead of working, although it was most definitely work. This warehouse and much more were part of President Roosevelt's New Deal: the WPA, FAP, TRAP, PWA, a whole alphabet of programs funded by the government in the hope of ending the Depression. Unfortunately, these programs had been going on for almost as long as Alizée had been in France, and still no one seemed to have any money.

Occasionally bureaucrats appeared at the warehouse and stood around looking decidedly ill at ease in their suits and bowler hats. The president's wife came once, but she was completely at ease. Mrs. Franklin Roosevelt climbed up ladders, unconcerned that she might get paint on her dress. She stopped and talked with the artists, asking questions and listening intently to the answers. Even answers from the assistants. You'd never see Mme. Albert Lebrun or Mme. Léon Blum do anything like that.

Alizée didn't much miss university in Paris or even the brief touch of success she'd had there, but she did miss her family. Often quite desperately: Oncle and Tante, who'd swooped in after her parents were killed and raised her as their own; Babette, who'd squeezed her hand and whispered, "I'm more than your cousin now, I'm your sister," on the night she first arrived; her older brother, Henri; little cousin Alain. All of them on the other side of the ocean.

But Henri would be coming to the States as soon he completed his exams, and Babette and her family, currently in Germany, talked of coming over, too. Alizée had given up a lot to return to America, but it was exactly where she wanted to be. She told herself this when the sorrow and loneliness she kept coiled deep inside pressed beyond the margins she worked so hard to maintain.

In New York, she was free to paint in the style of the moderns, something she'd been yearning to do. To study at the feet of Hans Hofmann with no fear of the octopus reach of Adolf Hitler's decrees against modern art, his desire to suppress anything that didn't smack of militarism and obedience. Especially if it was nonfigurative. The impact of his 1937 exhibition titled *Entartete Kunst* — Degenerate Art — deriding Picasso, Van Gogh, Matisse, Chagall, and many others, was unfortunately being felt across Europe, even in Paris. In New York, she could lose herself to the newness of abstraction, the fever of it, drawn to its insubstantial yet substantial nature, its difficulty and the wonder of the intuitive connections. This was worth everything.

It bothered her that there wasn't a single abstract mural being constructed in the warehouse. FDR didn't like modern art much more than Hitler did, and the president wanted the WPA paintings to be representations of what they were calling "the American Scene." *Putain.* Didn't they understand that you could represent the American scene without being representational?

The mural to the right of Alizée's, headed for a post office in Lexington, Massachusetts, was even more wooden than the shipbuilders. A completely flat depiction of Paul Revere's ride. The mural to the left was much better, in the style of the Mexicans, full of colorful ironworkers laboring

28

amid exaggerated piping and sprockets and looming machines. But for all its boldness and action, it, too, was completely figurative.

There was a commotion behind her, and she turned to see Eleanor Roosevelt striding through the door, followed by a cadre of men in business suits. The director and two supervisors swooped down on them, and soon more than a dozen men surrounded the First Lady.

"I thought she wasn't coming until next week," Alizée whispered to Lee, although there was no reason to speak softly: the room was abuzz. Mrs. Roosevelt was a moving force behind the WPA/FAP, and every artist on the floor revered her for that.

Lee stared at the president's wife. "She's so tall."

"That's all you can say about the most amazing woman in the world?"

Lee looked at Alizée with a straight face. "She's so tall."

They watched the First Lady with the fawning men. Although she was close to six feet, Mrs. Roosevelt stood upright and radiated an interest in her surroundings that was palpable. There was no doubt this was a woman who made things happen.

"Bet she'd like to talk to a girl," Alizée

said. "Let's go over there."

"Yeah, like those swelled heads are going to let us join their little coffee klatch."

It was even worse than that: when it was announced that the First Lady was coming, the rank and file had been ordered not to bother her. They were to pretend she wasn't there, to keep working, even harder than usual, and only speak if spoken to. Like good little children.

Alizée looked at their mural, at Paul Revere's ride next to it, at the ironworkers. All so uninspired and conventional. Someone needed to open horizons, to let new ideas in. And who better than Eleanor Roosevelt? Alizée touched her mother's engagement ring, which always hung on a chain between her breasts: a conduit. *Stay with me, Maman.* She stood.

"What?" Lee demanded.

"I'm going to ask her why there aren't any abstract murals. See if she can do anything about it."

"You could get kicked off the project," Lee insisted. "Don't."

Alizée strode toward the assemblage and edged in close to the First Lady. Exhilarated by her boldness, she waited for her moment, heart pounding.

One of the supervisors, an overweight

middle-aged man named Norton Zimmern, met her eye and gave his head a sharp tilt toward her desk. She hesitated. She couldn't afford to lose this job. But Norton was an old windbag, full of noise and little action, and this was important. She slipped to the other side of Mrs. Roosevelt.

When Mrs. Roosevelt stepped toward another mural, Alizée intercepted her. "I just want to thank you for this opportunity, Mrs. Roosevelt." Alizée's eyes were inches below the First Lady's, a rare occurrence for one who was used to being the tallest girl in any group.

"You're most welcome, I'm sure," Mrs. Roosevelt said politely, but kept moving.

"I'm Alizée Benoit," she said, thrusting her hand out. "And if it weren't for you, I'd be stuffing envelopes — if I were lucky enough to get that job — instead of painting."

The First Lady had no choice but to shake Alizée's hand. "I'm so happy to hear that, Miss Benoit. That was exactly our intention. If we're going to pay plumbers and carpenters for their work, why not pay artists to do theirs?"

"And this way you get original art in the places the plumbers and carpenters build." Alizée heard the artificiality in her own voice and flushed. "I have a question for you."

Mrs. Roosevelt began to move away. "It was very nice to meet you, Miss Benoit," she said. "Please continue your good work."

Alizée sent up another call to her mother and fell in step with the First Lady. "I noticed that all of the WPA murals are representational," she continued as if she hadn't just been dismissed, "and wondered why there's only one style. Why not some abstract murals, too? There are lots of us doing nonrepresentational work right here in New York. All over the country. It's innovative, forceful, and very American. So I was thinking it should be included, and I wondered if you agreed."

Mrs. Roosevelt's eyes flashed with merriment. "And what is it about this abstract art that makes it so innovative and forceful?"

Alizée took a deep breath. "It goes deep. Much deeper than just a picture of what we can already see. It's not easy to make sense of — or to paint — but when you do, there's nothing like it. It's magical, really. Interpreting what's going on inside." She tapped her heart. "And then putting it on the outside. The real experience of living."

The First Lady stopped walking. "I don't understand."

Alizée vibrated with the need to articulate this, to make Mrs. Roosevelt appreciate what burned inside her. "We want to get at what life *feels* like. The emotions we all share. Our commonality. To make our invisible life visible. Or," she added lamely, frustrated with her inability to put it into words, "or experienceable."

"I'm very sorry, my dear" — Mrs. Roosevelt gave a small laugh — "but the president likes pictures where he can recognize people. I'm not sure he'd recognize emotions."

"But you might." Alizée touched the ring again. "If you just gave it a chance."

Norton tapped her arm. "I'm sure Mrs. Roosevelt would like to see the rest of the murals."

"I'm sure she would," Alizée agreed, turning back to the First Lady. There was no point in retreating now. "I know you're very busy, but if you'd like to come to my studio, I can show you some of my paintings. That way you'll be able to understand better what I wasn't very good at describing."

"Why, that's a lovely offer, Miss Benoit," Mrs. Roosevelt said in a tone that conveyed she actually meant it. "I may just take you up on that."

"Please do," Alizée said. "And if you like

anything you see, I'd love you to have it. I'd give it to you, of course. A gift." She grabbed a small scrap of paper, scribbled her address, and offered it. "And maybe you'll decide that abstract art should be a part of the WPA."

Mrs. Roosevelt took the address and dropped it in her pocketbook, then looked at Alizée, obviously trying to contain her amusement. "And if the WPA did deem abstract art worthy, I'm guessing you have an idea of how you'd like to be involved?"

Alizée was stunned. Had she actually succeeded in convincing the First Lady? She didn't know what to say but had to say something. "I'd . . . I'd love to be the first one to design and supervise a nonrepresentational mural." She swept her arms around the warehouse. "And one for my friend Lee Krasner, too, please. Over there." She waved to Lee, who was watching them wide-eyed. "Miss Krasner's a wonderful artist. If the two of us could have our own abstract projects, I'd happily kiss your feet."

"I don't think that will be necessary," Mrs. Roosevelt said, swallowing a smile.

3
ALIZÉE

Alizée didn't go directly to the Jumble Shop after work. She wanted to clean up and change her clothes first. Both her stylish cousin Babette and coming of age in France had instilled a fashion sense that clashed with dirty overalls outside the studio. Lee's mention of Mark only served to heighten this.

She'd made a couple of scarves out of a piece of red-and-purple material she'd found at the five-and-dime which, when twisted together, would give some zip to her well-worn gray dress. Maybe that smart little hat Tante gave her the day she left Arles. "French chic," Lee always teased when Alizée showed up at the Shop or parties in her unusual outfits, which was fine with Alizée. The last thing she wanted was to dress like everyone else.

She also needed time alone to reflect on her conversation with Mrs. Roosevelt. Had she actually told the wife of the president of the United States that the WPA needed abstract murals? Criticized the ones that were being created? And then suggested that she, Alizée — who had been working non-representationally for less than two years — was capable of designing and overseeing the painting of one? *Merde.* Apparently, she had. She was both embarrassed and pleased by her daring.

When she reached her building in the Village, a letter with French postage was poking out of her cubbyhole. She saw it was from Henri and cried out in relief. She hadn't heard from him, or anyone else in her family, in almost two months. Henri was seven years her senior, born in France. She'd been born in Massachusetts, where the four of them lived until Henri returned to Arles to go to the *école secondaire* and stay with Tante and Oncle. She'd always idolized him. She still did.

Most of her memories of the days after her parents' deaths were mercifully hidden, vanished into unreachable folds of her brain. But there were a few, and they were painfully clear. Coming into the dining room right after the funeral, every surface weighed down by platters of food, the overwhelming odor of sugar and perfume, the horde of compassionate faces rushing toward her. Turning and running to the bathroom, vomiting what little she had in her stomach. Tante coaxing her back, the room falling into silence when she returned. In France, it had been just as bad. The teacher giving her a long hug in front of the whole class on her first day of school. The other children's wide-eyed awe and curiosity. The old woman in the *boulangerie* who always slipped her an extra cake and called her *infortunée.*

She'd detested the attention and pity heaped on her, despised the pathetic being she became under their weight. So she walled herself off from those who professed to understand what she was going through, from the sad doe eyes that went along with their untruths. She wrapped her head in scarves, drifted above them, didn't bother to respond. There was no reason to: they understood nothing. Only her family understood. Which was why she'd hadn't spoken about her parents to anyone beyond the family. Not to her new friends. Not to her teachers. Not to a single person in New York.

She headed up the stairs to her flat, clutching the envelope. Maybe he'd already taken and passed his exams. Maybe he was coming sooner than he'd thought. She wanted to open it, but there was so little light in the narrow and twisty stairwell that she was afraid she'd rip the letter. As she rushed to the fourth floor, she wondered again why it had been so long without any word from France. And why no news from Babette? She even missed Tante's predictable questions in her monthly letters: *Have you met any nice Jewish boys? Anyone closer to your own age?*

She thought about Mark and smiled. He was a nice Jewish boy, closer to her age than her French boyfriend, Philippe, who'd struck terror in her aunt's heart. But Alizée didn't think Tante would be any more pleased with a poor, married artist than she'd been with a Catholic who was five years older than Alizée.

Her parents wouldn't have been bothered by Philippe's age or religion, which Tante knew, and which was why she'd stopped talking about it but never stopped worrying. Maman and Papa had been scientists, bohemians uninterested in religion or conventionality, and they'd adored being part of what people were now calling the Roaring Twenties.

She remembered the parties, the high spirits, sitting on the floor of their tiny bedroom watching Maman get ready for a night out, putting on her makeup, her short dresses, ropes of fake pearls. And she remembered Maman baking *pain d'amande* cookies with Henri and her. The coarse golden sugar, stirring the almonds and flour into the butter, watching Maman slice the dough as thinly as possible. To this day, the scent of almonds meant safety, innocence. And excruciating pain.

Her social, high-spirited parents had been very different from her aunt and uncle, both of whom were teachers, introverted and studious, hardly ever going out unless it had something to do with university or the synagogue. It took a while for Alizée to grow comfortable with this. But in the end, it was their quiet and unwavering kindness, much more than all those psychiatrists she'd seen, that had saved her.

Alizée grunted. Her door was stuck, as always, but after more than a few jiggles, it finally clicked. She lived in what was called a cold-water flat. No hot water, no heat on the weekends. But it was big, huge actually, with a fifteen-foot ceiling, good light, plenty of room to paint, and somewhere to sleep. Most important, she didn't have to share it with anyone else. The better places had hot water, but they cost more than she could afford by herself, and privacy was everything to her. Sometimes she needed to sleep a lot and didn't want people around; other times she was so energetic, people didn't want to be around her. It was better to boil the water for her bath.

She shook off her coat and dropped it on what stood in for a kitchen table, a rough piece of wood centered above two piles of cinder blocks. That, along with a few battered chairs, a mattress and a couch that listed to one side was all the furniture she had. The remainder of the space was taken up with easels, finished and unfinished paintings, painting supplies. It suited her just fine.

She opened the letter, which had taken nearly three months to arrive.

3 January 1939
Arles

Ma petite soeur,
I am a horrible brother and an even more horrible correspondent, but as these are things you already know and forgive I will not bother to apologize. But I know you will not forgive me if I do not answer the many questions in your last letter.

Yes, I have seen Tante and Oncle. I had dinner with them and Alain three nights ago and everyone is as well as can be expected. You would not recognize our little cousin. He is now a teenager and is awkward and self-conscious and all arms and legs and so easy to tease. Tante brought out some pictures of you at his age. You look just as awkward and self-conscious as he does but maybe a little bit prettier. Ha!

And yes, Dr. Patenaude is confident I am ready to take my exams and has agreed to my choice of surgery, which as you will see by the end of this letter is very fortuitous. The rest of your questions will be answered as I bring you up to date.

I have not mentioned this before as I thought it would all blow over and there was no need to worry you, but things are getting more difficult here. Babette and Pierre are leaving Germany and are insisting we leave France also. When things did not improve after Kristallnacht, Babette declared that none of us can stay in Europe.

It has taken them almost a year and a small fortune to acquire visas to enter Cuba. They will take a ship called the

41

SS *St. Louis,* wait on the island for the American visas to arrive and then come to New York. They are scheduled to leave on May 13. Tante is worried baby Gabrielle is too young for the crossing, but Babette will hear nothing about it. I am sure they will contact you as soon as they arrive.

Although things are not so bad in France, Babette predicts the Germans will invade Poland and come here next. Most here believe if Hitler dares to step on French soil he will be immediately vanquished, but Oncle and I are not as convinced that we will be victorious against the armies of the Third Reich. So although none of this can be considered good news, you will be happy to hear that Oncle and Tante will come with me to America as soon as my exams are completed. And of course Alain.

I have already approached the authorities and discovered that French visas cannot be granted unless we have papers allowing us to enter the United States. Although we have heard this process can be challenging, it seems that as you are a US citizen you should have little difficulty. The sooner you can get the visas for us the more quickly the officials here will be able to work, and the sooner the whole family will be together again.

Please think of me often as I think of you and send a wire when you have the visas so we can prepare. I will let you know our plans as soon as they are set.

Ton frère qui t'aime,
Henri

Was it possible? Everyone here with her, in New York? Everyone she loved. She couldn't imagine anything better, and her mind raced. She would find an apartment. No, better to find two. One for Tante, Oncle, and Alain, the other for Babette and her family. If they weren't able to afford it, one would do to start. Henri could stay with her until he found a job.

Family dinners. Those beautiful little girls. Sophie would be almost four, full of words and opinions, a real person. Alizée had never met Gabrielle, and tears filled her eyes at the thought of nuzzling the baby. Of Henri's teasing. Of shopping with Babette. Tante's worry and hugs. Oncle's calming presence.

She reread the letter, and her exhilaration faded. Were things in Europe really that bad? Could her family be in danger this very minute? But no, Henri had always been overcautious, something their mother used to tease him about, referring to him as her "wise old man" when he was just a young boy: sober, thoughtful, ferreting out the cloud in every silver lining — another of her mother's lines. But Babette was a completely different story.

Babette was the wild one in the family, and everyone said she was just like Alizée's father: impetuous, fearless, a mathematical savant. She was four years older than Alizée, dark-haired and blue-eyed, and when Alizée arrived in France, she'd followed her flamboyant cousin around like a puppy. It almost broke Alizée's heart when Babette married Pierre and went to Berlin for graduate school, but after her cousin made a few trips back to Arles, Alizée was relieved to find that married or not, Babette was still Babette.

And this was the problem. For if Babette was afraid to stay in Germany, was willing to put her small children on some rickety boat to some godforsaken island, it meant the danger was real.

As she pushed through the door of the Jumble Shop, her eyes went directly to "their" table, long and narrow, covered with a flowered cloth. Artists of every ilk and political leaning filled the place nightly, but she and her cadre of modernists sat at a table where only those who thought Picasso was god were welcome.

It was late. She hadn't been ready to talk about Henri's letter, not the good parts and definitely not the bad. Nor had she been up for being cheerful and flirty, feigning light-heartedness where there was none. So she'd stayed home for another hour, circling the flat again and again, shards of ideas — steps to take, people to contact, potential problems — shooting through her head. Making plans helped her keep the darkness at bay.

Mark was at the table, along with Lee, Gorky, and Bill. Although the Shop was open until three in the morning, most of the artists had day jobs, usually on the project, so they came early and left early to work in their studios — also known as their apartments — at night. She waved to them and turned to the bar. She was going to need a drink, more likely three or four, to get through an evening of pretending nothing in her life had changed. She bought a beer and sat down next to Bill.

He gave her a slow, welcoming smile and touched his glass to hers. "And how is our lady of the mural tonight?" Bill was a beautiful man, tall and blond, with perfect features and an intense ice-blue gaze. Too pretty for her taste. She preferred Mark's large frame and crooked smile, his deeply intelligent, if brooding, dark eyes.

"Bushed." She threw her arms out in a theatrical gesture, flinging herself into the well-worn role of carefree Alizée, acting as if there had been no letter from Henri, no trips to Cuba, nothing to fear. "Totally and completely bushed." She looked at the sandwich Bill was holding. "And hungry." Which she wasn't. Her stomach was squeezed into such a tight fist that she wondered if she'd ever be able to eat again.

Gorky pointed his cigarette at Bill. "De Kooning here was just saying he was going to buy a few more for the table."

Bill, who couldn't work for the WPA because he wasn't an American citizen, was a commercial artist as well as a carpenter and made more money than the rest of them combined. He winked at Alizée. "I said no such thing."

"I thought you were coming straight from the warehouse." Lee eyed Alizée's dress and scarf with a smirk, then threw a glance at Mark. "What took you so long?"

She was saved from answering when Jack walked through the door and plopped himself down across from her. He was already tight, as was often the case, despite his fling last year with Jungian psychoanalysis and a lengthy stay at Bloom Sanatorium that was supposed to cure his drinking. Not that the others couldn't hold their own: by the end of the evening Mark, Gorky, and Bill would be, too. But Jack had an edge the others didn't have; he was volatile, and you never knew from moment to moment what kind of a jam he'd get himself in.

She'd met him at a party at Bill's. Jack, who she'd never seen before, grabbed her and whirled her onto the improvised dance floor. Slurring his words, he demanded, all loud and slobbery, to know if she liked to fuck. She told him she did but not with him. Everyone, including Jack, had roared. He was considered a wastrel by many, but she was fond of his bad-boy foolishness.

"Hey Pollock," she said with a grin she hoped didn't look as forced as it felt. "Heard you punched in yesterday wearing your pajamas."

"It's a rotten shame that those untalented government assholes expect an artist to be awake at eight in the morning." Jack waved his cigarette dismissively. "Or expect us to 'punch in.' " Both Jack and Mark were on the easel project, which allowed artists to work in their own studios during the day, checking in at the WPA office each morning.

"Especially when said artist has been tying one on all night," Lee noted dryly.

Jack raised his glass and gave Lee one of his most winning smiles. She colored slightly.

"Were your balls all shriveled up from the cold when you got home?" Gorky taunted Jack. "Did Ellie mind?"

"Hey, what about that sandwich?" Mark asked Bill. "Poor Alizée here is starving."

For the first time that evening, she looked directly at Mark. He locked his eyes onto hers, and although warmth began to spread between her legs, she turned away and quickly polished off her beer. She wasn't getting involved with a married man. Not now. Not ever.

"Can't have our most charming and talented artist succumbing to starvation," Bill said to Mark. Pretending to be sore, he pulled a dollar from his wallet, which Alizée plucked from his hand, glad for an excuse to leave the table.

She'd planned to get another beer along with the sandwich, but when she reached the bar she ordered a double shot of bourbon instead.

4
ALIZÉE

First thing the next morning, she went to the cramped, overheated office of the Emergency Rescue Committee, a private relief organization that arranged visas for European immigrants. A month earlier, she'd read about it in the *New Militant,* a Socialist Party newspaper, and was surprised she'd remembered the article. The plight of the workers was her concern, not European refugees. Until now.

She cleared her throat impatiently as she waited for the man at the desk to finish his phone call. He was slumped in his chair, tie loose around his neck, long hair curling into his collar. He was older, probably forty, with bloodshot eyes and a thick mustache. He looked as if he'd been up all night. And not because he'd been having fun.

When he finally put the receiver back in the cradle, he identified himself as Daniel Fleishman, the assistant director, and told her that yes, the fledgling group was trying to get refugees out of Europe.

"My brother, uncle, aunt, and cousin want to come here," she explained. "To New York. From France."

He nodded.

"They're afraid the Germans will invade France and make things difficult for the Jews." She paused for him to correct her assumption. When he didn't, she added, "Which I'm sure is an exaggeration."

He didn't correct this assumption either. "Are they originally from Germany?"

"They're all French, including my brother." She frowned. "Is that a problem?"

"Not necessarily. But we're focusing on people in the most immediate danger of persecution by the Nazis. Citizens, both Jewish and non-Jewish, of Germany, Austria, Czechoslovakia, Poland. People who've angered Hitler in some way and are trying to get out of the German-occupied countries. Does your family fall into any of those categories?"

"I can't imagine they've angered anyone. Which means they're safe, right?"

He ran his hand through his unruly hair, making it even more unruly. "At least for now."

She caught her breath. "For now?"

"To be frank, the visa situation isn't good." Mr. Fleishman laced his fingers together. "And probably isn't going to get any better. Not here and not in France. The US immigration laws are restrictive, and there are powerful individuals who want it to stay that way."

"What exactly does that mean?"

"People are afraid immigrants will take jobs from Americans. Or worse, that they're German spies in disguise, the Fifth Column, they call them. There's a lot of opposition."

"It doesn't have anything do with being Jewish?"

"Many of the people we hope to save aren't Jewish," he said, clearly weighing his words. "They're prominent politicians, artists, scientists, and others who've spoken out against the Third Reich."

She went rigid. "Are you saying the ERC's only getting visas for important people?"

Mr. Fleishman played with a pen on his desk. "It's our first priority at the moment."

"My uncle's a full professor at Université d'Arles," she told him. "Written many scholarly books and articles. My brother's just completing medical school. Is that important enough for you?"

"Have any of them written or said negative things about the Nazis?"

She crossed her arms. "I could tell them to."

Mr. Fleishman chuckled, but his eyes didn't look as if he'd found what she'd said particularly funny. "I'm not sure that would help — and it might put them in more danger."

"But according to you, that would be good."

He gave her a wry smile. "Miss Benoit, I admire your spunk, but you need to understand the situation we're up against. ERC's current plan is to raise at least three thousand dollars in contributions, which we hope will be enough to get nine, maybe ten, people out of Europe — if we're lucky enough to be able to get anyone out."

"And my family wouldn't be in that nine or ten." It was a statement, not a question.

"I'm sorry."

"So who else can help me? I've got to get the visas as quickly as possible."

"You could try the State Department, but I'm not sure they'll be of much use. The assistant secretary of state who oversees visas, a man named Breckinridge Long, appears to be more interested in keeping immigrants out than helping get them in."

She scrambled for a solution, her mind racing from one bad option to another.

"What if I could pay for the visas? Three hundred dollars for each one? That would be twelve hundred dollars. My aunt and uncle have some money," she said, hoping this was true. "You could just add them to the list of people you've already raised the money for. Get four more visas."

"I'm sorry but —"

"I'll send them a telegram today," she interrupted, not wanting to give him the opportunity to turn her down. "They'll send the money right away."

"That's not what we do. Not how it works."

"But it's something you *could* do."

"There's another group you might try. They're pushing for the US to take in more European refugees. It's called Americans for No Limits, ANL. They're larger and more political than we are. They hold rallies, run letter-writing campaigns, things like that." He scribbled down an address and handed it her. "They have weekly meetings. On Mondays, I think."

"Thank you." She took the paper. "But I still want to buy the visas. I'll bring you the money as soon as it's wired."

"I don't have the authority to approve something like that. I'd have to clear it with the director. But even if he okayed it, which

53

is unlikely, I don't know how many visas we're going to be able to get our hands on. As I told you, the State Department is essentially working against us."

She jumped up. "Thank you. I'll send my uncle a telegram right away."

"I'm not saying we can do anything for you." Mr. Fleishman stood and held up his hands as if to stop her. "Most likely won't be able to help you. I don't want to get your hopes up."

She left before he could say anything more.

5
DANIELLE, 2015

My ex-husband always claimed I would
never become a great artist because I had a
happy childhood. I blamed Sam for a lot of
things, but he wasn't the one who donated
my brushes and paint tubes to the middle
school on Bleecker Street. Nor was he the
one who went out and got a real job.

Frankly, it had been a relief to put down
my palette. It was liberating to allow myself
to be, rather than constantly striving to
become, living with the fear I'd never get
there, the humiliation that would follow
when I didn't. Still, when I find myself
caught up in some bureaucratic boondoggle
or catch a whiff of turpentine or feel that
gnawing emptiness in the back part of my
brain where I imagine my creativity lives, I
wonder about my choices.

I was trying not to wonder about choices
as I mentally prepared for my meeting with
Anatoly Armstrong, my boss's boss. I

needed his permission to pursue Alizée as a possible candidate in the quest to identify the artist responsible for the squares hidden behind the paintings. He and everyone at Christie's wanted them to belong to Mark Rothko, especially my own boss, George Bush — yes, that was actually his name, he was some kind of third cousin three times removed from the other three — and especially, especially the Farrell family, the owners of the carton. Everyone wanted me to butt out.

But I didn't want to butt out. Even though I was far from certain the squares were my aunt's, I needed to know either way. And if I didn't push it, no one else would give her a fair shot. It had taken me over a week, but I'd finally convinced George, who lived in terror of making a bad call that would halt his rise up the corporate ladder, that Anatoly should make the final decision. It was maneuvering like this that made me wish I'd inherited more of Alizée's talent so I could stay in my apartment and paint all day.

My family says I take after her. Or that's what Grand-père Henri always said, and he's the only one who actually knew her. Unfortunately, he died before I was old enough to figure out the right questions to ask. There are a few grainy photographs of her in her late teens, and even I can see the resemblance: the blonde curls, the excessively large mouth, an overabundance of freckles, the slight tilt of her head at the same angle as in photos of me. The genes work in strange ways.

As I said, she was the reason I studied art in the first place, and ever since I discovered a handful of historians who believed an unknown artist was integral to the development of the school of Abstract Expressionism, I'd imagined that artist was my missing aunt. These experts claimed, and I agreed, that there was an inexplicable gulf between the Abstract Expressionists' early work and their later work and that none of the artists' own work bridged that gap. Hence, the missing link.

I couldn't remove the squares from the building, as that would get me fired and possibly arrested for theft, so I'd taken photographs and then checked them against Alizée's paintings in my apartment. Not a particularly definitive means of authentication but also not without some redemptive value.

The semi-abstracted animals in one of the squares looked a lot like the semi-abstracted children in *Turned,* and the dying sunflowers in another had a similar attitude to the drooping clouds/lilies/fish in *Lily Pads*. The strongest support for my Alizée theory was the most elusive; there was an evolution in the third square, a subtle shifting from one form to another, which matched the emergent qualities of both *Lily Pads* and *Turned*. And then there was the restrained energy of the brushstrokes, the unusual mixing of styles.

Turned was too big for the subway, so I brought *Lily Pads* into work to support my argument and headed for Anatoly's office, a few floors higher but a skyscraper's distance in power from mine.

He frowned when I knocked on his half-opened door. "Oh, yeah. George said you'd be by. I thought you were coming later in the afternoon."

"He told me you said eleven o'clock." I walked in and rested *Lily Pads* on the edge of his desk so he wouldn't be able to put me off. "Shouldn't take more than a few minutes."

"That's no fucking Rothko," Anatoly growled. He loved to overact the part of the besieged executive, and he also loved to swear. I think he enjoyed the paradox of a cultured exec speaking like a street thug. "Thought we were talking fucking Rothko."

58

"George is, but I'm thinking we should keep our options open."

He crossed his arms over his chest.

I put the three squares on his desk, ignoring his pseudo-indignation. "He thinks these are Rothkos, but I think they might be Alizée Benoits, the same woman who painted this."

"The great-aunt." Anatoly smirked at me, then put on his glasses and scrutinized the squares. "Potent," he admitted. "There's a lot of Rothko in them."

"Benoit worked for the WPA, right before World War II, the same as the others. Allegedly very close friends. There are claims she strongly influenced them all —"

"You have any proof of these claims and allegations?"

"It's possible she affected the growth and thrust of Abstract Expressionism." I paused. "Might even be the missing link."

"That missing link crap is bullshit," he declared. "A bunch of white-tower academics jerking each other off over nothing."

I put *Lily Pads* on the desk next to the others, positioned it so it was closest to the two squares it most resembled, and pointed out the similarities.

"Don't see it," Anatoly said. "Look at the strength of the lines, the alienation in the faces of these men." He waved his finger over a cluster of abstracted, yet still clearly self-satisfied, lionlike creatures. "The hubris of these."

"Rothko didn't mix styles."

"We're talking early works here. He was a kid when he did this, probably just a student. Could have been an assignment. Could have just been screwing around. They had to hand x number of paintings into the WPA to get their paychecks. Could have been a slow month."

There was no way I could argue this, so I said, "There are rumors Benoit was Mark Rothko's lover, so he may have been influenced by her or —"

"Let's pursue the Rothko angle first. There's no need to consider an outlier when we have a perfectly legitimate contender."

"Why can't we do both at the same time?"

"We can revisit this if it's determined they're not Rothkos."

"But —"

"Give it up, Dani."

I knew exactly why he wanted me to give it up. If the squares were authenticated as Rothko's, Christie's was in line to make a fortune, but if they turned out to be the work of an unknown painter, there would be no line to stand in. "The thing is," I persisted, "she disappeared. Mysteriously. No one knows what happened to her. One day she was there, and poof, the next day she's gone. Never to be seen again."

"And the reason we care . . . ?"

"She was a friend of Eleanor Roosevelt's, that's where this painting came from. It seems that Eleanor bought them from Benoit and then gave them to my grandfather. Which means it could be —"

"This is getting convoluted."

"— an important find," I continued as if he hadn't interrupted. "Don't you think it's strange that three paintings by an unknown artist were attached to the backs of possible Pollocks and Rothkos and Krasners? That they might be the work of an artist Eleanor Roosevelt collected? Who happened to vanish without explanation? Who was hiding what from whom? And why?"

"Or, more likely, your so-called unknown artist is an extremely well-known one." He stood.

I didn't move. "I'd like to actively pursue this now. Maybe even go to Paris. They're setting up for that Early Abstract Expressionist show. At the Louvre. Must be getting tons of paintings from all over the world. We could ask for access. I could inspect the backs. There might be more squares." Desperate, I shifted tacks. "It could even work in your favor. Maybe I'll find proof they actually are Rothkos."

"Even if I agreed to this — which I'm not — it sounds like a job for someone with a little more experience." Anatoly came around from behind his desk. "Someone with a little less of a fucking point to prove."

I've never been very good at following directions, so as soon as I got back to my office, I logged on to a website called the Archives of American Art, the largest digitized compilation of primary sources on American artists in the world. If I could find a reference to Alizée in the Pollock, Krasner, or Rothko papers, maybe it would give Anatoly what he needed to let me follow up on her. He hadn't actually said no. All he'd said was "Give it up." Not exactly the same thing.

As I assumed, the materials on Pollock, Krasner, and Rothko were vast, and although they spanned from 1914 to 1984, the majority were after 1945. Rothko and Pollock weren't making real waves in the art world until the mid- to late 1940s, and Krasner even later than that, so it made sense that's where most of the substance and interest would be. Unfortunately, I was interested in 1937 to 1940, the years Alizée was in New York, when Jackson, Lee, and Mark were unknown artists working for the WPA along with thousands of others.

The deeper I dug, the more frustrating it got: useless business records, awards, family photos, and documents — Lee's social security card was particularly uninspiring — clippings; exhibition lists; résumés; correspondence with art historians, critics, gallery owners, artists, and collectors. As advertised, almost all from much later than my time period. There were audio and video interviews and recordings, which at first excited me, but it turned out only a few were with Mark and the others were mostly Lee, well after Jackson's death, talking about his legacy. The small number of interviews with Jackson were only about Jackson, clearly his favorite subject.

I clicked on "Sketchbook of Unidentified Artist," knowing it wouldn't be Alizée's but hoping it might. PDFs of the pages of the sketchbook were displayed, and I looked them over closely. I was pretty sure the drawings were of New York City, scenes of ordinary urban life circa 1940. They were very well done, with strong lines and great use of negative space: women and men reading newspapers on park benches, riding buses, in line at the grocery store, eating at what appeared to be a drugstore counter. There was a strong sense of detachment, a lack of outward emotion that was particularly haunting, Hopperesque. But it didn't look like anything Alizée would have done.

I searched through the correspondence, which was all handwritten, difficult to decipher, and mostly letters — lots of thank-you notes, how yesteryear — written to Lee or Jackson or Mark rather than anything they wrote themselves. Again, predictable. Who kept copies of letters they had sent? I switched to the interview transcripts, scanned for the words WPA, Alizée, Benoit. An hour later, all I had was a headache.

6
ELEANOR, 1939

Eleanor couldn't get her visit to the warehouse out of her head. What a fever that young artist had, what determination and pluck. She'd written down the girl's name, but for the life of her, she couldn't remember it. And why not something different, as she'd suggested? Something new? After all, wasn't the WPA/FAP itself revolutionary? She'd just have to persuade Franklin and Harry Hopkins, who headed the WPA, to see it her way. So she called her secretary, Malvina Thompson, and asked her to collect all the information she could on American modern art and leave it on her desk.

Malvina was nothing if not efficient, and when Eleanor returned to the White House, a pile of articles, books, and photographs were in her study. She had a couple of hours before an informal supper with Franklin and Harry, an unusual event amid the more commonplace formal dinners. Given the fortuitousness of the arrangements, she immediately sat down to go through the materials.

The paintings didn't look like anything and didn't make her feel anything other than perplexed. She'd imagined art similar to Picasso's reversed faces or the Impressionist paintings that became clear only when you stood at a distance. Works with a distinct focus, subjects that resembled what they were meant to portray. She had no idea how to interpret the pictures in front of her. Alizée was her name. Alizée Benoit. Alizée had told her to take her time, to give it a chance, so that's what she did.

Considering the photos longer and more carefully, she began to feel a stirring. She stared without blinking, burning the colors and images into her retina. She pushed to merge the impressions with emotions. And there was a shift, a flicker of understanding. She caught her breath.

Hartley's *Mountain Lake — Autumn,* vibrant colors and thick brushstrokes far more evocative of a Maine landscape than a recreation of how the foliage actually looked. *Moonlight over the Arbor,* summer light and a quiet breeze, so filled with longing for those fleeting days of sunshine and warmth that Eleanor could almost smell it.

Goin' Fishin', a tangle of bamboo and pieces of denim work shirts, Huckleberry Finn's Mississippi without a drop of water. And then there was Georgia O'Keeffe's *Large Dark Red Leaves on White,* an intense close-up of a leaf, tightly cropped, rendering it abstract in its exact depiction. Here were works by American artists revealing the heart of America through means beyond strict representation.

But it was John Marin's *Bryant Square* that finally brought it home for her. The drama and intensity of New York City emanating within its brash, searing lines. Abstracted skyscrapers leaning inward, pushing against each other, fighting for space, for supremacy, just like the tiny, sketchy figures rushing beneath them. Thin zigzags and thick black strokes, the excitement, the movement, the electricity of the city she'd just left, all there. All inside her.

When the butler arrived to announce dinner, Eleanor brought the photographs with her. When she entered the dining room, Harry was already there, but Franklin was still in the Oval Office. Harry didn't look well, and Eleanor was concerned. His clothes hung too loose on his bones, his hair appeared to be thinning before her eyes, and his face was pale with a slightly greenish hue. Both she and the president had begged him to see a doctor, and he'd finally promised he would. Although, as far as she knew, he hadn't yet.

"When I was up in New York, I visited a FAP site on the piers," Eleanor said as she sat down, hoping to cheer him up with his favorite topic. "Near Battery Park."

"Where they're painting all those murals? Isn't it the most amazing thing?" Harry lit up. "I wish I had the time to go up there more. I've only been once."

"Is there a reason why there aren't any abstract murals?"

Harry shrugged. "You know the murals have to be approved by a committee that includes the people who'll use the facility. Maybe they don't like abstract art. Frankly, I have to agree with them."

"But there's no official policy against it?"

"There's no official policy." He grinned at her. "Except common sense."

"Don't be such an old fogey, Harry," Eleanor retorted. "I did a little research. Look at these." She laid the photos of O'Keeffe's *Leaves* and Hartley's *Mountain Lake* on the table. "Nature in a completely different way. Not exactly what it looks like, as one of the artists told me, but what it feels like."

Harry shrugged again.

"Look at this one." Eleanor handed him *Bryant Square.*

He quickly glanced at it and gave it back to her. "Reminds me of everything I hate about New York." He shuddered in exaggerated revulsion. "All those people. All those buildings."

"That's the point!" Eleanor crowed. "This painting makes you feel what it's like to be in New York, to experience it, not just to see what it looks like."

"But I don't like how it feels."

She frowned at him. "I met a girl up there today, one of the artists, who wanted more than anything to paint an abstract mural." She paused. "There was something about her . . . She was so passionate, so fearless, yet oddly sad . . ."

"Another duckling to take under your wing?"

"Perhaps."

Harry sighed. "And I suppose you want me to make sure that she gets her abstract mural?"

"What's this about abstract murals?" Franklin boomed cheerfully as his valet pushed his wheelchair up to the table.

"I think we should expand the type of art we're supporting," Eleanor said. "We need to be behind all kinds of American art. All

American artists. Those of the future as well as the past."

The president picked up the photographs. "This is the future? Except for this one" — he pointed to the O'Keeffe — "I don't know what I'm looking at, and frankly I'm not sure this is really a leaf. Are these supposed to be buildings? They're all sideways, sloppy, something a kid would draw. Seems like taking up with this is going backward" — he winked at Harry — "not forward."

"She met an artist at one of the warehouses." Harry raised an eyebrow at the president. "An abstract artist."

"For forward-thinking men, you're both being extremely bullheaded," Eleanor declared. "The world is flat. Bloodletting cures diseases. Women will never win the vote." She glared at each in turn. "Is this where you want to stand?"

"I like pictures I can recognize," Franklin insisted.

"So you've said," she countered. "But maybe this isn't about what you like, it's about where American art is headed, with or without you."

The president looked sheepish. "Guess one abstract mural won't hurt anything."

"Two." She turned to Harry. "I'll give you

the artists' names. You vet them, and if all's well, please take it from there."

7
ALIZÉE

Alizée had gone to the ERC office on March 29, which meant she had to wait three days to send Oncle and Tante the wire about the visa money. An interminable delay. While her salary of seventy-nine dollars a month covered the basics, by the end of any given month her icebox was close to empty and she had no more than a few pennies in her change purse. Not nearly enough for a telegram. Just about everyone else on the project was in the same situation; a lot fewer beers were sold and a lot less levity ensued at the Jumble Shop when the calendar turned to thirty and thirty-one.

Although it was the first of April and yesterday it had been sixty degrees, as she headed north from the docks to the King Street WPA office for her check, a sharp wintery wind off the Hudson River bit through her cotton coat and cut into her fingertips, exposed by the fingerless gloves she wore in the warehouse. She'd brought a pair of wool gloves with her from France, but this was her second winter in New York, and they'd barely made it through the first. In another way, the blustery gusts were a welcome gift. Mounds of garbage sat on the streets and sidewalks and especially in the alleys, and without the wind to move the air, the stench would have been even worse than it was.

She did catch the aroma of roasting turkey as two women stepped onto the sidewalk in front of her, the door of a butcher shop closing behind them. Her stomach twisted, both from hunger and the reminder of Tante's home-cooked meals. She'd skipped lunch in order to leave early so she could get her stipend and make it to the telegraph office before it closed. She tried to peer into the shop, but it was impossible to see inside. The windows were completely covered by posters advertising the "sale" prices. Twenty-five cents for a turkey. Twenty-two for a leg of lamb. It wasn't much of a sale. She played with the thought of buying a turkey on her way home, but for that much money she could get at least five loaves of bread and a couple pounds of cheese.

It seemed as if food was all around her. Grocers with open bins of vegetables and fruit crowding the sidewalk. A bakery. A horse-drawn Sheffield Farms milk truck. Pushcarts filled with chickens. A kosher market. An Automat. Alizée tried to focus on something else, anything else, but even the red-and-white-striped barbershop pole reminded her of candy.

There were many stores peddling goods other than food: sign makers, gunsmiths, smoke shops, jewelers, Goldberg's Suits. But these didn't interest her nearly as much as the foodstuffs. As she crossed under the latticework of shadows cast by the elevated train tracks, she wondered how, when so many were unemployed, so much was for sale. But, of course, the shops were mostly empty. As were many of their shelves.

When she turned onto King Street, she balked at the long queue snaking two blocks from the WPA's door. She wasn't the only artist who'd run out of money. She looked to the west. Although buildings obscured her view of the sun, it was clear from the angle of the shadows that it was at least four o'clock. The telegraph office closed at five. She walked quickly to take her place at the end of the line.

She was standing in almost the same spot where she'd met Lee two years ago. After their first conversation, in which they discussed the brilliance of Picasso's antiwar mural *Guernica* but agreed that they both preferred their own art to be personal rather than political, Lee suddenly seemed to be everywhere. They lived only a few blocks from each other, and Alizée would see her on the street, in the grocers, sitting on a bench in Washington Square. Then it turned out they both had scholarships at Hans Hofmann's art school. And that was that.

A girl Alizée recognized from the Jumble Shop stepped next to her. "You sit at the Picasso table, don't you, sis?" She was tall and excruciatingly thin, her hair brushed back like a boy's. Still, with her high cheekbones and huge gray eyes, she was stunning.

"And you sit with those regionalists."

"Guilty as charged." The girl held out her hand. "Louise Bothwell, purveyor of the realistic portrayal of the miserable American condition."

"Alizée Benoit. Purveyor of the abstract portrayal of the —"

"Easel, mural, sculpture, poster?"

"Mural. I'm down at the docks working with —"

"I did mural for a year at the beginning, but now I'm on easel. It's okay but gets a little boring sometimes. I have to go out and find people to talk to in order to not go off

75

my nut."

Alizée could see that this might be a problem for her.

"But, my gosh, it's grand not to have to be at someone else's beck and call. Harder in the winter, though, when it's too cold to go to the park. And at the end of the month when there's no money for a coffee. But I find people. I go to the library sometimes. To the five-and-dime. Kresge's. Or I sit in the Jumble Shop and talk to the bartender until he kicks me out. Sometimes I burgle the poor box in the Catholic Church on Fourteenth Street just for something to do."

"Maybe if you tried something abstract, you'd find it more interesting," Alizée suggested.

Louise barked a laugh so loud half the line in front of them turned around. "You're a real hoot, Alizée. A real hoot. But for my money, I've got to go with what's there, with what's in front of me. That's the only way people are going to understand what we're trying to show them. Shapes and colors? Faces with eyes where the chin should be? Who the hell can figure that kind of thing out?"

"Maybe it's you who can't figure it out," Jack said to Louise as he walked toward them. He bowed. "Alizée. Louise. Gorky

76

and I couldn't help but hear you all the way at the front of the line, my dear Miss Bothwell." He winked at Alizée, then turned back to Louise. "There's no point in blathering on to Alizée. She's French and doesn't speak much English."

Louise narrowed her eyes. "She seemed to understand me just fine. We were having a very nice conversation about the differences between abstract and representational art, and I was explaining to her that if —"

"I'm guessing it was you who was having a nice conversation with yourself," Jack interrupted.

"You're just jealous, Pollock," Louise retorted. "And when you get jealous you get nasty. I've got three pieces in the Whitney exhibit, and you can't even get a gallery to show you or any of your lot. Just because you're doing something different doesn't mean you're doing something good."

"Just because you're doing something that pleases the old guard doesn't mean you're doing something good." Jack said, then turned his back on her, ensuring he had the last word. He offered Alizée his arm.

She hesitated for a moment, then took it. Although Louise had been nasty to him, Jack had been nasty first, and Alizée had been enjoying their conversation. She hated to be rude, but getting closer to the door was an advantage she couldn't ignore. She couldn't wait another day to send the wire. But she didn't like the feel of Louise's stare on her back.

"She's a lousy fake," Jack was saying as he led her toward Gorky. "Standing in line with the riffraff. Ha! She's got a father so rich he grew up with Roosevelt. Went to Groton Academy together." He spit on the sidewalk. "Although according to her, he can't stand the president now. Says he's a warmonger."

Gorky took a step back to let them stand in front of him. "Hate that such a beautiful girl is such a bitch," he muttered.

"I hate that such a bitch is such a talented painter," Jack replied.

At first, she was surprised to hear that Jack, who was a harsh critic, considered Louise to be a first-rate painter, but she'd been around artists long enough to know that an odd personality was more often a prerequisite for talent than it was a disqualification.

When she saw the flimsy airmail envelope in her mail slot, she assumed it was Tante's response to her telegram. But it wasn't. It was from Babette, dated six weeks earlier.

22 February 1939
Berlin

Ma Ali,

We are coming to you soon! We set sail on the thirteenth of May on the SS *St. Louis* and should be in America by fall. You will not believe how big Sophie is — and how beautiful, if I do say so myself. And wait until you meet my sweet Gabby! I know you will eat them both up. They are so delicious!

We have tourist visas to enter Cuba and have been assured that most of the paperwork has been completed for our American visas so our wait there should not be more than four to five months. It will be so wonderful to see you again, my dear, dear, dear *soeur-cousine.* I cannot wait to go shopping together in New York City! I hope you have not slipped back into your bad American styles. But if you have, I will quickly cure you of that!

You may think it strange that we are coming to America rather than just returning to France. It is because it is not safe in France or anywhere else on the continent. Hitler claims he is prophetic and that he foresees a world with no Jews. We believe he will do everything in his power to make his "prophecy" come true.

Pierre and I have been kicked out of university and Sophie out of kindergarten. I know you have heard about Kristallnacht. One of our professors was beaten to death and two others sent to a labor camp. Our shul and the tailor shop around the corner were burned down, and the tailor, along with many other Jewish men, has disappeared. No one has returned.

The only good to come out of this madness is that the Nazis have decided they want all the Jews out of Germany as soon as possible. Hence, their willingness to let us go to Cuba — that and the hefty sum we paid. You must get visas for the rest of the family as soon as possible. Hitler is not a man who likes to be wrong, and his ambitions are as grandiose as he believes himself to be.

I do not tell you these things to upset you but so you will understand what we are up against. But do not despair, because I do not. I see this as an opportunity to finish our studies in one of the great American universities and for our whole family to be in a place that is safe. I just hope many others will follow in our footsteps.

You and I will be able to talk and talk and talk and then laugh and laugh and laugh as we have always done! It will be so much fun to be together again. I cannot wait to see your beautiful face smiling at us from the dock in New York City. I also cannot wait to give you a big hug!

Je t'embrasse,
Babette

Ali. No one but Babette called her Ali. This tore at her almost as much Babette's tinny cheerfulness.

Americans for No Limits held its meetings in the cramped offices of *PM,* a newspaper that combined the magazine features of *Life* and *Time* with the editorial assertions, in this case left-leaning, and timeliness of a daily. Gideon Kannel, the man who ran things, sat on a desk, his feet barely brushing the floor. He was built like a jockey but was a math professor at NYU.

He had an academic air that reminded Alizée a little of Oncle, but the idea of Oncle leading a political group was patently absurd. Her uncle was an unassuming man, although rumor had it that Gideon had been also. Up until the Germans killed his parents, destroyed their home and kosher butcher shop during Kristallnacht, and took his three young brothers away. Babette's letter made this so much more real.

Although it was cold and rainy outside, the room was sweltering, filled with the odor of damp wool and too many bodies in too small a space. Alizée pulled at the collar of her blouse to expose more of her neck and hoped the meeting would be quick so she could discuss the visa problem with Gideon before she passed out from heat prostration.

Gideon's message was loud and strong: Hitler was going to conquer all of Europe, his mission was to kill off anyone who wasn't Aryan, and if the United States didn't intercede, a mass slaughter would occur in which millions would die. Her stomach went hollow.

"I've written a draft of the 'Defend America by Standing with Our Allies' letter," Gideon was saying. "It's what we agreed to last time: a warning of the danger to both Europeans and Americans if we don't step in and help them fight Hitler." He looked around the room. "We've got enough money to send out about two hundred letters. We just need volunteers to write or type them up. Who's got a few extra hours this week?"

She didn't want the United States to go to war. She wanted the State Department to authorize more visas, not send American boys, including Mark and Jack, off to fight thousands of miles away. She didn't raise her hand.

Gideon wrote the names on his pad and then moved on to urge everyone to participate in the next protest rally, planned for Thanksgiving weekend. It was to be similar to the one they'd staged last month at the New York offices of the America First Committee, an isolationist organization working tirelessly to keep immigration quotas low. This sounded better, and she made a note of the date and time.

The last item on the agenda was one Gideon was very excited about. "If we're to be successful, I believe we've got to hit the isolationist powers that be in the heart." He stood. "Bring them to their knees before they can do any more damage. These men are pressuring Roosevelt and demanding he stay out of Europe's business. Claiming that helping the refugees is akin to going to war. They must be silenced!"

She realized that if she said out loud what she'd just been thinking about not wanting

American boys to take up guns, everyone here would consider her an isolationist. The enemy.

"I know we've never done anything like this before," Gideon held up his hands, "and I'm not talking about hurting anyone. Physically, that is. These may be influential men with formidable friends, but they're also the kind of men who do what they want, when they want, and they're sure to have lots of skeletons in their closets. Sure to have greased a palm, told a lie, misrepresented themselves, maybe worse. And that's what we go after. We'll discredit them and undermine their ability to manipulate the president. We can't let them help Hitler destroy the European people!"

Henri. Oncle, Tante, and Alain.

"We'll go through their records, everything they've ever written or said. Newspaper articles, interviews, speeches, memoranda. Nothing in these men's lives is above scrutiny. We'll talk to their enemies, their colleagues, old girlfriends, do whatever we can until we get the goods we need to bring them down." He raised his arms in the air. "First and foremost are Charles Lindbergh and Joseph Kennedy!"

Shouts of agreement. Lindbergh and Kennedy were two of the most visible isolationists in the country, giving speeches and writing op-ed pieces, meeting with influential politicians. They were both high-ranking members of America First Committee, known anti-Semites who weren't shy about voicing this opinion. There was no doubt in Alizée's mind that everyone in the room hated them with a passion. And she supposed she did, too.

"There's another man, not nearly as well known, but he's been more effective at keeping European refugees from our shores than any other individual. He's turned away ships. Sent people — families running from occupied countries in fear for their lives — back to places where they no longer have a home, where they face bigotry, starvation, and almost certain death."

Babette. The little girls.

"As many of you know, his name is Breckinridge Long, the assistant secretary of state who controls all American visas. He flips his finger at the laws that allocate hundreds of thousands of visas each year. In direct defiance of official US policy and the president's wishes, he restricts visas beyond what makes any sense, refusing to authorize any to even the most qualified!"

Breckinridge Long. The man Mr. Fleishman said was responsible for limiting ERC's access to visas, the one who could, who would, consign her family to the Nazis.

"He's purposely leaving thousands of visas unclaimed," Gideon continued. "It's apparent to anyone who takes the time to notice that he's more interested in keeping immigrants out of the country than helping get them in. We must get him fired!"

Alizée sprang up from her seat. "Long must be stopped!" she cried. Embarrassed, she quickly sat down.

Gideon smiled at her. "Thank you, Miss . . . ?"

"Benoit. Alizée Benoit."

"Well, Miss Alizée Benoit, how would you like to be the first to sign up for the Discredit Long Committee?"

8
ALIZÉE & LEE

Alizée wanted to tear up the drawing paper on the table in front of her. Into many, many small pieces. Or at least throw it to the ground and storm out of the classroom. It wasn't working. *Merde* and *merde* and more *merde.* She was more than familiar with the concept of using color and shape to create motion and the illusion of multiple dimensions. She'd done it before. Many times. But somehow, with this piece, it wasn't translating to her gut. And if it wasn't getting to her gut, it wasn't getting to the paper. She was overthinking, and that always meant bad work.

The class was drawing from a nude model, overlaying and pasting cut-up pieces of tissue paper to create an abstraction of the voluptuous woman, reducing the actual figure to pure emotion and volume. Or that was what they were supposed to be doing. She was reducing the actual figure to complete *merde.*

Alizée glanced around the room to check where Hans was. Heading her way. He was going to trash her and her work into the scrap heap where they both belonged. She was used to criticism — and liked to think she took it well — but Hans could be tough, actually cruel at times, and she hated that he was usually right.

Saturday morning classes at the Hofmann School of Fine Art were held in the basement of a West Ninth Street building. Although the light wasn't great, Alizée liked it because the boiler was down here, and it was one of the only times during the cold months she got warm on a weekend. Lee was working next to her, and they shared a forlorn glance. Obviously, Lee was having problems with the assignment, too.

Alizée scrutinized the rectangles and triangles she'd cut out of brightly colored tissue paper. Maybe they were too neat. She moved them around to make it messier, but that just muddied up the image. She bit her lip, felt Hans coming closer. *Merde* and *merde* and more *merde.* Then she saw it. Tear up the tissue paper, not the drawing paper. She began to rip and paste.

Lee watched Alizée working next to her.

Completely absorbed. Alizée worked like Jack and Mark. With a directed passion that blocked out everything else, that took her from the external world and transformed her into the painting. Or maybe it transformed the painting into her.

There was a downside to this. Something Lee saw in Jack and Mark also. The three shared an intensity, almost an otherworldliness. It was as if a high-pitched vibration pulsed inside them, creating a scary kind of energy that drove them to brilliance but also seemed to drive them a bit mad. She often envied them their focus, their ability to completely separate from their surroundings, but she wasn't sure she'd trade places if she could.

Because there was the sadness, too. Alizée tried to vanquish this with jokes and brash confidence, but Lee sensed her friend's cockiness was often no more than a veneer. While Mark sank into deep depressions and Jack into alcohol, Alizée kept moving, pushing, as if through sheer force of will she could keep the wolves at bay. Watching her perform could be heartrending, particularly because Alizée wasn't one to confide. And Lee was certain there were things that needed to be said.

Lee leaned in and examined her friend's

work. Although everyone else was using scissors to cut rectangles, parallelograms, and triangles from tissue paper, Alizée had ripped hers into tattered abstracted shapes. She was covering her original pencil drawing of the model with the jagged forms, obliterating her sketch. The different shapes and hues quivered as the ragged pieces lay against each other, their juxtaposition causing the warmer reds and oranges to pop out while the cooler blues and purples receded, creating the pulsating push and pull Hans wanted.

But Alizée had gone beyond the assignment, for the model was still there, simultaneously present and absent, positive and negative — push and pull in multiple dimensions. You felt the great, yet imperfect, mother figure, the hugeness of her both in space and human consequence. And yet Lee sensed a longing, a deep loneliness within her. Perhaps grief over a lost child? Lee glanced up just as Alizée brushed a tear from her cheek. There was no doubt: Alizée and her painting were one. Both of them filled with melancholy.

Damn, the girl was good, which was clear to everyone but Alizée. This was partially due to the fact that no artist was capable of accurately assessing her own work — it was never as good or as bad as you thought it was — and partially due to the fact that Hans gave Alizée such a hard time.

Not that he didn't give everyone a hard time. Like now, he was ranting at Grant Mc-Neil, who sometimes worked as his class monitor. "Too academic," he cried, waving Grant's drawing in the air to show the other students. "We must get away from all this Renaissance nonsense." He slapped the paper back on Grant's board. "You've just clothed the naked image sitting in front of us. You've done nothing to make her speak beyond her own anatomy!"

Grant looked deflated, and the rest of the class turned away, each hoping that Hans would decide to critique someone else next. Hans stood behind Alizée, watching her working with her shapes. She was unaware he was there, so lost was she within the woman under her fingers. Lee guessed Alizée hadn't even heard Hans's tirade against Grant and steeled herself against another one directed at Alizée, although it was hard to imagine what fault he would find.

Hans grabbed the paper from Alizée's hands. "Not enough," he said. "Not nearly enough."

Alizée jumped, startled back into the room. She looked at him as if she didn't know who he was.

"Like this." Hans took a razor-edged ruler from a shelf, laid it down widthwise about a third of the way from the bottom of Alizée's picture, and ripped the paper in two, truncating the abstracted mother figure just below the swell of her hips.

Lee gasped, as did the rest of the students, horrified that he would so cavalierly destroy another artist's work in such a public way. Only Alizée remained silent, stone-faced, her eyes glued to her picture.

Hans took the bottom third and placed it against the left edge of the larger piece, thighs and legs at the end of the reaching arms, inducing both uneasiness and the picture's authority. "Now it's more dynamic," he declared. "Notice how it moves against the picture plane." He held the two pieces up. "Look at it now. The old way was to always work from the center. From the middle. As if that is the only heart a painting can have."

Alizée took her torn picture from Hans. "The heart, the heart . . ." she mumbled as she began to shift the two parts around to create different images. She grabbed Hans's ruler, placed it diagonally across the larger piece and ripped it in two. Then she did it again and again until there were a dozen geometrical shapes. Without a word, she bent over the colorful pieces of tissue paper and began moving them. In seconds, she was once again oblivious to anyone else in the room.

9
MARK & ALIZÉE

"This is ridiculous." Alizée pulled the belt of her terry-cloth robe more tightly around her. "Lee had no right to bother you." Two red circles of fury flushed her cheeks. "No right."

Mark held up his hands, although what he wanted to do was put his arms around her, crush her to him, devour her. "Sorry," he said. "She thought something might be wrong. That you might be depressed. Which I unfortunately know something about."

"Well, I'm not depressed," Alizée snapped. "I'm just tired. Have a headache. Maybe the flu. Can't a girl get sick around here without someone sending in the posse?"

He was relieved to hear the strength in her voice, irritation instead of the lassitude he knew so intimately, the downhill slope he'd suffered for years. "No gun," he assured her. "No posse."

When Alizée hadn't shown up at the

warehouse that morning, Lee went to her apartment to check on her. It had been well past noon, and Alizée was still in bed, mounded beneath a couple of blankets. She said she was sick and wanted to sleep, but based on her lethargy, dull affect, and lack of fever, Lee, who'd just seen her crying in Hans's class, guessed Alizée might not be suffering from a physical illness. So she'd called Mark and asked him to drop by that afternoon.

It was the first time he'd been to Alizée's apartment. His own living situation was pretty grim, but not as spare as this. After he and Edith had separated — for the third time now — he'd moved in with Phil Guston and Grant McNeil. They at least had a can inside their apartment, hot running water, and a kitchen with an actual stove instead of a hot plate. But Alizée had more light and space, and he figured she didn't like roommates any better than he did, which was one of the problems with his marriage and was growing to be a problem with Phil and Grant.

"I guess Lee overreacted," he backpedaled. "She's been known to do that. Just worried about you, I guess."

"I should've told her I wasn't coming in." Alizée sat down at the beat-up table and

95

pointed to the other chair. "I felt so crummy when I woke up, I didn't have the energy to go to the drugstore to use the phone. Should have."

"Happens," he said. There was something about her that touched him, more than her beauty, more than her talent, more than the fact that he desperately wanted to be inside her. It had something to do with her toughness, or maybe the vulnerability he suspected she used the toughness to hide. "Trouble getting out of bed is something I know something about, too."

"So I hear."

"But not you?" he asked.

"More the opposite. My problem is I get too up."

"Lord Byron once said, 'We of the craft are all crazy.' " He paused. "But would you want it any other way?"

"Sometimes."

"Sure. I get that. But I don't know if it's possible." His eyes swept the canvas-strewn room. Colors and quasi-geometrical shapes and arresting juxtapositions. There was no doubt Alizée was good, very good, and the canvases bore this out. Although she'd only recently started working abstractly, her instincts were deep.

His eye caught on a painting propped on

the north windowsill. What was she doing with that one? He studied it, trying to ferret out what made it so arresting. Thick swatches of pure blue and yellow, edges dripping into a mellow brown, titillating slashes of black. An abstraction, yes, but somehow instead of growing from a depiction of reality, which was how most of them were working these days, it felt as if it was rising from the abstraction into something else. This created a formidable combination of fascination and disquiet.

"Your work is damn good."

"Hans doesn't seem to agree."

He wanted badly to kiss her but held back. Lee had told him Alizée would never get involved with a married man, not even a separated one. And Mark wasn't ready to make a definitive break from Edith. Not yet, anyway. But he found it difficult to believe that a girl like Alizée, a girl who would leave everything she knew and come to New York on her own, would be such a stickler for propriety. Maybe with enough time she'd change her mind.

"Coffee?" Alizée stood and filled a soup pot with water.

She looked better already, and Mark was pleased to see it probably was just a touch of flu. His "bouts," as he'd come to refer to them, went on for days, sometimes weeks, spurred by nothing he could make out. He lolled mindlessly, miserably, in the dark place, not wanting to be there, but unable to go anywhere else. He was pressed down by anxiety, weighted in place by an all-encompassing self-loathing, his mind turned into crystalized molasses: sharp, impenetrable, and unbearably painful. But when the darkness began to loosen its hold, as it invariably did, the suicidal demands became more insistent. And that was where the real danger lay.

He thought back to the last time he'd decided he didn't want to live, a few years after he'd come to New York. He was living in an apartment without furniture or hot water and going to the Russian Bear almost every day to fill his empty stomach with rye bread and listen to the balalaika orchestra instead of painting.

He'd been struggling with his work, more than struggling, it was going nowhere, and he was desperately lonely. Despite his classmates and roommate, he existed alone in a dark, cold cave, huddled in the far recesses with only the damp rocks for company. He simply didn't want to be there anymore. If his roommate hadn't been let off early from his job as a busboy, Mark would have bled to death.

He stood to free himself from his thoughts and was again drawn to the painting against the window. "What are you figuring with this?" he asked.

"Just playing around. Trying something new. Not really sure, actually."

"It's the most compelling painting here."

She turned from the hot plate, clearly surprised.

"Whatever you're doing, you should keep at it. This grabs me and pulls me to it." He mimed punching himself in the stomach and staggered closer to the painting.

"You think so?"

"There's something unsettling about it, but in a good way. Like it's growing or maybe becoming something it isn't. Or maybe becoming something it already was, but that I didn't know it was until you showed me."

Alizée came to where he was standing. "That's what this makes you feel? That it's becoming a thing it already was?"

"I think that's the crux of it. Yes."

She stared at the painting. "That's exactly what I was trying to find. What was already there. To free it. Let it emerge."

"Looks like it's breaking out to me."

She was completely still. "Thanks for saying that. That helps. A lot."

"I'm not just saying it. I mean it. I mean it so much I'm going to talk to Aaron Seliger. Tell him to come down here and take a look." Aaron Seliger was the owner of the Contemporary Arts Gallery, one of the few galleries in New York willing to show modern art. Aaron had stuck his neck out and produced a one-man show for Mark last year. Everyone, including Mark and Aaron, had been surprised by how well it had gone over.

Alizée threw her arms around him. "You're a real doll." Then she just as quickly pulled away.

All Mark could see was the two of them naked, sweating and wrestling and groping, giving each other what they needed to give, getting what they needed to get. This was all he wanted. What he needed. Every other thought vanished from his mind. He reached for her.

At first she came toward him, but then she stopped. "I've got to think."

He leaned in and kissed her lightly on the lips. "Don't take too long." Then he left.

She stood in front of the canvas Mark had admired, stunned. This was the best work in the room? The lost-and-found dancers, risen from the depths? The flat was suddenly warm, and she dropped her bathrobe to the floor, trying to see what he had seen, to feel what he had felt, in what she'd never thought of as a painting, just as an experiment, a failed homework assignment.

A few months earlier, Hans told the class to go into the "urban environment" and draw scenes of people going about a daily task, oblivious to their surroundings. The students were then to turn the drawings into an abstract painting that evoked the feeling of detachment. So she went out with her sketchbook and penciled people reading newspapers on park benches, people riding on buses, people in the grocers and people eating lunch at a delicatessen. She came up with a dozen semidecent sketches and transferred two to canvas. One quickly became hopeless, and the other, the basis of this one, never succeeded in producing a feeling of detachment. It never succeeded in producing any emotion other than her disdain, and it joined her stack of failed canvases to be reused.

A few weeks after that, she was wrestling with yet another representational-to-abstract project, muttering under her breath, damning Hans and his repetitive, narrow-minded assignments. It was tedious and boring and, worse, futile. Stupid. What was so grand about going from representation to abstraction? Why not go the other way?

She'd snatched the unfinished urban canvas from the top of her pile and plopped it sideways on an easel, making what had been its right side, its bottom. She stared at what was now a complete abstraction, searching for recognizable images, mentally changing the focal point, the depth of field, the center. She marched to the far wall and studied it from there, then slowly drew closer. She turned away from it, then turned quickly back again. Nothing. She snapped the paintbrush in her hands in two. *Putain.* Could she do nothing right?

She dropped the broken brush on the floor and stomped back to the canvas, enraged by it, by herself. She grabbed another paintbrush and swirled gobs of blue paint over the original browns. She threw the paint on more vigorously than she usually did, applying it thickly, thinly, however she wanted. No thought. No assignment. She painted yellow over blue, let the two colors streak each other without allowing them to merge into green. She used navy, almost black, slashing lines where the new blue met the old brown, leaving whatever yellow edges there were to themselves. Why the hell not?

The animal ferocity of her movements was emboldening; she kept going, reveling in the pure pleasure of defying Hans. And suddenly, felt as much as seen, they appeared: dancers. Two dancers doing the jitterbug. She grabbed a fine brush, roughed out the figures, then stood back. They were there and not there, emerging into consciousness from a place that hadn't existed before. She'd turned back to her homework painting and saw the problem: it was too there. Ultimately, she did a good enough job on the assignment that Hans only criticized her privately rather than during class. She hadn't looked at the dancers again.

Now she looked.

Mark said it was becoming something it already was, that he hadn't been aware of it until she showed him. Which was exactly right. But she hadn't been aware of it either, not until the figures showed themselves. And maybe that was the point. She hadn't been trying to find them. She allowed them to find her.

A lightning flash of heat surged through her. She snatched a half-dozen old canvases from her failed pile, threw the paintings in progress off her easels and windowsills, replaced them with upside-down and sideways paintings. She grabbed up her palette, brushes and tubes of paint, then stood completely still, slowly inhaling, conjuring.

She moved from one painting to another. Splashing yellows here. Swirling greens there. Purple. Red. She flung one that wasn't working to the floor, picked it up, sliced it with a deep rose, threw it down again. She was still wearing the T-shirt she'd slept in the previous night, and it clung to her, damp against her skin. Sweat soaked her hair, ran down her face. She mopped her forehead with used paint rags to keep it out of her eyes, kept drinking water and kept painting. Time slipped. There was nothing but the canvases.

By midnight, nine hours after she'd begun, two paintings were complete. On one, lily pads emerged on a pond. On the other, the Empire State Building grew from a jumble of jagged rectangular shapes. She gulped down two more glasses of water and went downstairs to the johnny. When she returned, she placed the new paintings next to the one Mark had liked: dancers, lily pads, Empire State. Ghosts, perhaps, evolving, hovering, not fully formed, never meant to be. But there they were.

She tossed on the mattress, unable to sleep.

She could see the three paintings in the thin, city-night light, muted, in shadow, but very much present. She closed her eyes. They flew open, gobbling up the canvases, hungry to know. Were they good? Were they good good? One moment, yes. Then no.

When dawn began to seep into the corners, she finally gave up and made herself a cup of coffee. Lee had brought over a cake her boyfriend, Igor, refused to eat because he claimed it was too sweet, which Lee didn't want around because she was "watching her figure." Alizée forced herself to eat a piece. Even dunked in the black coffee, it was too sweet.

She went to the canvases, chewed at her paint-covered fingernails. She had a stack of failed canvases ready to be reversed. She had the vision and the driving desire. Yet she knew she couldn't count on the wonderful craziness that had fired her last night. These bursts of élan came and went, sometimes induced by fretfulness other times by nothing she could discern, impossible to summon at will. But she didn't need them. It was her passion, her ideas, her brushstrokes. She could do it either way. The series would be called Reversal. It would be the breakthrough she needed.

Mark had opened this window. Shown her

what was hidden within her experiment. Revived the boldness she needed to see the idea through. As Lee had said, he was a wonderful, sweet bear of a man. Alizée was touched by his kindness, thrilled by the way he lived in the moment, rejoicing in its heat and complexities, drawing on it to feed his passion. And he'd been able to look at her work and articulate what she hadn't known herself.

She visualized the way he'd reached out for her. Once again felt how much she'd wanted to reach back, the body-filling ache when she stopped just short of his arms. The soft touch of those lips. She wanted Mark, but she couldn't have him. She couldn't go looking for loss.

Every day she lived with the fear that she might have to again endure the piercing aloneness that had followed her parents' deaths, the rending of herself into so many pieces that she no longer felt fully human. She remembered pressing her fingernails so deeply into her arm that she drew blood, hoping to prove to herself that she did exist. And then wondering why she cared if she did or didn't.

She couldn't go looking for loss. Of any kind. Because it would awaken those old feelings, the ones she kept tightly coiled inside, the ones she knew she couldn't survive a second time. And they were already stirring. She could feel them as if they were living creatures, hibernating snakes sensing spring, sensing the dread that grew within her at every news report out of Europe, at every letter. Waiting to rip her apart.

10
DANIELLE, 2015

"You must remember something else," I said to my mother over the phone. I'd resisted talking to her about Alizée because I knew she'd give me a hard time, but my desire for information finally overcame my desire to avoid an argument.

"I don't know why we have to have this same conversation over and over again." Her sigh was highly theatrical, as was she. "Ad nauseam," she added. "To no end."

"Maybe because every once in a while you let something else slip. Something that makes me think you know a lot more than you're telling. Like how you casually mentioned that Grand-père got *Turned* and *Lily Pads* from Eleanor Roosevelt years after Grand-mère gave them to me. Or how you just recently told me Alizée went missing from a mental institution. Before that you only said she'd gone missing."

"Why would I keep anything from you?"

"Because that's what we do in this family."

"Not discussing painful things isn't withholding information, it's just good sense."

Now it was my turn to sigh. Like mother like daughter, the curse of the only child. "What would you say if I told you a few of her paintings showed up at work?"

"I'd say someone's pulling your leg."

"There's no one else. *I* think they might be hers."

"You've got to let this obsession with Alizée go."

I paused for effect. "What if it's not just an obsession?"

"Oh, Danielle, don't be so dramatic," she said. "I'm meeting Dad for dinner and have to walk the dog before I leave. Let's talk later in the week."

"I thought I'd ask Grand-mère."

"Even if she remembers anything, she's not going to talk about it."

"You can't be sure," I said, although my grandmother was a long shot at best.

"I've known her a lot longer than you have, Danielle. And if there's one thing I'm certain of, it's that she's not discussing anything that happened before or during the war. With you or anyone else."

"I'm asking her about after the war."

"Doesn't matter."

"Does that mean I can't borrow your car?"

"Of course you can borrow my car." Deep sigh. "God knows your *grand-mère* can use all the stimulation she can get."

On Saturday, amid a biting early March rain, I took the train out to Greenwich, where my parents live on the seedier side of town, a place that would be the good side just about anywhere else. My mother owns a small accounting firm and my father's the most dedicated high-school English teacher in the world. Although they both work their butts off, their household income has always fallen well below — well, well below — the Greenwich median.

I grew up feeling inadequate because I wore knockoffs while every other girl in my class wore Gucci and Versace. When I took up with the artsy crowd in high school, this fact became irrelevant, but I've never been able to completely get over that haughty disdain from the mean girls in middle school or the not-quite-good-enough feeling that came from all those perfectly plucked arching eyebrows.

When I got to the house, my mother was at the gym, so I jumped in the car and took off in case there was some kind of problem that might bring her home early — an instructor who called in sick, lower back pain, a fall from the stationary bike in spinning class. The last thing I needed was another discussion with her.

I don't want to give the wrong impression of my mom. She's actually quite funny, as sarcastic people often are, and I know, despite her caustic nature, when it comes to the big things she's always got my back. Another thing about her is that she's often right, which I recognized she probably was in this case.

Grand-mère was eighty-nine and for the past six years had been living in an assisted-living community; the use of the word *facility* or *home* was frowned upon. The doctors said it wasn't Alzheimer's, some other kind of dementia, but what difference did a label make anyway? She was in and out of it, recently more out than in, so that was one problem.

The other was that no one had ever heard her talk about anything that happened before she came to America as a new bride in 1945. I did know my grandparents met in a displaced-persons camp outside of Paris, that he was a doctor and she a wandering girl from somewhere in the French countryside, both the sole survivors of their

111

families. Other than that, silence had reigned on the subject for seventy years. The Benoit family has always believed that what remains unacknowledged doesn't actually exist. Even when I was a kid and we went on vacations to France, there were no investigations — actually not even any discussion — into what might have happened to our ancestors.

But some of us wanted to hear the story, our story really, mostly the cousins. Sticking with tradition, my mother and aunt maintained their parents' silence, and their husbands, third- and fourth-generation Americans, knew when not to intrude. But the four of us had speculated in whispers forever: Liz getting teary, Adam full of righteous anger, Zach thoughtful, struggling to understand the inexplicable.

My curiosity had been the most voracious. I read all the books. First the novels: Uris, Wouk, Styron. Then the nonfiction: Anne Frank, Elie Wiesel, Yehuda Bauer's *History of the Holocaust,* William Shirer's *Rise and Fall.* I tried to wrap my mind around what had happened, what it meant, but I became a jumbled-up fusion of my cousins' reactions: it made me cry, it put me into a rage, it frustrated the hell out of me.

Grand-mère was sitting in a chair in the

communal living room, sun brushing her right shoulder, the rest of her in dusk. When I was a child, my favorite thing was to bake with her. She taught me how to make *pain d'amande* and challah; dripping the melted butter over the braided loaf is one of my sweetest memories. I still bake the cookies, often when I'm feeling a little lonely; the intoxicating aroma of almonds and butter never fails to lift my spirits.

It hurt to see Grand so small, so pulled inward, so vacant. I wondered if the large woman who made potato latkes so rich and crisp they melted and crunched in your mouth at the same time, who beat the pants off her friends at the poker table, who loved her family with a fierceness that was scary at times, was somewhere inside this tiny husk of a woman. If she still existed at all.

I sat in the chair next to her and took her hand in mine. It was cold, the skin so transparent it almost wasn't there. "Grand-mère," I said. "It's Danielle. Dani. How are you?"

She looked at me with her still startling gray eyes. Blinked. Then a blazing smile. "Linda!" she cried. "Linda!"

"Not Linda," I corrected. "Dani. Linda's daughter. Your granddaughter."

"You look beautiful." She pressed my

hand between both of hers and leaned toward my neck, drawing in a deep breath. "Why do you look young when I look old? You even smell young."

"It's Dani," I repeated. "Not Linda."

"That beautiful girl of yours. *Syyn myydl.* The one with all those blonde curls? With the silly boy's name who does not eat enough? Such a firecracker. A real firecracker that one. Paints such pretty pictures."

Pretty pictures. This, of all things, she remembered. It hurt. "She's fine, but how are you? I came here to see how you are."

"I am dying," she said in a matter-of-fact tone. "Losing my marbles as —"

"Don't say that, Grand —"

"There is nothing wrong with dying when your time comes," Grand-mère declared, and I saw the woman she was push through the wrinkled skin and hunched body. "What is wrong is dying when it is not."

I hesitated. "You've seen a lot of that, haven't you?"

She stared over my shoulder, and I worried I'd lost her.

"Do you remember when you met Grand-père?" I asked, hoping to lead her gently into her memories.

She looked at me blankly.

"Henri," I said. "What was he like when you first met him?"

Her face softened. "Grand-père Cäin. He gives me milk right from the cow."

"Not your grandfather, your husband. Henri."

"The milk is very warm. At first I do not like it but then I do."

"You met Henri right after the war," I reminded her. "What was he like?"

"He is crazy. Everyone is. The war is over, but nothing is better. All he wants is to go all over France to find his sister. He is a good man, handsome, and I help him."

"In France? He was looking for Alizée in France?" This didn't make any sense. Alizée went missing in 1940 in New York; she'd never have gone back to Europe at that time. I didn't know what was worse, Grandmère's confusion, my disappointment, or the fact that I was going to have to admit to my mother that she was right.

"My Henri looks in America before he looks in France. Before I meet him. Then we come to America together."

I sat back in my chair. My grandfather immigrated to the United States in 1945. "I don't think so, Grand."

She nodded her head as if I'd agreed with her. "We come to America to look again."

"When you came to America to look again, did he talk to Lee Krasner or Jackson Pollock?" I asked cautiously. "Mark Rothko? Is that when he got Alizée's paintings from Eleanor Roosevelt?"

"He gets the painting from the other one."

I sat up, senses heightened. "What other one?"

"She gives him the one he carries with him all the time."

"Is it big?" I asked. "Red, white, and blue? Or does it look like lily pads?"

"Bloom. That is where we go first. We are worried she is . . ." Grand-mère made a circular motion with her forefinger. "She is not all there in the head."

"The painting looks like blooms? Like flowers?" *Lily Pads* could be interpreted that way. "Did you go with him to visit Eleanor Roosevelt?"

"We visit her and the husband way out in the country. In New York. But my Henri has the painting from her already from before. He brings it to France with him and then brings it back to America. He hates it."

I ignored her non sequitur. "You went to Hyde Park?"

"They make us apple pie." Grand shook her head. "She says her husband bakes it,

116

but I do not believe her."

"Her husband?" I asked a little too loudly, and Grand-mère pulled back into herself. Franklin Roosevelt was dead by 1945, she couldn't be referring to him. But Lee Krasner and Jackson Pollock lived on Long Island, not exactly "way out in the country," but maybe it was then. I knew it couldn't be, but I tried anyway. "Did you visit Lee Krasner and Jackson Pollock in Long Island? When you were looking for Alizée?"

"She is very nice, but I do not like him. Your father says he is an imbecile."

"Lee is very nice?"

"My Henri is so smart he talks to presidents," Grand said proudly. "The wife gives him pictures."

"The wife gives him pictures? What wife? Whose wife? Jackson Pollock's? Franklin Roosevelt's?"

"I like the pictures very much but they make him sad. He says we must make them go away. It is time to look forward and not back." Grand's face crumbled and a tear stumbled its way down a branching crevasse in her cheek. "I would like very much to see those pretty pictures again."

I took her hands, thrilled there was something I could do for her. "I have them, Grand. I can bring them to you. Or at least

Lily Pads, the one you like so much, the blooms, because I have to take it on the train and *Turned* is too big. But I can do that. Would you like that? Next Saturday maybe? I'll bring one of the pretty pictures for you to look at." I think maybe I'll bring one of mine, too.

Grand-mère's eyes flashed, and she lowered her voice to a conspiratorial whisper. "We cannot tell your father about this. He tells me to throw them away, but I do not. I hide them instead. How can I destroy such beautiful things? I save them for pretty little Dani. My Henri is so smart he talks to presidents, but he cannot bear to look at his poor sister's pictures."

11
ALIZÉE, 1939

"This is what we know." Alizée ticked off the items on her fingers. "Breckinridge Long controls all the visas. He has absolute power over who gets into the country and who doesn't. Perhaps who will ultimately die and who won't. He's an extreme nativist, staunch isolationist, doing everything he can to obstruct laws Congress has passed, to do the opposite of his job description. And he's completely committed to keeping as many immigrants out of the United States as possible."

It was the first meeting of the Discredit Long Committee. Gideon had recruited four other ANL members, and after a few discussions, he'd appointed Alizée to head up the group. She'd been surprised, flattered, and a bit nervous. But action was what she needed now, the best antidote.

The more she delved into Breckinridge Long, the more disgusted she was. The facts she'd uncovered were bleak: he'd managed to reverse a Roosevelt initiative to ease restrictions on immigration; since taking the job as assistant secretary, he'd slashed the quotas in half and was hoping to cut even more; he was out-and-out lying about how many visas he was authorizing, especially for Jews. If he wasn't removed from the State Department, it was sure to get worse. He had to be stopped before there were no more visas to be had.

"This could be the most important thing you ever do," she told her committee. "We get this man out of his job, and we can save thousands of lives." It was true, and what she needed to say, but inside she was crying: *Save mine, save mine, please save mine.*

They listened solemnly, and she forced herself to focus on them, on their sorrows. Nathan Heme was a veteran of the Great War who despised Germany. Aarone De Abravanel was an Italian trying to get visas for his family. Bertha Dryzen's German grandmother, aunt, and cousins had been killed by the Nazis in 1937. And William Stewart was a boy about Alizée's age who believed we were all God's children and therefore had to stand up against any evil perpetrated on innocents. Bertha and Aarone were Jewish, Nathan claimed his war experiences had turned him into a devout atheist, and William lived by Jesus's golden rule.

Alizée explained the general plan: they were to research everything Long had ever said or done that might be used against him. "We're looking for bribes, kickbacks, lies, underhanded or criminal activity. Anything we can find. Public and private."

"How are we supposed to do that?" Nathan asked. He was originally from England, born to Gypsies, a people Hitler was harassing almost as much as the Jews.

"I'll get to that," she said. "Just hear me out."

"I say we shoot the guy," Nathan grumbled. "Forget all this gobbledygook."

Alizée ignored Nathan; although his point about how difficult this was going to be was more than valid. "ANL has connections at the State Department and at the White House. Once we collect enough information, Gideon hopes his contacts will be able to convince FDR to fire Long. Replace him with someone who'll follow the law and actually try to fill all the visa allocations. Hopefully, someone more sympathetic to the refugees."

"There couldn't be anyone less," Bertha said, and both William and Aarone nodded.

Nathan scowled but sat up a bit straighter.

"A handmaid to the devil," William said. He was so good-looking, with high cheekbones and what Babette would have called "bedroom eyes," that Alizée had a hard time matching his piety with his movie-star face.

"You didn't mention that Long and FDR are good friends," Nathan pointed out. "Have been for years. So there's a good possibility whatever we find will end up being ignored."

Alizée recognized this negative attitude from her socialist groups; there was always one. Unfortunately, in this case, the defeatist voice was well informed. She gave Nathan her best smile. "That's a good point, and we'll need to take it into consideration when we're farther down the line, but the president's a good man, a great man. When we come up with enough ammunition, he'll listen."

"I've got ammunition," Nathan said. "And I can shoot. My way we don't need to worry about whether your *great man* will turn against his buddy. This way we can take it —"

"I am thinking the president is wanting to go to war," Aarone interrupted. "So there are other things that he and Mr. Long do not . . . How do you say? See with their eyes?" Aarone had come to New York when he was twenty-two and had been working for the past ten years in a shirt factory to bring the rest of his family over one by one. He'd managed to finance three brothers, but two sisters and his parents still remained in Italy.

"See eye to eye," Bertha said.

"Again, a good point, but let's concentrate on our first steps," Alizée said before Nathan could counter. "Our first hurdle is getting the goods on Long." She cleared her throat and picked up her notes. "The man's been in the public eye for years, which is helpful to us. A third assistant secretary of state under Wilson. Ran for Senate from Missouri twice — and lost. Ambassador to Italy and now assistant secretary of state. And there's been controversy all along the way. Some noise about campaign irregularities. He was considered overly pro-Mussolini when he was in Italy and —"

"Something that didn't seem to bother his buddy Franklin," Nathan interrupted. "Long stayed in that position for years."

"You're not being particularly helpful," Bertha said to Nathan in a soft voice coated with steel. She'd told Alizée that after her mother found out about the deaths of her own mother, sister, and nephews, she'd

123

gone mad and never recovered, that the suddenly old woman begged her daily to save her dead family.

Nathan snapped his head backward in surprise, Aarone winked at Bertha, and Alizée resumed as if there had been no interruption. "His lengthy career will make it easier for us to find articles, interviews, speeches, correspondence," she said. "It means he's had contact with lots of people — and that he's made lots of enemies. So let's go rattle some cages."

She divvied up the tasks. Nathan would take the early years: World War I, the Wilson administration, Long's senate defeats. William and Aarone were responsible for his tenure in Italy, and she and Bertha would handle the years between 1937 and the present. Each would scour the libraries for material, talk to reporters, the police, hunt down friends and enemies. They were to meet again in two weeks.

The next day, a month after her telegram to Arles, a response finally arrived.

1939 APRIL 30 AM 10 55 ARLES FRANCE

ALIZÉE BENOIT 303 WEST 10th
STREET NEW YORK NEW YORK
UNITED STATES

BANK WILL NOT RELEASE FUNDS
STOP NO EXPLANATION STOP CON-
TINUE TO DO WHAT YOU CAN STOP
LETTER TO FOLLOW STOP
TANTE C=

Days passed and no letter followed. Alizée
tried to convince herself that banks in
France had the same problems banks in
America did, that her aunt and uncle's inability to get at their cash was due to a
bureaucratic oversight, that the money
would arrive soon. She needed to stay calm,
allow time for things to work themselves
out. But fear gnawed at her.

Except for at ANL meetings, she hardly
ever heard talk of potential disaster in
Europe; almost everyone she encountered
was convinced any negative news was nothing more than an attempt to pull the United
States into a fight with Germany, which
America had no business getting involved
in. The waste of the Great War all over
again: hundreds of thousands of dead boys
followed by the hopelessness of the Depression. It wasn't that she couldn't understand

this position that bothered her; it was that she could.

So she threw herself into her work. Aaron Seliger came for a studio visit. He carefully inspected the six reversals she'd finished and claimed to be impressed. He explained that unfortunately he had shows scheduled through the end of December but that he would definitely come back in November to "reassess" when she had more paintings completed. Mark said this was extremely encouraging, and Alizée thought it was, too, so she went, rolled canvases in hand, to the few other galleries that sold abstract art: Montross, Rehn, Valentine Dudensing, A. E. Gallatin's.

The owners gushed over how talented she was, how original the work, but no one had either the space or the inclination to show any of them. Lee was certain the lack of interest was because she was a girl and had nothing to do with the quality of her work; Alizée could accept that was probably part of it. "Positive rejections," Mark called them, which, again, they were. But that didn't stop it from stinging.

She was thinking about this as she swirled red through the mostly blue tones of a failed painting when the door of her flat flew open and Lee bolted in, waving her hands and

126

talking so fast that Alizée couldn't understand what she was saying. Lee danced
around in a circle, singing a song about
jeepers and creepers and peepers, which
made absolutely no sense.

Alizée was mystified but pleased. Lee and
Igor had been fighting a lot lately, and it
was good to see her smiling again. "What?
What are you trying to tell me?"

"It's so fine, it's so fine, it's so fine!" Lee
sang. "You're so fine, you're so fine, you're
so fine!"

Alizée laughed. "I'm fine?"

Lee thrust a letter into her hands. "Look
what you've done."

Her heart pounded as she read. Commis-
sions from the WPA for two abstract murals.
Hers to be hung in the New York Public
Library and Lee's in the US Custom House.
They were to submit the preliminary drawings in early September. It was signed by
Burgoyne Diller, a supervisor on the mural
project, but it was clearly the work of Eleanor Roosevelt.

There was no one else who could have
achieved this. Despite the fact that most
people, even most artists, ridiculed abstraction and thought even less of female artists,
Mrs. Roosevelt had gone to bat for them
and managed to find these projects. It had

been two months since their conversation, and Alizée had almost forgotten about her request. Clearly the First Lady had not.

"Can you believe it?" Lee crowed. "The rotunda of the library? The ceiling of the Custom House?"

She reread the letter. It *was* difficult to believe. These murals weren't to be hung in some obscure high-school dining room or fifth-floor stairwell.

"You've got a lot of guts." Lee gave her a hug. "And you're one hell of a pal."

Alizée pulled her mother's ring from under her smock and curled her fingers around it, the familiar punch of loss taking her breath away. They would have been so proud. She didn't believe in heaven, but somehow she trusted her parents were looking down on her with pride. *I love you.* She sent the thought skyward. *Stay with me.*

She dropped the ring back between her breasts and looked at Lee's beaming face, heard Tante's voice in her ear: *Man tracht un got lacht.* Man plans and God laughs. "Let's go out and celebrate!" she cried.

There's nothing like a spring evening in New York, when the sun remains high and the lilacs perfume the air. Well, there's Paris on such a night, but Alizée wasn't going to

128

think about France or the dangers that lurked there; she was going to revel in their success, how grand it was to be an artist in this city at this moment in time. She would stay in the present. She and Lee figured it was too fine a night to be inside and that "anybody who was anybody," as Lee put it, would be up at Union Square Park, including the Jumble Shop crowd.

Arm in arm, the girls walked north toward the square, discussing their murals. According to the specifications outlined in the letter, the paintings were "allowed" to contain "nonrepresentational elements," but the murals were officially labeled as "decorative" to avoid that much maligned word: *abstract.* They found this distinction amusing and laughed gaily as Tenth took a forty-five-degree turn due east.

"I've got absolutely no idea what's exported from the port of New York," Lee said.

"And I know just about nothing about education in the United States." All WPA murals were based on a specific theme, usually related to the use of the building in which they were hung. Although why their current shipbuilding mural was going to a high-school cafeteria was a complete mystery.

Two blocks below Union Square, she

could smell the frankfurters and hear the buzz of the crowd. She'd been to the park many times. It was a hotbed of socialist and communist political activity, where she and Lee had gone to countless meetings and rallies. It was a gritty, wild place, roughly four square blocks between Fourteenth and Sixteenth, its bottom cut into a triangle by the slanting intersection of Broadway and Park. Few trees, lots of concrete, even more people.

When they stepped into the throng, it felt different from the other times she'd been here. Instead of the usual overcrowded, argumentative spirit, there was a festive air, as if they were all guests at the wedding of two people madly in love. Spring will do that. Lee treated them both to a frankfurter, saying it was the least she could do, and they ate as they wandered through the crowd. It didn't take long to find Jack, Bill, Gorky, and Mark sitting on a low wall, drinking beer with Phil and Grant, Mark's roommates.

Mark grinned when he saw her, and all she could do was grin back.

"We've got something grand to tell you," Lee said, waving the letter. "Alizée's scored a home run!"

The boys' happiness at the news was

touching. When she'd studied in Paris, there was a group of students she saw outside of class, drank with at the Dôme café, but it was never like this. Her modest successes there — winning a few awards, selling the most at a student show, two paintings purchased by actual collectors — had generated polite congratulations, but no real emotion aside from some barely disguised jealousy. Here, the boys whooped their approval, predicted their great success, toasted many times to Mrs. Roosevelt, and hailed Alizée and Lee as the "first ladies of abstraction." More beer was procured and pushed into their hands.

They all headed out of the park about an hour later to go work in their studios; Alizée and Mark fell behind. When a full block separated them from the others, he dropped his arm causally around her shoulder. "I'm very proud of you," he said softly, bending down to bring their faces closer together. "You're remarkable in so many ways."

His breath in her ear put her into a full body shiver, and when she looked up into his eyes, she was stunned by the burst of desire that filled her. *Man tracht un got lacht.* She raised her mouth, and his lips were even softer and more giving than she'd imagined. They slipped into the recessed doorway of a closed jewelry shop, and the inevitability of it, the rightness of it, obliterated everything else.

She didn't remember the walk to her flat. They were suddenly there, dropping clothes, reaching for each other, falling to the mattress, laughing like happy children. But they were far from children, and all those months of longing initiated an abandon she'd never experienced before. She pressed herself into his caresses, rose to his tongue. The feeling was so intoxicating she didn't ever want it to stop. And neither did he. It was dawn before they finally fell into exhausted sleep.

12
DANIELLE, 2015

It's called the Pollock-Krasner House and Study Center, a museum of sorts, and it took even longer to get there than the map suggested. It's in the Hamptons, way out on Long Island, Jackson Pollock and Lee Krasner's home, now a National Historic Landmark. Grand-mère hadn't exactly said she and Grand-père visited Lee and Jackson there, but I was hoping to find something that confirmed her implication. Plus I'd always wanted to see it.

It was the house where they lived and the barn where they painted, bought in the mid-1940s. Apparently, Lee convinced Pollock to move out there because she wanted to keep him away from his drinking buddies in the city. He was an alcoholic of the highest sort, putting to shame all the other alcoholic artists of the time, of whom there were many. He was killed at the age of forty-four in a drunken rage just a mile down the road by driving into a tree. Killed someone else, too. People quietly speculated it might have been suicide. I don't get the speculation part.

As I wandered through the house, a tiny thing, homely and uninspiring, surprisingly little light — apparently even after Pollock started making money, they had no interest in an upgrade — I wondered if Grand-mère's ramblings held any truth. Could my grandparents have sat in this very living room, on this lumpy couch, leaned against this kitchen counter? Hung out with people whose house had been turned into a museum?

I climbed the narrow steps that led to the master bedroom, which wasn't very master, and a cramped extra room where Lee painted while Jackson worked in his huge studio in the barn. A single bed would barely fit into her space while a Mack truck would be quite comfortable in his. No wonder her paintings from this period were small, in more ways than one, and his were gigantic, also in more ways than one.

I was surprised by how unfocused I was. Not connecting the way I usually do with artists' homes and studios. Typically, I'm so awestruck that I go into a state of intense mania, roller-coastering between stomach-rolling swoons and mad bouts of glee, jumping around like an eight-year-old at Disney World. But that day, I was more akin to a bored teenager being dragged on an educational excursion.

Until I went into the barn. The structure where Jackson created his drip paintings, the studio Lee took over after he died. When I was sheathed in the required slippers and climbed the steps to the studio, my heart began to race and my apathy disappeared. I was in the space of genius, and every part of my being knew it. A rush of excited heat filled me as I slowly turned 360 degrees.

On the floor were splatters and drips and streams of every possible hue, remnants from when Pollock laid his canvases flat and worked from above, circling, pouring house paints, throwing in bits of sand and shell, more paint. The floor lacked the intentionality of his creations, and yet it was art in its own right. Or at least the tracings of art, the makings of art, the remains of art.

And so, too, on the walls, empty squares and rectangles outlined by sunburst splashes of color, marking the outside edges of Krasner's masterpieces. It was difficult to take it all in. The frenetic energy. The command of the castoffs. Fabulous unintended consequences.

I took a deep breath, hoping to inhale the odor of paint and turpentine, what used to be my life's blood; but of course, there was none. It was a museum, after all. There were shelves loaded with jugs of turpentine, tubes of paint, hundreds of brushes, all of which, the guide assured us, belonged to Pollock and Krasner.

I saw my own apartment filled with the same and closed my eyes against the longing the image evoked. Who was I kidding? I missed it: the slipping of time, the pain–pleasure of a long day at work, the gratification of doing something difficult. Why had I been so sure giving up painting was the right thing to do? Why had I been so quick to fuel my insecurities with Sam's bitter judgments?

I pushed these questions aside and cruised the circumference of the barn with its huge window streaming north light, taking in the juxtapositions of the splotches, the colors pushing and pulling each other into three dimensions, picturing the paintings in my office at Christie's. Were they Jack's? Were they Lee's? I'd been working on this question for weeks now, ever since the carton first appeared, trying to create the beginnings of what's called the three-legged stool of authentication: provenance, forensics, and connoisseurship.

One problem was that there was no provenance: no papers detailing the lineage of owners, no sales receipts, nothing signed by the artist, not even a name on the paintings themselves. The second was that forensics are only marginally useful with a modern painting; it's a lot easier for a forger to get his hands on canvases, stretchers, and paints used in the twentieth century than it is for those used in the sixteenth. I was checking what I could, but so far there had been nothing definitive either way.

So it was probably going to come down to connoisseurship, the least verifiable of the three legs, as it's based on a gut feeling, coupled with experience, knowledge, judgment, and all kinds of other things that can't be quantified. I was in no way qualified to make this kind of determination. Which is why I was only tasked with the preliminary forensics piece.

There was little in the barn to help me with either this or my Alizée quest, so I wandered back to the house, where there was even less. I was hoping there might be some personal papers on site, maybe letters or journals Lee or Jackson wrote, maybe detailing their visitors or, even better, discussions about Alizée. But the director told me all the original papers were at the Study Center at SUNY's Stony Brook campus, which was closed to the public until the end of the semester, two months away. I asked her if she was familiar with the name Alizée Benoit. She thought for a couple of seconds, shook her head, and moved on to answer the next person's question.

I tried talking up the girl taking tickets at the back door, clearly an art student, but of course she'd never heard of Alizée either and appeared to have as little interest in her as she had in me. I looked around the small kitchen and remembered Grand-mère's mention of eating pie. "How about Jackson Pollock and apple pies?" I asked her, then laughed with false heartiness. "Someone told me he was into making them, but I can't imagine him doing such a thing. Seems completely out of character."

She gave me a withering look. "It's a well-known fact," she informed me, "that baking apple pie was one of his passions."

My jaw literally dropped. "Are you kidding me?" I cried, far too loudly for a recipient of such mundane information.

The art student took a step back. "No," she said, without a trace of humor. "Why on earth would I make up something like that?"

13
ALIZÉE, 1939

She was helpless against the passion, the power of being with Mark, a hunger, a raging thirst. He had a wife he might return to at any time, and while the thought of this terrified her, threw her back to the loss of her parents, she willed herself to live in the present. This was sometimes successful, sometimes not. They never talked about Edith, the estranged wife, who was unrelated to them or to the art they were so committed to making. Myopic, of course, and perhaps self-serving, but new love is selfish and so were they.

They hadn't ventured out much in the past month, preferring to hide out in her flat feasting on sex and conversation, but the Valentine Dudensing Gallery was showing Picasso's *Guernica,* his controversial antiwar mural. Although neither she nor Mark were keen on political paintings, she'd left France just weeks before *Guernica*'s first display at the World's Fair in Paris in 1937 and didn't want to miss it again. Picasso, after all, was Picasso.

They stood in front of the massive painting, eleven feet tall and over twenty-five feet wide, mesmerized. A wild-eyed bull loomed above a woman clutching her dead child. A horse fell to its knees, gored by a spear. The severed hand of a dead soldier still held a saber. An evil eye shone down on it all, a lightbulb as its pupil. Daggers rather than tongues. The bull's tail in flames. A shattered sword. The room's ceiling pressing down, crushing the people, the animals, and the objects below. Crushing her heart.

The painting was based on Hitler's bombing of Guernica, a small Spanish town of no strategic importance in a civil war that did not directly involve Germany. At the time of the attack, most of the men were off fighting, and the village was primarily inhabited by women and children. Hitler's intention was to impress Franco, to terrorize the populace, and to test his latest weaponry; he succeeded in all his ambitions and also destroyed the town, killing hundreds of people, but leaving standing, with cunning hubris, the only potential military target, a single factory.

In black, whites, and grays, Picasso had

created a heart-wrenching portrayal of this particular horror and the tragedies of all wars. Truncated animals and dismembered humans distorted in palpable agony filled the canvas in a nightmare miasma. It attracted and repulsed her at the same time, too horrific and too real to look at, but she couldn't turn away.

Mindless war. Mindless killing. The lust for power. Hatred of the other. The destruction of innocents. It hit her like a sucker punch. Babette was right: If Hitler had done this in Spain, he could do it in France. Do it anywhere. Everywhere. She sat down hard on a bench.

Mark sat next to her, still staring at the mural. "It's good," he said. "I'll give him that. But propaganda has no place in art."

"This isn't propaganda," she said, her voice rough with unshed tears. She had to get the visas.

"Even if it's true, that doesn't mean it isn't sending a political message."

She sat up. "Why can't it be both? A great painting and a provocative one?"

Mark turned and looked at her. "That doesn't sound like you."

"Why do you say that?"

"You don't like political art any more than I do."

She crossed her arms. "I like this painting."

He shrugged. "It shouldn't be about an artist's ideology. Real art needs to explore the soul, not politics."

"But Picasso's using politics to express what's in his soul," she said more vehemently than she expected and lowered her voice. "What he cares about. And to warn people."

"It's the warning part I disagree with."

"His warning is about the evil of war. It's a call to save lives. What's not to agree with about that?"

"Art isn't a weapon."

"Then why is Hitler chasing all the abstract painters out of Europe?" she demanded. "What about his horrid Degenerate Art show? If he didn't believe art could change minds, why would he care?"

"Come on, do you really believe a painting's going to stop Hitler?"

"No one knows what might or might not stop Hitler!"

Mark frowned, then his face softened. "I'm sorry, Zée. I forgot about your family."

She slumped on the bench. He'd forgotten about her family. About the thousands running for safe haven. So easy to forget what wasn't important to you, what wasn't

143

affecting you. So easy to forget what you didn't want to remember.

Mark turned her shoulders so they faced each other, his eyes latching onto hers. "I'm a dolt, and I wouldn't blame you if you never spoke to me again." He lightly kissed her lips. "But it would break my heart."

There was nothing to say, so she took him back to her flat where she hoped their lovemaking would drive away any thoughts of what was or wasn't happening in Europe.

As soon as Mark left, she went down to Telzonski's Hardwares and bought a used Philco radio for eighty-seven cents. She couldn't afford it, but she needed to keep better tabs on what was happening in the larger world. She unplugged the hot plate, hooked up the radio, and found a news station. Edward R. Murrow was reporting from London. In some magical way, the Philco played live broadcasts from across the ocean. Mr. Telzonski said it had to do with shortwave transmissions. Whatever those were.

As she listened to the dreary reports and somber prognostications, she tried to cheer herself by thinking about the letter she just received from a man named Hiram Bingham, whom Long had fired after Bingham objected to the number of visa applications the department was rejecting. She'd tracked him down with help from one of Gideon's contacts, and Bingham finally responded saying he was coming to New York next month and wanted to meet. Reading between the lines, she and Gideon got the impression he might have something specific to give them on Long. It wasn't much, but it was something.

A few days later, she came home and caught the tail end of a report. Murrow was talking about a ship with almost a thousand European refugees aboard seeking political asylum in Cuba. But when the boat got to Havana, the Cuban government hadn't let any of the passengers disembark, so it set sail for Florida hoping for a more hospitable reception. Instead, American officials refused to allow the ship dock, and now the passengers were "steaming back to Europe and an uncertain fate."

Long. It had to have been Long.

She turned up the volume. "What ship?" she cried out loud. "What ship?"

Murrow was describing the passengers. German Jews, mostly families with Cuban visas who planned to immigrate to America from there. The snakes coiled in her belly began to unwind, consuming her from within; she gagged. No. It wasn't the *St. Louis.* It couldn't be. She forced a deep breath, praying, hoping against hope. But Murrow soon confirmed that it was.

As a commercial for laundry detergent played, she felt slightly off kilter, as if she'd been in this moment before, heard this report before, strained to grasp its meaning before. Déjà vu, but not quite déjà vu, because it was both the same and altered. The circumstances were different; that was then, this was now. And yet there were the familiar sensations: the numbness, the disbelief, the tickle of terror. Now it was Babette. Then it was Maman and Papa.

Papa had walked her to school as usual that morning, but instead of Maman waiting for her at the end of the day, Mrs. Clouatre, her friend Colette's mother, was there in her place. This wasn't unusual as Mrs. C and her mother took turns walking them to the École française every Monday and Wednesday afternoon, but when they turned toward home rather than toward *l'école,* she and Colette both knew something was up.

The girls' first thought was that it was an unexpected reprieve, and they were thrilled at the prospect of a free afternoon when they thought they'd be stuck inside learning boring French. But there was something in Mrs. C's silence that quickly silenced them, too. And there was something in the way she looked at Alizée that turned her icy cold. Alizée didn't know it then, but what she saw in Mrs. C's eyes was pity. She would see it on many more occasions for many more years, and it would forever turn her icy cold.

Mrs. C may have taken them back to her house, or to Alizée's house, or maybe even over to the still smoldering lab building. She may have told Alizée or maybe she waited for Oncle to break the news. Alizée had flashes of that day, images, sharp and cruel, but mostly what she remembered were the feelings. That and Oncle sitting on her bed when she opened her eyes one morning. After the funeral, he and Tante had bundled her up and brought her back to France, a mass of twisting misery consuming her from within.

And here it was again. She dropped her head into her hands. All she could see was Babette's little family. Clutching each other and the meager possessions they'd brought from home. Sophie and Gabrielle fussing and crying. Babette and Pierre trying to be strong, crying inside. Looking to America with hope, finding only disillusionment.

Steaming back to Europe and an uncertain fate.

14
ELEANOR

It was deathly hot in New York; dirt and sweat mingled uncomfortably every time Eleanor stepped outside. She couldn't wait to get to the country, to swim, to ride her horse into the foothills. Over the last couple of days she'd dutifully met with the League of Women Voters, the planning group for the Roosevelt Presidential Library, among others, and now she was fulfilling her final commitment: the Good Neighbor Committee. All she could think of was Hyde Park and fresh air.

When the meeting ended early, she had the driver take her and her friend Hick to the gallery space on Fifty-Seventh Street. She hadn't expected to have time to stop at the opening of the July Federal Art Gallery exhibit but had wanted to. These juried shows were held monthly at a variety of venues to showcase the work of WPA artists. The judges were picky, and the work was always first rate. She and Hick would have to wait for the train anyway, so why not squeeze in the event that promised to be the most fun of the lot?

They entered the storefront while the chauffeur waited for them on the street. To the left, empty display cases were stacked on top of one another suggesting the store's previous life, most likely jewelry, but it now looked very much like the art gallery it was to be for the next few weeks. The artwork, hung on stark white walls, was impressive, and the room was so crowded that it might take a few minutes before anyone noticed Eleanor was there. In that short moment of anonymity, she surveyed the exhibit.

Although the work was primarily representational, Eleanor noticed a few abstract paintings in a far corner. She'd been intrigued by the articles and photographs of modern art she'd seen after her last WPA visit, although unfortunately, she hadn't had the time to pursue it any further. She nudged Hick. "Let's go over there before anyone spots us." They didn't get far.

"Mrs. Roosevelt!" A young man, shorter than both Eleanor and Hick by at least a head, shouldered his way through the crowd. When he reached them, he actually bowed. "We, we're honored that you accepted our invitation. The invitation." He pressed his hands together, forefingers to his mouth, took a deep breath. "I'm so surprised to see you. So surprised, but a swell surprise. A thrilling one. When I mailed out the invitations, I didn't think you'd actually come, but I decided it was worth the stamp. And now you have come, you're here, and the stamp was worth it. Please, let me take you around."

Eleanor suppressed a smile. "Thank you," she said. "And you are . . . ?"

"Oh." The boy was completely flummoxed. "Sorry. So sorry. I'm, I'm Milton Tripp. Milton. Please call me Milton."

"Well, then, Milton, this is my friend Lorena Hickok, and although we don't have much time before our train, we would love to see some of your favorite paintings. Are you an artist yourself? Working on the project?"

Milton answered both questions in the affirmative and propelled them to the front of the store. "I guess I don't need to tell you about all the talented artists we have on the project," he gushed. "They wouldn't be here if not for you. We wouldn't be here." He spread his arms to indicate the entire gallery. "None of this would be here without your belief in us."

151

Eleanor waved the compliment aside as he pointed out landscapes by Alexander Brook and Stuart Shirley, romantic sea-scapes by John Forbes and Jean Liberté, and the social scene paintings of Philip Evergood, Jack Levine, and Boris Margo. They were interrupted numerous times by well-wishers and waiters who kept offering Eleanor champagne, which she kept refusing.

She glanced at her watch; only forty-five minutes remained before their train left from Penn Station. "This has been just delightful, Milton," she said. "A great pleasure, but we have a train to catch and must go." She knew the train would wait for her if need be, but she didn't like taking unnecessary advantage of her position, especially if it inconvenienced others.

As they turned toward the front door, Eleanor again noticed the abstract paintings she'd initially wanted to see. "Those are very compelling," she told Milton. "Maybe we can stay an extra minute and take a look."

Milton bowed again, even more awkwardly this time. "I'd be happy to show them to you," he said, but it was clear that modern art was not what he thought the First Lady should be looking at.

"We'll be fine," Eleanor said, then remembering Harry Hopkins's similar reaction, she leaned into Hick. "Why is it that men are so afraid of anything new?" she whispered.

Hick laughed and linked her arm through Eleanor's as they headed toward the back.

Although there was no reason for Eleanor to expect so, she wasn't surprised when she saw the young French girl from the warehouse standing by the artwork, but she was pleased. "I'm so sorry," she said, her hand extended, "I've forgotten your name, but I'm delighted to see you again."

A million-dollar smile spread across the girl's face, and she grasped Eleanor's hand. "Alizée. Alizée Benoit, Mrs. Roosevelt. I'm happy to see you, too. Very happy. I sent a letter thanking you for the mural project, but I'm sure you didn't have time to read it."

"I'm sorry I didn't, my dear," Eleanor said. "I'm sure it was lovely." She'd also forgotten about the murals. "The project is going well, I presume? And your friend's also?"

"Swell," Alizée said. "Just swell. We're submitting our preliminary drawings to the committee soon."

"And these are yours?" Eleanor motioned

to the three colorful abstracts behind Al-izée.

Alizée nodded and pointed to the two next to hers. "And these are Lee's. Lee Krasner. But she's gone out for a sandwich. She'll be so sorry she didn't get to see you and thank you herself."

Eleanor looked at Lee's paintings. They were interesting, unusual she supposed, boxes and thick lines of red, black, white, and gray, but that was all they seemed to be: boxes and thick lines of red, black, white, and gray. Alizée's, on the other hand, were alive, abstract yet somehow also figurative, even as Eleanor struggled to understand what the figures might be. Dancers, perhaps. Blossoms? Floating plants? The works were bursting with movement, with vivacity, but somehow were also a little melancholy.

"Oh, Alizée," Eleanor said. "These are wonderful."

"You like them?" The girl's face was tentative, almost disbelieving. "You really mean it?"

"I do. Very much so," Eleanor assured her. Such a pretty child, so full of hope, and yet, Eleanor sensed, full of something not quite so cheerful. Like her paintings. Eleanor wanted to wrap her up in her arms, take her

154

back to Hyde Park, fatten her up, pamper her, watch her relax by the pool. "I hope your parents have had a chance to come by. They must be very proud of you."

Alizée shook her head.

"Oh, they live in France, don't they?" Eleanor smiled. "Where you're from. That would be a long way to come."

"It's not that," Alizée said.

"I'm sorry," Eleanor said quickly. "I didn't mean to pry."

"They died when I was younger."

Now Eleanor understood all too well where Alizée's sadness came from. And from where her connection to the girl derived. "Oh, my dear, I'm so sorry. Sorry that it happened and sorry I brought it up."

"It's okay, it was a long time ago."

"Then that makes it even worse," Eleanor said. "I was orphaned when I was nine."

Their eyes met. "You were?" Alizée asked. "Both at the same time?"

"No, not the same time. My mother passed away first and then my father. But I was nine when he died."

Alizée stared at one of Lee's paintings. "We were living in Boston, Cambridge actually, where both my parents were doing postdoctoral work, and where I was born. They were scientists, and there was an explosion, a fire, in their laboratory. They were killed along with three of their colleagues. I was twelve." Her eyes shown with unshed tears. "I'm sorry for your loss."

Now Eleanor had the excuse to give the child a hug. "It gets easier," she said, "but it never goes away."

Hick raised her watch.

Reluctantly, Eleanor let Alizée go. "Well, I'm happy to meet you again, sorry to hear your story, but I'm thrilled to finally see some of your work." She nodded at Hick, then turned back to Alizée. "I want to buy one — the one with the plants emerging, if that's what they are — but I don't have the time today. We're running to catch a train."

"I once invited you to my studio," Alizée said. "I'd be honored if you visited. Anytime. I have lots of other paintings. Many similar to this." She pointed to the floating flowers. "I'll save this one for you, but maybe you'll find one you like better."

"Please don't save it for me if someone else wants to buy it," Eleanor said. "But if it's still available, I'd be honored to own it. We're spending the month of August in Hyde Park. It's just too hot in Washington in the late summer, and I would like the president to get a little rest. But I have a speech to give in New York City on the third of September. May I come by that afternoon and perhaps make a purchase then?"

15
ALIZÉE

For the rest of the summer, Alizée kept the
Philco on, listening to news reports while
she worked: FDR's personal appeal to
Hitler on Poland, Franco's victory in Spain,
Churchill's call for a British-Russian alli-
ance. She had no idea where Babette and
her family were. If they were safe. If everyone else was. She wrote letters every week,
but none came in return. It tore at her.
Finally, at the end of August, after four
months of silence, a letter from Tante arrived.

2 August 1939
Arles

Ma douce nièce,
The mail is getting more erratic every
day, but I hope you have received word
that Babette and her family have been
allowed into Belgium. They are currently

in Antwerp but need to leave there as soon as possible. They are working with a Jewish agency helping the *St. Louis* passengers, and Babette says she is hopeful they will get visas to America soon. I am not sure she is being completely truthful with me about this.

I am grateful they are not still in Germany, but no Jew is safe anywhere in Europe. I thank God every day that they are alive. I lost ten pounds in the weeks after they were turned away from Cuba. I still have no appetite. Baby Gabby was very sick, but Babette says she is much better now. I just hope it is true. I long to hold my sweet baby girls. Soon, I pray, soon.

You are the only one I do not tear myself apart over, although I worry about you in a different way. Please write and tell me how your school and your painting are going. Have you met any young men? Perhaps someone Jewish? I long for good news.

The rabbi tells terrible stories not only from Germany but from Czechoslovakia and Lithuania as well. We all heard about the German police standing by while Jews were murdered in the streets, their homes and businesses burned to the ground, but now he says it is the same in Prague. And will soon be in many more places.

Do you know that Jewish children in France are being turned away from swimming pools in the heat of August? Somehow, despite the smallness of this, the image haunts me. How does a mother explain such a thing to her child? That she is not good enough to swim? That someone hates her so much they cannot share the same water? Hitler claims the biblical pharaoh did not go far enough and that he will not make the same mistake. Do Americans know about this? Do they care?

Even with all this, we continue to live our lives, and this is reassuring. Oncle and I are planning our fall classes, and Alain is starting to mope about the end of summer. Henri thinks he did well on his exams and is working at hospital while he waits for the official results. But I worry for us as I worry for all of mankind.

The bank still will not release our money. They claim it is red tape, but we believe it is anti-Semitism. It has been almost five months. Although most here are pretending to live in a world where

Hitler does not exist, there are also many who are so confident of a German victory that they are joining the Nazi Party and pushing for Hitler's policies before he even takes a step into the country. There is no way to prove this is related to the bank's refusal, so our hands are tied. Have you made any progress? Please let us know as soon as you have any news. We are prepared to leave immediately.

I am so sorry to burden you with our troubles and want to assure you that we are fine. We would just be more fine if we were in America with you. I know you are doing everything you can and thank you for that. I only hope that soon we will all be together as a family should be.

Oncle and I love you very much and think of you every day.

As always, I am *ta tante qui t'aime,*
Chantal

Babette and Pierre and the girls were in Belgium, a place Hitler wasn't. Oncle and Tante were preparing for school. Henri had taken his exams. Everyone was safe. Everything was good. In her head, she understood this was true, but her clenched stomach

161

knew better. Tante wasn't the only one without an appetite.

Breckinridge Long was the guest speaker at the October luncheon meeting of the New York chapter of the America First Committee. Gideon had arranged press credentials for her, and with these in her pocketbook, dressed in a drab skirt and the kind of cardigan sweater she thought a journalist might wear that she'd borrowed from Bertha, she sat at the back of the wainscoted room with the reporters.

Germany had invaded Poland. France and England had declared war against Germany. FDR had proclaimed the United States neutral and unaligned in the conflict. Alizée was knotted with fear.

She had no money for visas. Mrs. Roosevelt, who might have been able to use her influence to help with the visas, hadn't shown up for the studio visit, which wasn't surprising as it was scheduled for the day that the United Kingdom and France declared war on Germany, two days after the Nazis stomped across the Polish border. Hiram Bingham, Long's ex-assistant, had canceled their meetings, and the rest of her committee was struggling to come up with anything they could use against the assistant secretary. She was here today to try to change that.

"There are those," Long was saying, "mostly communists, extreme radicals, Jewish professional agitators and refugee enthusiasts, who claim that we are not doing enough to help the Europeans streaming to our shores from countries now under Germany's control. This is patently untrue. Since Adolf Hitler came to power, nearly a quarter of a million US visas have been granted to fleeing immigrants, a significant percentage to those of the Jewish race."

He was such a liar. She had numbers right here in her notepad that proved what *he* was saying was "patently untrue." According to the State Department, half of the visas in 1938 went to British or Irish immigrants, people who had nothing to fear from Hitler. And no more than a handful of the remainder had been granted to "those of the Jewish race."

Most of the others in the room were nodding their heads in agreement, including a substantial number of reporters. Why were they so willing to take Long's misinformation at face value? Why hadn't anyone done their homework? She clenched her hand tightly around her pen. Tante had asked if Americans knew what Hitler was planning, if they cared. The answer was all too obvious.

"But we must exercise our largesse with caution, for these are difficult and dangerous times. There is no doubt that many of these so-called immigrants are actually Fifth Columnists, Nazi spies masquerading as Jews, who come here to commit sabotage against our great and generous nation. And this we will not accept!"

There was a long round of applause.

"So to this end," Long said after a significant pause, "I have approved a new regulation. It mandates that every American sponsoring an immigrant be screened to determine their motives. And all would-be immigrants will undergo the same at their respective consulates." He put his hand over his heart as if reciting the Pledge of Allegiance. "I promise if any suspicions are raised, the visa will be refused. We cannot and will not take this chance! Our national security depends upon it!"

Now it was a standing ovation, and Alizée could feel the crowd coalescing into a single being ready and eager to follow Breckinridge Long. She had no choice but to haul herself to her feet. It was impossible to deny that the man was shrewd. Not only had he just declared he was going to make it even more difficult for European immigrants to get visas, but by focusing on those canny villains who disguised themselves as Jews, he'd devised a way to deny entry to as many Jews as he wanted.

She seethed as she waited for the question-and-answer session but grew more incensed by the snippets of conversation around her.

"That man's got his head screwed on right."

"They'll take all the jobs, and we don't have any to spare."

"They'll insinuate themselves until they've got their hands on all the money. You know how they are. That's always their goal."

These people were being brainwashed with untruths. Someone needed to set the record straight. And she had the numbers to do just that. Tante always said that honey caught more flies than vinegar. But Long didn't deserve honey. He didn't even deserve vinegar. Acid was more like it.

She was used to hearing anti-Semitic comments, growing up in Cambridge, in Arles, living here in New York. It was a fact of life, background noise, and she'd never spent much time thinking about it. When she was in first grade, she'd been completely bewildered when a boy started screaming on the playground that she'd killed Christ; she hadn't even known who Christ was. When her mother explained the situation and the lie, assuring her the boy was uninformed about history and that she should feel sorry for him, she'd taken Maman's words at face value. But now that a man representing the US government was turning that background noise into action, everything was different.

She busied herself with her notepad, trying to memorize her statistics.

"Probably ain't going to need that." The reporter next to her pointed at the notepad. "He's only going to repeat the high points of his speech. Not going to answer any questions either. Except from his own people." He tilted his head toward an older gentleman, who was better dressed than the rest of the group. "As if we don't know who they are."

Just as the reporter had predicted, Long, with a wide smile oozing friendliness, reiterated what he'd just said, and the first question he took was from the well-dressed man.

"When do you think your friend Franklin Roosevelt will promote you from assistant secretary to actual secretary of state?" he asked as if the question had just popped into his head.

Long chuckled modestly. "The president

and I have been friends since our navy days during the Great War, but as far as I know, he has no intention of taking the position away from Cordell, who is also a friend. Secretary Hull has, and will always have, my complete support." He scanned the crowd for another question from one of his own.

Alizée raised her hand, hoping the fact that she was a girl would fool him into thinking he could trust her. And it worked.

"The girl on the left," he said, pointing at her. "What's your name, dear?"

"Babette Pierre, sir," she said meekly, hoping to build on the edge his underestimation gave her. "And I just want to tell you, Secretary Long, how much I respect you for the help you've given to all those poor refugees." She'd purposely dropped the "assistant."

He beamed at her. "It is the least our great country can do for the poor souls caught up in a war not of their own making."

"But I'm a little confused about the numbers you just quoted." She smiled at him, fluttered a bit of eyelash. "I hope you can help me figure it out."

Long bowed slightly in her direction. "I'm always happy to be of service to a girl as young and beautiful as yourself."

The reporters chuckled, and one blew a loud wolf whistle.

She bobbed her head as if she were both pleased and embarrassed, cleared her throat, and purposely stammered, "I, ah, I understand that so far this year over three hundred thousand German refugees, mostly Jewish, have applied to come here. But then I read in the *Sun* that fewer than ten thousand visas have been granted by the State Department since January. Which doesn't sound right."

She frowned as if laboring to understand. "According to the Immigration Act, one hundred fifty-four thousand visas are available each year to citizens of European countries. So how can one hundred forty-four thousand still be outstanding with less than four months left in the year? I don't understand how a State Department as committed to helping 'fleeing immigrants' as you've described could have this kind of backlog."

Long appeared happy to explain. "You're absolutely right about the three hundred thousand German applications, Miss Pierre. It's the *Sun* that's wrong about the number of visas granted." He raised his eyebrows and chuckled. "As they so often are."

"I'm not sure I agree with you about the

Sun," Alizée said with a sly smile, "as they're my employer." She nodded at Long as the laughter began to subside: *I see what you're doing, and two can play this game.*

"But let's forget the *Sun.*" She glanced at her notepad. "You just said a significant proportion of the two hundred fifty thousand visas you've granted have gone to European Jews. So then we must be talking about at least sixty or seventy percent which would mean somewhere between one hundred and fifty thousand and one hundred seventy-five thousand Jews have been allowed into this country since Hitler came to power. That can't be right, can it? An awful lot of Fifth Columners, I'd think."

Instead of being angry or defensive, Long's eyes sparkled at the challenge. "I'm surprised you would say such a thing, my dear. We all know that the vast majority of the Jewish race pose no threat to the United States. They're just the unfortunate victims of that crazy man on the other side of the ocean."

The reporters were eating this up, all eyes following the verbal tennis match.

"So I take it that means you'll soon be authorizing visas for many more of these unfortunate victims." For a moment, she caught herself thinking that maybe he could be reasoned with. He was clearly smart enough to appreciate the facts.

Then her head cleared. What a ridiculous notion. Breckinridge Long was a man whose actions were based on hatred not logic. He was the man putting her family in danger. So many others. *Merde.* If he could charm her, whom couldn't he charm?

"Touché, Miss Pierre, touché. You're not only beautiful but clearly intelligent. Unfortunately, you're also very naive." He doffed an invisible hat. "I'd love to discuss this with you further, but that wouldn't be fair to the rest of the reporters here. Please feel free to call my secretary to schedule a private meeting." He winked at her knowingly, then pointed to a woman whose clothing was a few stripes above that of the other members of the press. "Mrs. Appleton, do you have a question for me?"

16
DANIELLE, 2015

I borrowed my mother's car again and went back to visit Grand-mère the following weekend. I brought *Lily Pads* and a painting of my own, a brightly colored collage made of paint, string, canvas, and cloth, which I thought she'd like. I hadn't seen it in over a year and regarded it impassively: it wasn't half bad. The idea for it had come to me in a flash. I pulled an all-nighter, and when the first smudge of dawn appeared I couldn't have been more surprised; I thought only seconds had passed. How I missed those moments when passion muddied time, when the painting and I were one.

As I pulled into the parking lot, I thought about how Grand was going to perk up when she saw Alizée's "pretty painting" again. How, like hearing a favorite song, it might spark a whole range of memories. Who knew, the sight of it might give her a blast of real joy, free her, even for a moment, from the haze. She'd cared enough about this painting to save it from my grandfather's heartbreaking demand to destroy what was too painful for him to see. And maybe she'd be happy to see my work, too.

Whistling — which is very uncharacteristic for me, especially in the morning — I lugged the two unwieldy canvases into the elevator and gave the button a punch with my elbow. When I got to the living room, I found Grand-mère sitting in the same chair in half shadow, but she was slumped completely to one side and her eyes were closed. She wasn't moving.

I ran to her, picked up her wrist, felt a fluttering pulse, shook her. "Grand!" I cried. "Grand, wake up. Are you okay?"

This was a mistake. She startled, stared at me uncomprehendingly for a moment, then started to scream. She flailed her arms, pushed me away with surprising strength. "I hate you, Stephanie," she yelled. "Go away!" She pointed to the two paintings in my hands. "And take your ugly children with you!"

Nurses and aides rushed toward us, tried to calm her, and then quickly took her to her room. An aide apologized to me — although I knew it was my fault for disturbing her — sat me down and brought me some tea. I pressed the mug between my hands, hoping it would stop the trembling. It turned out that Grand had mistaken me for a nurse she was none too fond of. So much for joy.

Pretty much everyone I know, including my mother and my cousin's five-year-old, uses their various electronic devices for all the necessities of daily life from checking the weather to getting on a plane. I'm equally guilty. Last week I raced back up three flights of stairs because I'd forgotten my phone, and I was taking a two-minute trip to the grocery store. Who knew who might text? What breaking news I might miss? What trivial question I might desperately need an answer to?

Still, there's a Luddite part of me that can't give up my file cards. Yes, file cards, those three-by-five rectangles made of thin cardboard. They used to be ubiquitous, but I'm not sure anyone but me uses them anymore. Maybe elementary school teachers, but probably not. I'd bet my life there's an app for that. Anyway, the cards help me think, to focus in a way nothing with a screen can. I like the weight of a pen in one hand and a pile of cards in the other.

So that's what I used to get a handle on where I was with my search for Alizée. On the top of a card, I wrote: *What do I know about Alizée?* Returned to the States in 1937 at nineteen. Lived in Greenwich Village. Maybe hung out with Jackson Pollock, Lee Krasner, and Mark Rothko. Was a talented painter. Probably knew Eleanor Roosevelt. Had some kind of nervous breakdown. Went into a mental institution and was never seen again. I doodled a picture of a young woman with blonde, curly hair painting a canvas in one corner of the card, a sketch of Eleanor Roosevelt in another.

Family lore has always centered on the Alizée-was-crazy explanation for her disappearance. After leaving the hospital, the thinking went, she either got lost or had an accident or had amnesia or killed herself, maybe all of the above. I wrote these choices on another file card.

Grand-mère, granted not the most reliable of sources, had suggested Grand-père was looking for Alizée in France before 1945, which would mean she'd left the States and returned to Europe before Pearl Harbor, probably sometime in early 1941. Unlikely, but I wrote it down and drew a caricature of Adolf Hitler, mostly mustache.

What else? I started a new card. Maybe

she did it on purpose, just disappeared because she wanted to disappear. Maybe she'd had it with all those nutso artists and wanted to start a new life somewhere different. I'd had the desire myself, more than once, although obviously for much more mundane reasons. Like when I got pregnant when I was eighteen. Or when I had to tell my mother I'd failed three courses in college because I was more interested in partying than studying. And definitely when I discovered Sam cheating on me for the second time.

While I was living within each of those situations, I'd yearned for that long highway heading west, looping over all those rivers and mountains and plains, bringing me to a new place, a place where I could be a new me. Obviously, I'd never done it, being the same old me that I'd always been. I reminded myself that Alizée wasn't me; she seemed just the type who could pull it off.

It was also possible she'd never left the hospital, which no one knew the name of. Maybe she fell in love with a fellow patient — better yet, a doctor — and decided to stay there under an assumed name. Maybe she was so drugged she couldn't leave, and the staff faked her discharge papers because they didn't want to admit what they'd done to her. I began to draw a 1940s electroshock machine but stopped myself. Too ghoulish. What if she'd died there, and the hospital had covered it up?

Orphaned at twelve, all of twenty-two in 1940, without her family and with a tortured artistic soul. It was possible that any of these awful things had happened to her. Or something equally awful I hadn't thought of yet. Clearly nothing good. Probably nothing I even wanted to know.

But I did want to know. About Alizée, her story, her art, her demise. I also wanted to know who painted the squares, and if it turned out to be Alizée, to get her the recognition she deserved.

It would have been a lot easier if Anatoly and George had given me permission to pursue this through Christie's. But they couldn't control what I did in my free time — or even what I did on the side at work — and I was damned if I was going to let their self-interest hold me back.

So I Googled the hell out of every possibility on my file cards. Not a single hit on Alizée Benoit and, unfortunately, as with the Pollock and Krasner papers, few other hits because most of the online information started in the mid- to late-twentieth century, more late than mid. The frantic twenty-first-century digitizing of every possible piece of data hadn't yet reached that far into the past.

I was surprised to discover that in 1940 passenger ships and commercial airplanes were still traveling between New York and Europe. So theoretically, Alizée could have gone there, but as no passenger manifests were available, it was impossible to know.

No mention of an Alizée Benoit in the smattering of marriage and death records I found for the New York area in that time period.

I called various police departments: in Greenwich Village, where she'd lived; in Cambridge, Massachusetts, where she was born; in DC, in case she went there after her release to see her good buddy Eleanor. I left multiple messages that mostly weren't returned. And when they were, I found myself quickly dismissed or sent to hold hell.

I turned back to the Archives of American Art database, checking on other artists in New York City at the time: reams and reams of material, no mention of Alizée.

I stared at *Lily Pads* and *Turned.* Who was the woman who'd painted them? Had she also painted the squares? Was she the conduit who carried the Abstract Expressionists into their new school of art, the so-called missing link? I was no closer to an answer than I'd been the first day the carton appeared.

And then, one night as I was absently scrolling through some of the Krasner papers, I came across a transcript of a video interview Lee did with Bruce Landau in 1982 about her early years in the WPA. As my eyes scanned down the page, Alizée's name jumped out at me as if it were highlighted.

BL: The image of all of you at the time was that you were wild and crazy. Is that a fair assessment?

LK: More than fair. It was a wonderful time. Youth, hope, art. Very heady stuff. Most of us were on the project. Not de Kooning because he wasn't an American citizen. But Pollock, Mark Rothko, Arshile Gorky, Phil Guston, Alice Neel. So many great talents. Such fun. Sure, we partied, hung out at the Jumble Shop, were what might be called sexually promiscuous, but mostly we worked. We worked hard on the project and we worked hard on our own art.

BL: Can you talk about how you influenced each other? About the beginnings of Abstract Expressionism?

LK: (frowns) We never thought we were the beginning of anything so specific. Not in that sense. We were working in a way that was meaningful to us, not trying to start something that could be named.

BL: But you did. Abstract Expressionism is the first true American school of art, when we began to export our artistic ideas to Europe instead of vice versa. You should be proud of that.

LK: (crosses arms over chest) It's not a matter of pride or not pride. It's all semantics. Not worth discussing.

BL: So then let's get back to the influences. Who was your single greatest influence?

LK: There's never any one greatest, it's not possible. I studied with Hans Hofmann for a long time, so him. And of course Pollock. But we were always in and out of each other's studios. In each other's faces about what we were doing. Or not doing.

BL: Did you ever work together on a single project?

LK: No, never. It wasn't like that. Except once, I guess. If you could call it that . . .

BL: Once?

LK: Well, not really. But there was another influence I didn't mention, Alizée Benoit, a true talent. Her work had a huge effect on all of us. Especially her ideas about transformation, about pulling the abstract into the real. And about the big canvas.

BL: Never heard of her.

LK: She disappeared in 1940.

BL: What do you mean, disappeared?

LK: (sighs) She went to a sanatorium for a rest — one where more than a few of the gang ended up at different times — and never came back.

BL: And her work?

LK: Also gone. A real loss.

BL: (hesitates) That's too bad, but let's get back to the people we do know about, you and your friends. I'm really curious about how it all worked. The cauldron, so to speak, that started a movement. Who was at . . .

17
ALIZÉE, 1939

8 October 1939
Arles

Ma petite soeur,
This is a very difficult letter to write.
Two nights ago three policemen came to
the house and arrested Oncle. They said
he'd been fired from university and was
being detained because he was teaching
communist propaganda in his American
literature class. Apparently he was discussing *Call of the Wild* and *An American
Tragedy.* When he told them the books
had nothing to do with communism,
they sneered, put him in handcuffs, and
took him away.

Tante called and we went directly to
the police station. There they pretended
to know nothing about his arrest, but
one of the policemen who I recognized
from *l'école* told me Oncle was already

on his way to Drancy. We had no idea why they would send him to a tiny village outside of Paris but have come to learn a *camp d'accueil* is located there. I will go as soon as my shift ends tomorrow.

We have heard of many cases in which people are arrested with no basis and are let free after a few days, and hope this will be the case. Maybe by the time you are reading this Oncle will be home safe with Tante and Alain. She will send a telegram as soon as this happens.

I know I should try to cheer you with lighthearted stories, but I cannot think of any. As you can see, things are growing more dire here. Please try to get the visas as soon as possible. Leaving France and the rest of the continent is getting more difficult every day.

I have received only one letter from you since June, and Oncle and Tante have received none. In the one dated August 15, you said you weren't receiving mine either, so I do not know if this will ever reach you. Tante mailed one yesterday with this same news, and I am sending this with a friend who is going to England. He will mail it from there.

Ton frère qui t'aime,

Henri

The letter fluttered to the floor. *Camps d'accueil?* What did that mean? A reception camp? A euphemism for something much more grim, she was sure. Oncle arrested for being a communist? Another euphemism.

She paced in large circles around her flat, touching a canvas, a cluster of paintbrushes, the table, a chair. She needed to be sure the objects were real, solid and tangible, because nothing else seemed to be. She herself felt ephemeral, not of the world. Or not of a world she recognized. Arresting a professor for teaching literature?

She picked up the letter and studied the hands holding it. The fingers were different. Someone else's? They were thinner and longer, more clawlike than hers. When had this happened? She held up the hand mirror sitting next to the sink and cried out. Maman was staring back at her.

Of course it wasn't Maman, whom she resembled, it was her own reflection. She was not going to allow herself to succumb to fear. It was not going to happen again. It was not. Could not. She splashed water on her face and went to the drugstore to call

Gideon. He agreed to meet her at a bar on the Lower East Side, near his apartment.

The bar was a hovel within a labyrinth of narrow streets that made her neighborhood seem well appointed. She'd never been in this area before and wasn't planning on coming back anytime soon. As she told Gideon what had happened, she ran Maman's ring up and down its chain. Oncle in handcuffs. In prison. Or worse. She fought back the images. "Do you know of any way to help him?" she begged. "Anyone who might know how?"

"I've heard about this," Gideon said. "French Jews arrested on trumped-up charges. But I've also heard they aren't being held long. It's not Germany, after all," he added, then checked himself. "At least not yet."

"I need your help," she said, the words *not yet* reverberating in her ears. "We have to get him out. Right away."

"I'm sure he'll be home in a few days. Like I said, it's the French police, not the Nazis. But even if he isn't, I wouldn't have any idea how to go about it. The resources for that kind of thing are completely different from those that ANL —"

"But we have to," she protested. "He's not the kind of man who can survive long under

184

those —"

"I'm sorry about your uncle, you know I am, but we're a political organization. In the United States. Committed to finding political solutions to political problems, not personal ones."

"But this *is* a political problem," she argued. "He wasn't arrested for personal reasons. He was arrested because he's Jewish."

Gideon shook his head, but his eyes were full of compassion.

"Couldn't you make an exception?" she begged. "They might . . . they might . . . You never know what they might do to him. He's got a young son. A wife . . ."

"I'm sorry, Alizée, really sorry, but I wouldn't know how to go about it. And anyway, we can't be about a single individual." He placed his hand over hers. "As terrible as this is for you and your family, ANL can't be diverted. We've got to stay focused on what we know how to do, what we do best."

When she left the bar, Alizée headed west toward the Emergency Rescue Commission office to speak with Mr. Fleishman again; the ERC *was* trying to help individual people. She pulled her coat tightly around her as she made her way along the shabby blocks filled with even shabbier people. Pushcarts filled the streets and the sidewalks, blocking store entrances and forcing her, as well as a stream of other pedestrians, onto the cobblestones to fight for balance while watching for horse droppings.

If only someone had killed Hitler years ago . . . If only her paintings were selling . . . If only she had money to give Mr. Fleishman toward the visas . . . If only that graduate student hadn't left the gas open on the Bunsen burner in the lab . . . But after so many years of "if onlys," she knew these thoughts were pointless.

Out of the dreariness, Judy Garland smiled luminously from a theater marquee, beckoning viewers to *The Wizard of Oz*. If only she had twenty-three cents to lose herself in a movie . . . A newspaper boy ran by, calling out the news. "Dutch passenger ship hits German mine! Sixty-nine dead! SS *Simon Bolivar* sinks. Sixty-nine dead!"

Amid the cacophony, she noticed a storefront. UNCLE JOHN'S PAWN SHOP: YOU CAN PAWN ANYTHING FROM A SHOESTRING TO A LOCOMOTIVE. She stopped on the sidewalk. A man bumped into her, swore under his breath, then moved on. She stayed where she was.

Handwritten flyers were splattered on the windows. BUY & SELL & LOAN; CASH FOR DIAMONDS, SILVER & GOLD; HIGHEST $$$ PAID FOR ANYTHING OF VALUE. Behind the signs were racks of guns and musical instruments, shelves laden with radios, silver tea services, tools, cameras, and just about everything else.

She pulled her mother's engagement ring forward and looked at it. Closed it inside her fist. How many times had she heard the story of her father, all awkward and blushing, pushing the ring box into her mother's hand and disappearing into the restaurant's bathroom before she could open it? It was all she had of Maman. Of Papa, too.

"Vienna must be 'Jew-free' by March 1!" another newsboy cried. "Four thousand Jews sent to reservations in Poland!"

She crossed the street and entered the store.

18
MARK

Mark and Edith had split up three times during their seven years of marriage. The most recent separation began the previous spring when Edith, furious that he wasn't making more money, told him if he couldn't contribute to the rent, he couldn't live in the apartment. It was now early November, and he hadn't returned since. Edith was always peeved at something, usually at him, and he didn't think he could stomach listening to her complain about how Macy's and Gimbels were taking too large a cut from the jewelry she sold there.

The problem with Edith, one of the many problems with Edith, was that she always wanted things. She wanted a toaster. She wanted a couch. She wanted to live in a larger apartment that wasn't above a synagogue. He thought about Alizée's sparse apartment without a bathroom or hot water and felt a rush of tenderness for her. Edith wanted him to wash the dishes. She wanted him to iron his shirt. She wanted him to help her sell her jewelry instead of working on his painting. The bohemian artist he'd fallen in love with, the girl who'd gloried in their relaxed, unconventional life together, had transformed into a middle-class nag.

Not that he didn't sometimes need nagging. It was just the relentless constancy of it. She'd been aware he was an artist when she married him. Hell, she once was an artist herself. But now that her aesthetic sensibilities had turned commercial, she expected him to follow suit. Something he wasn't prepared to do. Ever. He couldn't imagine Alizée considering such a thing. It would be as blasphemous to her as it was to him.

Mark wouldn't even be here now if he hadn't been inspired by Alizée's reversal paintings. He wanted to try something like them, although focused on the emergence of form and color rather than objects. The problem was that all his failed canvases were stored in their apartment, and Edith both lived and worked there, the back room given over to her business. He knew she preferred to design jewelry early in the day and make sales calls in the afternoon, so it was two o'clock when he climbed the crumbling granite stairs of the dilapidated brownstone on the Lower East Side. He hoped she hadn't changed the locks.

"Mr. Rothkowitz!" a voice called up to him. "It's so nice to see you again."

Mark turned and smiled at the sight of the tall, thin man at the bottom of the stairs. They had enjoyed many conversations, sitting on the stoop, discussing philosophy, art, and to Mark's surprise, physics. Rabbi Fuchs was a brilliant man. "Rebbe," he said. "Nice to see you, too."

"You are here on a Friday, Mr. Rothkowitz." The rabbi's blue eyes were playful. "Does that mean you'll join us for Shabbat services this evening?"

Mark grinned. This was a game they'd been playing since he moved into the building, including the part where the rabbi referred to him by the name he'd anglicized to Rothko years earlier. "Maybe next week."

"I'll look forward to seeing you then," the rabbi said cheerfully, then ducked into the street-level door of his synagogue.

Mark had forgotten how much he liked this neighborhood. The arguments in Yiddish, the smell of corned beef and pickles, the tenements spilling over with immigrant families. Kaplan's Fine Jewelry, Schapiro's Kosher Winery, Gould's Deli, which was owned by his friend Norm, who was fascinated by art and was always happy to lend his truck when Mark needed to move large canvases. Mark had been raised in Portland, Oregon, in a nonreligious family and didn't remember much about the shtetl in Russia where he was born, but there was something about this place that made him feel like he was coming home.

So he was in better humor when he let himself into the apartment. It was the second floor of what had once been a single-family house, and the rooms and windows were large, an uncommon thing in an area better known for its dark, crowded tenements. He missed painting here. The brightness and space, nothing like his current place in the Village, third man in a two-man apartment, half the size of this with a fraction of the light. It also smelled better here. But just about anywhere would.

He listened and heard nothing. He'd timed it right; Edith was out, and he'd be able to grab the canvases and be gone well before she returned. He headed straight for the bedroom, where his paintings were lined up against the walls and stacked in the closet, and began to gather them up.

He figured he could manage around twenty if he took the smaller ones, fewer if he went with the larger. He scanned the unfinished works, searching for ones that might hold the best possibilities for his emergent forms, but then stopped. Alizée said it was better not to try too hard, to just let it happen. So he focused on getting the largest number of canvases he could carry.

"Well, look who the cat dragged in."

Mark whirled around. Edith leaned against the doorjamb in her loose-limbed, supple way, her long brown hair pulled back in a bun with tendrils falling around her face. Her smile was half mocking, half pleased.

"You're here," he said stupidly.

"Very observant of you." She was wearing her smock, which meant she'd been working in her back room. He just hadn't heard her.

"How are you?" he asked, surprised that he actually cared. "How was the camp?" He'd heard, unfortunately after the fact, that she'd taken a job teaching art at a summer camp in Woodstock, New York. If he'd known earlier, he would have painted here while she was away.

"I'm sure much better than spending the summer in hot, sticky New York."

He thought back to his hot, sticky summer, and heat rushed to his cheeks. Was he actually blushing? From guilt? Or perhaps from the pleasure of the memories.

Edith narrowed her eyes. "It wasn't hot and sticky?"

"Oh, yeah. It sure was. Very hot and, ah, very sticky." He tried to maintain eye contact and look innocent, but the description of his summer as hot and sticky was just too funny, and he started to laugh.

"Are you tight?" she demanded.

Mark forced himself to think about Nazis. "Perfectly sober."

"You're not acting like yourself." She crossed her arms. "Although that's not entirely a bad thing."

"Oh, you know," he said, regaining his composure. "My usual ups and downs."

"More of your bouts?" she asked with real sympathy. "Are they affecting your work?"

He hesitated. If he told Edith he'd been suffering, which he had, her mothering instincts would take over as they always did, and a part of him wanted that. Alizée was wonderful, but she wasn't particularly indulgent with his anxieties. "They haven't been too bad."

"Oh, Mark," she said, taking a step closer. "It's the darkness, isn't it? The shorter days?"

"Yeah, I guess. You know how it gets." He

examined his hands. "Been kind of rough, to be completely honest. A real battle at times." Although he was telling the truth — he'd had more than a few dark moments, despite Alizée — he felt as if he were lying. Or maybe exaggerating, which he supposed he was. He just needed a bit of coddling. And what was wrong with that? "The painting, too."

Edith reached her hands up to his shoulders and began to massage the tight muscles.

He groaned and leaned back into her expert, knowing fingers.

"What are we to do with you?" she asked in the deep breathy voice he knew meant sex.

And suddenly, he wanted her. Edith was a stunning woman, always had been, and God damn it, she was his wife. He envisioned himself swooping her into his arms, carrying her to the bedroom, laying her on the bed . . . But no. She'd assume it meant he was moving back in, that this separation, like the others before it, was a thing of the past. It would break her heart when this didn't happen.

And although he wasn't ready to officially declare the marriage over, he was not returning to her anytime soon. In truth, he loved Edith, maybe not with the passion he had for Alizée, but he cared for her deeply, for their history. She was a good person, and hurting her was the last thing he wanted to do. Even as he acknowledged that was exactly what he was doing.

He pushed her hands away and stood. "I've, ah, I've got a meeting with Aaron."

"Really?" Edith asked, pleased. "Another show at Contemporary Arts? That's swell. I thought you said the work wasn't going well."

"It is and it isn't." He began to pick up the canvases. "But no. No. Not another show. But maybe. I guess. I don't know."

"Then what is it?" Edith eyed him suspiciously.

"Just a meeting," he said, and it came out more sharply than he intended.

"What kind of fig have you got?" she demanded.

"The work *is* coming well," he said, hoping to get back to her original question. "Had a couple of bouts. But before and after I've been productive. Surprisingly so. But I never asked: how's *your* work going?"

She waved her hand dismissively. "Oh my gosh, that commercial stuff?" Her laugh was thin, hard, and mean. "Why would you have any interest in something as ragged as all that? It's not real art, not like yours. Just doing it to make money. To pay the rent, you know. Which, by the way, Mrs. Segal raised in September."

"And that's my fault, I suppose?"

"I didn't say that it was, but if you were able to help out in the money department, it wouldn't be such a problem."

He jammed as many canvases into his arms as he could, even wedged a few under his chin. It was always the same. Nothing ever changed with Edith. It was a rotten shame, but there was nothing he could do about it. "So move to a cheaper place."

Her eyes widened. "Without you?"

"If I'm not 'helping out in the money department' then what do you need me for?" He marched across the living room and out the door.

19
ALIZÉE

"And what exactly is this Drancy?" She fingered the thick envelope in her coat pocket.

Mr. Fleishman was still slouched in his chair, but the piles of paper on his desk had grown since the last time she was here. He looked even more troubled and overworked than before, still in need of a haircut, and the expression on his face only grew more uneasy when he heard the word Drancy. "It's a town outside of Paris." He cleared his throat. "But it's also the name of a prison in the town. Why?"

"My uncle was arrested," she said with a calmness that surprised her. "He may have been taken there."

"Who arrested him?" Mr. Fleishman straightened. "When did this happen?"

She once again explained what little she knew. "I was told it was a *camp d'accueil.* A reception camp? What does that mean?"

He played with the pen on his desk. "Never heard the term before."

"So what would you call it? What kind of camp do you think it is?"

"An internment camp, I guess. More like a jail, but maybe this new name means they're not keeping people there for as long. Our understanding is that the French government holds political prisoners there. Mostly people they suspect of being communists."

"My uncle isn't a communist."

"Yes," he said dryly. "I never thought of *Call of the Wild* as a communist manifesto, but I'm sure this didn't happen because of the books. The word *communist* is a catch-all phrase they apply to anyone they want to detain."

"Jews?"

"Sometimes. But we think it's more about imprisoning political dissenters. Right now, they're arresting anyone they think is anti-Nazi and charging them with being a communist."

Oncle involved in politics? It didn't seem possible of a man who loved nothing more than sitting on the couch with a novel in his hand. But he was a man of conviction. And he did have a passion for fairness.

"What's your uncle's name?" Mr. Fleishman picked up his pen. "Maybe I can get some information."

"Benoit, Professor Edouard Benoit. In Arles." She leaned forward and touched his hand. "Thank you. I don't know how —"

"As before, I can't promise you anything, but if he's been taken to Drancy, we might be able to get him on our list." He pulled out a file folder and began writing on the tab. "B-e-n-o-i-t?"

"Without the money?" she asked. "We wouldn't have to pay for his visa?"

"Not for his. But the director's still insisting that an individual paying for visas is not ERC's mission and that it might even be ill —"

"The last time I was here you said it was possible —"

"I said it was *possible,* not that it would happen."

Of course he was right.

She dug into the pocket of her coat and pulled out the cash. The pawnbroker had given her far less than the ring was worth, but it was enough to cover one visa and half of another. "For one," she said, holding it out to him. "Three hundred dollars. For my cousin, Alain Benoit, also in Arles. His name and address are on the envelope. He's just a boy."

"I can't take your money." Mr. Fleishman held up his hands. "It wouldn't be ethical. Not until the director agrees to it."

"He needs a chance at a life."

Mr. Fleishman hesitated, clearly wrestling with the dueling obligations of conscience and job, of wanting to help and not wanting to raise false hopes.

"Please."

"I'm sorry, Alizée," he said slowly. "Really I am, but —"

She placed the envelope on his desk. "Show this to the director. Please. Show him I've got the money. That I can do this. That I mean it."

"That's not the point." Mr. Fleishman stood, tried to hand it back to her.

Alizée stood also, arms tight to her sides, fists clenched. "Alain's fifteen years old."

He slowly lowered the envelope. "This is indeed a terrible moment in time."

"I guess I should be happy Oncle might get on the ERC list," she said, her tone thick with sarcasm. "Such great news."

Mark had come down to the pier to meet her for lunch, and they were in a small booth at a deli a block from the warehouse. "At least this Fleishman fellow seems willing to go to bat for you," he said. "That's something."

She didn't tell him about her equally futile conversation with Gideon. Neither Mark nor any of the others knew she was going to ANL meetings. The organization was perceived as fiercely interventionist, willing to do whatever was necessary to get America involved in the war, legally or illegally. Which wasn't true. Aside from a few extremists, people there just wanted to help innocent European civilians who were getting caught up in the fighting. Although both Lee and Mark were Jewish, and Bill was from the Netherlands, they and pretty much everyone else she knew in New York insisted that America had no business in other countries' disputes.

Mark pointed to the pastrami on rye in front of her. "Eat."

She picked up the sandwich, but the rich, spicy smell turned her stomach. She knew she was losing weight she couldn't afford to lose, so she took a bite, almost gagged, and dropped the sandwich back on the plate. "Goddamn bastards," she sputtered. "Communist, my eye. Blatant anti-Semitism is more like it." *Putain.*

Mark didn't say anything. He'd told her he'd experienced anti-Semitism his whole life, claiming Hitler was nothing new. His family had emigrated from Russia out of fear of czarist pogroms; he'd been bullied and called a kike throughout his school years in Oregon, and he'd left Yale after two years because of the obstacles the university put in his way because he was Jewish. Whenever they passed one of the many restaurants in New York with a RESTRICTED sign in the front window, indicating that neither Negros nor Jews would be served, Mark was the first to say that he wasn't interested in eating anywhere he wasn't wanted. But there was always a particular set to his mouth, a hardness in his eyes, as they passed on.

"Throwing a man like Oncle in jail," she continued to rail. "A good man. Locked in some tiny, filthy cell crawling with rats for no reason whatsoever. Who knows what they might be doing to him? Starvation, torture or even . . . Even . . ."

"This wouldn't be so hard on you if you weren't so damn creative," Mark said with forced joviality. "You can't help spinning all these bad possibilities and then pumping life into them."

"Oncle is in prison," she reminded him. "I'm not making that up."

"Your brother said he could be home in a few days. Why don't you picture that? How happy they all are to be together again?"

She knew she was being unkind, but she wished Mark would go back to work, leave her alone to imagine whatever she wanted.

He picked up the sandwich and held it up to her nose. "How can you resist that smell?"

"You eat it."

"Zée, please . . ."

How could she eat? *It's not Germany,* Gideon had said. *At least not yet.* She thought about *Guernica,* of the helpless people and animals lit by an evil eye with a lightbulb inside, of the ceiling pressing down on them all. This is what Hitler could do. What he'd already done. Was doing. *This is indeed a terrible moment in time.*

"You managed to get your uncle on the ERC list and found money for your cousin's visa." Mark cupped her chin in his palm. "Both of which are amazing. I know it's tough to sit still and wait, but you've done everything you possibly can — and driving yourself crazy isn't going to get your uncle home any faster."

She twisted her face from his grasp. *Guernica.* She would start working on a painting about France. About Drancy and what it all might mean. Pour herself into the paint and canvas. Give the fear a place to go. An anti-

Hitler painting like Picasso's, but a notice of future danger rather than a picture of what had happened in the past. No, that was wrong. It would be about refugees struggling to get out of Europe, the international disinterest, the ships being turned away by country after country. She would call it *Turned.* She looked at Mark and smiled.

"That's my girl. Flip it around, take it from the other side. Nothing bad has actually happened yet and most likely nothing will." He leaned across the table and gave her a light kiss, closing the discussion. "There's something else I want to talk to you about."

She didn't want to talk about anything. She wanted to think about her new painting. About putting the fear to work.

He popped a pickle into his mouth. "I saw Edith the other day."

"She's okay?"

He sighed. "She's like she always is."

Alizée pictured a large canvas. She would create an homage to *Guernica.* But push beyond it. Like Hitler was pushing beyond Spain into the continent. Start with surrealist elements. Maybe even some Picassoesque imagery. Use the principle of her reversals, but turn it on its head. Pull the surrealistic representations into their natural abstraction. Build them back out into their new devastating reality. She could see it in its entirety. Ripping apart like war was ripping apart Europe. Seizing, slashing, reordering —

"Alizée," Mark interrupted her thoughts. "This is important."

Guilty for not listening when he'd listened to her, she forced her attention on him. "You and Edith had a fight . . ." This was a safe guess as every time Mark saw his wife they fought. And every time he told Alizée about their fights, she found herself hoping that this would be the last fight, that Mark was finally ready to let go of Edith. But it never was. Edith had a hold on him, and it wasn't just guilt. Alizée feared it was love. And that fear uncoiled the snakes.

"I was saying that this time it was different . . ."

She caught her breath. Different. He was finally going to divorce Edith. No. She couldn't start thinking like that. But he'd said different.

"It's just that when I walked out of the apartment, I felt as if I was walking out for good. And I liked the feeling."

He liked the feeling. This time *was* the last time. He was leaving Edith. Blood pulsed in her ears. He was going to ask if he could move in with her. Relief. Joy. Emotions she hadn't experienced for so long she almost hardly recognized them.

"So I'm going to stay on with Phil and Grant."

"Stay on with Phil and Grant," she repeated, trying to take in his meaning. "But I thought maybe you would, you know, now that you're actually leaving her, you could always move in with —"

"It's best this way for now." Mark took her hands in his. "I don't want to be with her, I want to be with you. I love you, but Edith's so fragile, and if she found out I was living at your apartment . . ."

Alizée untangled her fingers. "You're not leaving her."

"I will, I promise. But not just yet. You should have seen her face. She's all alone. She's only got me. I can't ask for a divorce until she's more stable. She's not well, not well at all, and I don't know what she might do if I told her it was over."

Although Mark was directly across the table from her, no more than a foot or two away, it seemed as if his voice was coming from far off. No, not far off. It was more like there was a wall of glass between them. She could see his lips move, hear his reedy voice, but she couldn't touch him. Nor could his words touch her.

20
DANIELLE, 2015

My first piece of hard evidence that Alizée had been a major player. In writing. In Lee Krasner's own words. *A true talent. A huge effect.* I was thrilled. But when I showed the interview to George, he was much less impressed.

He pointed out that it proved nothing about Alizée's relationship to the squares, although he did acknowledge it put her "among the circle." He reminded me — as if I needed reminding — that I was not to pursue this on company time but conceded that if I had no other pending assignments, I should feel free to poke around. Big concession. In all the time I'd been at Christie's, I'd never had fewer than a dozen pending assignments.

But the interview got me thinking about the whole Alizée-was-crazy angle, about the sanatorium where *more than a few of the gang ended up.* So I went back to Google.

Aside from being famous, what do Beethoven, Mark Rothko, Hemingway, Francis Ford Coppola, Van Gogh, Alvin Ailey, Robin Williams, Sylvia Plath, Balzac, Jackson Pollock, Edgar Allan Poe, Axl Rose, Mark Twain, and Virginia Woolf have in common? They all suffered from some form of mental illness.

Even more interesting, there are those who believe this isn't wholly a negative thing. Apparently, there's a strong statistical association between what we consider the artistic soul and the disease: compared with the general population, creative people — writers, painters, dancers, musicians, actors, directors — are much more frequently diagnosed with a psychiatric condition. Some researchers even contend that genius and these ailments go hand in hand.

The most common "creative" diagnosis is bipolar disorder, which used to be called manic depression, an illness the high-functioning can hide so well their closest friends may be unaware they have it — or at least unaware that it's anything serious. The second is depersonalization/dissociative disorder, in which a person feels as though she's an outside observer of her own thoughts and actions. Also difficult for a layperson to detect. Both tend to be sporadic, episodic, disappearing within long stints of normalcy then exploding outward, often for no objective reason.

The bipolar argument is that mania — high energy, increased productivity, speed of thought, willingness to experiment — is a key to inspiration. Unfortunately, these same traits often lead to addiction, screwed-up relationships, and suicide. And that isn't counting the depressive piece, which can send you to your bed for weeks with lethargy, slowed thinking, apathy and a general all-around misery.

As far as depersonalization goes, it's assumed that because the out-of-body experience produces an altered worldview it also enhances thinking outside the box. Symptoms include distortions in the appearance of things. Like looking in a mirror and seeing pieces of your own face but not all of it — or see someone else completely. One author wondered if this might explain Picasso's work. Sounded a bit lame to me. Especially when I read depersonalization often stems from PTSD. I'm thinking not all of those traumatized vets and abused children end up as famous artists.

I was blown away when I stumbled on an article called "Mind and Mood and Modern Art," which analyzed fifteen Abstract Expressionists who worked in New York City in the 1930s and '40s. I'm not making this up. It concluded that more than half of the artists suffered from some kind of mood disorder, 40 percent ended up in mental institutions, two committed suicide — this had to refer to Mark Rothko and Arshile Gorky — and two were killed in single-car crashes while driving; clearly Jackson Pollock was one of these. It included a quote from a psychiatrist at Bloom Sanatorium in White Plains, New York, who had taken care of a number of them, explaining the positive effects he'd achieved using electroshock therapy on manic-depressive patients. I hated to think my aunt Alizée might have suffered like this.

I immediately searched for the hospital. Unfortunately, Bloom Sanatorium was no more; it had been transformed into Bloomingdale Farms, an over-fifty-five playground for the upper-middle-class tennis and golf set who summer in New York and winter in southern Florida. Fortunately, when the hospital was sold in 2005, the small number of remaining staff and patients were transferred to an inpatient psychiatric facility in Yonkers called Wellspring Ranch.

When I called Wellspring, the data coordinator explained that the Bloom records were in storage with Wellspring's inactive files and that it would take up to a month and a notarized document attesting to my relationship to the patient before I could get access to any information — including whether or not my aunt had ever received treatment there. It took closer to six weeks, and it was late April by the time I was granted an appointment to review the records of Alizée Benoit.

Records was as much of a misnomer as was *Ranch*. Wellspring was housed in a concrete building at the end of a strip shopping center, and Alizée's records consisted of two thin sheets of paper, one pink, one blue. The first was an admission form dated December 18, 1940, which contained her name, address, and a diagnosis of depersonalization, mania, melancholia, hysteria, paranoia, and delusions of grandeur. The other was a discharge form dated December 20, 1940 — just two days after she'd arrived.

21
ALIZÉE, 1940

"I've been working on a new painting," Alizée told Lee. "A political." It just popped out. She hadn't planned on mentioning it, but she knew enough about Dr. Freud's work to believe he'd think she had.

They were sitting next to each other in the chilly warehouse examining their partially completed murals, which were hanging side by side. The wind off the river blew through the rickety structure, freezing their exposed fingertips and making painting difficult.

Lee raised an eyebrow. "You are?"

Alizée hadn't told anyone about *Turned.* She didn't want to hear the arguments about art being emotional not political, rooted in the "always," not in the specific state of now. But she needed to talk about her process and progress with another artist. "Yes."

"Still no telegram?" Lee asked.

She shook her head. It had been two months since Henri's letter about Oncle, three months since he'd written it. No wire from her aunt. Just silence.

"All sorts of things are buggered up over there," Lee said. "Maybe she sent it but it just never got here."

Alizée was all too aware there were a lot more things than just communication "buggered up" in Europe. "I've only sold one reversal in the last two months." She shrugged. "Just wanted to try something new, I guess."

"What's the topic?"

"Refugees."

Lee hesitated. "Abstract or representational?"

"Both. Like the murals. But more complicated."

"I guess it'd be tough to do an abstract political." Lee's voice was a little too cheerful.

"Did you know a bill to allow more refugee children to come here was just voted down?" Alizée was sorry as soon as the words were out of her mouth but felt compelled to continue now that she'd started. "Congress thinks Americans don't want to bring refugee children into the country. That they're dangerous. Especially if they're

Jewish."

"I know you want to help." Lee shifted in her chair. "But what's been going on forever isn't likely to be changed. And definitely not by a painting."

"I'm not trying to *change* anything," Alizée protested. "I just saw the finished image in my head and had to paint it. I'm an artist. That's what I do. What we all do. All we can do."

"Well, then good. Good for you," Lee said. "Really."

Turned was three feet tall and six feet wide, much smaller than Picasso's *Guernica* but a similar shape. Still, it was the largest painting she'd ever attempted. Most challenging, too. After more than two months, it wasn't close to finished. The library mural swallowed her days, the reversals her evenings, so *Turned* was a child of the deep night.

The painting flowed through time from left to right, and also, both literally and metaphorically, from light to dark. On the same plane, it surged from surrealist representation to pure abstraction and back into an emotional realism all its own. The ships, the children, the families, the sea. The nos, the *Neins,* the turning backs. The transformation into statelessness, hopelessness, and finally, nothingness. In red, white, and blue.

She'd hoped the project would be cathartic, a way to shift the emotions coiled in her belly to the canvas. And although she believed *Turned* drew its power from these feelings, there had been no dislodging, no lessening within her. If anything, as the days progressed, she was more distressed than ever. Sometimes it was a battle to get out of bed and other times it was a battle to go to sleep. Work, her usual remedy, was of little help.

She glanced at the clock. Mark was late. Or he wasn't coming. He'd been struggling badly over the past couple of months. The ups, the downs, the look in his eye that told her he was in there but couldn't get out. Disappearing for days, not completing his work, refusing to talk to anyone, including her. And when he did, he was cranky and argumentative, rude, sometimes aggressive. His symptoms might be different from hers, but she recognized the underlying similarities.

A pounding on the door. It sounded upbeat. She covered *Turned* and let Mark in. He had no idea she was working on a political. He'd been depressed almost the entire time she'd been painting it, and small things could set him off, so she just told him it wasn't ready to show yet. She knew he would never look until invited.

And indeed he was upbeat. More than upbeat. He was as vibrant and cheerful as she'd seen him in a long time. "Eureka!" he cried, gathering her up in his arms.

"I have found it!" He kissed her hard on the mouth, let her go, and then spun himself to the other side of the room.

She laughed. "And what exactly is it you've found?"

"The compositional potential. The emotional content. It all becomes possible when your preconceptions are put away." He grabbed one of the reversals. "Like this. Like you figured out. It's when you're not looking, when it comes looking for you."

She sat on the mattress and patted a spot next to her. "Start from the beginning."

He sat, nuzzled her neck, then jumped up again. "I used your idea. But instead of looking for objects, I went looking for emotions. Emotions in color and emotions in shape. But like you warned me, I couldn't see them when I looked." His eyes glistened with pleasure. "I had to wait for them to find me!"

She stood and wrapped her arms around him. "A breakthrough." He felt warm, almost feverish in his delight. She recognized élan when she saw it.

He whirled away. "More than a break-through. A crossing to the other side. A seeing like I've never seen before. Colors conjured in space like we're conjured in our own lives. Just like Jung says. It all grows out of our collective unconscious. Swimming within something so much larger and greater. So great it can't be comprehended by the color or the shape or by us, yet it is us."

Someone else might perceive Mark's words as nonsense, but she recognized the mania and understood exactly what he meant. That's what she'd experienced with her reversals. Her images, like his colors and shapes, did seem to emerge from nothingness into somethingness, and the process felt both magical and purposeful. He'd just expressed it far better than she ever could. "Mark . . ."

He stopped roaming the room and came to her, immediately apprehending what she hadn't said. He knelt in front of her, linked his hands around her waist and pressed his face into her belly. "It's you, Zée," he murmured. "It's us. We're muse to muse."

His warm breath through her thin pants buckled her knees. They made love, but it was beyond the fusing of bodies. It was the fusing of artistic souls.

She couldn't have been more surprised when she received a note from Mrs. Roosevelt's secretary informing her that the First Lady was sorry she'd missed her visit and wanted to reschedule. Alizée had assumed Mrs. Roosevelt had forgotten all about her, and was thrilled on many counts. Primarily because the visit might provide an opportunity to ask for help with the visas.

"This is quite an education you're giving me, my dear," Mrs. Roosevelt said as they circled the flat while Alizée tried to explain what she was doing with the paintings. Although not all that much taller than Alizée, it seemed as if the First Lady towered over her, her presence as large as her standing in the world. "And quite a pleasure to see your work now that I understand it better."

Alizée searched for an opportunity to bring up the visas but so far had found none. "I'm thrilled you found the time to look into abstraction. John Marin's *Bryant Square* is one of my favorites, too."

"It was a marvelous moment when I finally began to see," the First Lady said. "When it started to crack open. If only a little."

"I think lots of people would like abstract art if they took the time to look at it."

"That's certainly true of me. I'll have to get my friend Harry Hopkins up here so that you can educate him, too."

Alizée cleared her throat. "I'd, ah, I'd hate for you to think I would ever impose on you for a special favor, but there's something I just have to ask —"

"And what's this?" Mrs. Roosevelt asked, standing in front of *Turned.* "It looks very different."

"It is. Inspired by current events. Something I've never done before. Much larger, too."

Mrs. Roosevelt's brow furrowed as she stared at the painting. She looked at Alizée, then returned her attention to the canvas.

"I'm trying to draw the viewer into —"

The First Lady held up her hand. "If you tell me then I won't be discovering it for myself. And I won't be able to really experience it."

Alizée fell silent, impressed by Mrs. Roosevelt's perceptiveness.

"It's the *St. Louis,* isn't it?"

"Yes."

"I know that's a bad first question, that it's the emotional impact you want from me, not the intellectual. And that's there, too.

'In spades,' as my friend Hick would say. The *St. Louis* is a particular heartache for me."

"It's all the horrors rolled into one. Not just guns and soldiers but families . . ." Alizée's voice grew hoarse. "The children."

"And the world's refusal to help. It breaks my heart to think we turned our backs when they asked so little of us."

"I'm calling it *Turned.*"

Their eyes met, and Mrs. Roosevelt said, "It hurts to look at it, but I can't stop looking." She swept her hand over the width of the painting. "By this dreadfulness into this, this emptiness . . ."

"My cousin and her family were on it," Alizée blurted.

The First Lady snapped around. "Where are they now?"

"Antwerp. At least the Belgian government was willing to take them in. They're working with Jewish agencies, but we don't know how long they'll be safe there."

"You're Jewish?" Mrs. Roosevelt appeared surprised, then concerned.

"Yes."

"And your family, the family who took care of you after your parents died, they're still in France?"

Alizée nodded.

"Have they made plans to leave?"

"They'd do anything to come here," she said in a rush. "I've been trying for months to get them visas, but so far nothing. My uncle's on the ERC list — the Emergency Rescue Committee — but he's far down. I've offered to pay them for visas for my brother, aunt, and cousin, but the director hasn't approved it. I've got the money for one, saving for the second. The director hasn't said no yet, and he's had the opportunity, so I'm hoping he's going to let me do it."

Mrs. Roosevelt's expression told Alizée she believed this was unlikely.

Alizée had planned to be subtler, but now it spewed out. "Is there anything you could possibly do to help them? Please. I . . . we . . . we're all very scared." She reached for her mother's ring, but of course it wasn't there. "I . . . I don't know where else to turn."

"Their names are Benoit?" The First Lady took out a small notepad and pencil from her pocketbook. "What are their first names?"

"Henri, Edouard, Chantal, and Alain Benoit. And my cousins are Monteux: Babette, Pierre, and their little girls, Sophie and Gabrielle. In Antwerp. The others are

222

in Arles. Arles, France. Except for my uncle." Alizée hesitated as Mrs. Roosevelt wrote the names down, gathering strength. "He was arrested and sent to a detention camp outside Paris last November."

"For what?"

"For being a communist."

"Which he isn't?" Mrs. Roosevelt placed a hand on Alizée's shoulder.

Alizée felt the First Lady's sympathy through the warmth of her palm. This was a woman who appreciated, really appreciated, her terror of losing her family for a second time. "No," she managed to say around the lump in her throat. "Not a communist."

Mrs. Roosevelt dropped her notepad into her pocketbook and clicked it shut. "Unfortunately, I know the ERC has very limited resources, but I did talk with a young congressman the other day who confided he's getting visas to Polish Jews and secretly bringing them into the country through the port of Galveston, Texas. This is, of course, very dangerous business, and frankly I was surprised he took me into his confidence — not that my sympathies aren't well known."

"Do you think he could do it in France?"

"There are so many over there who need help . . ." The First Lady smiled sadly. "But there's no harm in asking now, is there?"

"No, no," Alizée stammered, overwhelmed by Mrs. Roosevelt's many kindnesses. "No harm."

"What's the price for this one?" Mrs. Roosevelt asked.

"Price?" Alizée was confused. "For what?"

"Why the painting, of course."

"*Turned?* If you want it, it's a gift. Of course, a gift. The lily pads, too. It's the least I can do when you're —"

"Absolutely not," Mrs. Roosevelt interrupted. "I won't take either unless you allow me to buy them. Does one hundred dollars for the pair seem fair?"

"One hundred dollars?" This was an absurd amount, a third of a visa.

"Sold," the First Lady declared. "I won't be able to put *Turned* in the White House, it's far too controversial for that. But I could hang it at Val-Kill . . ."

"Val-Kill?"

"My house in upstate New York. It's in Hyde Park, on the Roosevelt family estate." She paused. "Perhaps I could have a get-together. A bit out of character, but we can come up with some plausible excuse."

"You have your own house there?" Alizée felt like a fool for her repetitive questions, but she was having difficulty grasping the enormity of what was being offered and

224

needed some extra time to take it all in.

Mrs. Roosevelt stood back, studied the painting, then turned to Alizée. "I'll invite a number of artistic types, you and your friend Miss Krasner included, and some others who share our opinions — and some who don't. People who have the power to make things happen. *Turned* might be able to get them to think. To talk. Possibly raise awareness of the danger of doing nothing."

Although raising awareness was part of the purpose of any political painting, Alizée had created *Turned* as an expression of her own turmoil, not as a political device. "You think people will take it seriously?"

The First Lady's smile was mischievous. "That's where I come in."

Alizée, for once, was speechless.

Mrs. Roosevelt laughed merrily. It was the first time Alizée had heard her laugh, and it was a lovely, throaty sound. "It's a remarkable work, my dear. And now we shall see if we can put *it* to work."

As if Mrs. Roosevelt's largess wasn't enough, the following week the WPA/FAP informed her that *Light in America* was not just going to be hung at the New York Public Library but officially installed on the evening of December 23 during a gala fête to kick off a six-month celebration commemorating the library's fortieth birthday. She was dazed, bedazzled.

"And it's only up from here." Mark raised his beer, and everyone at the table followed suit. "Once everyone sees what Alizée can do, there's nowhere else for her to go."

"I'll drink to that," Jack said.

"You'll drink to anything," Lee said.

Jack grinned. "But for our wonder girl here, I'll drink twice." And he did.

"Enough," Alizée said. "You keep this up and my head's going to get so big I won't be able to get it through the door of my flat."

"Of all the damn luck," Gorky grumbled, but everyone knew it was his way of congratulating her.

Bill leaned over and kissed her on each cheek. "Couldn't happen to a better person. Or to a better artist."

This was making her uncomfortable. "It's seven months away. In France, there's a saying, *'Ne pas vendre la peau de l'ours avant de l'avoir tué,'* which roughly translates to 'Don't sell the bear's fur until you've shot the bear.' "

Mark stood and raised her arms like a winning prizefighter. "I say we sell the fur and count the eggs. That we celebrate what's happening now."

She wrestled her hands from his grip but had to laugh. Their response to her good luck was touching.

"I'll drink to that," Jack said.

Lee looked up at the ceiling, and Alizée watched her carefully. After Igor moved to Florida, she'd noticed the heat between Lee and Jack increase. Although their exchanges were mostly sarcastic, and Lee claimed Jack was the most loathsome boy she'd ever met, Alizée had the feeling that Lee "doth protest too much." As much as Alizée adored Jack, it was clear he'd make an awful boyfriend.

Louise Bothwell, along with Becky Tomlin, who Jack referred to as Louise's lap dog, came up to the table. "Alizée," Louise said, "I heard a rumor that the First Lady — or should I say First Prune? — bought one of your paintings, but I wasn't going to believe it until I heard it straight from the horse's mouth."

Mark, who still stood behind Alizée, put his hands on her shoulders, gave a playful squeeze, and said to Louise, "You, as always, have your ear to the ground, don't you? Could it be your father's famous friends keeping you up to date? Or are they too busy making more money than Midas on the backs of the workers?"

Louise and Becky exchanged glances.

They were both from wealthy Connecticut families. "What's eating you, Rothko?" Louise asked. "I'm just asking *Alizée* a question."

"The answer is yes," Alizée said quickly. She didn't think Louise was such a bad egg. Although she couldn't understood why, given Louise's snobbery and conservatism, she'd chosen to bamboozle her way into the WPA and spend her days with poverty-stricken socialist artists.

"Not only did Mrs. Roosevelt buy Alizée's painting," Mark continued, "for a lot of money, I might add, but the First Lady's going to throw a party for it at her house. And invite lots of art types and political powerhouses."

"Why, that's fabulous." Louise swooped down and gave Alizée a hug. "That's just marvelous. But a party for a single painting? I never heard of such a thing."

"Me either," Alizée agreed. "It was Mrs. Roosevelt's idea."

"*Turned* raises interesting questions about current events," Lee said as if she actually agreed with its underlying premise.

"So she bought it for the politics." Louise's relief was obvious.

"She bought it because it's a masterpiece," Mark corrected, as if he'd actually seen it.

22
ALIZÉE & LEE

A month after Germany invaded France, and days after Paris fell, Alizée received the most disturbing letter to date.

1 June 1940
Pyrenees, Spain

Ma petite soeur,
  I am sorry to tell you that I am on the run. This is the first opportunity I have had to write and as another may not come again for a very long time, I will tell you everything I know. I am currently hiding in a barn in northern Spain and the kind farmer here has given me paper and pen and promised to mail all the letters I write. I hope at least some arrive safely.
  I went to visit Oncle at Drancy right after the Germans invaded. I know it was foolish, but we needed to make sure

he had not been shipped off to the camps. Or worse. I was led by a soldier who looked no older than Alain through the filthy prison toward the room where I had spoken with Oncle before.

But instead of taking me there, the boy pressed a bayonet into my back and shoved me into a foul-smelling closet. "Rot like the rest of your kind, kike," he said, and then locked me in.

It was stiflingly hot and smelled so bad I was sure I would vomit, making it that much worse. I have no idea how long I was in there, but it was long enough that I was so thirsty I was ready to pee in the least smelly boot — if there was such a thing — and drink the urine. I was spared this additional indignity when the door was thrown open. I was yanked out and thrown onto the concrete floor.

A lumbering German soldier with sweat running down his bloated face stood over me, gun in hand. His expression was so filled with hatred that I was sure I was a dead man.

Instead of shooting me, the soldier started yelling. I know enough German to understand he ordering me to stand up and walk. With his gun in my back, I did, although my arms and legs were so stiff and numb from the closet, I could barely stagger in front of him. But as I pulled the comparatively fresh air into my lungs, my head began to clear. I was alive, I was not in handcuffs, and from the sound of the panting soldier behind me, I could outrun him. Of course, there was nowhere to go. And the man had a gun.

But I kept my eyes open, watching for possible escape routes as we traveled through a labyrinth of dank hallways. Then we were in some kind of courtyard. Only about half the floodlights were lit, and it was surprisingly quiet with no other soldiers in sight. This seemed odd, ominous even, but I was not about to argue with my luck.

When we got close enough to a post with a blown light, I ran. I heard shots behind me, yelling, footfalls, the whiff of a bullet. Alizée, I admit to you, I have never been so scared.

I kept moving, darting, weaving, my eyes always on the barbed-wire fence, looking for a hole. The place was poorly maintained and I figured if I could keep from being shot, I would be able to find a gap in the wire. And suddenly, there it was. A breach in the fence. Between two supports. It was narrow, but I thought I could make it. And I did.

I spent days working my way on foot through the woods on the outskirts of Paris, hiding in basements and barns and trash receptacles, evading both German soldiers and French police, not trusting even the most ordinary looking peasant. It was not my country anymore, and these weren't my countrymen. I could not afford the luxury of trust.

I did not contact anyone, could not contact anyone. Although I knew it would break Tante's heart and devastate the rest of the family, I could not take the chance of stopping in Arles. The Germans could be there, lying in wait for my arrival, and if I showed up, the soldiers would arrest them all. I felt terrible for leaving them behind to their fates, perhaps securing their fates, but I did not know what else to do.

I am on my way to Portugal, which thus far has managed to remain neutral. I do not know what will be next. I might try to get to the Dominican Republic or Argentina, both I have heard are accepting immigrants, or maybe Palestine. Although there is nothing more I want than to get away from this wretched continent, I also wonder if I should stay and fight with the partisans. America is also a possibility, but a far-fetched one at best.

I will write again whenever I can. Try not to despair, as I try, although it is difficult. But please, please, please get the visas for the rest of the family. This is crucial and must happen immediately.

Ton frère qui t'aime,
Henri

Once again, Alizée detached and watched from above as the girl reread the letter. She knew the girl was herself, but also not herself. It was odd, almost as if she were watching a movie or play. The girl placed the letter on the table, got up, and made herself a cup of tea. Her actions were calm, purposeful, yet covered with a patina of worry. The poor thing. What a terrible turn of events. Alizée wondered what would happen next.

German troops marched down the Champs-Élysées and through the Arc de Triomphe in celebration of their occupation of France. Jews were ordered to wear yellow stars, their French identity cards confiscated. Nighttime curfews were established. Thousands of Jews were rounded up by the SS and French police and imprisoned in Drancy. And this was probably only the beginning. *Please, please, please get the visas . . . This is crucial and must happen immediately.*

She raised her fist along with roughly fifty other ANL demonstrators and chanted, "Don't help Hitler! Save the refugees! Don't help Hitler! Save the refugees!"

They sat on the sidewalk in front of the New York office of the US Bureau of Foreign Missions chanting and waving placards that mirrored their words. The building was squat and unassuming and had nothing to do with the granting of visas, but it was the only State Department office in the city, so Gideon figured it would serve their purpose.

They'd been at it for about half an hour. A couple of bored reporters and a few policemen stood alongside the group; the people walking by threw them curious glances, at most, and moved on. Except for three teenage boys shouting *"Heil Hitler!"* and thrusting their arms straight out from their bodies. She didn't know what was more infuriating, the hate or the indifference.

The only encouraging thing that had happened of late was that Hiram Bingham, the assistant Long had fired, finally made it to New York. He told Gideon and her that

Long, illegally and without the president's knowledge, had been writing memos to his trusted lieutenants with specific instructions on how to keep the maximum number of immigrants out of the country, Jews in particular. This was in direct violation of legislation approved by Congress and signed by the president. Insubordination at the least. Possibly a criminal action.

Hiram said he would do everything he could to get one of the memos to ANL, but he made no promises, citing myriad difficulties. If he was successful, the plan was for Alizée to get it to Mrs. Roosevelt, who would then give it to the president. Hiram was convinced FDR would fire Long immediately. Who knew, maybe he'd even be arrested.

"Clear the sidewalk!" a cop yelled through a bullhorn. "You're trespassing on public land. Clear the sidewalk or you'll be arrested!"

Gideon climbed the steps at the front of the building and pulled out his own bullhorn. "This is a peaceful demonstration against the State Department's policy of systematically denying entrance visas to European refugees!"

Alizée threw an arm around the shoulders of the boy to her left and the girl to her right. They did the same, and more did the same, and soon they were all linked physically as well as politically. It was as if they were one body, one force, a powerful momentum of fair-mindedness, of honor, building and growing, making itself heard. And she was within it, absorbed by it, not a single person anymore but a piece of something much greater than she ever was or could be.

"This property belongs to the City of New York," the policeman said. A dozen additional cops materialized and stationed themselves at strategic points around the group's perimeter. "You and your group have no permit. Therefore your occupation is a violation of the law. You have one minute to disperse or you will be arrested!"

"We are citizens of the City of New York!" Gideon cried. "We are citizens of the United States of America! And we will exercise our First Amendment right to protest the policies of a nation that willingly allows the slaughter of innocents!"

"You have one minute to clear the sidewalk or you *will* be arrested!" the policeman yelled. "One minute. Sixty seconds!"

Gideon raised his bullhorn. "Fifty-nine, fifty-eight, fifty-seven," he began, and they all joined in, taunting the cops. "Fifty-six, fifty-five —"

Two policemen stepped out of the door behind Gideon, and one of them hit Gideon on the back of his head with a billy club. The bullhorn flew from Gideon's hand, and he dropped straight down to the concrete.

Alizée roared out her rage along with the others. As a single organism, they raced toward the building. Up the steps. At the cops. How dare they beat a man leading a peaceful protest? A college professor? Had everyone gone mad? *Merde.*

Suddenly there were as many police as there were demonstrators, maybe more. Cops with their billy clubs swinging, hitting, kicking. Dragging those on the edges by their feet toward paddy wagons, which appeared from nowhere. Alizée flew to the top of the stairs, dropped to her knees next to Gideon.

He was bleeding badly. She ripped off her sweater, pressed it to the wound just below his hairline. "Help him!" she screamed. "He needs a doctor!" But her voice was lost in the cacophony.

Sirens. More cops. More beatings. Handcuffs. It made no sense. No sense. No sense. All this to punish them because they wanted to save blameless people? No sense.

After two medics put Gideon on a stretcher and rushed him to a waiting ambulance, she scrambled to her feet, for a moment an island of stillness within the melee. Alone. Horrified. Only barely able to grasp what had happened. What was still happening. Police rounding up protesters as if they were criminals. Beating them. Hurting them. It was the cops who were criminals. That was for certain.

She went to help a woman who had fallen. But before she got there, she was hit by a hard blow to the stomach. She was flat on her back. Gasping for air. Which was nowhere to be found.

Lee hurried toward Alizée's apartment. It was her lunch hour, and she hadn't seen Alizée since she was arrested two days earlier. The bust-up at the rally had made all the newspapers. There was even a blurry photograph of Alizée lying on the sidewalk, a stunned expression on her upturned face. The caption read, *Alizée Benoit, an Americans for No Limits agitator, was arrested along with 51 others during a riot at the US Bureau of Foreign Missions.*

Fifteen people had been taken to the hospital, fortunately none with serious injuries. Mark said Alizée was thrown into a

Black Maria and tossed into a cell with a dozen other girls. She was booked, held for hours without access to food, water, or a toilet, then released, all charges dropped. Although her injuries were minor — apparently the police were told to use rubber truncheons on the girls and hit them in the midriff so no bruises would be visible — it was abundantly clear that this was neither the best nor the healthiest way for Alizée to get her family out of France. Lee figured Alizée would now see it that way, too.

Lee had trouble believing that the worst rumors out of Europe were true. Although she was aware of what had happened during Kristallnacht, she had to believe Hitler was more interested in conquering the world than harassing Jews. Why would he bother? What were they to him? It wouldn't be easy for Alizée's family in occupied France, for anyone over there, particularly the Jews, but anti-Semitism had existed throughout history, and somehow the Jews had managed to survive. They would survive this madman, too. Lee glanced at a clock over a jeweler's and picked up her pace.

She found Alizée painting. Although she looked tired and painfully thin, she was in better shape than Lee had feared. "Hi," Lee said, giving her a hug. "Looks like you're bouncing back just fine. Guess you're tougher than those coppers expected."

"It takes more than a blow to the stomach to keep me down," Alizée said, but Lee detected a note of falseness in the bravado.

"Does it hurt?"

Alizée shook her head, but when she placed a hand on her stomach, there was a cautiousness in her touch. "It wasn't that bad."

"Assholes," Lee said.

"That, too."

"You feel up to going to the Jumble Shop? Taking a break? We could grab some drinks and dinner. See the gang."

"I'm up to it, but I've got to keep working. Get some money for the visas."

Lee paused. "I thought that the guy said his boss wouldn't do it."

"That's not what he said," Alizée protested. "He said he was still working on getting the director to agree to it."

Lee didn't know what was more absurd, Alizée's assumption that she would sell enough paintings to pay for the visas, that the director would take the money if she did, or that the visas would be of any use in German-occupied France. But she said, "Good to see you focusing on getting the visa money and staying away from that crazy

240

ANL lot. You're not going to be involved with them anymore, right? Now that you've seen what can happen. Those people could get you in serious trouble. Have gotten you into serious trouble."

Alizée nodded as if she agreed, but Lee had the impression that, as was so often the case, her friend was not being completely forthcoming.

23
DANIELLE, 2015

Aside from the specifics of Alizée's diagnosis, the result of my visit to Wellspring Ranch was primarily confusion. A patient with symptoms of depersonalization, mania, melancholia, hysteria, paranoia, and delusions of grandeur would never have been allowed to leave after just two days. Something fishy had definitely gone on. There had to have been some kind of cover-up. But cover-up of what? Side effects from electroconvulsive therapy? Mistreatment? Death? Grand-père must have visited Bloom during his search; he was a doctor and wouldn't have been easily fooled. Some kind of conspiracy then? Right, an unknown twenty-one-year-old painter caught up in clandestine intrigues. I was clearly watching too much television.

It saddened me to think that Alizée had been so sick, and yet it also felt like an affirmation of her talent. There she was, committed to a mental institution along with all her genius friends. But the others had managed to get out, gone back to their lives for however short a time. She'd never returned.

Although I doubted it held any secrets, I searched *Turned* for the answer: the devastating emptiness at its core, the vortex that swallowed itself and everything else, then spit it all out in a different form. I recognized that it was about the run-up to World War II, about children and families who might not survive the war. But could Alizée have also been referring to her own situation? Pointing to potential causes of her demise? Her feeling that she, too, might not survive?

It occurred to me that in some ways the painting was similar to *Guernica* — although it wasn't nearly as large — for *Turned* also told a story, could almost be considered a mural. I conjured the three squares at Christie's, and it suddenly became clear. The squares weren't separate paintings; each was a piece of a greater whole, possibly huge. And together they told a different story. But if I was right, where was the rest of the mural, and why the hell had it been chopped up in the first place?

One night, after I made sure both Anatoly

and George had left, I stayed late at the office. The notion that the squares were dismembered pieces of a larger mural intrigued me. And mystified me. Obviously, I had no idea how big the original might have been, but if it existed that meant more squares were out there. Or had once been out there.

I logged into Christie's database of artworks owned by museums and collectors and searched for paintings by Rothko, Pollock, and Krasner. There were hundreds all over the world. The artists' respective catalogues raisonnés contained even more extensive listings. But I couldn't just walk up to curators and millionaires and ask them to check for a two-by-two-foot piece of canvas attached to the backs of their masterpieces. Maybe someone higher up could do it, but not lowly me. And obviously neither George nor Anatoly would be willing to help.

Then the real problem struck me. Any painting by artists of this caliber would have been well vetted prior to entering a collection. Probably multiple times. Every time it was sold. Every time it went out on loan. Every time it was returned. So I wasn't going to find squares behind any of the works in the database. They would only be hidden behind paintings owned by someone who wasn't an active participant in the art market. Someone who might have no idea they even owned a valuable painting. And how the hell was I going to find any of those?

Later, as I sipped my wine and ate my Indian take-out, it occurred to me that the reason I hadn't found any information on Alizée was because I didn't have access to the richest data sources. As a Christie's employee, I could log into all kinds of information not available to the general public — such as the database on art owners I'd accessed earlier — none of which would show up through the simple Google searches I'd been using. Same for academics with access to expensive research journals only a university could afford. Same for journalists.

Even better, my closest childhood friend, Diane Arenella, wrote for the *New York Times.* Plus, she was well versed in my Alizée obsession as we'd lived next door to each other through high school, and she'd listened to me blather on about my aunt for years. When I finally caught up with her, she got a good laugh out of my request, but I immediately heard the sound of keys clicking.

Diane whistled. "Bingo. Right here in the inner records. A photo even. Who would've thought?"

"Of Alizée?" I couldn't believe this.

"It says under the picture: 'Alizée Benoit, an Americans for No Limits agitator, was arrested along with 51 others during a riot at the US Bureau of Foreign Missions.' Really bad-quality PDF, though. Can't see much of anything. Can't read much of the article either."

Agitator? Riot? Arrested?

"June 26, 1940." Diane continued typing.

"She's real," I breathed.

"Of course she's real, you nitwit. You already knew that. She's your aunt."

"Yeah, but somehow, somehow . . . What else does it say?"

"I just emailed it to you. But there's another hit here. Something about Walter Winchell. It looks like he might have mentioned her in a column."

"Walter Winchell?" I echoed. "The gossip guy? That doesn't make any sense. Alizée wasn't a movie star."

Click. Click. "Shit," she said. "It's coming up empty. Nothing's here." Click. Click. "These damn databases. Sometimes I think they put links in to pretend that there's stuff there when there's not. Like someone's getting paid by the link. Or it's a hacker who wants to make journalists' lives miserable.

As if we weren't miserable enough already."

"What's Americans for No Limits?"

"Maybe in our outer records," Diane muttered. "Or Lexis Nexis . . . Lots of times it's just not there. Nineteen forty was a long time ago. Bad records. Bad record keeping. Bad microfiche. Bad links."

"Maybe it's the wrong Alizée Benoit," I suggested. "It sounds like an unusual name to us, but maybe it's not all that uncommon in France . . ."

The typing stopped. "You don't want it to be her?"

"Well, yes, of course I do," I said. "I asked you to do this, didn't I? I just can't believe she was famous enough to get into the newspaper and no one in the family knew anything about it."

"Were they reading the *Times* in 1940?"

I hesitated. "Alizée was the only one in the States then. Everyone else was in France."

"There you go." Click. Click.

My computer beeped, and I opened Diane's email. Incredibly grainy photograph, impossible to read the article. Except for the caption.

"My grandparents were here in 1945," I told her. "Looking for Alizée. If it's really her in these articles they would've found out about it."

"You're talking a different world, Dan. What would they know about something written in a newspaper five years earlier?" Click. Click. "And if — Holy shit!"

"What? What?"

Silence.

"Holy shit what?" I demanded.

"There's an op-ed here from the *Washington Times-Herald,* June 1940, written by Joseph Kennedy and Charles Lindbergh . . ."

I stopped breathing.

"And it looks like it's all about your aunt."

24

WASHINGTON TIMES-HERALD OPINION-EDITORIAL, JULY 1, 1940

Mrs. Roosevelt's Painting
by
Ambassador Joseph P. Kennedy,
Court of St. James, Great Britain
&
Colonel Charles A. Lindbergh,
United States Army Air Corps

It has come to our attention that a painting recently purchased by Mrs. Franklin D. Roosevelt promotes American involvement in the European War, a position in direct conflict with the best interests of our country and the desires of the majority of Americans.

Said painting, *Turned,* is the work of a Jewish French artist called Alizée Benoit, who is an active member of Americans for No Limits, a communist organization that recently rioted in New York in protest against visa quotas that have been federal law for decades.

Miss Benoit's painting is in concert with these ideas, sending a clear message that if we do not welcome all the European refugees, each and every one will perish. This is complete nonsense, and this we cannot do. For once we allow foreign ships to unload their human cargo, we are allied with those nations.

America must not be drawn into the European Conflict because that is what the French, the British and the Jews desire. We are not attacking the Jewish, French or the British people, all races we admire. We are saying that the leaders of these races, for reasons that are as understandable from their viewpoint as they are inadvisable from ours, wish to involve us in their war.

We cannot blame them for looking out for what they believe to be their own interests, but we also must look out for ours. We cannot allow the natural passions and prejudices of other peoples to lead our country to destruction. Nor can we allow Mrs. Roosevelt to stoke the natural kindheartedness and sympathies of the American public to the same disastrous end. No outside influence can solve the problems of European nations or bring them lasting peace. They must work out their destiny, as we must work out ours.

We believe Mrs. Roosevelt should return said painting to Miss Benoit posthaste. Now is not the time for the First Lady of the United States to stake claim to a position in opposition to the welfare and safety of her countrymen.

Nor is it appropriate for her to use her position to impose her will on a people who did not elect her. She may be the wife of the President, but she is just like every other woman who has neither the knowledge nor the aptitude to take her husband's chair at the office or his hammer at the construction site.

Or to put it another way: Is the cause of a communist French Jew worth the life of your son?

25
ELEANOR

"I can't tell you how sorry I am." Eleanor had invited Alizée to lunch at the *Pavillon,* the new French restaurant owned by the manager of the French pavilion at the New York World's Fair. She thought the stylish atmosphere and familiar food might cushion her news about *Turned,* but from the way Alizée was playing with her coq au vin, she guessed she'd thought wrong.

"It's not important," Alizée replied. "All I care is that you liked it. That you bought my painting. That's enough for me."

"Well, it's not enough for me."

Alizée put her fork down. "You'd think they'd be embarrassed to admit they believe these things. Let alone put it in a major newspaper."

"One would think." Eleanor sighed. It had been a disastrous week for the administration on many fronts: from the *Washington Times-Herald* op-ed, to Britain's sinking

French ships to keep them out of Hitler's hands, to Wendell Willkie's warning to the American people that if Franklin were elected president in November rather than himself, "you can count on our men being on transports for Europe six months from now." And after all this, Franklin was still stubbornly insisting that although he was running for a historic third term against tough opposition, given current international events, it wouldn't be appropriate for him to actively campaign for office.

"I so much wanted *Turned* to be seen," Eleanor said, "but Kennedy and Lindbergh have tied my hands for the moment. Exactly as they intended."

"Powerful men get what they want."

Eleanor was saddened to hear Alizée's cynicism, but what the girl said was true. "Politics is a nasty game, my dear. Clearly someone on either my staff or the president's leaked the information. No one else knew about it." She frowned. "And Franklin worries about spies coming in on the ships! That Fifth Column nonsense. What we have to worry about are spies in our own house."

"Do you think that's true? The idea that some refugees are German spies. Or is it just a way to keep more people out?"

Eleanor didn't want to get into this discussion because that was exactly what she believed. "I've made some inquiries about your family, and although I don't have anything specific to tell you yet, there are possibilities."

"Possibilities?" The girl's face lit up.

"Remember I told you about that congressman who's trying to get Jews out of Europe? Well, this is not to be discussed, but I have it on good authority he's not just trying, that he and an envoy have rescued close to a hundred Jews from Poland."

"And brought them here?"

Eleanor hesitated. She'd debated telling Alizée about Lyndon Johnson's activities, for if they became known, this brave young man would be thrown out of Congress and possibly into jail. But she felt that after the Kennedy-Lindbergh fiasco, it was important for the girl to know that there were good people fighting along with her.

"Apparently," Eleanor said, "he's buying passports and fake visas in Cuba and Mexico, some South American countries, too. I've been told they're using both ships and planes to smuggle the refugees into Texas and then setting them up with lives there. The Galveston area mostly. Remarkable. He's taking quite a chance."

"What about France?"

"I'm putting feelers out, but as I'm sure you can imagine, this is delicate business. And I can in no way be directly — or indirectly — involved." Eleanor didn't want to get Alizée's hopes up, but she also wanted to give her hope; it was a difficult balance. "If that comes to nothing there's another possible, but also challenging, option. I'm working with a number of refugee agencies to find people with spotless paperwork who want visas. Once we have all the documentation in hand, we plan to use every means to expedite the applications to the State Department. I've put all your names on the list."

"You did? You'd actually do that for us?" Alizée lowered her eyes, but Eleanor caught the flash of tears. "Thank you," she whispered.

"My pleasure, I'm sure." There was a good chance Breckinridge Long and his fascist cronies would reject the majority of the visas, almost definitely the uncle's application. And although this might give her the ammunition she needed to convince Franklin that Long had purposely created a system that denied entry to almost all foreign nationals, especially if they were

Jewish, it wouldn't do much to help Alizée's family.

"There are no guarantees," Eleanor cautioned, "but this should put your family in a more favorable position."

Alizée cleared her throat, looked a bit stricken. "You've been so wonderful to us, so truly wonderful, that I —"

Eleanor waved her thanks away. "Really, my dear, there's no need."

"That's not it. Although I'm so grateful, so very grateful. It's . . . it's just that I have another favor to ask." Alizée raised her chin, looked into Eleanor's eyes and spoke quickly. "If I had something I needed to get to you, a letter for you to bring to the president, is there a way I could do that? Without anyone knowing?"

Eleanor had been involved in politics long enough to expect the unexpected, but Alizée's question threw her off balance. What could the child possibly need to get to Franklin? Something that no one else could see?

"It's about the refugees." Alizée lowered her voice. "It might be a way for the president to help them."

This seemed highly unlikely, but one look at the girl's face made it clear that whatever it was, it was crucially important to her.

Eleanor prided herself on her strong instincts, so she took out a piece of paper and scribbled down the information. "Make sure to include your name and return address on the envelope and address it to Malvina Thompson, my secretary, not to me. I'll have her look out for it."

26
DANIELLE, 2015

I hadn't dated since my divorce over two years ago, and I didn't plan to anytime soon. Gun shy, they call it. I had a core group of friends — embarrassingly similar to the cadres on the *Seinfeld* and *Friends* reruns we often spent Saturday nights watching together — and I was fine with that.

I'd met Sam in college, and against my mother's advice, we married right after I graduated. The first year was great — mostly because of the constant sex — the second less so, and the last two were pure torture. I would have ended it sooner, but it took me that long to get up the nerve to hand my mother yet another I-told-you-so moment. When I finally confessed, she was surprisingly kind. That's what I mean about having my back in the tough times.

One night the group planned to meet up at a bar in Brooklyn, but then it turned out that Nguyen, my Christie's buddy, was recruited at the last minute to attend a fund-raiser for the Grey Art Gallery, NYU's art museum. A stand-in for Anatoly, whose wife was in the hospital having a baby. He begged me to come with him, promising I would be out of there by ten and off to Brooklyn before anything got going at the bar. I felt sorry for him, so I agreed.

It was a full-plated, place-carded, sit-down dinner, and I was squeezed between a middle-aged professor of military history and an elderly donor wearing way too much makeup. The heat was turned up too high, and her foundation was starting to streak. I was starting to seriously regret my largess.

Nguyen was at the far end of the table, and I tried to catch his eye — maybe I could get rushed to the hospital for heatstroke — but his dinner companions were apparently as boring as mine, and he was completely focused on the wine. I decided to do the same.

A couple of glasses later, I was feeling much more loquacious and turned to the professor. I would have needed more than a couple glasses to turn to the donor. "So," I said, "military history, huh?"

He tried to hide a smile at my pathetic opening gambit but gamely played along.

"Not too popular these days, but I like it."

"What do you like about it?" I asked in my best cocktail-party voice.

"War."

I gaped at him.

"Killing, especially," he continued. "And many of the attendant atrocities: burning down villages, torture, rape."

I was starting to think I should have talked to the donor.

"Twentieth century is my specialty. Some of the best wars happened then."

It finally occurred to me that he was kidding, and I laughed for far longer than the comment warranted. It was clearly the wine, but the guy was also funny. Nguyen lifted his glass at me from his side of the table.

The professor grinned and reached out his hand. "Charlie Nolan. Had you going there for a few."

"Dani Abrams," I said trying to gather myself. "You sure did."

"When you dedicate your life to a subject women hate, you have to come up with some kind of shield. It's either that or succumb to dinner-party ridicule and poor student evaluations."

I lifted my glass. "I'm sure you get neither."

"And what's your connection to our

esteemed university?" he asked in his own best cocktail-party voice.

"None. I'm here on a date." My usual cover to ensure I'd never have to go on one.

"I'm sorry to hear that," Charlie said, then turned to wink at a handsome woman across the table. "But I'm sure my wife won't be."

"A liar and a flirt. A deadly combination."

"And here we are at my specialty again."

"Twentieth-century death."

"To make things even worse, my particular area of interest is World War II. A premier death machine if ever there was one."

A World War II expert. Ever since I found the op-ed and deduced the squares were pieces of a larger mural, I'd been pre-occupied with the idea that Alizée's disappearance was due to her politics. Granted, I had trouble believing she'd been an agitator, but it did fan the fire of my conspiracy theories. Maybe Bloom Sanatorium was involved in a cover-up. Maybe Joe Kennedy and Charles Lindbergh were in on it.

If *Turned* had been her first effort, then the squares could have been a later attempt to use a painting to raise political awareness. On a much larger scale, perhaps on a much larger stage. Could the mural have been the source of the trouble? Was this why she'd been forced to cut it up? Not that I knew she'd cut it up. Not that I knew there'd ever been a mural.

Could she have escaped from Bloom to protect herself from her tormentors, forged the discharge papers to hide her getaway? She could have gone anywhere, but what if she went to France as Grand had told me?

I turned to Charlie. "Can I ask you a weird question?"

"Shoot," he said with a straight face.

"Would, ah, would it have been possible for an American, a Jew, to go to Europe — to France, say — in late 1940 or early '41?"

"Probably wouldn't want to. Most people were desperate to go the other way. Especially Jews." He shrugged. "Planes and ships were still traveling then, probably without many tourists aboard. But I suppose, theoretically, one could have. If said person had a lot of money."

I didn't know much about Alizée's finances, but I was pretty certain she didn't fall into the having-a-lot-of-money category. "And if one didn't?"

Charlie grinned at me, clearly enjoying this absurd conversation. "Then one would need friends in high places."

"Would it have been possible for a regular

person to be friends with Eleanor Roosevelt?"

"You've got an awful lot of would-it-be-possibles," he said, but his voice was encouraging.

"Like now, it wouldn't happen. Michelle Obama couldn't just go out and find an unknown artist and invite her to dinner."

"Well, she could if she wanted to."

"You know what I mean," I said, feeling foolish.

"It was different then. It wasn't as much of a celebrity culture. The media as we know it didn't exist. Just newspapers and radio. No Internet. No CNN. No twenty-four/seven. So yes, Eleanor would've been able to come and go a lot more easily than a First Lady now. And she would've been able to take an unknown under her wing. Which apparently she did quite often. She was a great lover of all those lost causes."

"You know the isolationists, right? Joe Kennedy, Charles Lindbergh, the America First Committee?"

"Think I've heard of them," he said slowly, rubbing a thumb and forefinger back and forth along his chin where there was no beard, his eyes bright. "Yes, yes, I'm pretty sure that I have. Correct me if I'm wrong, but weren't they the guys who didn't want

Roosevelt to get into the war? Did everything they could to stop him. That was them, right? The guys you're talking about."

I pulled a face. "I heard they were getting pretty desperate in 1941. Before Pearl Harbor."

"Think I've heard that somewhere, too," he deadpanned.

"How desperate do you think they were?"

"I'm not sure what you're asking."

"This is going to sound crazy . . ." As if this entire tête-à-tête didn't sound crazy. "But if there had been someone, say someone who really pissed them off, an American, someone who wanted us to enter the war, wanted, let's say, to help European refugees get into the US. Jews. Maybe got into some trouble over it . . ."

"Still confused."

"Okay." I sat up in my chair. "There's this family rumor — actually, it's more than a rumor — that a great-aunt of mine, a Jew and an American, got into that kind of trouble trying to get her brother and some cousins out of France before the war started. Then she disappeared. From New York. Like poof. No one saw her go. No one ever saw her again. Late 1940. Early '41."

"And you think Lindbergh did it?"

"No, no, of course not," I said. "But I did

find an op-ed that Lindbergh and Joe Kennedy wrote together about a painting of my aunt's that Eleanor Roosevelt bought. They thought it was incendiary."

"Incendiary," Charlie said, rubbing his hands together. "Now you're talking my language."

"And I found a newspaper photo that shows her being arrested at some kind of pro-refugee riot."

"She disappeared right after that?"

I thought back to the photo: June 1940. "About five, six months later."

"Probably not that then," he said. "Where was she the last time she was seen?"

I hadn't wanted to get into that part. "A mental institution," I admitted.

He raised his eyebrows. "Seems a lot more likely you'll find your answer there."

27
ALIZÉE, 1940

1 July 1940
Arles

Ma douce nièce,
Oncle has not returned and now Henri is gone, too. We have had no word from Babette. Alain and I are leaving Arles first thing in the morning. One of Oncle's friends from university, Gaston Begnaud, is bringing us to his brother's farm outside of Antibes near Juan-les-Pins where we should be safe. I will send you the exact address when we arrive so you will be able to contact us when you get the visas. People are still getting out, but the situation is growing desperate and we must work fast.

Every day they are taking more Jews away. Sometimes they shoot people. Whenever they want. For no reason. You remember Monsieur and Madame Milhaud from the pharmacy? Jean Plante? Old Mrs. Lunel? All gone just in this past week. We think to Drancy. So many others, too. The rabbi and his family have disappeared. There are terrible stories about trains going from Drancy to labor camps in Poland. I am sick with despair and worry, but try to stay brave for Alain.

I am sorry to burden you with all this, but it is vital you know what is happening so you can tell people in America. All of the rumors you hear are true. Even the ones you cannot believe. And there is worse to come, of this I am sure.

I cannot tell you how relieved I am that you are safe in New York. If only we had understood the danger and left earlier. But please do not despair and please continue to pursue the visas. Even though it is more difficult now, I believe once we have all the papers in hand, we will be able to come to you.

I have always loved you, my Alizée, deeply, completely, as a mother, and I always will. You must remember that our family is within you, that you will be able to carry all of us into the future. No matter what happens.

Now we no longer need just visas from

America, now we need the United States to come to our aid. There will be horrors beyond anything anyone can imagine if your President Roosevelt does not declare war on Germany. There may be these same horrors even if he does.

I find myself unable to pray, for a god who would allow this to happen is no god of mine. I cry for my babies. I cry for the world.

Je t'embrasse fort,
Chantal

Alizée reached for her mother's ring, grasped nothing. The room flattened, drained of color, became almost two-dimensional. She gasped for breath. Tante didn't believe in God anymore.

28
ELEANOR

It wasn't often that Eleanor had the opportunity to be alone with Franklin. He was consumed with the war in Europe and the looming election, neither of which was going well. At first, seeing exhaustion written all over his face, she tried to keep the conversation light, talking about their daughter and an upcoming state dinner. But things were too dire for idle chitchat, and she was bursting with fury at Breckinridge Long.

"Almost every visa request is being turned down," she said, trying to keep the stridency out of her voice. "Even for people with spotless credentials. I've seen the rejected applications myself. Something does seem wrong."

"*What* does seem wrong?" Franklin asked. "Your SS *Quanza* passengers got their visas."

"They weren't *my* passengers. They were

Jewish refugees from occupied France. And they were only eighty-some odd souls out of the tens of thousands who need our help."

"They were allowed into the country," he said stiffly.

"Only because we went around Long."

"He's just doing his job. What he thinks is best for the country."

Eleanor knew Franklin could be loyal beyond reason, but this was far, far beyond reason. "I don't believe that and neither do you," she declared. "He's anti-Semitic and mean-spirited to boot."

"Eleanor! That's —"

"People are dying, Franklin, and we can do something to stop it. You can do something to stop it."

"It's not that simple, and you know it." His voice was cold.

She tamped down her anger, knowing it would only hurt her argument. "I'm not saying it'll be easy or we won't face opposition. I'm saying this is something we need to do as human beings. That if we don't, it might be the greatest regret of our lives."

Franklin stared over her shoulder, clearly trying to see into a future that couldn't be seen.

"I know you find the situation just as appalling as I do."

"And you also know my hands are tied. Willkie and the Republicans are out for blood, and one false step is all they need. Look what Kennedy and Lindbergh did when you bought a simple painting."

"Which was absurd, and all the more reason that you need to get out there and explain your positions before the election."

Franklin ignored her rebuke to his contention that the American people needed a working president more than they needed a working campaigner. "You'll be happy to know that Harold and I were discussing ways to encourage our supporters to become more active and vocal."

Eleanor believed he had to do much more than this, but at least it was a start. "And?"

"Everything's on the table. Direct solicitation by me — and you — to all Democratic senators and congressmen. Events hosted by the campaign to bring these people together to strategize. Smaller gatherings at exclusive venues for the press and our biggest contributors."

"What kind of venues?"

"We were thinking hotels in various cities for the larger events and maybe Hyde Park for the more intimate." He eyed her warily. "Perhaps even Val-Kill . . . You know how the reporters are always begging for a chance to see it."

Eleanor hesitated. Val-Kill was her private retreat, not a place for political maneuverings, but if Franklin was going to win the election, they all had to make sacrifices. Plus, his reference to Lindbergh and Kennedy reminded her that Alizée's *Turned* was hanging on the wall of her dining room. No one had seen it beyond a small group of her friends, and an event like this would be the perfect opportunity to put it in front of a large number of influential people, not to mention the press. It had been almost two weeks since the *Herald* op-ed, and so much had happened in the world since then that perhaps no one would make the connection.

"Let me think about it," she said to Franklin's obvious surprise.

29
ALIZÉE

Through the train window, she watched the voluptuous hills of upstate New York rise and fall. Although it was broiling hot in the car, on the other side of the dusty glass it looked cool and green and welcoming. The landscape was reminiscent of the north of France, of carefree summer vacations before her parents died: Maman, Papa, and Henri, along with Oncle, Tante, Babette, and baby Alain, hiking through the hills, picnicking by the river. She wondered what that countryside looked like now. Not cool and green and welcoming, she was sure. Nor was her family without care.

She focused on the colorful names of the places passing by: Spuyten Duyvil, Dobbs Ferry, Ardsley-on-Hudson, Croton-Harmon, Peekskill, Manitou, Breakneck Ridge. So many different languages, so many different peoples, lending names to towns that stood side by side. America at its best, with open arms. She only hoped the country would somehow recapture that spirit.

Lee was asleep beside her, snoring softly, sweat gathering into dots on her forehead. Alizée had been up until three in the morning painting and wished she could sleep, too. But sleep wasn't coming easily these days. She was constantly fighting off visions of hulking German tanks rolling across the soft French countryside, devouring everything in their path. Of Oncle in his grimy cell. Of Tante and Alain huddled together, alone and scared. Of Henri making his way over the inhospitable Pyrenees. And what of Babette in Belgium, which had also surrendered to Hitler?

Tante's last letter was always with her, the words seared into her brain. *All of the rumors you hear are true. Even the ones you cannot believe.* Alizée forced her eyes closed, but within seconds they popped open again. *A god who would allow this to happen is no god of mine.* She needed Mrs. Roosevelt to have encouraging news about the congressman bringing refugees into Texas. About the accelerated visa program. She needed hope.

When they arrived at Wolfe's Cove Station in Hyde Park, she ran her fingers through her hair, hoping to calm her damp curls, and looked out the window. Mrs. Roosevelt said they would be met at the train, so she was expecting a cab or, if they were really lucky, maybe a chauffeured limousine. What she didn't expect was the First Lady to be waiting on the platform.

Mrs. Roosevelt raised her arm and waved when Alizée appeared at the open car door. Alizée stopped in disbelief, momentarily blocking the traffic behind her. She stared at Lee in wide-eyed wonder.

"Whoa, Nelly," Lee said, then looped her arm through Alizée's. "You done good. Damn good."

When they stepped onto the platform, the cool breeze was literally a breath of fresh air after the stifling train and even more stifling city. Alizée greedily pulled it into her lungs.

Mrs. Roosevelt came toward them, a porter on her heels. Surprisingly, no one in the station appeared either excited or nonplussed by the First Lady's presence. Perhaps this wasn't an uncommon occurrence. Although it sure was for her.

"Girls, girls," Mrs. Roosevelt said. "I'm so happy you could make it." She was wearing, of all things, a riding habit and looked so much more relaxed and happy than she had in the city. "You must be hot and dusty, let's go right back and have us a swim before dinner."

Alizée looked at Lee, who appeared as stunned as she was. "We'd love to," she finally said. "But we didn't bring bathing suits."

"That won't be problem." The First Lady waved them into the backseat of a large car, which wasn't a limousine but did have a uniformed chauffeur at the wheel. "If there's one thing we don't lack for at Val-Kill, it's swimming costumes." She turned to the driver. "We're going to go home please, Lester."

As they drove, Mrs. Roosevelt pointed out the places she loved best: where they hiked, where they rode, where they picnicked. The car turned down a long drive, and she gestured toward an imposing mansion. "That's Springwood. We just call it the big house. It's been in the Roosevelt family for generations."

Alizée stared at the huge brick residence with its columned porticos and what seemed like hundreds of mullioned windows. "Why would you want another house if you could live there?"

Mrs. Roosevelt laughed. "I stay there when Franklin and the children are up, but it's my mother-in-law's house, and she rules the roost. I prefer my own little cottage."

Of course, it was no little cottage, but neither was it anywhere as grand as Springwood. They parked in front of a sprawling but casual two-story house set within a grove of trees. It had screened-in porches on two sides, multiple chimneys, and was completely and delightfully unassuming.

As the chauffeur brought the suitcases inside, Mrs. Roosevelt showed them the brook that ran along the side of the yard. "It's called Val-Kill. Dutch for valley stream or waterfall or water stream. The house is its namesake. Lovely, isn't it?" She raised her arms and wiggled her fingers in a girlish gesture of delight. "Isn't the peace just divine?" she cried while waving them to the front door.

The inside was as modest as the outside, with wood-paneled rooms full of comfortable furniture scattered willy-nilly in an inviting, unpretentious way. The girls' second-floor room was small but spotless, a painted wooden dresser and two iron-post beds covered with mismatched but colorful spreads. The windows were thrown wide, and the aroma of woods and rushing water wafted in on the breeze.

Within minutes, the housekeeper brought up a half-dozen bathing suits for Lee and Alizée to try on. After donning their swimming costumes, the girls headed out. The housekeeper pointed them toward the pool and said that Mrs. Roosevelt was in her study but would join them soon.

Alizée felt ridiculous wearing a shirt that was too short to cover her bathing suit, which was at least two sizes too big. Babette would be horrified. In contrast to their usual fashion choices, Lee had found a red suit that was a perfect fit for her curvy figure and was wearing it under a silk bathrobe Igor had given her as a consolation prize before he left for Florida. Alizée's only comfort was that given Mrs. Roosevelt's obvious lack of interest in her own wardrobe, she'd probably never notice, and if she did, she wouldn't care.

They were sitting on the edge of the pool, legs dangling into the water when Mrs. Roosevelt arrived. The First Lady dove in and swam a few lengths in a strong crawl, then hoisted herself up next to them. She squeezed the water from her hair. "Marvelous. Just marvelous."

"We can't begin to thank you for inviting us," Alizée said.

"It's you girls who are doing me the favor. Adding a little youth and beauty to the company. Not to mention talent."

"I've got to tell you that we're a little

intimidated by your important guests," Al-izée said.

Lee nodded. "And we don't intimidate easily."

"Almost every famous person was once just an ordinary person, kings and queens excluded," Mrs. Roosevelt told them. "And I'll tell you a little secret: just about every one of them is afraid someone's going to figure out that they're still just as ordinary as they've always been."

"I know more than a few artists who fit that description," Alizée said.

Both Lee and the First Lady laughed.

"And the whole op-ed thing?" Alizée asked. "You don't think it'll be a problem?"

"Let's hope not, but if someone brings it up, so what? Most of the guests are much more concerned with themselves than with you. I'll let it be known you're the artist responsible for *Turned,* and people will want to talk with you about that. But feel free to tell your family's story, too. People forget that Americans suffer when we turn our backs on other countries." Mrs. Roosevelt sighed. "But if you're not comfortable talking about your personal situation or politics, don't."

"I'm comfortable talking about anything that might help."

"Good." Mrs. Roosevelt patted her hand, then stood. "But we must go and get ready."

As they walked toward the house, Mrs. Roosevelt fell back to allow Lee to get ahead of them. "I'm sorry, but the young congressman I told you about isn't able to expand his efforts into France. At least not for the foreseeable future. He doesn't have the resources. Nor, I presume, the visas." She touched Alizée's shoulder. "And that expedited visa project is being put off indefinitely."

At least sixty people, laughing and talking, drinking and nibbling, flowed through the rooms onto the porches and lawn and then back again. Although this was the First Lady's house on the Roosevelt's estate, there was none of the stiff decorum Alizée had expected. It felt more like a large family gathering than a political event. But she supposed that was the point.

Mrs. Roosevelt introduced them to many of the guests: senators; congressmen; admirals; generals, one of them a Negro; cabinet secretaries, one of them a woman. There were also activists, labor leaders, speechwriters, journalists, friends, neighbors, and even the Roosevelts' daughter, Anna. To Alizée's great disappointment, the president was in Washington.

Alizée and Lee kept exchanging amazed glances as they passed each other in the crowd. Alizée had suggested they go it alone so both of them could meet more people, which was working just fine as far as successful mingling was concerned. The problem was that hardly anyone seemed to notice *Turned,* which hung by itself over a credenza far wider than its six feet. Lee had said no one would remember anything about the op-ed in six months, but it had only been a couple weeks. Although Alizée supposed this was a good thing, and had no illusions the painting would actually influence opinion, she'd hoped for a little more attention than this.

She plucked her second martini from a passing tray, took a long draw, and approached a thin man standing by himself near the painting. "What do you think of it?" she asked.

He assessed it. "How can I think anything about it when I don't know what I'm looking at?"

Two women wearing jackets cut like those of a businessman walked over. They examined *Turned* with a detached, almost professional, interest. Clearly not artists. Journalists?

"I don't understand the colors," the taller woman said. "Why is this ship red? And this child blue?" She leaned closer. "Or maybe it isn't a child?"

"It's modern art, Natalie," the smaller woman told her. "Like Picasso."

"He's just lazy," the man said. "Anyone can draw a face with the eyes in the wrong place. You don't need to be an artist to do that."

Alizée took another, bigger draw on her martini and looked around for someone who might appreciate what Picasso, and she, were trying to do. She caught Mrs. Roosevelt's eye.

Natalie gave the painting a careful study, walking its length, taking in the details. "I guess it just isn't my kind of art," she finally said. "But even I can see the artist's skillful, maybe even very talented."

"And that she is." Mrs. Roosevelt came up and stood next to Alizée, guests following in her wake. Alizée recognized a general and a cabinet member. The First Lady put her hand on Alizée's shoulder and said to the smaller woman, "You're right, Katherine. It's in the modernist style, or as I understand it, in a number of different modernist styles. Styles at which Miss Benoit here obviously excels."

Everyone looked at Alizée. She swallowed hard and tried to smile as if it was the most natural thing for the First Lady of the United States to praise her work.

Natalie narrowed her eyes and stared at Alizée as if looking at a specimen under a microscope. "Where have I heard . . . ?" She paused. "I know. You're the one Joe and Charlie wrote about. In the *Herald*." She turned back to the painting. "And this must be your famous — or infamous — painting."

Alizée drew herself up to her full height, cleared her throat. "Yes," she said, "it's my infamous painting. If you believe this is what infamy looks like."

Mrs. Roosevelt chuckled softly and whispered in Alizée's ear, "She's with the *Daily Worker*." The *Daily Worker* was a right-leaning newspaper.

"It's like a mural," Alizée said. "But smaller. It tells a story."

The cabinet secretary squinted at the painting. "I don't understand the story."

"I think it's marvelous," a large woman boomed. "An extraordinary accomplishment in both form and statement."

Alizée recognized the speaker as the friend who'd come with Mrs. Roosevelt to the WPA show. "Thank you, Hick," she said, pleased that she was able to pluck the name out of nowhere.

Hick beamed. "I love how the objects start as one thing on one side and end up as something altogether different on the other."

"I still want to know what the story is," the cabinet secretary insisted.

"It's about the SS *St. Louis,*" Alizée explained. "The ship full of refugees that was denied —"

"So you think we should take all of them in?" Natalie demanded. "Even if it's a prelude to war? To thousands of American boys getting killed?"

"It's not a prelude to war," Alizée said. "And it's not swapping some lives for others. These are innocent people, families, running from Hitler and being sent right back to him . . ." She began to choke up. "And . . . and if we don't help them, they're the ones who are going to get killed."

"Only the Jews," someone murmured.

The small group went completely silent, although it wasn't clear if the comment was just a statement of fact or if it was, indeed, anti-Semitic.

"There's no reason for that kind of talk," Natalie said. "I may not agree with either the style or the message of this painting, but we live in a country where religious persecution is never acceptable."

Alizée couldn't help wondering if maybe they didn't.

30
Danielle, 2015

Grand-mère died in her sleep. The family was shocked, then sad, then relieved. "She didn't have any quality of life," my mother pointed out. "I lost my mother a long time ago," my aunt Susan declared. "It's exactly the way I'd want to go," we all told each other. But when I moved beyond the platitudes, I was surprisingly bereft.

I guess it was partly because of that last time she spoke to me about Alizée, how many of the things she said turned out to be true: Lee Krasner, Jackson Pollock, apple pie, *Turned,* Eleanor Roosevelt. She *did* have a quality of life. She *wasn't* lost a long time ago. She was as present as I was. And now she wasn't. I'd been planning on visiting her again, telling her about the Pollock-Krasner House and the op-ed and the newspaper photo. I'd been looking forward to a possible reaction, maybe a few more nuggets of information. But I'd never got around to going. The lesson was not lost on me.

As absurd as it seems, given our single conversation, it appeared I'd been viewing Grand-mère as my partner in this quest to answer the mysteries surrounding Alizée and the squares, imagining we were coconspirators in a great adventure. Which was ridiculous. This adventure had always been mine alone. Still, I couldn't shake the notion that Grand had been cheering me on, and I felt guilty that I hadn't been able to follow through, that I'd let her down.

A week after Grand-mère's funeral I got a call from my mother. She sounded odd: slightly giddy, which was unlike her, yet guarded, which was very much like her. "I have something I think you're going to want to see," she said, then paused theatrically.

"What is it?" I was far from sure I wanted to see whatever this was.

"I've been going through Grand-mère's storage unit." Heavy sigh. "It seems that maybe I was wrong about a few things . . ."

Now this was intriguing.

She wouldn't tell me any more over the phone, so I jumped on a train and was at her house in a little over an hour. She handed me a letter written in a cramped but exacting script.

12 April 1944
New York City

Ma petite soeur,
Although I have no idea where to mail this letter, I am writing it anyway and will give it to you when I see you, along with any others I write. This way you will be able to follow my search, and we will be able to laugh together at all my false turns. But first I suppose you want to know about the strange journey that has brought me here.

I have written some of this to you before, but I have no idea if you received the letters. So please bear with me. After Oncle was sent to Drancy, I went to check on him and was arrested myself. I escaped and have spent the past four years getting to America, most of it on foot. I walked across France, climbed the Pyrenees into Spain, and then made my way into Portugal.

I hid in the hold of a ship in Lisbon, which took me to Cuba. I was planning to go to Argentina or the Dominican Republic, but an opportunity arose and I was able to slip into the United States

288

and get to New York. You do not want to hear the details nor do I wish to write them down.

I found your friends Lee Krasner and Jackson Pollock in New York, and they told me you have been missing for almost as long as I have been traveling to you. I do not understand how a person in America can just disappear, and although they cannot either, they have convinced me it is true.

I went to the Bloom Sanatorium and saw the papers with your diagnosis, which I know has to be wrong — except for the depersonalization that you suffered after Maman and Papa died. I am sorry to hear it has returned, but that does not change the foolishness of the rest. Just because you stay up all night painting and then sleep for a day to recover, to me, this does not mean you suffer from mania and melancholia. It is just how you unleash your creativity. Americans do not understand that artists are different from ordinary people. That this does not make them insane. This is what makes them artists.

I also do not understand why you left the sanatorium after only two days. If that is what you did. I did not like the nurse I spoke with and am not certain she was telling me the truth. She acted strangely and would not say anything more than was on the papers. I am going to return to the sanatorium when a doctor is on duty. Maybe he will be more forthcoming.

I also went to Cambridge to see if you had gone there, but found nothing. Lee told me Mrs. Roosevelt tried to help find you, so I went to Washington, DC, to speak with her but was not able to get an appointment. I am at a loss as to what to do next.

I was so despondent that Lee gave me one of your paintings as a gift to try to cheer me up. She said it is the only piece of your work that is left. As with so many things I am discovering, I cannot believe this is the type of work you are doing now. It is so different from your paintings in France. But Lee assured me she watched you paint it.

I did not want to take the painting as it reminds me that we are both very different people than we were when you left for America in 1937. But she told me you would be very happy to see it, so it is now in my rucksack and I will give it to you along with this letter when we are together once again. I have decided to return to France and search for you there. It will be nice to see your big, lopsided smile.

Ton frère qui t'aime,
Henri

Stunned, I looked up at my mother, who nodded. Grand-père had never mentioned any of this to anyone, nor had Grand-mère, who surely must have known the story. He'd been arrested and escaped from a prison camp? Walked across Europe at the height of the war? Stowed away on a boat to Cuba? Gone to Bloom and read the same papers I had? It broke my heart that he wrote letters to the sister he never found.

We had a good cry, and then my mother said, "There's something else."

She handed me an unframed painting depicting abstracted barn animals under a blazing sun. It was a two-by-two-foot square with red undertones and a tantalizing emergent quality. The colors were fierce and energetic, and there was a piece of newsprint in the right corner. I began to cry again.

31
ALIZÉE, 1940

The Rose, a saloon on the corner of La-
fayette and Bleecker, was small, dark, and
mostly empty, except for a half-dozen men
lined up along the bar speaking with strong
Italian accents. It was four thirty in the
afternoon, and they were clearly laborers
just off their shifts. Gideon had recom-
mended it as an out-of-the-way spot to meet
Hiram Bingham. It was a step up from the
last place Alizée had been to with Gideon
but not by much. Hiram ordered two beers
while she grabbed a table as far from the
bar as possible.

Hiram was a good-looking man, with high
cheekbones and thick, curly hair. His unease
and twitchiness were apparent. He sat
down, took off his hat and twirled it around
on his finger. He lit a cigarette, glanced
around. When he saw that neither the men
at the bar nor the bartender were paying
any attention to them, he slipped her an

envelope from inside his coat.

Alizée pulled a single sheet of paper from its casing. This was it. What they'd been waiting for.

"It's a duplicate," Hiram told her. "I've got the original. I'll give it to you after you've contacted Mrs. Roosevelt and set up a safe way to get it to her."

She read it quickly and shook her head. "This can't be real. No one would put something like this into words. On official stationery. I don't believe it."

"Believe it." He crushed his cigarette into the ashtray and immediately lit another. "I worked in Long's office for over three years. And I've seen worse. He violates the law with impunity — thinks he's above the rules. Even Congress and the president's. He's a completely immoral man. Fixated on his career and his hatreds."

"How do you know someone didn't just write this to get you in trouble? Or ANL?"

"I got it from a friend I trust, and I can assure you Long wrote this himself. The bastard."

"But —"

"I tried to get my hands on one of the wires he sent to consulates in Europe ordering them to stop granting visas to Jews. Can you believe it? Written orders. Completely illegal and against FDR's policies. Unfortunately there were none to be had. Long knows what he's doing. It was only because of a slipup that I was able to get my hands on this."

"Consulates in Europe?" she croaked. "Which consulates?"

"I know he was in contact with consuls in Lisbon, Zurich, and Marseilles, and I'm sure —"

"Marseilles," she repeated, stunned. "And Antwerp? Antwerp, too?"

Hiram looked at her for a long moment. "You have family in Belgium," he said. It was not a question.

"And France." She heard her words as if from inside a long tunnel, far away, distorted, not connected to her. "My family, all of them, are over there."

"I'm sorry," he said, and his eyes told her how sorry he was. How bad it was.

She dug her fingernails into her arm. Pressed them deep, but she felt nothing.

"This memo could change things," Hiram added quickly. "Make a huge difference. When FDR sees it, realizes that Long's directly disobeying his orders, disavowing the oath he took to uphold the laws of the land, well, he'll have to get rid of him. How could he not? It's outright insubordination.

And I'm thinking a federal crime."
She reread the contents.

UNITED STATES DEPARTMENT OF
STATE INTERNAL MEMORANDUM

CLASSIFICATION: TOP SECRET

FROM: Breckinridge Long, Assistant
    Secretary of State for Visa Division
TO: James Dunn, Assistant Secretary of
    State for European Affairs; Adolf
    Berle Jr., Assistant Secretary of State
    for Latin American Affairs
RE: The Matter of European Refugees
DATE: June 12, 1940

We can delay and effectively stop for a
temporary period of indefinite length the
number of immigrants into the United
States. We could do this by simply advis-
ing our consuls to put every obstacle in
the way and to require additional evidence and to resort to various administrative devices which would postpone
and postpone and postpone the granting
of the visas.

Top Secret. The Matter of European
Refugees. Long was sitting in his big office,

writing his secret memos with impunity. Killing thousands with his administrative devices and then going home to play with his children. Killing Babette and the babies. Oncle and Tante and Alain and Henri. Killing her.

She looked down and saw tiny crescents of blood welling up on her arm. "I'll write Mrs. Roosevelt as soon as I get home."

She worded the letter so it would be clear to the First Lady she had something of great consequence to bring to the president's attention, but she didn't get into specifics, which she and Gideon decided was the safest way. They also decided not to involve her committee. The fewer potential tongues, the better.

Over a week passed, and there was no response. It didn't make sense that Mrs. Roosevelt hadn't had a few moments to get back to her. Clearly, she was an extremely busy woman, but she knew it was about the refugees and she'd told her secretary to watch for it. So Alizée figured it had been lost in the mail and wrote another one, putting her name and return address on both the front and the back of the envelope.

After two more weeks, there still was no reply, so she met Gideon at the Rose. The same line of Italian men sat at the bar, and they settled in with their backs to them.

"Still nothing," she said before he could ask. "The only thing that makes any sense is for me to go to Washington and give it to her in person."

"We can't sit on this any longer." He didn't look happy.

"Do you think your contacts could get me in to see this Miss Thompson, the secretary? I'm sure I can get it to Mrs. Roos— to her from there."

Gideon looked nervously around the bar. "Do you know for sure that she's in Washington?"

"She told me at Val-Kill she was planning to do a lot of campaign —" Alizée caught herself again. "Traveling. During the late summer and fall. But there must be an official schedule. You can get a hold of that, right?"

"I'll let you know as soon as I do."

She stood on the platform wearing a nondescript gray skirt and a slightly faded blouse, carrying a small suitcase with nothing in it. No scarves, no costume jewelry, no French chic. She tried to look as nonchalant as possible, as if taking a train to Washington to give the First Lady a stolen memo to bring down an assistant secretary of state was an everyday occurrence.

After the long wait, it had all fallen quickly into place, and she was still spinning from the suddenness, the realness, of it. When Gideon got access to Mrs. Roosevelt's schedule, it turned out that today was the only day the First Lady was going to be in Washington until late September. Hiram gave her the original memo, and she once again met Gideon at the Rose. Same empty tables, same Italian workingmen. Same bad beer.

Gideon handed her a round-trip train ticket and cab fare. "This isn't like pretending to be a reporter."

She put the papers in her pocketbook. For the first time in ages, she wasn't anxious or afraid. She felt strong, ready.

"The consequences if it doesn't go well could be, well, they could be . . ." He ran his hands through what little hair he had. "It's dangerous."

"It's worth the risk." *All of the rumors you hear are true. Even the ones you cannot believe.*

"These men are fierce and as passionate about their beliefs as we are about ours. They'll do whatever's necessary to get what they want — and they can do it with impunity."

"If you're trying to be encouraging, it's not working."

"I'm trying to impress the seriousness of this on you. If you get caught who knows what might happen."

"What might happen — what will happen — is that we're going to get Long out of the State Department."

"If you'd rather," Gideon offered, "we can have someone else carry it to Washington."

"Because I'm a girl? Absolutely not. I'm the one who got the damn memo in the first place. I'm the one who knows Mrs. Roosevelt, and I'm the one who has the best chance of getting it to her. Which is exactly what I'm going to do."

Gideon didn't contradict her, but the furrow had grown deeper in his brow.

Now she waited for the 5:30 B&O, restless energy jangling inside every nerve. The trip took roughly six hours, with at least a dozen stops between Grand Central and Union Station. She willed herself not to look around. To act normal.

The train was scheduled to arrive a little before noon, and she would take a taxi directly to the White House. There she would speak with Mrs. Roosevelt's secretary, Miss Malvina Thompson, and hopefully to Mrs. Roosevelt. Then she would hand over the memo and return home on the 4:15. It was simple and clear-cut, as the best plans were, and Gideon had oiled a few wheels, probably also some palms, to make it run smoothly. What a day it was going to be.

The train screeched into the station full of noise and smoke, like a living being, filling the gaping space with its massiveness. There was a frenzy of porters and passengers and luggage. Everyone surged toward the doors and up the metal steps, ignoring the conductors' admonishments to wait until those disembarking had made it off the train.

Alizée raced forward with the crowd. She had to get on. Had to be on her way. She couldn't be left behind. No waiting politely while others claimed all the seats. So much depended on the success of her trip. Much more than on anyone else's, she was certain. She pushed her way into a car, threw her pocketbook and suitcase on a seat, grabbed on to the overhead rack to steady herself, drew a deep breath.

As the aisles began to clear, the hubbub subsided and she regained her composure. She couldn't allow herself to get so easily undone. There was much more ahead. As she lifted her almost weightless suitcase to the overhead rack, a boy in his teens, dark-haired and smiling, offered his assistance.

"No thank you," she said, afraid that if he felt how light it was he might get suspicious. She should have packed some clothes to weigh it down.

But he wouldn't take no for an answer and yanked the suitcase from her hands. Before she could respond, he grabbed her pocketbook from the seat and began to shove his way toward the front of the car.

Alizée lunged for her belongings, but he was too quick. In barely a second, he was striding down the aisle, her suitcase in one hand, her pocketbook in the other. "Thief!" she cried. "Stop! Someone stop him!"

She elbowed a businessman out of her way and seized the back of the boy's jacket. He wrenched himself from her grasp. Then a large woman at the front of the car stood up and faced him, legs apart and arms crossed over her ample chest. There was nowhere for him to go. He dropped the bags.

After the conductor and a cop escorted the boy from the train, Alizée sat down hard on her seat. The woman placed a hand on her shoulder. "Are you all right?"

"Thank you." She clutched both the suitcase and her pocketbook tightly to her. "I'm fine. Fine now that you saved my things. Thank you."

The other passengers clucked and smiled at her sympathetically, and she nodded her appreciation. As the train picked up speed, the others turned back to their concerns, satisfied all had ended happily.

She was furious at herself. She'd been so caught up in her own self-importance, in her daring and the magnitude of "her mission" that she'd become cocky. If the boy had managed to get off the train with her belongings, the memo would have been lost. Stupid, stupid, stupid girl. She sat straighter in her seat but kept her arms locked around her belongings. What if the memo had been his target?

When the conductor returned, she asked if she could speak to him privately. He motioned her to the tiny space at the end of the car. "I'm a little afraid someone's going to try to take my things again, sir," she said. "Is there anywhere on the train where maybe I'd feel safer?"

The conductor grumbled but led her the first-class car. After he settled her into a wide velvet seat and inspected her ticket, he pointed to a broad-shouldered Negro porter. "Jacob here will make sure you're safe while you're here. He's leaving the train in Washington and will give you whatever help you need when you get there."

At first she was on edge, her watchfulness spiking at every station, whenever anyone got on or off. When a man reached for his luggage, when a woman came or went from the toilet. She startled at loud noises, of which there were many. But by the time the train pulled into Washington's Union Station, she'd convinced herself it had just been a case of bad luck, that there was no way the boy could have known the memo was in her pocketbook, that everything would go smoothly from here on.

She was calmer, but still watchful, as Jacob helped her down the steps and led her toward the cabstand. She glanced surreptitiously around the station, but saw nothing out of the ordinary. Still, she was relieved when she slammed the taxi door behind her and they pulled onto the wide boulevard. Time to get Breckinridge Long.

When she arrived at the gate of the White House there were a slew of uniformed guards, which initially gave her confidence. Until they wouldn't let her in. "I've got an important message to deliver to Mrs. Roosevelt," she explained. "Very important."

They pointed her toward the exit.

"Miss Malvina Thompson is expecting me," she said with her most engaging smile.

One of the guards, a boy about her age whose eyes roamed down her body, made a phone call. He grinned at her wickedly when he put the receiver down. "They said it's okay," he told the others.

She followed another guard through seemingly endless corridors, some very grand with marble walls and flooring, others quite ordinary. They rode what appeared to be a service elevator, and then she was standing in the office of the First Lady of the United States.

The anteroom was huge, the ceiling at least twenty feet high with moldings that appeared two-feet thick. An enormous Persian rug covered the floor, and the cobalt-blue curtains against the stark white walls added elegance and solemnity. The White House. It was difficult to take in. *Stay with me, Maman.*

At first the room appeared to be empty, but then she noticed a small desk in a far corner. A woman sat behind a typewriter, and Alizée approached briskly. It was actually happening. She was doing this. It was going to get done. "Miss Thompson?" she asked.

"I'm Mrs. Cartwright," the woman corrected her. "Miss Thompson's secretary. How may I help you?"

The secretary had a secretary. "I have a message to give to Mrs. Roosevelt. I was told to see Miss Thompson."

"Your name?"

Alizée told her, and Mrs. Cartwright rose and turned the handle of a door Alizée hadn't noticed: it sat flat against the wall without any molding. The door opened into a smaller but just as elegant office. A minute later, Mrs. Cartwright returned with an older woman who said, "I'm Malvina Thompson, please follow me."

Alizée stared at Miss Thompson's impossibly straight back, did the same with her own. "Is Mrs. Roosevelt in?"

Miss Thompson didn't answer her question, just pointed to a chair in front of her desk, and Alizée sat. She put her pocketbook and suitcase down and realized this was the first time she'd done so since leaving New York.

"I was told to expect you. You have something for Mrs. Roosevelt?"

Alizée placed the envelope on the desk.

The secretary read it quickly, then read it again. "Are you telling me this is an original memorandum from Breckinridge Long?"

She glanced at the date. "Written earlier this summer?"

Alizée kept her voice calm, although her heart was pounding. "That's my understanding."

"Where did you get it?"

"To tell you the truth," she lied, "I'm not sure."

Miss Thompson stood. "Please stay right here." She took the memo and hurried through yet another door, which she closed behind her.

Within minutes, the First Lady strode into the room. Alizée jumped up, and Mrs. Roosevelt threw her arms around her. "I don't know how you did this, my dear." She held Alizée at arm's length. "All I can say is that the hand of God is at work here. And I am deeply grateful. To both of you."

They stared into each other's eyes, grinning. "Me, too," Alizée said.

Mrs. Roosevelt dropped her arms. "Tell me everything. Where you got this. From whom. I won't be able to do anything until we're absolutely certain this came from Long's office."

After Alizée explained what she knew, Mrs. Roosevelt handed the memo to Miss Thompson and whispered a lengthy list of instructions. Then she turned back to Alizée and smiled affectionately. "I wish I had more time to talk with you, to take you to lunch at least, to thank you properly. Unfortunately, I'm leaving first thing tomorrow morning, and my schedule is more over-scheduled than usual."

"No thanks are needed," Alizée assured her. "As you would say: it's my pleasure."

Mrs. Roosevelt pressed Alizée's hand between her own. "Once this is verified, I promise you I will show it to the president immediately. And if all goes well, very soon Breckinridge Long will no longer be at the State Department."

32
DANIELLE, 2015

Although I was still responsible for the larger paintings, after our last meeting, George reassigned the squares to a recent hire named Ryan. Obviously, George preferred a staffer who would follow his directions and not make waves like someone else who shall not be named. So I borrowed the three original squares from Ryan and lay them on my desk next to the square Grandpère got from Lee.

There was no doubt all four had been painted by the same artist: Alizée Benoit. Nor was there any doubt the four two-by-two canvases were part of a larger mural. Or, to be more precise, there was no doubt in my mind. George's mind turned out to be another matter altogether.

"First of all," he told me, "all the testing so far points to Mark Rothko. The brushstrokes in particular. And the colors. Ryan's been focusing on the alienation in the animal and human faces. Doing a convincing job using Rothko's WPA paintings for comparison."

"Look at these." I placed the four squares on his desk. "You can't deny the square Lee Krasner gave my grandfather is part of this same work. And we know for sure Alizée painted it." I thought if I mentioned Lee's name he'd take it more seriously.

Wrong again. "Not necessarily," George corrected. "His letter about a seventy-year-old conversation with Krasner doesn't put it in the 'know for sure' category."

"What about that interview I showed you when Lee said Alizée was a major influence on them?"

"And exactly how is that interview connected to this square?"

It was slowly beginning to dawn on me that, despite the unassailable evidence, George was going to stonewall. "What are you trying to say?"

"I'm not trying to say anything," he said with a calmness that infuriated me. "I'm just pointing out that you can't be certain this square is your aunt's work. It could just as easily be Rothko's. Wasn't it you who told me they were lovers? Krasner could have been confused. Or lying."

"Why would she do that?" I practically

309

shouted. "You can't really —"

"And your theory that these are pieces of one mural is just that: a theory. You might be right or they could be part of a series or separate —"

"I've got two other paintings I know are Benoit's. I'll bring them in and we can have them all authenticated."

George was shaking his head. "You know we don't have the budget to spend on that kind of speculation this early in the process. Given Ryan's initial results, I say we go through our usual procedures, and if there's no definitive answer after the authenticators have completed their evaluations, we'll take this new evidence into consideration and give your aunt Alizée a second look."

I poured out my frustration to Nguyen. He was sympathetic, but I needed more. I wasn't going to let George and Anatoly's ambitions — no matter how well hidden under calm or expletive-laced practicality — keep Alizée from getting the recognition she deserved. Nguyen and I brainstormed possible ways to get around Christie's but didn't come up with much.

It was obvious to us that George was posing, looking for any way he could to stop me from interfering before the authentication process moved beyond his direct reports. If the experts — who were wrong more than you might think — determined the squares were Rothkos, there wasn't much a low-level employee like me, or even a midlevel one like Nguyen, could do about it. Clearly, finding more squares before the others went to the specialists was the best option, but exactly how to do this wasn't nearly as clear. And really, what were the odds?

Nguyen suggested I contact a friend of his who was working on the Early Abstract Expressionist show at the Louvre. The show was opening in a couple of months, and Jordan Washor, whom Nguyen had gone to graduate school with, was an assistant to the assistant to the curator.

Jordan was happy to talk to me but explained that he had more contact with paperwork than he did with artwork. I was further disappointed when he told me that due to the value of the art and all the recent thefts, over half the committed pieces hadn't been received yet — particularly those from small collectors. Exactly the paintings that might harbor a square.

We did share a few laughs over Nguyen's successful suck-up antics at Christie's, and Jordan promised he'd look at the back of any painting he came in contact with. He also invited me to visit the show if I got to Paris. Like that was going to happen anytime soon. Anatoly had nixed this idea when I'd raised it when the paintings first came in — not that I'd ever thought it was a real possibility — and when I talked Nguyen into trying to get permission to go, his boss gave him the same answer.

Dead ends everywhere. Lee's square. Alizée's politics. Even Grand-père's letter, which had seemed so promising at first, fell short under closer scrutiny. His flight through Europe was interesting to me but shed no light on his sister's whereabouts. His mention of trying to meet with Eleanor Roosevelt, which at first I'd taken as proof that she'd given him *Turned,* in the end meant nothing of the sort; Grand-père hadn't been able to see her. And while his suspicions of Bloom Sanatorium echoed mine, there was no more Bloom Sanatorium.

I was thinking I needed a vacation, but when I checked around, none of my friends had the time, and the idea of going somewhere by myself wasn't particularly appealing. The truth was, aside from Paris, I couldn't think of anywhere I wanted to go and didn't really have the energy to figure it out. I started spending more time at work, more time watching *Seinfeld* reruns, more time drinking wine.

Frustration and the waning light of late summer always do that to me.

33
ALIZÉE, 1940

Alizée's success swallowed her worries whole. More visas would be available soon, and that was all that mattered. Mrs. Roosevelt would surely insist some of the first be assigned to her family and hopefully use her influence to make sure they got out of France and Belgium, Drancy, too. Soon they would all be in New York. Safe. Together. And maybe Henri would find his way here, too. Or at least to safety in Palestine.

Her happiness was difficult to contain, and she could barely sit still as she listened to her committee reporting on its progress, or lack thereof. Nathan was by far the most industrious, coming up with page upon page of details on Long's early public life. Although Long was plainly a despicable character, rife with bigotry and narrow-minded arrogance, he had an amazing way of getting exactly what he wanted and then wrangling free from the repercussions.

Like the way he'd bamboozled Roosevelt into not imposing an embargo on Italy after Long's buddy Mussolini invaded Ethiopia. Or when he'd convinced the House of Representatives that it wasn't necessary to establish an agency to rescue refugees by giving testimony that was patently untrue. Or when FDR supported a plan to save thousands of French and Romanian Jews, and Long delayed acting until it was no longer feasible. But now it was going to be different. Breckinridge Long was going to get his due.

When everyone finished their reports, Alizée pressed her palms on the table. Gideon hadn't wanted her to say anything about the memo until Long was out of the State Department, but she'd insisted her committee had a right to know. "I've got something to tell you," she said, trying to keep her voice calm, failing. "But you can't talk about it to anyone until it's all confirmed." She looked each in the eye. "Okay?"

They glanced at one another, clearly attuned to her excitement, and nodded expectantly.

When she explained what had happened, the room was completely silent. No one moved. Then they all roared to life.

William pressed his hands together and cried, "Praise the Lord!"

Nathan, who usually had only antipathy for William's piousness, punched him lightly on the shoulder. "Praise whoever you want, my boy. This is a great moment!"

Bertha rushed to Alizée and threw her arms around her. "You've done it," she kept repeating. "You've done it!"

Aarone, as bighearted as he was imposing, began to cry.

34
ELEANOR

Eleanor waited impatiently for the meeting to end, Long's memo in her hand. When everyone left the Oval Office, she went in and closed the door. Franklin took in her expression, the sheet of paper she held, and frowned. "I don't suppose this can possibly wait?"

"No." She slapped the memo on top of the papers covering his desk. It was still difficult for her to believe that Alizée Benoit was the one to bring this to her, and she wondered if there was perhaps a larger purpose for their seemingly random meetings or the bond they'd formed. "Read."

The president slipped on his reading glasses and did as she asked. He read it a second time, folded the page in half and then half again, put it into his jacket pocket. "Where did you get this?"

"More important, what are you going to do about it?"

"I need to know where it came from. It could be a hoax."

"I had it checked out," she said, not liking the tone of his voice. "Look at it. Touch it. That memo sounds just like Long. Looks just like a State Department memorandum. I can hear him saying those exact words — and I know you can, too. It's incomprehensible that he would put something so despicable in writing, but then he probably didn't think it was despicable. He's in direct violation of Congress. In direction violation of the law — not to mention your wishes. If this doesn't finally prove to you that the man's a dangerous bigot, I don't know what will."

Franklin shook his large head. "He's worried about jobs. And it worries me, too. Unemployment's still at fifteen percent, and we've got to be careful about immigrants taking jobs from Amer—"

"This isn't some political speech!" she exploded. "You're talking to me, not the America First Committee. And these aren't 'immigrants taking jobs from Americans'; these are political refugees who are going to die if we don't do something to help them."

"We can't know that."

"Long took an oath to uphold the law. Laws made by Congress, not by him. His

318

actions are illegal, immoral, dead wrong. And he's going behind your back. 'Secret memorandum,' my eye." She glared at Franklin. "What are you going to do about this?"

The president sighed. "I'll talk to him."

"Talk to him? That's all?" She was incredulous. "He's breaking the law. Worse, he's taking the law into his own hands. He's blinded by his own hatred and doing whatever he wants with impunity — and now with your tacit approval!"

"These things aren't always what they seem to —"

"What it *seems* is that your man in charge of visas is illegally conspiring not to approve any!" She knew Franklin's heart in a way no one else did. And she knew this response was not coming from his heart. "And what about the Jews running from Hitler? Many with families here. American families. They need more than talk. They need us to help them."

"You know," Franklin said pointedly, "this is a Protestant country, and the Jews are here under sufferance. It's my decision who gets visas and who doesn't, and it's up to the citizenry to go along with what I want."

She grabbed the back of a chair, her knuckles white. "You're going to let him keep out qualified refugees because that's what he chooses to do? Because he's an anti-Semite? Even if thousands of people die? You can't be serious."

The president sat tall in his wheelchair. "This isn't just what Breckinridge chooses to do. There are many others who agree with him and many valid reasons for their caution. It's more complicated than you know."

The long years in the political spotlight had taught her to hold her tongue, and the long years of being married to a politician had taught her not to upset his opinion of himself. But these lessons were vanquished by her fury. "What I know is that you're not willing to take the political risk of standing up to them. That that's what this is all about!"

"That's quite enough, Eleanor!" Franklin roared.

"It's inhumane, and you're not an inhumane man. You're going to live to regret this — and so am I."

"You are to say nothing about this memo to anyone," the president ordered. "Nothing. And you will not have any more contact with whomever gave you the damn thing in the first place. Do you understand me?"

Rage surged through her, and heat flushed

her face. But she recognized her rage was futile. As futile as it was for her to continue the argument. It wasn't only the citizenry of the United States who had to go along with whatever the president wanted. She had to also. No matter how wrong she believed he was.

35
ALIZÉE

When a week passed with no announcement out of Washington, Alizée's optimism began to wane and dread to wax. Gideon was even more worried than she, frantically checking in with every contact he had. There were no rumors, no gossip, no nothing. Alizée and Gideon constantly reassured each other it was just the bureaucracy, that the government was a large ship that turned slowly. They heard nothing from Hiram Bingham.

She wished she hadn't told her committee. Initially they'd been all over her with questions, but at the last meeting, she'd been forced to silence their inquires with a shake of the head. William said he would pray about it, a comment Nathan growled at, and both Aarone and Bertha had turned away, hiding anxious expressions. Alizée, of course, couldn't talk about any of this with her friends, and Gideon was such a wreck, talking to him was worse than talking to nobody.

When the letter arrived from Mrs. Roosevelt, apologizing profusely for her inability to sway the president and explaining that they couldn't be in contact anymore, Alizée observed herself reading it from above the icebox, just as she'd watched herself reading Henri's last letter. She gazed down with equanimity as the girl shook her fist at the god she didn't believe in. As the girl cried out her fury to the ceiling. As she pounded the walls.

Alizée stared into the mirror, searching for herself, but what she saw was a Picassoesque collage: a nose, an eye, a cheekbone. She knew this wasn't her true reflection, yet it resonated. Her doppelgänger, her fractured, frightened other. A tear rolled from the eye.

She dragged herself to the next ANL meeting. Gideon said nothing about her failure to the larger group, none of whom knew of the attempt, but she had to give the bad news to her committee, whom she suspected knew the truth already. This time the silence was stunned. This time it was Bertha who cried.

Nathan jumped up from his chair. "No!" he yelled. "We're not going to sit around and let this happen. That man has got to be stopped!"

Alizée watched him dispassionately, said nothing. The anger and sadness had depleted her, as had her doppelgänger, and now she didn't feel much beyond exhaustion, a deep, profound tiredness.

Bertha dabbed her eyes with a handkerchief. "Where will they all go?" she asked softly, almost to herself. "What will become of them?"

"These are our people we are talking about," Aarone said. "So many people. We are having to get rid of him."

"Yeah." Nathan, who was none too fond of Aarone, scowled at him. "We know that."

"That is not what I am meaning. He will be killing many, many people, and he is only one man."

"We'll just continue on with what we've been doing," Alizée said dully. "We'll find something else, I'm sure."

Aarone shook his head. "I do not believe this way is working so we must be doing it a different way."

"Are you saying what I think you're saying?" Nathan asked with more respect than he'd ever shown toward Aarone.

"We cannot break God's commandments," William said. "Even in a case like this."

"It is one death exchanging so many thousand can live," Aarone declared. "In this situation God would be thinking twice. He knows that it is what is in the end that is important."

"That's not up to us to decide," William argued. "If it's his will —"

"You said you have guns?" Aarone asked Nathan.

Nathan puffed out his chest. "I was a sharpshooter in the Great War."

"We're not shooting anyone," Alizée said. "ANL isn't an organization that —"

"It's like Aarone said, thousands of lives are at stake," Nathan interrupted. "This is bigger than ANL. Bigger than just about everything."

"I think we should at least talk about it," Bertha said.

Alizée stared at Bertha. "You think we should talk about shooting Breckinridge Long?" She looked at the others. "Have you all lost your marbles?"

"My grandmother, my aunt, and all my cousins are dead. My mother's out of her mind with grief." Bertha folded her hands. "I don't want this to happen to anyone else."

Alizée couldn't believe the conversation.

Couldn't believe they were actually considering such a thing. There had to be another way. "There's something else we can try," she said, surprised her brain was still capable of making logical connections. "Gideon has the duplicate of Long's memo, and he's got friends at the *Times.* He can get it to them. We'll go around the president without any guns."

They grudgingly acquiesced, but it was not to be. It turned out that Gideon, fearing retribution, had destroyed the copy after she'd brought the original to Mrs. Roosevelt. Alizée refused to allow the committee to continue the discussion of Aarone's proposition at the next meeting, but she knew Aarone, Nathan, and Bertha were discussing it without her.

15 August 1940
Antwerp

Ma Ali,
I have no idea if this letter will reach you, but I am writing because I need to feel we are still linked together, although I know we are linked always in our hearts. I also wanted to let you know we are alive. And that that is all I want for us.

How things have changed! No thoughts of clothes or parties or mathematics, only of survival. I cannot imagine I once worried about my haircut or my inability to solve the Birch and Swinnerton-Dyer conjecture. We are living with three other *St. Louis* families in a small apartment in the western part of the city. One family is nice. From the roof I can see a bit of the sea.

Sophie and Gabby are good little troupers, especially Sophie, who tries very hard to make us laugh. She is kind to her little sister. Much kinder than I was to you! Pierre is having a difficult time because he is not able to work or to make anything better for us. I am taken up with the children and household tasks so it is not so hard for me.

We do not know what the future holds, and I try not to think beyond the present. Which is easier than you might think as just finding enough food and water — or soap — can take an entire day. But we are alive. We are together, and we are safe for now.

I have not heard from my mother in over a month but assume she and Alain are out of harm's way on the coast. Perhaps my father is with them. We can only hope the same for Henri.

It helps to know you are in America, far from this insanity. I daydream of you painting in your warehouse, drinking with your friends, walking freely down the sidewalks of New York. This makes me very happy.

The agency is working hard on our visas, but the Germans have been here for almost four months now, and things grow more difficult by the day. They have imposed their so-called anti-Jewish regulations, including yellow stars, curfews, and the unimpeded looting of shops. The police, the royal prosecutor, and the citizens of Antwerp stand by and do nothing. Cowards all. It is hard to believe that we so recently lived in Berlin, had friends and associates there who thought nothing of our being Jewish. Or so we supposed.

I look at my beautiful girls and know they have full lives ahead of them, that this ugliness is a momentary hiccup, not a forever. For who could hate such sweet little faces? Who could look in their eyes and then do them harm?

So please, try not to worry, for I believe we will be together soon. I will wire when we have our visas in hand and are steaming toward you!

Je t'embrasse fort,
Babette

36
ALIZÉE

She stared at the huge, unfinished panels headed to the library to be fêted in front of hundreds, covered by major newspapers: *Light in America.* The library rotunda was a subdued, although elegant space, and she'd used deep reds and earth tones with small splashes of green to complement this. The mural told the story of the triumph of public education in a previously unschooled land, a theme and subject matter best suited to a more literal, surrealistic style combined with a bit of abstraction.

It consisted of four panels, each four feet high and four feet wide, each representing a different century, the seventeenth at one end and the twentieth at the other. She'd used recognizable objects, books and desks, students and teachers, but slightly abstracted and juxtaposed them in unexpected ways. Some of these odd combinations were strewn across all four panels, depicting the evolution of knowledge through time, while others were singular and stationary, rooted in their own century.

It was good, she was proud of it, but only four months remained until the installation, and she was falling behind. Far behind. But even the time pressure couldn't move her brush any faster. Her hand felt heavy, her head and heart heavier still.

It was deep into afternoon, and as was all too common lately, she'd barely made any progress all day. It often felt as if she were living inside a dream: slices of images, voices, smells, juxtaposing in ways that made little sense. And then there was the inverse: when she wasn't sure whether the things she remembered, the memories that made her who she was, had actually happened or were part of last night's nightmare. Maybe hers. Maybe someone else's. Her fingernails dug into her arm, a habit now, but like her memories, they seemed to belong to someone else.

She glanced over at Lee, who was completely absorbed in her own mural. It was impossible that Lee hadn't noticed her lack of forward motion, but Lee was too kind to mention it. Which Alizée greatly appreciated. In an attempt to get herself back to work, she pictured the library event, the dignitaries, literati, and celebrities all in attendance, champagne circulating, flashbulbs popping. But all she could think about was Babette's little girls. Tante, Alain, Oncle. Henri. About how she'd let them all down.

And then she saw it, fully formed, just as *Turned* had first come to her. Instead of *Light in America*'s four panels hanging in the library rotunda, in front of her hung four canvases depicting life for victims of Hitler's megalomania: refugees, soldiers, Arles and Antwerp, ships, Tante and Babette, horses, cows, crops. Jews. Gypsies. Sophie and Gabby's eyes. Abstract, surreal, and realistic images flowing from one to the other. Compelling, riveting and horrifying, yet touched with compassion for lives lost, for innocence lost, pleading for help.

"Sit," Lee ordered Alizée. "You're white as a ghost."

She sat, a kaleidoscope of colors swirling around her.

"Are you okay? Are you sick?"

"I'll switch them." Swap. Exchange. Substitute.

"Switch what?" Lee demanded.

"I'm going to paint another mural!" she said jubilantly. "A political. About Hitler and war and the refugees. I'll hang it in the library instead of this one."

Lee knelt at her desk; they were face-to-face. "I'm not sure what you're talking about, but if it's what I think it is, you've got to talk about it more quietly."

"Something has to be done. And I'm going to do it!" Babette might believe the face of a little girl would sway the Nazis, but Alizée did not.

Lee grabbed her hands. "Take a deep breath and lower your voice."

"They'll all be there," she said more quietly but with no less urgency. "Politicians, press, photographers. They'll report on it, take pictures, and everyone will see it. Then people will understand how terrible the situation is. And like Mrs. Roosevelt said, they'll respond from the heart. They'll demand more visas. We'll get around Long."

"Around what?" Lee asked, her face flushed with concern. "What's long? Wrong? You're not making any sense."

Focus, Alizée ordered herself. *Merde.* She had to stay focused.

"You said you didn't agree with Mrs. Roosevelt," Lee continued. "That a painting couldn't do that. Plus how can you complete a whole mural in just four months? And even if you could, they'll take it down as soon as you get it up."

"The point will be made."

"But how will you switch them?" Lee pushed her hands downward to indicate Alizée should whisper. "It's a bad idea. It's wild, dangerous, reckless. There are so many —"

"It's a good idea." Alizée slapped her palm on her desk, and it shuddered. "A great idea."

Lee shifted backward, her eyes filled with compassion. "Think about it, doll. Think about the difficulties. Technical and otherwise. The danger. Do you really believe this can work? That it would actually make a difference?"

Alizée didn't bother to answer. She'd been searching for a solution that didn't involve murder, and suddenly it had appeared right before her eyes. What more proof did she need?

She decided to call the mural *Montage,* which was exactly what it was: a mosaic of war created through a medley of her own evolving techniques. She planned to use the deep red underpainting and overlays of the first series of politicals, the transformative motion of *Turned,* the advancing panels of *Light in America,* and the pull from nonfigurative to figurative of her reversals.

The ideas flowed from her fingers as if by

sorcery, and she worked feverishly on colors and composition, sketches and mock-ups. It had to dig deep, bring the viewer into the center of the heartbreak, focus on more than just the victims, include the perpetrators — who would ultimately became victims themselves — and on those who stood apart from the melee, sanctioning with their indifference. As she worked, she became Babette and the little girls, Henri, Tante and Oncle and Alain. Aarone's sisters. Nathan's brothers. Bertha's mother. She was inside them, and *Montage* was inside her. She would bring it to life, give it life. Give them life.

She only had four months, but *Montage* wouldn't take as long as *Light in America*. No more planning was necessary, no approvals, no bureaucracies, no meetings, no lazy assistants coming in late or developing sudden stomach ailments on Fridays. Still, she couldn't do all the work by herself.

She could hire assistants, but whom could she trust? Mark and Lee were the only people she'd told about the switch, and both were adamantly against it. Even after they'd finally accepted she was going to replace the mural whether they liked it or not, they continued to question the plan's practicality and legality as well as point out its futility. So, just as she'd done when faced with their disapproval of ANL, she stopped talking about it.

But they were the only ones she could count on not to betray her. She needed their help, and she needed Jack and Bill, too. Although both of them were against political art, Bill would have trouble saying no to her and Jack would be tickled by the intrigue.

So she told them all she wanted their take on the preliminary drawings for her new project, and although she wanted to save as much money as possible, she sprang for some bread, cheese, and beer to put them in a more receptive mood. And indeed, the four of them gobbled up the food, were happy to drink the beer, and their reactions to her sketches and mock-ups were very positive. They all knew about her family. Understood her passions. But once Alizée explained about switching the murals silence filled the flat.

"Even though I like the whole switcheroo thing on principle," Jack said, "it's . . . I don't know . . . fraudulent to use art this way."

"You sound like those people horrified by naked statues." Alizée kept her voice light.

"Or the ones who hate abstract art. Should artists stop creating these things because someone thinks they're inappropriate? Fraudulent even? No one has the right to make those kinds of decisions for someone else."

Jack laughed. "Ouch."

"As I told you before, you could easily end up in a lot of trouble with nothing to show for it," Lee said. "At the least, you'd be thrown off the project. And what about *Light in America*? What will happen to it? You can't just destroy —"

"I'm not going to destroy it." Alizee was actually quite proud of this. "I found a type of mild glue that will be strong enough to hold *Montage* for a short time and won't hurt *Light* at all. They take one down, the other will still be intact."

"I don't understand why you can't just paint it," Mark said. "Show it without all this switching nonsense. You'll still make your point."

"Does seem kind of crazy to take the risk," Bill agreed.

Alizée winked at Mark. "Aren't we of the craft all crazy?"

"Not this crazy," Mark grumbled.

Jack blew smoke rings, feigning an indifference his movements were too exaggerated to support. Mark paced the perimeter of the room, thumbs locked behind his back. Lee watched the mock-up as if it might suddenly grow to full size.

Only Bill met her eye. "Just so you know, I think it's a terrific project, kiddo. More than terrific. Virtuoso. But Mark's got a good argument: let it stand on its own. It's more than strong enough."

If this was the way they felt about the idea, how were they going respond to her request for help? Without their assistance there could be no *Montage.* So she plunged on. "None of this is why I wanted you to come here. I've got a huge favor to ask you. All of you. And I mean really huge. As in: I've got a lot of nerve."

"I knew all this cheese and beer was going to come with a cost," Jack griped. Everyone else merely looked curious.

"As you can see, I've got the mural all planned out, and I've bought almost all the supplies, but I need help with the actual painting."

Four pairs of eyes focused on her.

"I know it's a lot to ask, but it's a good project. An important project. And if you could give me a hand I'd be forever grateful."

"You want *us* to work on it with you?"

Lee was clearly astonished.

"I can't do it by myself," Alizée explained, swallowing her annoyance. Why was Lee so surprised? It wasn't that outlandish of an idea. "There's just too much painting that needs to be done. The canvases are large, and the deadline's December. So I was thinking that if each of you could find a couple of hours, maybe a couple of nights a week, then you could come here, and together we'd be able to finish it on time . . . I'll supply dinner."

Their expressions ranged from disbelief to incredulity.

"Please help me do something I care very much about. It would mean everything to me."

"You know it's not that simple." Lee studied her paint-stained fingers. "In so many ways. Just painting a mural is incredibly complicated. You know that, we do it every day. There's so much more than just applying paint to canvas."

"I've made a detailed schedule, and I'll take care of all the other things," she said. "It'll be more like you're one of my assistants."

"You're offering me a demotion?" Lee asked with a fleeting smile.

"What if it gets out that you're planning

to switch the murals?" Bill asked.

"The five of us are the only ones who know," Alizée said. "The only ones who are going to know."

"I'm not saying we're going to be blabbing all over the city," Bill said. "But things like this have a way of getting out. Look at what happened when Mrs. Roosevelt bought *Turned*." He chuckled. "Guess we'll have to make sure no one talks about it in front of Louise."

Mark threw his arm around Alizée's shoulder. "I know you're thinking about your family, about all the refugees, but you've also got to think of yourself and what kind of toll this will take on your heath and —"

"Forget about the risks or the logistics or my health." Alizée looked each one of them in the eye, allowed them to see her, to connect with the portion of the project she knew they'd understand. "Sure, this is about my family and what's going on in Europe, but it's also about art. My art. About what's in my soul. About how I have to get it out. About how I can't do it without you."

Jack finally broke the silence. "What kind of dinners are we talking about?"

37
ALIZÉE

The gang was being grand. Not because
they approved of the switching but because
they had great respect for *Montage* and felt
bad about her family. Which was fine. Even
though it annoyed her and she wished it
wasn't so, Alizée understood they felt safe
and secure on their side of the Atlantic,
content with a worldview that didn't cross
over much to the other. And they were
wonderful friends; despite their initial
reluctance, once they committed, all four
began coming to her flat on a regular basis.

Mark was there almost every night, Lee
and Bill once or twice a week, and even Jack
showed up now and then. He was fascinated
by the size of the canvases, the whole
concept of scale, and he relished the opportunity to argue about art and politics.
Which wasn't what she needed from him,
but he worked hard and fast, was always
entertaining, and he was good. All she could

do was thank him for his efforts and try to avoid getting pulled into the quarrels he worked so hard to stoke.

Mr. Schmidt, a retired carpenter who lived downstairs, had helped her construct four lightweight two-by-three-foot easels on which she placed the canvases. She could easily move them around by herself, and if need be, there was room for all five of them to work at one time.

Never had she been more pleased with her large barren flat. Nor with the seemingly endless energy that fueled her. The drive to create. Élan like she'd never experienced it before, perhaps with a touch of mania, but that was just semantics. She didn't need sleep, didn't need food, all she needed was to paint. And this she was doing every second she could.

Most evenings, only one person worked with her, but once in a while everyone came at the same time, and when that happened Jack was in his element. One particularly hot Indian-summer night, the five of them were working together. It was early, but Jack and Bill were already drunk. She, Mark, and Lee were catching up quickly. There wasn't any ice, and the warm beer was far from refreshing, but that didn't stop them. It was wet.

The underpainting was complete on all the canvases, and working as she did with her assistants at the warehouse, she'd sketched the major elements over the underpaint and told her friends which color and style she wanted them to use. She'd decided to use pieces of newsprint in spots, which they were all having a blast with, although if anyone noticed the articles were about the war and the refugees — one even about Drancy — no one mentioned it. They were all sweating profusely and kept bumping into each other as they maneuvered around the oversized canvases, but their spirits were high, and the work was progressing masterfully.

She leapt from canvas to canvas, singing *"Frère Jacques"* at the top of her lungs to everyone's great amusement. She sketched changes. She ground pigment. She climbed ladders. She moved canvases. She painted. She instructed. It was wild, it was wonderful, and it kept thoughts of anything else at bay.

"Jesus." Bill, who was painting a series of abstractions of fearful farm animals on canvas 2, wiped his forehead with his arm. "What a box to sweat in."

Alizée didn't raise her eyes from the row of sunflowers she was working on. They stretched from canvases #1 to #3, starting out tall and affirming and ending bowed and defeated. "There are a few bottles of warm beer left."

"Tastes like piss and makes you piss." Jack put down his brush and pulled two beers from the icebox that contained no ice. He threw one to Bill and opened the other. "Might as well head downstairs to the can before I drink it 'cause that's where I'm going as soon as I do."

Everyone laughed, and Lee asked, "So why bother to drink it?" She was painting a surrealistic depiction of a group of men in tuxedos so intrigued by their own conversation that they saw nothing beyond the small circle of themselves.

Jack poured half the beer down his throat without swallowing, one of his many drinking skills. He grinned at Lee, their eyes locking. "Now what fun would that be?"

Lee grinned back. "What about the rest of us? It would be a hell of a lot more fun for us if you weren't lurching around here pontificating." The caustic acidity of their conversations had increased lately, and although Lee still denied she cared anything for Jack, the heat between them was as sweltering as the night.

"I take great umbrage with that position,"

Jack declared, downing the other half of the bottle. "I have not been pontificating at all this evening. I have been hard at work helping the sad-sack refugees wheedle their way into a country that doesn't want them — and wheedle us into a war we don't want any more than we want them."

The room fell silent.

"Is that what you really think?" Alizée knew he was an isolationist, but *Montage* didn't have to do with war; it had to do with innocents suffering. "Helping the refugees has nothing to do with going to war."

"Yes, yes, pretty Alizée, please forgive me," Jack said with the sweeping bow of a nineteenth-century nobleman. "I completely agree. I was just pon-ti-fi-cating as the devil's advocate."

Her grip on her paintbrush was so tight the edge dug into her skin.

"You're tight, Pollock." Mark moved in close to Jack. "Time to go on home."

"But Alizée needs me." Jack pushed by Mark, stumbled, then pulled himself up and pointed to the canvas he'd been working on. "Look at the brilliant way I've rendered this corner of #4 so it flows from #3, just as our oh-so-talented girl ordered. 'Pulling the deep tones of sadness across the sky of the canvas' as she so artfully directed." He started to laugh. "*Artfully* directed, that's a good one, don't you think?" He sat down cross-legged on the floor and grinned up at them. "Good one."

"Do yourself a favor and do what Rothko says," Bill told Jack.

"Oh," Jack slurred, "you're all just a bunch of wet towels."

"Better a wet towel than a horse's ass," Lee said.

Jack stood and pounded his chest. "Apologize, woman!" he cried. "You don't mean a word of what you're saying. You know you have a yen for me."

Mark grabbed Jack by one arm and Bill took his other, but Jack was both wiry and wily, and he easily slipped from their grasp. Bill started to lose his balance, but Mark caught him with an awkward lunge before he could topple over. They both straightened up and started to laugh. Jack plopped himself down on the floor again and began to howl. Lee threw Alizée an apologetic glance and joined in. Tears streamed from their eyes as paroxysms of laughter distorted their faces.

Alizée put down her paintbrush and walked out of the flat.

It was cooler on the street than it was inside,

but she barely noticed the difference. Without any real awareness, she headed down Christopher toward Washington Square Park. But she never got there and somehow found herself walking in circles within the blocks of Grove, Barrow, and Jones. But the roads kept intersecting at odd angles. Hadn't there been hard corners before? Nothing looked familiar. And her friends. They were suddenly alien to her as well. As apparently she was to them.

The streets were deserted, but here and there shadowy figures seeking a nonexistent breeze sprawled on the fire escapes that crisscrossed the fronts of the brick buildings. These people were unconnected to her, too, distant and strange.

Images bombarded her brain, so fast and so distinct that her head felt like it was exploding. Playing rounders with Henri. Painting in the fields of Arles. Reading at the house with Oncle. Alain. Tante. Shopping with Babette. The avenues of Paris. These were her memories. Yes, they were hers. In France. But when had she been there? One moment yesterday, another decades ago. Or maybe she'd dreamed it all.

She saw the despondent horses, the lost children, the wilting flowers, the arrogant men concerned only with themselves. Saw her friends relishing a carefree bout of hilarity while her family was being held hostage by madmen and bureaucrats. Saw Breckinridge Long, giving a speech, blustery and self-righteous. Saw Nathan shooting him in the head.

A surge of exhaustion almost knocked her over. She was so tired. More tired than she'd ever been. She looked around at the unfamiliar landscape. Where was she? What was she doing in the middle of the night, standing alone on a cracked and grimy sidewalk in front of row upon row of dark tenements? Drenched in sweat, covered with paint, lost in the bowels of a foreign city?

Her knees gave way, and she was sitting at the bottom of a towering set of stairs that reached into the darkness above her. She pulled into herself, dwarfed by the stairs, the buildings, the city, by the sense that she was truly and deeply alone.

Then she felt it. She wasn't alone. Someone was watching her, someone with evil intent. Someone who had heard about the memo? Who'd found out about *Montage*? Or worse, someone who knew they'd been discussing assassination.

Every hair on her body flared, the sense of impending doom so strong it thrust her into a stand and then a run. She could hear his breathing behind her. Or was it her own? Either way she had to keep moving. Fast. Even though she had no idea where she was going.

38
DANIELLE, 2015

After my exasperating meeting with George, I tried to put both Alizée and the squares out of my mind, but this proved impossible. Especially now that I had Lee's square, carried with such hope in Grand-père's rucksack across thousands of miles, tossed aside in heartbreak. I'd been looking at it for months now and never failed to find something new.

I took out my magnifying glass and managed to pick out a few words from the newsprint embedded in the paint. One of which was *Drancy,* followed by *camps d'accueil.* A reception camp? Whatever that meant, it was the place where Alizée's uncle had been imprisoned, from where Grand-père had escaped.

So Alizée knew about Drancy, about her uncle perhaps, maybe about her brother. Could this mean she did go back to France in 1940? That she tried to find them? I thought about my conversation with Charlie Nolan, the NYU historian; he'd said it was unlikely but not completely out of the question.

I'd checked out Drancy after I read Grand-père's letter. It was an unremarkable town outside of Paris with a troublesome history. Home to one of the most brutal World War II transit camps in France, the Drancy Deportation Center was the main terminus from which French Jews were sent to Auschwitz. It was run by the Gestapo and manned by French guards, many of whom were more than happy to oblige their Nazi commanders, humiliating and beating prisoners, separating small children from their parents and sending them off to the death camps by themselves. Not the best moment in French history.

When Grand-mère's will was read, it turned out she left each of the grandchildren ten thousand dollars with the stipulation that we use it for something we'd always wanted but didn't have the money to buy. An indulgence, she said. I knew she'd been thinking about an object, but I figured a trip would also qualify. Reenergized by this windfall at this particular time, I put in for the six days of vacation I'd accrued. Maybe

Jordan Washor at the Louvre could be persuaded to look a little harder. Maybe more paintings from small collectors had arrived. Maybe I'd take a trip to Drancy.

I hit the Internet to prepare. But soon I found I wasn't looking at websites for cheap airfares or centrally located hotels. I was cruising sites for ways to find missing persons. And boy, were there lots of ways. Searchable arrest records and prison databases abounded, as did sites belonging to private investigators who are more than happy to take your money to find — or most likely, not find — your missing loved one. There were frequent references to "loved one."

I studied photographs of the lost, most images so poor I couldn't imagine they would be of help to anyone. I found myself worrying about these blurry souls, about the families who wanted to find them. It was all very sad. Where are you? Who are you? Did you want to be lost?

Had Alizée wanted to be lost? Maybe. But if she'd gone to France, she wouldn't have wanted to be lost there; she would have gone directly to Arles, maybe to Drancy, to her family. I shifted over to websites specializing in finding Holocaust survivors — or as many tactfully described it: getting closure on the fate of the victims.

There were almost as many Holocaust sites as there were in the general missing persons category, most of which started with the disclaimer that they couldn't actually help you find a particular person. You could register your missing relative, add them to existing databases or visit the hundreds of blogs dedicated to this purpose. There were Jewish genealogy sites, the International Tracing Service, the Yad Vashem central registry, the databases at the US Holocaust Memorial Museum in DC.

I learned that most concentration camp deaths weren't documented by the Nazis — and here I'd thought they were such anal-compulsive record keepers — but there was something called the "Death Books from Auschwitz." If your relative had been lucky enough to survive the selection process on arrival at the camp but unlucky enough to have been killed there, it was possible he or she was one of the eighty thousand murder victims listed in one of the three volumes. There might even be a photo. You could purchase the boxed set for $365.

The American Red Cross had a Holocaust and War Victims Tracing Center whose staff actually did attempt to find individual people for you. A caseworker was assigned, and he or she searched all the victim databases and registries as well as the archives of hundreds of organizations and museums across the world. And it was completely free. According to the website, the Red Cross had confirmed the missing person's fate almost a third of the time, and in one thousand cases the relative had been found alive and the family reunited. Not that I expected that to happen, but still I got goose bumps reading about it.

I didn't have any specifics on any of the other Benoits, so I spent the rest of that beautiful Saturday afternoon going down the list of websites and entering what little of Alizée's information I knew — name, nationality, date of birth — into every registry, database and blog I could find. I contacted my local Red Cross chapter and filled out the Tracing Inquiry Form (1609). Then I turned my attention to websites for cheap airfares and centrally located hotels.

39
LEE, 1940

When Alizée didn't come right back, Lee and Mark decided to go look for her. Bill and Jack went also, and the four of them fanned out in different directions, agreeing to meet back at the apartment at three o'clock. No one had much confidence that Jack would do anything other than stagger home and pass out, but Lee, and she presumed Mark and Bill, was propelled into that painfully clear sobriety that follows a drunken scare.

She took Christopher toward Washington Square Park; Mark headed to the river; Bill went south toward SoHo; Jack stumbled east. They all ended up on the steps of Alizée's building an hour later, empty-handed. Lee wasn't surprised they hadn't found her — it was a vast city, after all — but she was worried. Everyone was. Jack was in the worst shape.

"This is all my fault," he moaned, holding

his head in his hands. "It was just a joke. I had a little too much to drink. Just because I don't like political art doesn't mean I like Nazis. I'm an idiot. Why did I say such a stupid thing?" He looked up. "What exactly did I say?"

No one answered him.

"I checked upstairs," Lee said. "She's not there."

"I think one of us should stay here in case she comes back," Mark said.

"I'll stay," Jack offered.

"No you won't," Bill snapped. "If she comes home and finds you here, she'll turn around and leave again."

"It should be Lee," Mark said. "We don't need two girls wandering around alone in the middle of the night."

Although Lee walked through the Village at all hours, tonight she'd been unnerved moving through the deserted streets, looking into alleys where bedsheets swayed like hovering ghosts from their overhead clotheslines, afraid of what she might find. "Okay. I'll stay. You boys go out for another hour, and I'm sure she'll be here when you get back."

"Right," Mark said, although he didn't sound convinced. "Where else has she got to go?"

No one answered this question either.

Lee walked in circles around Alizée's apartment, taking in the bareness of it, even filled with the towering canvases. Although far from finished, there was no doubt *Montage* was revolutionary. They were right to help her with it. For Alizée and for themselves; Alizée's ideas were opening up new avenues for their own work. They all felt it.

When Mark and Bill returned, there was still no sign of Alizée. And now Jack was missing, too.

"Calling Jack a horse's ass turns out to be a compliment," Lee grumbled to take their minds off Alizée, although the truth was she was a little worried about him, too. "A horse is a noble creature."

"I'm going back out," Mark said. "You'll stay here?" he asked Lee.

When Lee nodded, Bill said, "I'll go with you."

Lee lay down on Alizée's mattress, hoping to sleep. But her eyes flew open with every sound, and there were many coming through the open windows as the city began to wake. She sat up and was once again caught by the command of the mural. Even though she'd watched Alizée work it out, she wasn't sure how it had become so large, far bigger and weightier than its sheer size.

It had something to do with its physical massiveness, yet it was more than that. The experience of the colors was almost tactile. And there was the unexpected punch the juxtaposition of so many disparate elements created. The newspapers. The mixed textures. The transformations. It generated a raw emotion, a visual message that slammed you. And it wasn't complete yet.

For the first time, it occurred to Lee that maybe, just maybe, the idea that this painting could have an effect beyond artistic merit wasn't such an ill-fated notion after all. Maybe Mrs. Roosevelt had it right. And maybe the plan Alizée had devised was a potentially credible scenario to get it out to as many people as possible.

She stood and stared at the low roof of the building next door, which was littered with broken furniture and piles of old tires. Alizée would be home any minute. She had to be. Lee leaned her body far out the window but saw only the city's early risers: the bakers, the newsboys, the bus drivers, a chambermaid. Abruptly, she left the apartment and went outside. She needed air.

To the east, the sun was still low behind the buildings, but light oozed at their tops and sides, cutting into the shadows at street level. She sat on the front stoop. Apprehension caught between her lungs, pressed toward her throat.

And then, there was Alizée, walking slowly toward her, fatigue written in every slope of her body. Lee raced to her, gathered her up in her arms. "Are you all right?"

Alizée nodded into Lee's shoulder.

Lee held her at arm's length. She did appear to be all right, although she was sweaty and dirty, and there was a scary deadness in her eyes. She was breathing hard, as if she'd been running. "You look like something the cat dragged in," Lee said as cheerfully as she could muster, turning Alizée toward the front stairs. "Let's go up to your apartment."

Alizée followed without saying a word.

"She was really scared," Lee said to Mark, her voice low. They were walking away from Alizée's; Mark on his way to punch in at the WPA office, and Lee headed to the warehouse. Alizée was taking a bath and had promised to meet Lee at work within the hour. "Which, as you know, isn't like her."

"And you said she'd been running?" Mark asked. "Do you think someone was chasing her? Trying to hurt her?"

"I said she *might* have been running. There are lots of scary things in the city in the middle of the night."

"Jesus!" he cried, slamming one fist into the other. "How can she be so irresponsible? She could have gotten herself killed!" Then he caught himself. "Sorry. That was unfair. It's just that, ah, that I love her."

"Yeah, I kind of figured." Lee had to smile. "There probably wasn't anyone there. She probably just imagined it. Easy enough to do."

Mark frowned. "Extra easy for Alizée."

"What does that mean?"

He hesitated, looked like he wanted to say something, stopped. Then began, "You know she's different . . . And I worry. She . . . she told me that sometimes she feels like she's floating in the sky, watching herself painting or shopping in the five-and-dime. That she looks in the mirror and doesn't always recognize her face."

Lee stopped to collect herself. Lit a cigarette. "Are you telling me she's seeing things? Or not seeing things?"

Mark took her cigarette and lit one of his own; his hands trembled slightly. "You said when she first got back, her eyes were all funny. Dead, you said." He took a deep drag. "I've seen that look. Like she's not with me. Like she's on the other side of a window, and I can't reach her. Even when

I'm touching her."

"She's just working too hard," Lee said as much to assure herself as to assure him; she'd seen that look, too. And not just last night. "And think about what she's producing — it's tough to pull that kind of passion out of your soul."

"*Montage* is great, I'll give you that, but this idea of switching it just adds to the whole, well, you know . . . She's sick over her family, I get that, but taking on the weight of all the refugees? Of the whole goddamn war in Europe? It's unhinging her. She wants to do something so badly that she can't see what's possible and what isn't."

"I'm starting to think that maybe it isn't so impossible," Lee said. "If she could pull it off, if *Montage* were seen by lots of people, discussed, maybe that would create more interest in the refugees. It wouldn't be an overnight thing, but it's possible something could change."

Mark was shaking his head. "Don't let the fact that *Montage* is shaping up to be a possible masterwork blind you. The mural's brilliant, but the rest of it's pure delusion. She can't change US policy with a painting — no matter how good — and she can't hang a sixteen-foot mural without someone finding out." He threw his cigarette to the sidewalk, crushed it with his shoe.

"Mark —"

"And when she fails, she's going to be devastated. Broken. And then what's going to happen to her? How's she going to be able to withstand that?"

40
ALIZÉE

Alizée managed to leave the warehouse a little early, but it was on the other side of dusk by the time she reached her street. She hated the waning sunlight of autumn even more than the chill in the air. She hurried up the stairs of her building, but inside there was little relief. It, too, was gloomy and dark, the foyer full of cobwebs and grime. The smell of onions was overwhelming.

She peered into her mailbox and saw envelopes. Her heart jumped, and she quickly drew them out. A five-page supplement to the Sears-Roebuck catalogue. An electric bill. A letter from Ruth, a girl she'd shared a room with at a woman's hotel when she first came to New York. Another from Sheri Rhodes, who'd also won a scholarship from Hans Hofmann but had dropped out and returned to Michigan to get married after the first semester. Alizée couldn't remember what either of them looked like. She trudged up to the flat.

Hitler was running riot over the continent. The Warsaw ghetto had been cordoned off from the rest of the city. And then last week the ERC director officially rejected her money-for-visas scheme. Mr. Fleishman had returned the cash, which was now hidden in an empty paint can, waiting to be used if another opportunity to get her family out of Europe arose. *When* another opportunity arose.

This was looking bleaker by the day. The Vichy government in France had repealed the law barring anti-Semitism and reversed one protecting Jews from deportation to Nazi camps. The ERC had sent an emissary named Varian Fry to France to bring as many refugees back to the United States as was possible, but the lack of visas was severely hobbling his efforts. And Long was cutting the number of available visas by the thousands, last week to European immigrants coming through Cuba and Mexico.

To make matters even worse, her powers of concentration were slipping. Ever since the night she'd been followed, instead of narrowing in on a problem, her mind jumped from one thought to another. She'd try to find the solution for a particular challenge, get stumped, leap to the next, go back to the first to reconsider, resolve nothing. This bouncing created an almost constant sense of déjà vu: she felt as if she was where she'd once been, but in a slightly different way. It was interfering with *Light in America,* with *Montage,* and with her decision about what they should do about Long.

The committee continued to debate, secretly of course, not even Gideon knew about it. Aarone insisted saving the refugees superseded all other concerns. Nathan bragged about his sharpshooting abilities and the five guns he owned, how he could "knock off" Long with a single bullet. Bertha was the most reasoned by far, balanced in her thoughts and statements, focused on what was best for the refugees, but her pragmatism seemed to be leading her to support Aarone and Nathan. Astonishingly, even William was starting to shift a little, pointing out Jesus's overwhelming concern with the downtrodden and with man helping his fellow man, but he appeared quite troubled by the words coming out of his own mouth.

She let herself into the flat and put the mail on the table, then picked it up again. Something struck her as odd. She turned over the letter from Sheri. It looked as if it had been reopened after being sealed and then pasted shut again. She dropped it back on the table without reading it. Sheri must have decided to add something she believed was too important to miss. It could wait until later.

She walked over to *Montage,* pleased and panicked at the sight of the panels, her emotions as willy-nilly as her judgments. The flow of the flowers and soldiers between #1 and #2 was good. But the cows reaching from #2 to #3 didn't mesh at all. Number 1 and #4 were in better shape than #2 and #3, as they were more straightforward than the other two, requiring fewer details as well as fewer layers of color and texture. Still, even #1 and #4 needed a huge amount of work.

She checked the Betty Crocker calendar nailed to the wall, counted up the remaining days: sixty-eight. That was a long time. She could do it. She counted up the weeks: less than ten. That wasn't nearly long enough.

She eyed the mail, wondered what Sheri's news might be, picked up the letter. But then she saw that Ruth's letter had a similar lumpiness under the back flap. As did the electric bill. She laid the three envelopes side by side on the table. The same small tears, same lumps of glue, same unevenness where the flap met the body. The flat expanded around her, the ceiling flying up into the dark night, the walls stretching across the street. Then with a whoosh, like an accordion, it collapsed back into its usual dimensions. *Putain.* Her mail was being opened.

She paced, fists pushed hard under her arms, mind jumping. She'd known someone was following her the other night. Had had the same feeling just last week walking to work. And the boy on the train who tried to steal her bags . . . Had he just been a pickpocket or something more ominous?

The committee might have been overheard talking about Long, or one of the members might have spoken outside the group. Either the America First Committee or Long himself might be aware she was the one who brought Mrs. Roosevelt the memo. That trusted colleague of Hiram Bingham's might have had second thoughts. And then there was *Montage.* She recognized her little paintings and schemes were too unimportant for this kind of treatment. But Breckinridge Long's life was not.

There was a pounding, then a scratch at the door. She raced to the far wall and squatted behind one of her larger canvases. They were here. Already. What did they want from her? What would they do to her? She made herself as small as she could.

"Alizée?" Mark's voice boomed across the flat. "Are you here?"

She thrust the canvas aside and ran to him, so relieved she threw herself into his large, reassuring body.

"What? What?" he demanded, holding her away so he could see her face. When he did, he led her to the mattress. "Sit."

She sat. It was nothing. She'd overreacted. "I'm fine," she assured him. "Fine."

He pushed a curl off her forehead, which was noticeably damp. "You don't seem fine."

She took a deep breath and blew it out slowly. "Just gave myself a little scare. Silly."

"What kind of scare?"

"It's nothing." She scrambled for an explanation. "I . . . I fell asleep is all. And when you came through the door I must have still been dreaming, thought you were in it, or you were someone else who was in it . . . You know how dreams can do that sometimes."

"Zée . . ."

"No, no, I mean it," she said. "I was so tired. I thought I'd just lie down on the floor for a minute. But then . . . then I guess I must have actually fallen asleep, and then you just startled me. That's all."

Mark held her tightly, and she burrowed into him, hoping he'd just hold her and say nothing more. But he kissed her forehead and whispered, "You weren't asleep, you were hiding behind a canvas, alone in your own apartment. You've got to talk to me, trust me. Please let me help you."

She needed to sort through this on her own, needed to figure out what was real and what wasn't. Then she would talk to him. Part of her wanted to confide in him now, tell him her fears and her secrets, unburden herself. But he'd been so upset when he couldn't find her that night. How would he feel about someone chasing her, stalking her, reading her mail? And there were his bouts. He didn't need any more to worry about. "I do trust you," she finally said. "But there's nothing to talk about. I just need a good night's sleep."

She found the idea of someone tampering with her mail even more unnerving than being followed. At least if she was being followed, it was outside, in public; her mail was inside, her private self. She watched herself more closely now, hovering higher to view a wider swatch, to see who was behind her, who was coming toward. She was spooked, jittery, and her nerves felt as if they were on the outside of her skin. This made it more difficult to sleep, and the weight of accumulating tiredness was crushing.

The physical incongruity of restlessness and exhaustion was particularly acute late one night as she and Bill worked in silence. She was like a whirling dervish, ready to fall over but unable to do so because of her own cyclonic motion. She checked to make sure she wasn't messing up the mural, and was surprised to find she wasn't.

Bill was immersed in painting an abstracted image of a pride of lions scanning the horizon, impervious to the dead lions at their feet. He didn't look like he was going anywhere soon, which was fine with her. Not only did the lions need to be completed, but she wasn't looking forward to being alone.

"Working on this mural has changed my mind about a lot of things," Bill said into the stillness.

Alizée was caught unawares by the sound of his voice and jumped as if she'd heard a gunshot. "What? What?"

He grinned at her startle, leaned back on his haunches and looked hard at his panel. "For one, I never liked merging styles in a single piece. I always thought it muddied up the works, but now I see that it can be additive. Like how when you let paint dry between layers the colors become more vibrant. Not less like you'd think."

She nodded.

"But it's the political stuff I really get now." Bill turned and looked at her, his ice blue eyes filled with what appeared to be gratitude. "Like we always say, art's about evoking emotion, about exploring the human condition." He waved his brush at all the panels. "And this *is* the human condition. The details might be specific to 1940, but the emotions, the underlying themes, are about who we are. Unfortunately, probably who we'll always be."

To her great surprise, she burst into tears.

"What? What did I say?"

"Nothing," she managed through her tears.

Bill threw his hands up in the air. "I thought I was giving you a compliment."

The expression on his face was one of such complete bafflement that she started to laugh. And once she started, she couldn't stop.

As he watched her, Bill's face changed from perplexity to concern. "Are you okay? Should I go get Mark?"

She rocked on the floor, holding her knees to her chest, howling up at the ceiling. Bill filled a glass of water from the tap and tried to hand it to her, but she waved it away, sure she'd spill it. It occurred to her that Bill, Mark, Jack, and Lee had been laughing the same way the night she'd stormed out of the flat. But this concurrence only made her laugh harder.

"Alizée," he said, pleading. "Please stop. You're scaring me."

Somehow, the idea of frightening this big, self-confident man did it. That and the realization that he was sure to tell Mark about the laughing fit. She sobered, mirth draining from her as rapidly as it had come. She hiccupped and wiped her eyes with the sleeve of her shirt, not caring that she was smearing wet paint on her face. *Merde.* This was the second episode in less than a week that Mark was sure to worry himself to death about. He was having enough problems. Maybe it was time to come clean.

Bill handed her the water again, and this time she drank it gratefully.

He knelt and tentatively touched her shoulder as if afraid the slightest touch might topple her.

She looked over at him with what she hoped was a reassuring smile. "Someone's been going through my mail."

41
LEE

Lee and Mark sat on the stoop in front of Alizée's building. Alizée was expecting them and the night was chilly, but instead of going up, Mark had suggested they share a cigarette first. He wanted her help convincing Alizée to go to Bloom Sanatorium, but Lee wasn't having any of it.

"It'll be horrible with her gone," Mark said, "but it'll be worse for her if she stays."

Lee took the cigarette from him, inhaled, and handed it back. He was panicking, overreacting. "She's having a tough time, sure, but it's nothing some good news from Europe won't cure. She just needs to handle it in her own way. You suggest this now and I guarantee it'll backfire. She's fragile. You never know what might set her off."

"And that's exactly the problem," he said. "I'm worried about what she might do to herself if nothing changes."

"That's crazy. The poor girl's exhausted.

Worried sick about her family. Furious that she hasn't been able to help them. Feeling impotent. She doesn't need to go anywhere. She just needs to paint, to finish *Montage*. To believe she's doing something to help."

"What if you're wrong?"

She worried about this. "What if taking her away from her work is the worst thing for her right now?"

"Have you noticed the marks on her arms?"

Lee shook her head and motioned for the cigarette.

"Rows of them. Some are scabbed over. Or thin lines of red. Slightly curved."

"What are you saying?"

His voice was husky. "She's been digging her fingernails into her skin so hard she's drawing blood."

Lee swallowed hard and handed the cigarette back to him. Could this be true? "Bug bites maybe?"

"I knew a girl in college who used a pocketknife to carve hash marks on her thighs. She said she did it so she'd know she was alive."

"Alizée knows she's alive." Even if sometimes she looked out at the world with dead eyes.

Mark leaned against the railing and blew

smoke skyward. "Jack says Bloom's a good place. Not so much a mental asylum as a hospital where you can get away from the world. Out of your own head, was how he put it. He said there are all kinds of regular people there. That it was actually fun. Claims the doctors helped him a lot."

"Except that he started drinking again three months after he got out."

"It's the part about her smiling that gets me." Mark crushed the cigarette into the concrete without asking Lee if she wanted another drag. "As if she were proud, Bill said. Happy even, that someone might be going through her mail."

"That's Bill's interpretation," Lee reminded him.

"Bill's not prone to exaggeration. If anything, he tips the other way."

This was true. Lee strained to find other arguments that might sway Mark from starting this conversation with Alizée.

"Bill said he looked the envelopes over carefully," Mark continued. "That they seemed perfectly normal to him."

Lee took another stab. "Maybe we just need to convince her to take it a little easier."

"We've been telling her that for months and getting nowhere!" Mark exploded. "She won't sleep, she won't eat. She thinks she can fly around like a ghost and that someone's following her and reading her mail!" He punched his left fist into his right palm. "You understand what a psychiatrist would say about that kind of behavior, don't you?"

"It's not that —"

"What if she decides her fingernails aren't enough? That she needs a knife?" Mark stood. "We can't take the chance of letting this go on. Even for a few more weeks. She's too unstable." He touched Lee's shoulder. "I'm scared for her."

They headed up the stairs. Suddenly, Lee was scared, too.

Alizée greeted them as always, pleasant and thankful for their help, but distant, preoccupied. She kissed Mark and smiled at Lee, then immediately returned to her painting. Lee and Mark took up where they'd left off the previous night.

They continued this way for over an hour, then Alizée put down her brush and said, "I've got another favor to ask you both."

"Oh?" Lee asked as naturally as she could. This wasn't going to be good.

"I went to the library yesterday," Alizée began, growing animated for the first time that evening. "Met with the director, talked over the plans for hanging *Light in America.*"

"I knew you'd change your mind," Mark said. "This is swell —"

"I found a way in — and a way out." Alizée was clearly pleased with this feat. "They're going to bring *Light in America* to the rotunda before hanging it, going to prep the walls, put it up a couple of days before the fête. So I'm going to bring the *Montage* panels to the warehouse and roll them inside of *Light in America* right before they move it, which is all fine, and I even talked the director into hanging velvet over the *Light in America* panels so no one can see them before the fête, and that way no one will see *Montage* until the draping is pulled off!"

Lee and Mark looked at her with gaping mouths.

Alizée took a deep, excited breath. "There's a door, a door into the basement that no one uses. It's at the back of the library. I couldn't believe it when I found it. The exact thing I was looking for! And then the bookshelves! It's meant to be, I tell you. Clearly meant to be."

Alizée was making less and less sense, acting more as Mark feared and less as Lee hoped.

"That way we can go in and out with no one seeing us!" Alizée cried. "Isn't that amazing?"

"We?" Mark edged closer to Alizée.

"Into the library!" she chortled. "That's the favor. Obviously, I can't hang the four panels by myself, but I think that the three of us should be able to do it easily. They're actually not that heavy, and we can smuggle in all the materials and tools that we'll need through the door I found and hide them in the basement behind the bookshelves like the panels beforehand, and then we go over after the library's closed the night before the fête, and like I told you before, I've got some glue that isn't too thick so that it won't hurt *Light* when we put *Montage* up on top of it."

Alizée's breath was coming in gasps. "I don't think it should take more than a few hours. We're in at midnight, out by three, and no one will be the wiser until the next night when it's revealed to all!"

Lee had absolutely no idea what to say. Alizée's ramble had more than a hint of madness to it. Bookshelves? Velvet curtains? Back doors?

Mark cleared his throat. "Zée, you're looking a little tired."

Alizée stared at him blankly.

"Tired," he repeated. "You look tired."

"Will you help me?" Alizée's eyes swung

from Mark to Lee and then back to Mark.

"It's impressive you figured this all out," Lee said. "All those details. Very —"

"Will you or won't you?"

"Sure we will." Mark turned to Lee. "Right?"

"Yeah, yeah," Lee quickly agreed. "Sure we will."

"Thank you," Alizée said, reaching for her paintbrush. Her face looked so haggard Lee didn't know how long she could go on.

"So now that that's all agreed," Mark suggested, "how about the three of us sit for a minute and have a beer?"

"You two go ahead," Alizée said, already focused on her painting. "I've got to finish this section tonight."

Lee shook her head at Mark. After that barely comprehensible babble about the library, she didn't think this was the right time to bring up Bloom. Even if the babble suggested Alizée needed to go there.

Mark cleared his throat again. "Bill said you think someone's been reading your mail."

Alizée continued to paint.

He hesitated. "I, ah, I hate to ask, but are you sure this is really happening? That you're not, ah, misconstruing things? You haven't been sleeping, and that can confuse a lot of things."

Alizée stiffened but kept painting.

"Maybe it would be good for you to take a little break," Mark offered. "A rest. Away from all this."

A barely perceptible shake of her head.

"You told me about the flying around," he continued. "The mirror . . ."

Alizée started to laugh, an oddly vacant sound. "Oh, I can just see you all at the table at the Shop, huddled together and whispering about whether poor Alizée has lost her mind. 'First she cried and then she laughed.' 'She took a walk at night.' 'She looked at me funny.' Well, I'm happy to tell you that it's not true. I see reality as clearly as you do. Perhaps more clearly."

"Maybe a break isn't such a bad idea," Lee said. "You wouldn't even have to go anywhere, you could —"

"Or you could go to Bloom," Mark interrupted. "Just like Jack did. Get lots of rest, lots to eat, and then you'll be able to come back and finish up the murals."

Alizée picked up a dab of yellow from her palette and touched it lightly against the gnarled trunk of a tree. She stood back. Added a wisp of a line rising to the leaves, skimmed a few branches. When she turned and looked at them, her cheeks were flushed a deep red, but when she spoke, her voice was hushed. "I appreciate all the help you're giving me," she said. "I do. And I thank you for that. But just to be clear, I'm not going anywhere."

42
DANIELLE, 2015

It was with a bit of trepidation at traveling alone, and more than a little at what I might or might not find, that I landed at Charles de Gaulle Airport. Also with a heavy dose of exhaustion: It was 7:30 a.m. Paris time, 1:30 a.m. Dani time. More than seven hours wrenched into a seat between an overweight woman who kept leaning in — and not in the good way — and a teenage boy who sang along to the rap songs on his iPod the entire trip. I kid you not.

After I cleared customs, I hesitated before taking a cab to my hotel. I wasn't used to spending money so frivolously, but I reminded myself that this was Grand's gift, that she'd want me to enjoy myself. I handed the driver what seemed like an exorbitant fare, roughly a hundred dollars with tip. Didn't *seem* exorbitant, *was* exorbitant. My room wasn't ready and wouldn't be until noon. I contemplated stretching out on one of the red couches ringing the lobby but figured this would be perceived as a gauche American thing to do. Instead, I handed my luggage over to the bellhop and headed out to the street.

I picked this hotel on rue du Roule because it was near the river and walking distance to the Louvre and the Paris Holocaust Memorial, which I discovered contains the largest cache of Holocaust-related materials in France. The Drancy deportation camp museum would entail a train or bus trip. I'd been in Paris a bunch of times; we came here a lot when I was a kid, and my high school graduation present was a bus trip around Europe. But I hadn't been back since. The Holocaust Memorial didn't open until 2005 and the Drancy museum until 2012, so I'd never been to either one. Not that my family would have visited had they existed.

When I got outside, the sky was gray, as it so often is in Paris, but my spirits began to rise nonetheless. Rue du Roule is narrow and one way; bicycles, mopeds, even cars, were parked on the sidewalk, as there was no room for them on the street. Men in green uniforms swept what little asphalt there was with their green plastic brooms, deftly avoiding vehicles as well as the cell-phone-glued pedestrians streaming off to work in their fabulous shoes. Women in impossible heels, perfectly wrapped scarves, hair swept up in ways both chic and effortless-looking, although I guessed these coifs were quite time-consuming. Men dressed much more colorfully than at home.

I took a deep breath, caught the mingled scents of perfume, motorbike fumes, baking bread, and *pain d'amande* from the *boulangerie* across the street. Ah, Paris. The cream-colored facade of the hotel, which matched just about all the buildings on the block, was laced with wrought-iron flower boxes spilling red carnations. The screech of motorbikes and mopeds, the rumble of buses on a nearby boulevard, the rolling vowels of the French language. A beguiling assault on the senses. Thanks, Grand.

My meeting with Jordan Washor at the Louvre wasn't for two more days. What to do first. Sightsee? The Holocaust Memorial? Drancy? I figured I should leave sightseeing for last so I'd have something to look forward to if my other endeavors didn't pan out, but it was by far the most appealing.

I decided I didn't have to decide and turned south toward the Seine on rue de Rivoli, a wide and busy street, also one way, lined with clothing stores, shoe stores, banks, cafes, and the old Samaritaine department store. Tourists, Parisians, taxis, cars, motorbikes, a cacophony of image and sound. I passed a Métro stop, the exit littered with discarded tickets. Where were the men in their green suits?

And then the Louvre was on my left. I stood in the expansive courtyard, taking in the massive Italian Renaissance museum with its distinctively French design: the vertical lines, the elongated windows, the double-sloped roof. Cream-colored, of course. Fountains, of course. Hordes of tourists, of course. I was pulled toward I. M. Pei's fabled glass pyramid by the early-morning crowd, but stepped aside before I reached the entrance.

I was too tired to waste the money on a ticket. I'd need at least a full day inside, and this was definitely not the day for it. It was home to some of the greatest art ever created, and I was, after all, still an artist. I pulled out my cell and hit Jordan's number in the hope he had some good news about the squares.

"Great to hear from you, Dani," Jordan said in a rush. "All hell's broken out here, and we've been working twenty-four/seven. I don't even know what day it is." He paused. "Oh, shit, is our meeting today?"

I laughed. "No, not until Friday."

"That's a re—" He mumbled something to someone else. "Good. Good," he said to me, clearly distracted. "What time did we say? Can we do it over lunch? I'm totally jammed."

"That's fine," I assured him, although I was disappointed. If he'd found any squares he surely would have mentioned it. Most likely, he hadn't had a chance to give them a thought.

When Jordan hung up, I checked my watch. It was almost ten, and I had at least two more hours before I could fend off my jet lag with a nap and shower. It was more than enough time to visit the Holocaust Memorial. It wasn't far, near the Hôtel de Ville, the Marais district, the old Jewish quarter. I hesitated, then turned in that direction.

I got a little lost, which was okay with me; I wasn't sure I was up to coming face-to-face with the world's worst genocide. As I wandered, I was, as always, charmed by the city, its magnificent architecture, and this area of sixteenth-century buildings had many of its finest. Unfortunately, some of the buildings' histories weren't the finest.

Like Saint-Germain-l'Auxerrois, a church begun in the twelfth century that grew into a brilliant blend of Romanesque, Gothic, and Renaissance elements. Beautiful to look at, which I appreciated as I stood in front of it, but it was also at the center of the Saint Bartholomew's Day Massacre — a riot in which thousands of Protestants were killed by a mob of Catholic Parisians. Sixteenth century, twentieth century, twenty-first century. Some things never change.

When I reached the Mémorial de la Shoah — *Shoah* is Hebrew for "Holocaust" — I was struck by how cold and hostile it looked, walled in, foreboding. But clearly that was purposeful. The outer courtyard contained a huge cylinder, evocative of the Auschwitz chimneys, chiseled with the names of the European concentration camps to which French Jews were sent. Ahead of me was the Wall of Names. I cautiously approached.

Seventy-five thousand names carved into stone, the French Jews deported to Nazi camps. Only twenty-five hundred had returned. Three percent. And there was space on the last slab for more names to be added if more deaths and deportations were discovered. How forward-thinking. How hideous to have to think that way. The names were inscribed along with date of birth; place of birth; and the number, date, and destination of the convoy in which they rode to their deaths. Row upon row upon row. Panel upon panel upon panel.

I couldn't look for Benoit. Not yet. Instead, I stumbled through the barred doors into the museum, taken aback by its light and spaciousness, almost an affront. So many photographs. So many shoes. Eyeglasses. So many suitcases packed with clothes never worn. A sham. "One valise per person," the Nazis had said. "Bring what you need." And then they stole it all. Why so many eyeglasses?

There was a crypt in the shape of a Jewish star, black marble, topped with an eternal flame. It was filled with ashes from the camps, the Warsaw ghetto, too. Ashes now buried beneath dirt brought in from Israel, kaddish finally said for the now-nameless dead.

Even worse was a room filled with drawers. Drawer upon drawer upon orderly drawer, a card catalogue of law-abiding French Jews — grocers and carpenters, doctors and lawyers, students and housewives — kept by the French police. Parisians ordered by the Germans to register as Jews in 1940, picked up, and herded into trains over the following years, herded into oblivion. Some of those who refused to comply with the order weren't taken away because they weren't known to the authorities. Saved by bucking the rules.

And then there were the children. Photos of eleven thousand murdered children: they grin; they cavort; they hug their brothers and cousins, their mothers; they smile shyly. I sat down hard on a bench and started to cry. A woman lightly touched my shoulder and handed me a box of tissues. I took them without meeting her eyes. She said nothing and moved on.

43
ALIZÉE, 1940

A letter arrived from Tante. The handwriting was frenzied. No date and no salutation. Alizée read it three times before she fully took it in.

> I know you are doing everything you can, but you must find a visa for Alain. Immediately. We are going into hiding tomorrow. With Oncle's arrest and Henri's disappearance, we feel it is our only option. When you get the visa, contact the man I told you had helped us before. He knows where we are and will get it to us. I cannot impress upon you how vital this is. I am not being hysterical when I tell you that if we do not get out now, we will die. I love you. I have always loved you. I will always love you.

This wasn't her family being cut down. That couldn't be happening again. No. This story belonged to the girl clenching a letter in the cold glare of a December morning, waiting to speak her next lines, take her next action, follow the script. Alizée watched from the audience, the first row actually. It was an amazing performance and Alizée felt for the poor thing, but it was just a play. In a play the heroine always overcomes the obstacles. Always finds a way to save her loved ones, to save all the others, too. It would be hard, it would be dangerous, but she would do it. Because that's what heroines do.

"I'm willing to take that chance," Nathan said.

"It's not a chance," Alizée pointed out. "You do it this way, you're going to get caught." After Tante's letter, she'd put her questions behind her. Long, a single individual, was going to murder her family and thousands of others with his bureaucratic prevaricating, his anti-Semitic schemes. One man. Aarone was right: the ledgers did not balance. She saw that now.

"But Long will be dead," Nathan insisted.

"And so will you," Alizée said. "After a long stint in jail."

Aarone crossed his arms over his chest. "If Nathan is willing, I am thinking this is what we should be doing."

The four of them were sitting in the *PM* offices, hours after the general ANL meeting had ended, arguing about the final details of "the project," as they now referred to it. William wasn't there. He'd told Alizée that although he would pray for their success at removing Long from the State Department, he couldn't be personally involved in the taking of a life. Then he admitted he was starting to question his faith when he found he wanted Long to die. Everyone felt better without him around, the weight of his conscience weighed on them also.

"We've got to come up with a better escape route," Alizée said. "*An* escape route. The room Long's speaking in is too tight, too crowded. We need somewhere with more space. Where there's at least the possibility that Nathan can get away."

"We've already been through that." Bertha sighed. "It's the only place we know for sure Long's going to be. What are the choices? Should Nathan follow him around the city with a gun in his pocket?"

"What you don't seem to understand, Alizée," Nathan added, "is that I *want* to do this. I'm an old man, my wife's gone, my kids grown." He puffed out his chest. "It will be the crowning achievement of my life."

She wasn't convinced. They'd agreed Nathan would be the face of the project, that it wasn't necessary to put more than one person in danger. Nathan had the gun. He was the sharpshooter. He wanted to do it. But maybe there was another way.

She thought about her last encounter with Long, how he'd smiled into her eyes, looked admiringly at her chest, called her beautiful. And she had the answer: she would be a decoy. The carrot to bring Long somewhere Nathan wouldn't be such a sitting duck. Granted, there was the risk that whoever was watching her might follow her there. But she could be cautious. Take a circuitous route.

"What if I asked Long to meet with me?" Alizée said, thinking out loud. "At that last AFC meeting, when I was pretending to be a reporter, remember? He told me to contact his secretary if I ever wanted to continue our conver—"

"If you're so afraid for me, why would you want to put yourself into the mix?" Nathan interrupted.

"I could set up an interview for the evening of the speech." She was warming to the idea. "At night. In some bar or restaurant . . . Near his hotel so he'd have to walk over. Alone. In the dark."

"But there is your incident about the memo. What if he is remembering that?"

Alizée waved her hand at Aarone. "He doesn't know anything about it because nothing ever came of it. Ditto with ANL. And me. He thinks I'm a reporter. Has no idea what my real name is."

"That's a great idea," Bertha said, her eyes gleaming. "It sounds like the Shadow and decoder rings, but Nathan could be waiting in an alley — an alley with an entrance and an exit — and he'd know what time Long will be there." She turned to Nathan. "We'll find a restaurant that fits that description, and you could get him on the way out. After the interview. And then you'd be able to get away."

"What about Alizée?" Nathan asked. "How would she get away?"

"I wouldn't need to get away. I'm just a reporter interviewing the assistant secretary of state, who leaves when he does, walking in the opposite direction. And even if someone checked — which is unlikely — it's going to be difficult to track down a Miss Babette Pierre who works for the *Sun.*"

The arrangements went more smoothly

than she could have imagined. Long's secretary got back to her within a few days to set up a time for the interview, explaining that Mr. Long remembered Miss Pierre and was looking forward to talking with her again. He was staying at the Waldorf-Astoria but would be happy to meet her at the time and location she'd suggested: the Haven Tavern and Restaurant on Lexington at 5:00 pm. Alizée hoped no one would bother to check on her affiliation, or nonaffiliation, with the *Sun.*

This time, for her reporter impersonation, she dressed up rather than down. She added an orange scarf with black polka dots to partially hide the suggestively low neckline of her black silk blouse, a birthday present Tante had sent the first year she was in New York. When things were so different. She fingered the shimmery lapel, and tears filled her eyes. Where was Tante? Where were the others? She whipped her head back and forth. This was no time for easy emotion, for self-pity or doubt. She may have failed at her first attempt to get rid of Long, but she wouldn't fail tonight.

Instead of going out the front of her building, she slipped down the back stairs and left through the alley door. She forced herself to walk at a leisurely pace as she switchbacked between blocks until she reached a subway station she'd never used before. When the train arrived, she stood on the queue for a particular door, then darted to the next car at the last moment. Although she was pretty sure no one had followed her, she changed subway lines three times before finally arriving, quite pleased with herself, at Lexington Avenue. She tried not to but couldn't keep from looking into the alley between South Brookside and Park, but of course Nathan wasn't there yet. Or if he was, he was hiding himself well.

Long was already inside the restaurant waiting for her. When he saw her, he stood and pulled out the chair next to him at the table. "Miss Pierre," he said, "I can't tell you how pleased I was to hear you wanted to interview me. After our last conversation, I admit I was surprised."

She smiled at him, completely calm. She believed what they were doing was necessary. A necessary evil perhaps, but an acceptable bargain. Thousands of innocent lives saved. One not-so-innocent lost. "If I only interviewed people whose views I agreed with, I'd be a damn poor reporter."

"According to that description, there are a hell of a lot of bad reporters out there." He was handsome in an ordinary-looking way, tall and lean with intelligent dark eyes.

"Glad not to be considered one of them." As she took off her coat and rearranged her scarf, she noticed him glance at her cleavage. Good. Let him look. Let him enjoy himself, grow inattentive, complacent. Then she would close down the interview at five forty-five. He would go to the left, she to the right.

"Neither a bad reporter nor too hard on the eyes."

She opened her notebook. So far, he appeared to accept her for whom she presented herself to be. And her job was to keep it that way, to make the interview feel normal to him, to raise no red flags. And to send him back to his hotel on time. "Will you join me for a drink, Secretary Long?" she asked, again dropping the "assistant" from his title.

He ordered a Scotch on the rocks and she a beer, which she planned to sip very, very slowly.

"How did your speech go today?" she asked.

"I was quite pleased with the reception, thank you." He took a swallow of Scotch. "But I'm guessing you wouldn't have approved of the content."

"You seem to be quite certain of who I

am and how I think based on a very short conversation."

"Am I wrong?"

"Not necessarily wrong on the face of it, but my questions go deeper, my uncertainties, too." She looked at him over the rim of the beer mug she wasn't drinking from. "And I enjoy delving into the many sides of an issue. Especially with an intelligent, well-informed adversary."

"Are we indeed adversaries?" He winked at her. "I'd like to think we might be friends."

"Not necessarily mutually exclusive," she said. "But I'll be candid with you, as I hope you'll be with me. My family's originally from Arles, so of course I'm worried about my grandparent's homeland, about the French populace. You may not want us to get involved in the European War, and frankly I don't either. But my concern isn't with soldiers and guns, it's with those blameless people running from Hitler with nowhere to go."

"I understand completely." Long leaned back in his chair and finished off his Scotch. "And I'm glad to hear you're not in favor of rushing our boys onto the battlefield."

She got him talking about all the reasons the United States must remain neutral, taking copious notes, flattering and flirting gently with him.

He ordered another drink, downed that one pretty quickly also, become loquacious, dropping names, hinting at promises of higher office. It was all working perfectly until a waiter brought a telephone to the table.

"Assistant secretary Long?" the man asked, unfurling the long cord, his face flushed with the weight of his responsibility. "There's a call for you." He lowered his voice. "From the White House."

Alizée went rigid. They'd only been talking for fifteen minutes. Nathan wasn't expecting Long for another half an hour. This couldn't be. She could not fail again. Would not. She lit a cigarette and took a long swig of beer, trying to act naturally while her mind flew in a million directions. Act like a heroine.

Long frowned self-importantly when he hung up the phone. He waved for the waiter to take it from him and said, "I'm so sorry, Miss Pierre, but I'm afraid we won't be able to finish our interview. As you heard, that was a call from the White House, and I'm needed back in Washington immediately." He clucked his tongue but didn't appear displeased.

She removed the scarf from around her neck and pouted. "But I have so many more questions for you, Secretary Long. Could you possibly give me just a few more minutes?" She gazed into his eyes, and he hesitated. "I want so much for our readers to understand, truly understand, your positions. The deep thought and reasoning behind them."

For a moment, Long looked wary, and she thought she'd overstepped, but then he said, "There's nothing I'd like to do more."

She raised her pen. "Wonderful. I'm sure we can finish up quickly."

But instead of settling back into his chair, he sucked the last of the Scotch from the ice cubes, took a lingering look at her breasts, and stood. "Unfortunately, in my position I often don't get to do what I want. Perhaps you could ask your paper to send you down to the capital so we can finish at some other time?"

She drew herself reluctantly to her feet. She had no idea if Nathan was in position. She had to slow Long down. A minute could be the difference between success and failure. She held out her hand and smiled up at him. "I'm so sorry you have to leave, but obviously an important man like yourself has grave responsibilities."

"Thank you for understanding." He took her hand and held it longer than necessary, which was just fine with Alizée.

She pressed her left hand over his right as she scrambled for ways to keep him in the restaurant. "And don't worry about the bill. I'll pay for the drinks. You hurry on."

"Absolutely not," Long declared, waving at the waiter. "I'm never in so much of a hurry that I'd let a lady as lovely as you pay for her own drink."

"No," she protested. "I set up the interview and I'm —"

"I won't have it any other way." But he didn't wait for the bill and instead placed two dollars on the table. Then he put on his hat, touched the brim, and started toward the front door.

"Wait!" she called out.

Long turned, and Alizée saw annoyance mingling with wariness: she had indeed overstepped. "Yes?" he asked.

"I'll walk out with you," she said. "Hold on." She slowly wrapped her scarf around her neck and handed him her coat. He had no choice but to hold it for her as she fumbled a few times to find each sleeve. After she buttoned it, she took his elbow, smiling up at him again. "Thank you, kind sir."

He nodded and walked her briskly to the door.

The cold December wind hit them when they reached the sidewalk. Long pointed to the left. "I'm sorry again that I have to rush off, but I really must get to my hotel as soon as possible."

There was nothing she could do but go to the right.

44
ALIZÉE, 1940

A gunshot. A second and then a third. Alizée had never heard the sound before, but she had no doubt what it was. She pressed herself into the recessed doorway of a small haberdashery a block down from the Haven. She should keep walking, that was the plan, to get away as quickly as possible.

But there was only supposed to be one shot. And already there were sirens. So fast. Was he dead? What about Nathan?

She crossed the street and circled back toward the restaurant. A crowd forming. A woman screaming. A body lying at the mouth of the alley, but moving, trying to sit up. He wasn't dead. For a moment, she was relieved, then realized she shouldn't be. But she was. And wasn't. Where was Nathan?

She was pulled toward the commotion. A bad idea. The murderer returning to the scene of the crime. But she wasn't a murderer. Not yet at least. Maybe never. Again the relief. Then devastation. Tante. Alain. The little girls.

She elbowed herself closer to Long. He was sitting up, clearly not dead, but bleeding. A man held a wadded shirt to his shoulder. They were talking. Not dead. She had to go before he saw her.

As she worked her way toward the edge of the crowd, she suddenly froze. Nathan. Maybe five people separated them. Their eyes met, held, horrified to see each other, horrified at what had, and hadn't, happened, sending silent messages to run. Run quickly. She turned back toward the way she had come, caught a glimpse of Nathan turning the other way.

Then a shout. "That's him!" a woman yelled. "He came out of the alley!"

Alizée kept walking.

She couldn't go to her apartment. Couldn't go to Mark's or Lee's. Couldn't go to any of her usual haunts. They might be looking for her, maybe even following her. Her mind spun with empty possibilities. She couldn't go to Gideon either. He'd be furious at them for the attempt, for keeping it a secret, for failing. She couldn't face his wrath or the hysterics sure to follow. She needed someone calm. Someone who might be able to help. So she took the subway to the ERC office, hoping Mr. Fleishman would still be at his desk. He was.

He nodded absently when he saw her in the doorway, but when she closed the door and told him about Long, he went rigid with attention. "You tried to kill Breckinridge Long?" he whispered. "With Americans for No Limits? I can't believe this. What were you thinking?"

She raised her chin. "That would have saved thousands of lives."

"Gideon Kannel approved this?"

"We didn't tell him."

"You didn't tell him," Mr. Fleishman repeated slowly, as if saying the words would give them meaning.

She sat in the chair opposite him. "I think they caught Nathan. They must have. He was right there."

"My God, Alizée. Do you understand what you've done? The repercussions? The police, the government, they're not going to let this be. They're going to investigate every connection." He ran his hands through his hair. "Breckinridge Long, for Christ's sake. A goddamn assistant secretary of state."

"That's why I came here." Seeing their plan through Mr. Fleishman's eyes was throwing her into a panic. "I . . . I couldn't go home. Or to anyone involved with ANL."

"You've got to leave the city. Immediately."

That made sense, but it was impossible. The murals. Mark. If the visas came through, she had to be here. *If we do not get out now, we will die.*

"This isn't negotiable," Mr. Fleishman declared. "I should call the police right now."

Her chest tightened, and her breath came in short gasps.

"You promise to leave and I'll pretend we never had this conversation."

All she could do was stare at him. She had nowhere to go.

"I can't, the ERC can't. We can't get involved in this. There are too many people depending on us to take that kind of risk."

She knew he was right, was sorry she'd come. What would become of her? Of her family? She tried to stop it, but a tear rolled down her cheek. And there were many more behind that.

"Okay," he said. "Okay, don't cry. What's done is done, and we can be thankful that it sounds like he's going to live, that there's no direct connection between you and the shooting. Right?"

"No." She shook her head, then caught herself and nodded vigorously. "I mean yes.

Yes, that's right. No connection. Not really. His people knew I was meeting him at the restaurant, but they . . . they think my name is Pierre and that I work for a newspaper."

"Pierre?"

"Babette. Miss Babette Pierre. She's my cousin and he's her husband. His first name is Pierre and hers is Babette. So I combined them —"

"Alizée," he said sharply. "Do you have any family or friends outside New York? Someplace you could go where the police wouldn't think to look for you?"

"Everyone I know is here. There isn't —" Except she did have family outside New York. And they were in a place no one would ever think to look for her. "I . . . I could go to France."

"That's even more dangerous than staying here," Mr. Fleishman said dryly. "I'm sure there are other solutions that don't —"

"I have money," Alizée interrupted, her thoughts narrowing, growing focused. "Quite a lot actually. The three hundred you returned. The rest from the ring. Mrs. Roosevelt's paintings. I can use it to bribe officials, for visas, to get us all back here. I can —"

"Money doesn't matter as much as you'd think. It's almost impossible to get anything

407

done over there — with or without it."

"You're using money to get people out."

"Not easily and not in all cases. Plus the ERC's an organization, not a lone individual." He shook his head. "It's too risky. Complete folly."

"Your Varian Fry's in France, and he's perfectly fine."

"He's not a girl. Or a Jew."

Suddenly, everything took on a startling sharpness. The streetlight slicing between the edges of the venetian blinds was blindingly white. Conversations on the sidewalk outside fully audible. The bitter odor of old coffee lining Mr. Fleishman's empty mug. This could work. With Varian Fry's help, and some luck . . .

"Varian's having a lot of trouble," Mr. Fleishman was saying. "The Vichy police watch him constantly. Often, they refuse to issue exit visas even when he has US entrance ones in hand. He's hunkered down somewhere in Marseille, hiding people, trying to get them out of France legally or send them through Portugal and Martinique. The authorities harass him and wait for him to make a mistake so they can expel him from the country." He gave her a steely look. "With you, it would be much worse."

All those months of indecision were gone

in a flash of clarity: this was the heroine's choice. "Tell me where he is and I'll go to him. I have more money than I need for my family. I'll share what's left with him. With the ERC. We'll all be able to help each other."

"He's not going to be able to help you, and you're not going to be able to help him," Mr. Fleishman insisted. "All his visas are already assigned. And you've got no business running around a war zone on a fool's mission."

"I'm fluent in both French and English. I can translate for him. I know the country. I'm sure he'll find lots of ways I can be useful."

"That's not the point. Varian's got his hands full." Mr. Fleishman crossed his arms over his chest. "And how exactly would you get to France anyway?"

"How did he do it?"

"He flew. On an American passport with Eleanor Roosevelt's support."

"I have Eleanor Roosevelt's support," she said, although of course she didn't anymore. "She bought two of my paintings. Invited me to Hyde Park."

"You know Eleanor Roosevelt?" He was clearly astonished. "Paintings?"

"She came to my flat to buy them. I'm an artist."

"Can you contact her? Tell her what happened . . ." He shook his head as if to clear it. "Of course you can't."

Of course she couldn't. "But I have an American passport," she persisted. "And enough money to take a ship."

"There aren't many ships still carrying regular passengers."

"But it sounds like there are some."

"I shouldn't be doing this," he mumbled as he began to flip through files on his desk. "But I'll make some calls. Find someone who can put you up for a few days. That way you can take some time to sort through all the options before you make any decisions about which one's the best."

"This is the best option."

Mr. Fleishman looked at her, and she saw both sorrow and compassion in his eyes. "I'd like to help you, Alizée. I really would. What you did was wrong, but you're just a kid. A desperate kid trying to make your way through an unendurable situation. But I promise you, this is going to be even more unendurable. And I'm begging you not to do it."

"My mind's made up."

"It's no way to protect yourself. And not

the way to help your family."

She saw he was weakening. "It may be the only way left."

He sighed and stopped looking through his files.

"I can do this," she said. "And I'm going to do it with or without your help."

"Please think this through. Take a little more time."

She shook her head.

Mr. Fleishman raised his hands in a gesture of surrender. "I've got to be out of my mind, but fine, okay. I'll give you Varian's information and some papers that should help you reach him. But only because if I don't, you'll have no chance at all."

"Thank you," she said. "I'll make it work."

He hesitated, clearly wanting to continue his warnings, holding himself back. *"Gyyn myt g'át,"* he finally said. Go with God.

Within an hour, Mr. Fleishman had found a temporary apartment and someone, as he said, "to keep her safe." Her guardian angel, a man named Sy Lubin, would periodically patrol both the building she was staying in and her flat, as well as accompany her anywhere she needed to go. Which was to be as few places as possible. Mr. Fleishman also told her that under no circumstances was she to let anyone know where she was or where she was going.

The magnitude of his concern and the swift pace of the changes were disorienting. Mr. Fleishman confirmed that Breckinridge Long had taken a shot to his shoulder and was expected to make a full recovery, that Nathan had been arrested, that an assassination attempt on a federal official was a crime that would be pursued to the full extent of the law, perhaps even meriting the death penalty.

And she was on the run, a fugitive, in hiding. On her way to France. Everything she'd done over the past three years, everyone she'd known, set aside. Left behind. Images of New York jumbled with those of Arles, Cambridge, the French countryside. A kaleidoscope of times and places. Faces. Which had come first? Which were real and which imagined? Had she dreamed a train ride through rolling green hills? Standing in an enormous room with a Persian rug and cobalt-blue curtains? Shooting a man in the head?

She was still uncertain when Sy Lubin came to the ERC office to take her to the apartment. A man of few words, he didn't tell her anything about himself and didn't ask any questions. He was wide-shouldered, thick, with the look of a longshoreman, which for all she knew, he might be. The apartment was small and well furnished, the home of a vacationing colleague of Mr. Fleishman's, a vast improvement on her own living situation. Then she wondered why she had thought this. Her bedroom in Arles with its French provincial furniture and bright yellow rug was nicer than this. As was Tante and Oncle's big house.

She gave Sy the key to her flat, and he returned with some clothes, her passport, the paint can containing her $573, and a corned-beef sandwich. She gulped it down, surprised she was so hungry. Tante had made a wonderful brisket that she'd devoured just a few hours ago at lunch.

When he asked if she needed anything else, she hesitated. She desperately wanted to be alone and just as desperately didn't want him to leave. She shook her head, and he walked out the door. She took a blanket and broom from a tidy closet and pressed herself into the alcove next to the front door, blanket across her shoulders, broom across her knees. If they came for her, they'd expect her to be in the bedroom. This way she'd see them first and smack them with the broom before they knew what hit them.

A heroine's plan. She stayed up all night, waiting.

The next morning, Sy purchased her ticket. She put it in the paint can along with the rest of the money and the papers to help her find Varian Fry. But her movements were awkward and rigid, controlled by someone else. She heard Sy explaining that she was not to leave the apartment until he came back after his shift, but it was as if she were eavesdropping on another person's distant conversation. The words had nothing to do with her.

As soon as she was alone, she called Mark. She couldn't leave without seeing him one more time. She told him she was working at the flat and if he had a few free minutes she had an idea of how he might like to spend it. He said he'd be over in less than an hour. If she left now and hurried right back, Sy would never know she'd been gone.

They made love, and it was incredibly pleasurable and incredibly sad. She watched them from above, but she lived within the sensation, the deep wetness of his kiss, the length of his body pressed along hers. She was of two states, split apart, splintered from her core. She loved him, and she was going to vanish from his world, disappear

414

without warning. A cruelty of mammoth proportions. But she was actually doing him a favor. He deserved someone who was whole.

She wrapped her legs around his waist and pulled him even more tightly to her. She gasped and fell back into herself as he touched a spot deep within her. The sensation obliterated all sound, all thought.

Mark groaned, shuddered, and then lay still. He kissed her lightly on the lips. "I love you."

She jumped up and started to dress, as aware as she had been unaware only a moment before. She had to get back to the apartment. Fast. This had been a mistake. What if she'd been followed?

"What is it?" Mark asked. "Why so jumpy?"

"Not jumpy. Just busy."

Mark sat up and pulled on his pants. "I've got to get back to work, too," he said. "But I need you to come by when you get a chance. I need a critique. I'm doing something new and need to talk it through."

Alizée buttoned her shirt, missed a button, started all over again, her fingers fumbling, not moving under her own volition, suddenly damp with sweat. She would not be coming by. Might never be coming by. "What new?"

"The big canvas. Like yours. I wanted to give it a try, but something's off."

She grabbed a pair of overalls from the pile of dirty clothes on the floor. What had she been thinking? They could be outside the door. "Your color blocks?" she asked vaguely.

"I'm not using the scale to its best advantage."

"Scale, scale," she repeated as she climbed into the overalls, trying to grab on to his meaning. "The thing is, the big canvas, well, it dwarfs the viewer. The image is all there is."

"Which is why it seemed perfect for my blocks. People want to dismiss them like that idiot at the *Times* who said they were something 'a housepainter could do,' but if the scale's larger maybe people won't be able to walk away as quickly. They'll have to stay, even for an extra minute, and look. See the vibrancy. That it's not static. That it's alive."

"Yeah, that's good." She would use a different route back to the apartment. Wear a different coat. Then they wouldn't know it was her. "You'll hit them between the eyes."

"But I don't think the painting's as powerful as its size," Mark said. "And I don't know why."

She could do this last thing for him. She closed her eyes and visualized one of his color block paintings. She distorted the canvas into a taller and wider version of itself, then added more canvases that grew progressively bigger. She made them dance with each other so she could see them from all angles. "Are you keeping the shape of the blocks the same?"

"Yes," Mark said slowly.

"Well, maybe you shouldn't." She clicked the overalls shut and reached for her boots. A hat. The big floppy green hat. It would hide her face. She'd look completely different than when she came in. "Make them wider, maybe more square than rectangular."

"Or narrower . . ."

"Try both." She yanked her spring jacket off a hook, too light for December, but it would have to do. "See what happens."

He kissed the end of her nose. "You haven't even seen the damn thing and you've got better ideas than I do about how to fix it." He buried his face into her neck. "I don't know what I'd do without you."

She pulled away and pushed him toward the door. "Shoo," she said. "I've got work to do and so do you."

But as with Mark, she couldn't leave without a final good-bye to *Montage*. She turned in a semicircle, scanning the four canvases, taking in the elements that gave it power: the colorations, the juxtapositions, the fragments of style and imagery she'd put together in unusual combinations, the sand she'd mixed into the red paint. It was part of her. Her art. Her family. Her hopes. Her passion. Her doppelgänger.

She grabbed a small pot, filled it with water, pulled the plug out of the Philco and put it into the hot plate, turned it on. She'd have a cup of tea, stay with *Montage* a moment longer, love it like she'd just loved Mark, let it go, too. It broke her heart, but she knew Mark and Lee would take good care of it until she got back. If no one got to it first. *Merde.*

The mural was in danger just as she was.

It needed protection. The police, Long's people, the isolationists, who knew who else. They were going to come after it the same way they were coming after her. Perhaps kill it as they wanted to kill her.

She grabbed a screwdriver and a bread knife. She approached #1, lifted it from its easel, stopped. How could she? How could she not? She was the heroine. She'd accepted the part. It was her responsibility to rescue everyone. It was her role.

She quickly removed the canvas from its stretchers, taped the edges to the floor, lifted the knife. Better in pieces than dead. With a rapid slash of the blade, she sliced the canvas from top to bottom. She did it again in the opposite direction. She did the same to #2, #3, and #4. Sixteen two-by-two-foot squares. Fragmented, but still alive.

Then she noticed her other politicals, her reversals. They thrust themselves at her, called to her, beseeched her: we are you, too.

Her body of work. She couldn't leave them here to die either. She took the two cloth bags she used for shopping and put eight squares in each, hefted them to her shoulders. Unwieldy, but she could make it to the ERC apartment. It was only thirty blocks. But it was all she could carry. She would drop these off and return for the others.

45
MARK

Louise confided in Becky, who was so appalled at her friend's revelation that she told her boyfriend, Phil, and it was Phil who informed Mark when he got back from Alizée's. Mark was also appalled. He'd never liked Louise, no one but Becky seemed to, and even Becky was sure to avoid her after this. How could she do such a thing to a fellow artist? And how did she find out about the mural switch in the first place?

He had no answers to these questions as he raced back to Alizée's apartment. He'd been gone for almost an hour. What if someone was already there? Scaring her? Hurting her? Taking *Montage* away? But no, Phil said Louise hadn't contacted anyone until this morning. There hadn't been enough time. He slowed down, tried to figure out how to break the news.

When he turned the corner, Alizée was hurrying away from her building. He ran to catch up with her. She had a bulging cloth bag over each shoulder, was slightly bent forward beneath the weight. And why was she wearing that ridiculous green hat? He grabbed her arm.

Alizée spun around, her eyes full of fright. When she saw it was him, relief flooded her face, but the fear quickly returned. "What is it?" she demanded. "What's wrong?"

Even though no one was in earshot, he pulled her closer. "I've got some bad news."

Alizée's hand flew to her throat. "They found me? They know what we did?"

"Found you? Who? No, it's nothing like that. It's about *Montage.*"

"Oh, oh. Okay. Good."

"No, it's not good." Mark took a deep breath. "It's Louise. Bothwell. Somehow she found out about *Montage* and the plan to swap it."

Oddly, Alizée appeared almost pleased by this news. "How could that be? Only the five of us know about it, and no one would ever say anything. Especially not to her."

"Maybe she overheard something. Put things —"

"Jack," Alizée said. "It had to be Jack."

"That occurred to me."

"It wasn't Lee or Bill."

"He'd only have said something if he were

drunk . . ."

Alizée nodded.

Mark hated to think this, but knew it was the most likely explanation. "What matters now is that Louise told someone high up at the WPA. And as wild as it sounds, whoever she talked to said he was going to call the police."

Alizée took both bags from her shoulders and held them out to him. "Here's *Montage,*" she said. "I need you to hide it."

"What?" He looked in the bags, and it took him a moment to realize what he was seeing. No. She hadn't. She had. "What the —"

"It'll be fine. Like Humpty Dumpty."

"Humpty Dumpty?" Mark repeated, his stomach clenching. This was bad. "Alizée, please, you're not making sense."

She glanced behind her, behind him, across the street. "Just take them," she hissed. "Give some to Lee, to Bill, to Jack. Split them up. Hide them. I'll put them together when I come back."

"Come back?" Mark dropped the bags and grabbed her by the shoulders. "Come back from where?"

"Pick up the bags!" Alizée twisted from his grasp. "If you let them go, even for a second, they'll take them from you. Try to destroy them!"

Mark did as she asked and tried to keep his voice soft and calming. "I'll keep them safe. I promise. But where are you going?"

"I'm, ah, I'm going to the WPA office. I never got my check this month. Too busy." She looked over her shoulder again, up at the darkening sky. "It's late. I have to get there before they close."

"I'll come with you."

"No, no. You can't. You have to go to your place. Hide the squares. I'll meet you there when I'm done."

"I can do that after we go to —"

"No!" Her voice was shrill, on the edge of panic, or maybe already there. "You promised me, you promised. You need to do it now!"

"Okay, okay," Mark said. He'd follow her, stay out of sight, make sure she was okay. "You go by yourself. I'll take care of the squares."

Alizée's eyes narrowed. "If you follow me, if you don't hide the squares, I'll never forgive you."

Mark bowed his head in defeat. "I'll be waiting at my place." She knew him too well.

46
ALIZÉE

Dusk was seeping out of the city. The sky was almost completely black, starless, leaden with heavy clouds she couldn't see. It was four thirty in the afternoon, but it felt like midnight. She moved quickly, hurrying from lamppost to lamppost, from one splatter of tepid light to the next. Her shoulders hunched against the sharp wind, her light jacket doing nothing to protect her. But she had a ticket and the papers to take her to Varian Fry. Mark had *Montage.* It was going to be all right.

When she returned from France with her family, the whole Long fiasco would be forgotten. She'd retrieve the squares and put the mural back together again. Humpty Dumpty. It wouldn't be perfect, not as good as if it were whole, but stitching the pieces would give it another dimension, a gravitas it might lack without it. Yes. She would make it even more powerful than before.

Mix up the pieces. The way Hans Hofmann had mixed up her tissue papers, rearranging them to increase the intensity.

A blast of cold threatened to steal her hat, and she clamped it down hard on her head. All the king's men hadn't been able to put Humpty back together again, but that was just a nursery rhyme.

She was almost to the apartment. She would make it back well before Sy got off his shift. Good. No. She stopped. She didn't have the squares. Her hands and arms were free. She should have grabbed her politicals and reversals when Mark took *Montage.* Stupid. Stupid. Stupid. It was so important to concentrate. *"Merde!"* she yelled into the night as loud as she could. Then she flung herself around and retraced her steps.

An angry, acrid smell brought her back to the world. She had no recollection of her trip across town but recognized she was only a few blocks from her flat. It was as if she'd been sleepwalking while she was awake. She heard sirens in the distance, noticed a strange glow in the sky ahead, tried to comprehend what all her senses were screaming. She began to run, but she already knew it was too late.

When she reached her building, the entire

structure was engulfed in flames. The heat was intense, as was the smoke, and the firemen kept yelling and pushing people to the other side of the street. How could this have happened so fast? She'd been gone less than an hour.

She thrust her way to the front of the crowd. She recognized a number of her neighbors, most swathed in blankets, faces streaked with soot, either crying or staring in glazed fascination as their homes were destroyed. The black night was now filled with light, but it was a harsh, orangey light, flickering and mean.

Someone grabbed her arm, and she turned into Lee's fierce bear hug. Lee was sobbing. "Oh, oh, I . . . I . . . I thought you were in there. I was on my way home, and I saw it, and you didn't come in today . . . I . . . I'm so happy to see you."

Alizée patted Lee's shoulder, craning her neck to take in the scene, trying to understand, knowing the answer but not allowing herself to think it. She stepped out of Lee's embrace. "What happened?" she asked Mr. Schmidt.

He opened his hooded eyes wide and puffed out his chest. "Went off with a tremendous boom. Like a train roaring into the building. Or maybe a plane falling from

the sky. Only good thing, they think everyone got out before the fire got down the
stairs. Good thing you weren't home. Being
on the top floor and all. I was the first in
the hallway. Called up really loud. Banged
on some doors." Mr. Schmidt shook his
head and clucked. "And it's a damn good
thing. Never seen anything go up so fast. A
miracle, it is. A damn miracle."

"It came from the fourth floor?" she
whispered. "My floor?"

Mr. Schmidt shrugged and pointed to the
flames rising high into the night sky. "Don't
much matter now."

She followed his finger. It did matter. This
was her fault. She crumpled to the sidewalk.
They had come for her.

Lee crouched beside her and gathered her
up. "It's okay, sweetie," Lee murmured. "It's
okay. You'll come stay with me. I'll take care
of you. It'll be fine." She pushed Alizée's
hair from her forehead. "Stay as long as you
want. I'll lend you some clothes. We can be
roommates. For as long as you need."

Alizée's eyes remained fixed on the soar-
ing conflagration. A bee was buzzing in her
ear. She shook her head to make it go away.
Her parents. Their laboratory.

"What you've lost you'll paint again," Lee
continued crooning. She rubbed Alizée's

back with wide swirling motions. "It can all be remade. Nothing's irreplaceable but people. Nothing but people. And you're fine. All your neighbors are fine. All your people are fine."

Had she heard what she thought she'd heard? She tried to focus on Lee's face and failed. She blinked, tried again. How could Lee say such a thing? How could she even think it? Her parents were dead. And all her people were far from fine.

Something huge crashed through the building with a roar, sent up a wild flurry of sparks, sent Alizée back to another fire. To the smoldering ruins of her childhood. She grabbed hunks of her hair, yanked on it, just as she'd done then. She heard a shriek, a wail, a keening, and realized the sounds were her own. Just as they had been then.

Lee grabbed her by the shoulders and shook her, gently at first and then harder. "Don't do this. It's going to be okay. You've got to stop this. This isn't the end of the world."

Alizée broke from Lee's grasp and started punching her. Just as she'd punched at Mrs. Clouatre, the bearer of bad tidings, that long ago afternoon. "Are you crazy?" she cried. "Crazy mad? Crazy crazy?" One part of her recognized that Lee knew nothing about how her parents had died, was only trying to help, but the fury was so strong, a living thing inside her, and she was lost between there and here, then and now. "They're dead!" Alizée howled, pummeling Lee's shoulders. "Oh my God. Oh my God. They're dead!"

What felt like a hundred hands grabbed at her. She elbowed and kicked and tried to wrestle away from them. She broke free and sprinted toward the building, raced up the outside stairs, ignoring the smoke, the heat, swinging with superhuman strength to keep her path clear.

Maybe they were still alive inside. She could still save them. She pushed through the arms and lunged toward the front door. Then everything went black.

47
LEE & MARK

Lee pulled Mark into the hallway, closing the door of her apartment softly behind her. "Jack had some pills he called horse tranquilizers. Said he takes two and they knock him out for the whole night, so I gave her half of one. She didn't want to take it, but I forced her. She should be sleeping well into tomorrow."

Mark sat down on the top of the staircase and stared into the shadowy depths below. After a few minutes, he asked, "So do you think this was it? A real breakdown?"

Lee joined him in the narrow space. "I'm no doctor," she answered carefully, "but yeah, I guess. The shock of the fire on top of the exhaustion on top of the Louise thing on top of her family on . . . I guess I've got to say on top of her, her instability."

"She gave me those squares *before* the fire." Mark's voice was gruff with concern. "Said something about *Montage* being destroyed. You don't think . . . ?"

"No, I don't think," Lee said with all the surety she could muster. "Alizée would never do something like that. The rest of her work was in there. And someone might have gotten hurt." But what did she know?

"Tell me exactly what happened."

She hesitated.

"Tell me," he said more insistently.

Lee let out a long breath. "She was babbling, not making any sense —"

"That's not so surprising, right?" he interrupted. "Given the circumstances?"

Now it was Lee's turn to stare into the stairwell. Maybe she'd gotten it wrong. Overreacted in the intensity of the moment. Maybe he was right. Maybe it was a normal reaction to a shocking experience.

"But you don't think so," Mark said.

She shrugged. "I've never seen anyone watch their home burn down before."

"What else besides the babbling?"

Lee tried to reconstruct the events through a less emotional prism. "When she first got there, she was pretty calm, asking people what had happened. The usual stuff you'd expect. But then she kind of dropped to the ground and started moaning."

"Moaning?"

"Yeah, she kept saying 'No, no, no,' which

I guess also isn't that strange, but all of a sudden she started crying, but more than crying, howling. It was the kind of crying you'd do if you just found out someone you loved had been killed. Like a mother with a dead baby. It was scary. People started moving away."

"And?" Mark pressed.

"And then she got this crazed expression in her eyes. Her whole face changed, and she didn't even look like herself. She started grabbing hunks of her hair, trying to pull it out. And I mean really trying. All the time she kept getting more hysterical, crying louder and louder. Screeching, I guess." Lee closed her eyes and pictured Alizée at that moment. No. She wasn't overreacting. Alizée had gone mad.

"So I started shaking her," Lee continued. "I thought maybe I could shake her out of it. Or shake it out of her. Get her to see it wasn't as bad as all that. I kept telling her everything was going to be okay. Over and over.

"And that's when, well, that's when she sort of snapped. She started punching me, yelling at me, calling me crazy. Screaming that everyone was dead." Lee's throat felt thick, and tears pressed hard and scratchy in her eyes. She took a wavering breath.

"But no one was dead," she whispered. "And it was only a fire . . ."

Mark bowed his head. "How did she get knocked out?"

"That was the craziest part. All these people were trying to keep her from hitting me, including the firemen, and she, I don't know how, but she just burst out like she was Superman, knocking everyone away, and ran into the building. Apparently, when she got inside, she ran headfirst into a wall." Lee couldn't stop the tears any longer, the image of Alizée as a madwoman was just too awful. "It was so scary," she sobbed. "I . . . I didn't know what to do."

Mark wrapped his arms around her just as she'd wrapped her arms around Alizée a few hours earlier. "You did everything right," he said. "Everything you could do."

Lee didn't say anything, grateful for his kindness.

Mark spent the night on the floor alongside Lee's couch so that when Alizée woke he'd be there if she needed him. Which he was sure she would, even if she refused to admit it. He'd slept little, but Alizée had been dead to the world since Lee had handed him some blankets and a pillow to create a makeshift bed for himself. For hours at a stretch, Alizée hadn't moved, her breathing barely discernible. More than once, he'd checked her pulse to make sure she was still alive. Maybe Jack hadn't been kidding, and his pills actually were horse tranquilizers.

The morning was late in coming, winter solstice only days away, and Mark wished it would remain night forever. Asleep, except for her blooming bruises, Alizée looked as she always did, like an untroubled girl. Awake, he knew that was not going to be the case. He didn't want to face the day ahead, didn't want to see Alizée in such a state, didn't want to force her to do what must be done.

The time without her would be agony for him, not having her close, his touchstone, his heart. But it would be worse for her if she stayed. He sat up and dropped his head to his raised knees, cushioning it with his crossed arms. His beautiful, talented girl, tormented from both within and without. What was to become of her?

There was a soft tap on his shoulder. Mark looked up to find Lee holding out a cup of coffee. He'd been so deep into his thoughts that he hadn't heard her, hadn't even known she was awake.

"Here," she whispered. "I've got to get to the warehouse. There's some bread and jam

434

in the icebox." She threw a look at Alizée's still, pale form, at her face, swollen and streaked a painful purple. "Call over there if you need me. I can be back here in twenty minutes."

Mark took the cup and thanked her, although he knew he wouldn't be able to eat anything.

Lee leaned down and kissed his cheek. "I'm sure she'll be better today."

They looked at each other in silence, clearly thinking the same thought: How could she be any worse?

48
ALIZÉE & MARK

She swam upward through mud, groggy, nauseated. Her head pounded. Her entire body hurt. Where was she? A fire. Maman. Papa. No, not them. But fire. Flames inside her nostrils. Smoke piercing her lungs. Another fire? At her flat. In New York. Not Cambridge. Not her parents.

She caught a flicker of light. Closed her eyes. Kept her breathing at a still-sleeping tempo. Lee's. Mark looking out the window. His back was to her. If he saw she was awake he'd want to talk. Talk. And more talk. No talking. Too exhausted to talk. She shifted her weight. Pain seared through her skull, and she moaned involuntarily.

She heard Mark drop to his knees next to the couch. "Alizée?" he said. "Are you awake? It's me, Mark. Can I get you anything? How are you feeling? Are you okay?"

She kept her eyes shut. So many questions. So much noise. Too much noise. She affected a small sigh and settled into the pillow. He'd think she'd cried out in her sleep. Leave her be. His hand was cool on her cheek. She snuggled in tighter.

"Good morning, Sleeping Beauty," he said. "Time to rise and shine."

She didn't move.

"I've spent enough nights with you. I know you're awake. Might as well open your eyes."

She sighed, this time for real, and looked up at him. He knew her too well.

"How are you feeling?" he asked again, clearly relieved.

"Headache." She touched her forehead. A lump the size of a golf ball. She tried to sit, but Mark gently pushed her down.

"Going to have a real shiner, too," he said with a thin smile.

Disembodied images flashed at her. Mr. Schmidt. Arms. Lots of arms. Lee. The crash of falling timbers. Had this actually happened? Had she dreamed it? There was no doubt her pain was real. "How?"

"According to witnesses, you ran into a burning building and smack into a wall."

Burning building. Right. Her burning building. Smoke. Thick, black smoke. But no wall. She reached for the memory, but the farther she stretched, the faster it shattered. Leaving her empty but for the throbbing soreness.

Mark went to the sink and filled a glass with water, returning with it and a couple of aspirin. "Take these," he ordered.

She did as he asked, lay back against the pillow with another moan.

He took her hands in his. "I'm so, so sorry this happened. What a crushing piece of bad luck. But don't worry, we'll have you back on your feet in no time."

She tried to ferret out his meaning through her wooziness. "It wasn't bad luck."

He hesitated and then, with the false lilt in his voice one uses with a child on the verge of a tantrum, asked, "You think it was good luck?"

"Of course I don't think it was good luck." She bolted upright, which hurt like hell, and she dropped back down just as quickly. "I don't think it was luck at all."

"Not luck?" His eyes widened as he caught her meaning. "Oh, Zée, you don't think someone did it on purpose?"

"Why wouldn't they? After Louise ratted to the WPA? To the cops?" How could he not understand this? It was so obvious. Then she remembered it wasn't *Montage* or the WPA. It was far worse than that. The police must have gotten Nathan to rat her out. They were after her, the fire was their warning: We know what you've done and you're going to pay. Oh baby, are you going to pay.

Now Mark ran himself a glass of water. He downed the entire thing, refilled it and sat in the chair across from her. "It was probably the furnace. An electrical fire. Some other mundane cause."

"They wanted to punish me," she insisted. "To destroy *Montage,*" she added so he wouldn't think it was anything else. He might have read about Long in the paper, might put it together.

Mark swallowed hard. "Whatever it was, you need some rest, some care. You need to get away from here. Maybe go to the countryside —"

"I'm not going anywhere. I'm staying right here until I leave for —" Vigilance. She couldn't let him trip her up. "Until we've hung *Montage,*" she said triumphantly.

He covered his face with his hands. "We're not hanging it."

"What are you talking about? The fire has nothing to do with the plan."

"Did you forget that you —"

"You can't back out now. *Montage* has to be seen. Mrs. Roosevelt said so."

Mark dropped his hands. "Mrs. Roosevelt

doesn't know *Montage* exists."

Whoops. That was *Turned*. Here it came: Alizée needs help, Alizée is sick, Alizée has to go to the sanatorium.

"You cut *Montage* into squares," Mark said, his voice flat. "Sixteen squares. Don't you remember?"

Squares? Squares? It came tumbling back. Mr. Fleishman. Sy Lubin. The ticket to Marseilles. She was to sail in a couple of days. She had to think. What to do. Think. "Did you hide them like you promised?" she challenged him. Time. Time. She needed time. "Did you?"

"Yes," Mark said. "They're safe. Where no one would ever think to look."

"Where's that?"

"Behind my canvases. Taped to the back, in envelopes, between the stretchers. Lee's going to do the same. Bill and Jack, too."

She nodded, pleased. That was a good hiding place. Poor, sweet Mark. He loved her, and she loved him. But now was not their time, and she had to let him go. A tear rolled down her cheek. "Thank you," she whispered.

He knelt at the side of the couch so his eyes were level with hers. "*Montage* is a great painting. An important breakthrough, and yes, it does need to be seen, just not right now. You're a major talent, and that's why you have to take care of yourself. For you, for me, but also for the world." His eyes sparkled with unshed tears as he wiped hers away with his hand. "I know you want to do something to help, and I love you for that. I know this means a lot to you, but you need to help yourself before you can help anyone else."

She had failed. Completely. In every possible way. Let everyone down. Not a heroine. What little energy she had began to seep out of her. Leaving her limp and confused. So tired. Deep down in the blood tired. Her eyes closed.

"Please, Zée," he begged. "Let me bring you to Bloom. Just for a little while. You'll rest, you'll get stronger, better, and then when you come back we'll figure out a way to help your family. All the other refugees."

Buzzing. Familiar buzzing. Like from before. But when? In a dream or real life? No more talking. Please, no more talking. He had to leave. Let her go. She had to get to France. She had a ticket.

"We can still use *Montage,*" Mark persisted. "Put the squares back together. Show it the right way. In the right place."

She had to stop the buzzing. She needed it to be quiet. She needed silence.

"They'll take good care of you," he murmured as if he were soothing a frightened child. "Help you get your thoughts straight, your strength back."

He'd never let her leave here without him. Never let her be on her own. He'd keep her from going to France unless, unless . . . She wracked her mind. There had to be a way. But she couldn't reach it.

"It's going to be good," Mark soothed. "It'll be good for you to have some time off. With no demands, no pressure. No one pushing you. So good, so very, very good."

Quiet. Quiet. Quiet. She had to think. Think.

"I'll take you there today. And when you come back, after all that rest and time to yourself, we'll be happy. We'll do great work together. After you get a good rest."

Bloom.

"Please, Zée . . ."

He would take her there. Leave her there. She'd be free of the buzzing. Free of the police. Free of Mark.

"For me?" he begged.

She nodded, then fell into a deep sleep.

When Mark told Bill what had happened, Bill offered to pay the hospital fees, so Mark borrowed his friend Norm Gould's truck and drove Alizée to Bloom that very afternoon. He was afraid she'd change her mind if they didn't go immediately.

He kept shooting glances at her as he navigated the barren hills pimpled with stalks of skeletal trees. The sky spit sleet, and the roads were treacherous, but it was the pale, silent girl in the seat next to him who terrified him. He'd watched her rapid-fire changes in just the past few hours: the childish avoidance strategies, the bravado, the distortions of reality, the confusion, the paranoia. And then, suddenly, acquiescence. He didn't have any idea what might be next.

Lee had told him that when she went to the warehouse that morning, she'd found *Light in America* in shreds. During the night, maybe at the same time Alizée's building was burning, someone had broken into the warehouse and slashed the mural into hundreds and hundreds of narrow strips. Nothing else had been touched.

Light in America must have been mistaken for *Montage,* and Louise Bothwell was lucky he was too concerned with Alizée to contend with her at the moment. But contend he would. He didn't mention any of this to Alizée. If she found out she had indeed been targeted, she'd feel vindicated and refuse to go to Bloom. And targeted or not, she clearly needed help.

For the moment, she was calm, but it was most likely a wafer-thin veneer. She stared straight ahead, her eyes focused on the road, hardly blinking. Mute. But her breathing was even, and she didn't appear distressed. He hoped it would last until he got her safely to the sanatorium.

And it did. Strangely so. When they pulled into the circle in front of the palatial building, Alizée looked at it with little interest. He helped her out of the car and, an arm around her shoulders, guided her into the spacious rotunda. Again, she appeared indifferent, and he steered her toward a desk at the back of the chamber where a receptionist sat.

He explained that he'd called earlier, that they were expected, and she escorted them to a small room whose walls could barely contain a metal desk and two chairs. "Please take a seat," she said. "Someone will be with you shortly."

Mark looked pointedly from the receptionist to Alizée. "As quickly as possible would be best."

She nodded and made sure the door was securely latched behind her.

Alizée sat with her hands folded on her lap, as if at a station waiting for a train.

Mark wondered if this was yet another explosion, the reverse of the others, turned inward instead of outward.

A matronly nurse in a uniform stretched tightly across her large bosom bustled into the room. She introduced herself as Mrs. Delahanty, knelt next to Alizée's chair, and waited for Alizée to make reluctant eye contact. "We're going to take good care of you, Miss Benoit," she said in a respectful yet soothing voice. "You did a brave thing, coming here, and I promise we'll help you get better."

Alizée smiled slightly at the nurse, the first smile Mark had seen in days. He felt a stab of jealousy that this stranger had a greater capacity to reach Alizée than he did.

Still kneeling, Mrs. Delahanty leaned across the desk and slid a piece of paper, along with a pen, in front of Alizée. "This says that you're voluntarily committing yourself to Bloom Sanatorium for a period of three months. Although by law we can't require this for a voluntary commitment, we ask that you remain here for that entire time, accept our treatment protocol, and" — she glanced at Mark — "have no visitors until the three months is up."

"What?" Mark exploded. "That's unacceptable. She needs to see me before that.

445

I'm her fiancé."

"Do you agree to these conditions?" she asked Alizée.

"But I can leave earlier if I want to," Alizée said, for a moment sounding like her old self.

"As I said before, you may." The nurse brushed back a curl that had fallen in Alizée's eye. "But we don't recommend it. We've found that it's best for our patients to stay with us for the full three months — if not longer." Mrs. Delahanty checked the calendar on the wall behind her. "That will be until the end of March. Are you willing to give it a try?"

Alizée took the pen and signed her name.

At first Mark was filled with relief, but then he noticed the gleam in Alizée's eye. She looked pleased with herself, a completely inappropriate response to the circumstances. He tried to console himself with the thought that this confirmed his decision to bring her here. But it didn't make him feel any better.

49
DANIELLE, 2015

I'm not sure how long I sat on that bench at Mémorial de la Shoah, but it was quite a while. When I'd cried my last tear, a good-sized mass of damp tissues was nested in my palm. I found a trash can and made my way back to the courtyard. I needed to know who had survived and who hadn't. I needed to know if Alizée was on the list. I took a deep breath and searched out Benoit on the Wall of Names.

There was Émile, *Monsieur Benoit Émile né(e) le 07/12/1863 à Marseille déporté(e) par le convoi n 64 le 07/12/1943 à Auschwitz.*

There was Rosalie, *Madame Benoit Rosalie né(e) le 06/05/1869 à Saint Avold déporté(e) par le convoi n 64 le 31/07/44 à Auschwitz.*

There was Adrian, Edouard, Jean, Chantal, Martel, Alain, Joseph, Rivka, Estella, and Arnold. Edouard and Chantal were born in Arles, he in 1896, she in 1900. Alain, also of Arles, born 1926. Edouard was deported in 1942, Chantal and Alain in 1944, all three on convoys headed for Auschwitz.

These must be Alizée's aunt and uncle, her cousin. My aunt and uncle, my cousin. A corkscrew of pain twisted inside me, and I pressed my hands to the carved letters, as if the letters were the people, my people. I wanted to touch them, to hold them, to let them know that something of them still survived. My DNA ached, and a sob ripped from my chest.

As I'd expected, both feared and hoped, there was no Alizée.

I didn't want to go to Drancy. My visit to the Holocaust Memorial the day before had been crushing, to say the least, and I wasn't looking forward to that kind of experience again. But Alizée's uncle had been imprisoned there, Grand-père, too. Perhaps Chantal and Alain, at least for a short time. So I had to go. Maybe I'd find more there than a few tragic lines carved into marble.

The town is northeast of Paris, outside the *périphérique,* the beltway surrounding the city. I thought about taking a taxi, but even with Grand's money, I just couldn't bring myself to do it. The bellman directed me to an RER station called Châtelet–Les

Halles, promising a commuter train would get me there in less than a half hour. Disappointingly fast. I climbed into a car, hoping for traffic, perhaps an accident — in which no one was hurt — but in the way these things happen, because I didn't want to get there, we arrived in what felt like a nanosecond. The good news was that I had to take a bus to reach the museum.

Unfortunately, the bus was waiting and that trip was also quick. After a short drive through a series of nondescript streets lined by nondescript buildings, we pulled up to the memorial, which appeared to be an apartment building. Excessively nondescript. I double-checked with the driver, who assured me I was in the right place and pointed to three sculptures atop a small rise to the side of the building. Apparently the camp had been an apartment complex before it became a deportation center and now was an apartment complex again. That creeped me out.

I climbed toward the sculptures, behind which steps led down to a forty-foot section of railroad track and a lone boxcar. The central sculpture was a carving of intertwined people, embodying both suffering and dignity; the outer sculptures symbolized the doors of death. After all the emotion of the day before, this left me strangely cold. I walked down the steps and along the shortened piece of track, stopping before the boxcar. Two signs were painted on it: CHEVAUX 8 and HOMMES 40. Eight horses. Forty men. Except that a flyer explained that this car regularly carried groups of four hundred to the camps in Poland and Germany.

Inside the boxcar was a small museum. Very small. A smattering of photographs, a few texts, inexpertly matted and taped to freestanding walls. No specific information on the individuals who'd come through here, who died here, or who died on the next lap of the journey. Oncle Edouard, Tante Chantal, Cousin Alain. But for a split-second decision and a bit of luck, Grand-père. Four hundred people in this tiny space? The walls squeezed in on me, the low ceiling dropped. I rushed outside.

In front of me was a street so commonplace that if it weren't for the signs I wouldn't have been able to identify it as French. Small stores and houses, working-class people living their everyday lives just as they do all over the Western world. I turned my back on the boxcar and crossed over to the ordinary, stepping into the present, hoping to put the past behind me.

But that wasn't possible. As I walked I found myself wondering when I looked into the creased face of an elderly woman if she'd lived in Drancy then. If she'd condoned what was happening in her hometown. Stood by and said nothing. Maybe even helped.

I headed toward the bus stop, passing tired shops and empty storefronts, kicking small stones on the crumbling sidewalk, the late afternoon shadows flitting like lost wraiths, ghosts walking along with me. In the streets. In the museum. In the boxcar. Permanent specters caught in a netherworld of apathy and cruelty. There would be no closure for them, none for Alizée, none for me.

The Benoits had been murdered at Auschwitz, and Alizée had disappeared, as they say, without a trace. All that was left of her life were two paintings and a handful of mismatched canvas squares. It was all so unbearably sad.

The weight of all I'd seen pressed down on me, like the roof of the boxcar, stealing my breath. I had my meeting with Jordan tomorrow, but if he didn't have anything on the squares there was no point in staying. I had no stomach for sightseeing. I wanted to go home.

50
MARK & LEE, 1941

It had been a difficult three months for Mark. He spent January drinking heavily. February was consumed by fear that taking Alizée to Bloom had been a horrible mistake — and drinking more heavily. Much of March was lost to this continuing fog of self-reproach, partially caused by, and resulting in, drinking even more heavily.

But that was all behind him now. He'd gone cold turkey a week ago, been to the barber, and bought a new shirt. He was on his way to Bloom to see Alizée, hopeful he would be bringing her home with him this very afternoon, that by tomorrow they'd finally be able to start their life together.

As he drove out of the city and into the hills, it struck him that this trip was a complete turnaround from the last time he'd traveled these roads, the catatonic Alizée at his side. Then, the weather, which had been cold, dark, and hissing sleet, had mirrored their disheartened state. Today, the red fuzz of leaves ready to unfurl softened the edges of the tree branches, promising more forgiving days ahead.

Although the hospital refused to provide patient information over the telephone, Mark was guardedly optimistic that Alizée would be well enough to be discharged. She'd been worn down by work and worry — not to mention the fire — and twelve weeks away from these pressures were sure to have built up her strength. That along with three balanced meals a day and lots of sleep. It wasn't as if she had an actual disease. Just a little breakdown in the face of extreme strain.

He couldn't wait to see her, to touch her, to kiss her, and when he pulled into the circular drive in front of the sanatorium, he was elated. All winter, everything had been so bleak, but now as the warm rays of early spring sun tickled his shoulders, he felt renewed along with the grass and trees. He sauntered up to the desk in the rotunda and smiled at the receptionist, who had the look of an old nun who'd witnessed too much in her years. "I'm here to see Alizée Benoit," he announced.

She nodded crisply and ran the back end of her pencil down a list of names, frowned, and did it again. She looked over the narrow rims of her glasses at him. "I'm sorry, sir, I don't think that will be possible. Her name isn't on today's register."

"That can't be right." Mark waved his hand, indicating the room thronging with people in street clothes. "It's visiting day, right?"

"Yes," the receptionist said carefully. "But not all patients are cleared for visitors."

A knot began to take hold in his stomach. "Please check again. She's been here for three months, and I was told that after that time I'd be able to see her."

She did as he asked, but he could tell she wasn't actually reading the names. "She's not on here, and I don't have any more information for you."

"Is there someone else I can speak to?" He drew himself up to his full height, aware his size could be intimidating, especially to a diminutive older woman. "Someone with more *information*?"

The receptionist was unfazed. She shrugged and told him she would get Miss Horning, the head nurse.

Mark paced the rotunda. It was some kind of mistake, a clerical error easily made in a place with hundreds of patients. It was nothing. It would be cleared up. But as the minutes dragged on, his apprehension grew. He rubbed his sweaty hands together and glared at the patients, some in pajamas and slippers, crisscrossing the marble floor chatting with or ignoring their loved ones. Why did they get to be together? Why wasn't he with his loved one?

An efficient-looking nurse bustled into the room and introduced herself as Miss Horning. "You are Mr. Rothko?" she asked. When he nodded, she said, "Please come to my office and I'll see about your patient."

"Why isn't her name on the list? Alizée Benoit. I was told she could have visitors after three months. She came here December 18."

"Frankly, I have no idea," Miss Horning said. "I can't tell you anything until I review her files. She's not one of my patients."

Mark grudgingly followed her into an office so fastidiously neat that it made him even more uncomfortable than he already was.

"Benoit, you say?" she asked as she opened a file drawer. "B-e-n . . . ?"

"O-i-t."

Miss Horning pulled out a file, scanned it, then closed it. "I'm sorry, Mr. Rothko, but she's gone."

"Gone?" It felt as if every bone in his body

had turned into icy liquid. He forced himself to remain upright as his brain attempted to grapple with what he was hearing. It couldn't be, not his Alizée. "She's . . . she's dead?" he whispered.

"No, no," Miss Horning said quickly. "She's not dead. She's just not here."

Now he was completely confused. "Not here?"

"She signed herself out two days after she was admitted."

"The last time I talked to him was on Monday," Lee told the group nursing their beers at the Jumble Shop. It was Thursday. "Has anyone seen him since then?"

"I went back to the apartment a couple of days ago to get some clothes," Phil said. "He was passed out. Lots of whiskey bottles and beer cans. The place smelled like a garbage dump and didn't look much better. Neither did he."

"This isn't exactly what we signed on for," Grant groused. "I can't stay with Doris much longer. She threatened to stick a knife in me yesterday." Doris was his sister. She had three kids, a husband in the navy and a two-room apartment.

Ever since he'd returned from Bloom without Alizée, Mark had been flying into rages at no apparent provocation and then, just as abruptly, spending days ensconced on the couch in his apartment, sometimes sleeping for twenty hours at a stretch, other times staring dully at the ceiling for similar amounts of time. He'd threatened both Phil and Grant and had punched Phil in the face when he asked for a swig of his whiskey. It got so bad that Phil and Grant temporarily moved in with family because they were afraid of him but couldn't bring themselves to kick him out.

"And what do you suggest we do?" Phil asked Grant. "Throw him out on the sidewalk?"

"I didn't say that. I just don't think we —"

"So no one's heard from him in the last two days?" Lee interrupted the argument, which had been going on for at least a week. She looked around the table. Everyone shook their heads.

Lee sighed. She'd been almost as devastated as Mark when they discovered Alizée had gone missing. Even though she'd been missing for three months, they'd searched for her everywhere they thought she might possibly be. And many places they didn't think there was a chance in hell they would find her: the train station; the airport; the wharf; the charred ruins of her apartment building; the benches and outbuildings of Union Square, Washington Square, and Central Park; every museum, gallery, restaurant, and bar she'd ever visited and all the streets and alleys in between. Nothing.

Jack, Bill, Gorky, and the rest of the gang did the same. Nothing. Then they retraced their steps. Lee even managed to contact Eleanor Roosevelt, who promised to do everything she could to find Alizée. Still nothing.

Mark took the train up to Boston but came home empty-handed. A woman who lived in the neighborhood where Alizée grew up remembered the family — or more correctly, she remembered that Alizée's parents had been killed in a fire at their laboratory at Harvard. "A goddamn fire!" he cried to Lee, his face haggard with grief. "No wonder she went crazy. Her parents! Why the hell didn't she tell me? Tell us?"

Lee shook her head, indicating she had no answer, but she wasn't all that surprised. Alizée held her secrets close. She was almost glad that her friend wasn't around to hear what had caused the fire. The fire department concluded that it had started in Alizée's apartment, but not by Louise or the WPA or whomever Alizée thought was trying to punish her. It was much more mundane: something electrical, most likely paint and turpentine ignited by a random spark, combusting all that was left of her oeuvre. So sad.

Mark complained that Harvard was less than forthcoming when he'd visited and admitted he'd wept all the way back to New York. As soon as he got home, he burst into Louise's apartment yelling that if she didn't get the hell out of the city, he would strangle her with his bare hands. Louise had cried, begged his forgiveness, claimed she had nothing against Alizée, hadn't meant anything to happen to her, just thought the WPA should be informed that their property was going to be destroyed. Mark screamed, "Bullshit!" and punched a hole in her wall. She was gone the next day.

Lee and Mark took another ride up to Bloom, but there was no doctor on duty, and the nurse he'd spoken with before wasn't there. The young receptionist shifted terrified glances between Mark and her hands, repeating in a shaky voice that Alizée wasn't listed as a patient and that she had no further information.

The girl had good reason to be scared: Mark was a fright. He'd been drinking constantly, picking up where he'd left off before he went to bring Alizée home. His face was ravaged by sorrow, alcohol, and fury, and he didn't appear to have showered in weeks, or at least he didn't smell like he had.

"Someone's got to check on him," Lee said. "He may be sick."

Phil rubbed his right cheek, which was slightly bruised. "I'll do it."

"He might still be sore at you," Bill said, standing. "I'll go."

"You'll need this." Phil handed Bill a key. "He won't answer."

"I'll come." Lee stood also. "Two's better." As she turned to go, she couldn't help but notice the relieved expressions around the table. The young girl at Bloom wasn't the only one afraid of Mark.

They pounded on the apartment door, yelled for Mark. As Phil had predicted, there was no response. Bill raised an eyebrow and took the key from his pocket. Lee nodded, but she was squeamish about bursting uninvited into someone's private life, private space, private hell. And she was afraid of what they might find.

"Hello!" Bill called out as they entered the main room. "Mark! It's Bill and Lee. Hello?"

No answer. The couch was empty, surrounded by upended glasses as well as empty and half-empty bottles. A basement apartment, it was stuffy, overheated, and oppressive with its low ceilings and low light. She wondered how he could paint here. And it did smell like garbage. Maybe something worse.

Lee caught Bill's attention and put a finger to her lips. "Mark?" she said more quietly. "Mark, it's Lee. We just stopped by to see how you're doing. Are you here?" She walked toward the rear, calling softly, Bill at her heels.

They poked their heads into the two small bedrooms, back-to-back in the railroad-car apartment. Neither smelled much better than the living room. "You'd think they'd never heard of a Laundromat," she muttered. The silence was ominous. Why wasn't Mark here? Where could he have gone? Where had he found the energy? Something was very wrong.

As soon as she stepped into the kitchen, she saw what it was. There on the floor, in a pool of blood, lay Mark. He was faceup, and his arms were flung out as if he'd unexpectedly fallen backward. But the incisions on both arms and the two empty pill vials beside him revealed there was nothing unexpected about it.

The doctors told Lee that if she and Bill hadn't found Mark when they did, he would have bled out in another hour. When he recovered enough to leave the hospital, Edith took him home with her. It was a long time before Mark returned to the Jumble Shop.

51
ELEANOR, 1946

Eleanor received Alizée Benoit's brother at the New York apartment where she stayed when she wasn't at Val-Kill. "I can't tell you how happy I am to meet you, Dr. Benoit." She clasped his hand in hers. "I was a great admirer of your sister's." It still rattled her senses that Alizée had never been found. She'd tried to help, done what she could, but everything was going haywire then. It was 1941, right before the war, and no one had the time to help her find a missing girl. She longed to know what had happened to that lively child, so talented, so troubled. Was she gobbled up by the war like so many others? Or more likely, gobbled up by her own demons?

Dr. Benoit swallowed hard, clearly nervous in her presence. "I . . . I, too, am pleased to meet you."

She could see a family resemblance, the height and the strong chin, although his hair was dark where Alizée's had been light. "I only wish it were happening under happier circumstances," she said.

"I have spoken to everyone else I could find who might have information on where Alizée went. You are the last. I understand you came to her home and she came to yours."

"Yes. Yes, we did." It had been over six years since Alizée disappeared, yet the girl was in her thoughts surprisingly often.

The brother's face was guarded as he waited for her to continue, hopeful still. After all this time.

"I'm very sorry I don't have the answers you want, Dr. Benoit. But you can rest assured that I, and a great number of Alizée's friends, searched everywhere we could."

"It is as I expected," he said with great dignity.

"You've been to that hospital? What was it called? Bloom Sanatorium?"

"There is nothing there." He paused. "I have been many places, and there is nothing anywhere."

Eleanor started to tell him again how sorry she was, but caught herself. It had already been said. It changed nothing. "I have a gift for you."

"A gift?" His voice croaked as if he were a

boy on the edge of puberty. He cleared his throat. "A gift for me?" he asked in a more normal tone.

"Come." She gestured for him to follow her into the parlor.

Alizée's two paintings were propped up against a set of chairs: *Turned* and *Lily Pads.* Eleanor hated to part with them, particularly *Turned,* which was her reminder, along with her memories of Alizée, to stand her moral ground above all else. But the paintings belonged with the family. It was all they had of her.

Dr. Benoit knelt in front of them. He reached out and touched one signature then the other: A. Benoit. "These are nothing like the paintings she did in France. Lee Krasner gave me another like this," he pointed to *Turned,* "but it is very hard to believe this is my sister. It troubles me that I do not understand what they are."

"At first I didn't understand them either," she told him. "But Alizée taught me that just because there aren't any objects in a painting, that doesn't mean there isn't a subject. She said you're not supposed to recognize what's in it as much as feel the artist's emotion."

He stared hard at the two paintings. "I am afraid all I feel is sadness."

Eleanor wanted to reach out and hug him, take him under her wing as she had Alizée, but he was a grown man, and she had nothing more to give.

"These are for me?" he asked, looking neither at her nor at the paintings.

"I'm certain she'd want you to have them."

He rocked back on his feet, as if to put some distance between him and the paintings. "Thank you," he said after a long pause. "That is very kind. These mean very much to me."

Eleanor didn't believe him; he was just being polite. It was clear the paintings made him uncomfortable as well as sad, and he was sad enough already. But this wasn't her decision to make. "I'll send them to your home tomorrow morning. When you look at them more, maybe they'll start speaking to you as they do to me."

He stood. "I do not understand how such a thing could happen. I looked for her in New York City when I was here during the war, and I looked for her in France when it was over. Then I came back to America to look again. But she is nowhere. Poof in the air."

"You can take some comfort — and much pride — in the fact that your sister was fighting for what was right," Eleanor said. "She was a brave girl who took dangerous chances for what she believed in. And it wasn't just for her family, she wanted desperately to help everyone running from Hitler. She tried through activism and she tried through art. Her passion was a wondrous thing to see." Eleanor took a deep breath. "I failed her. Let her down. Along with many others."

Dr. Benoit looked doubtful. "You?"

Eleanor had never said this out loud, although she'd been thinking it for many years. And who better to hear than Alizée's brother? "The truth is that neither Franklin nor I did enough for the refugees. He was unwilling to take the political risks, and I didn't try hard enough to change his mind." Her voice caught, and she had the unchristian thought that if Breckinridge Long had been killed instead of wounded in that assassination attempt back in 1940, so many lives would have been saved.

"I am sure this is not true. You have done much for so many people."

"We could have saved tens of thousands, hundreds of thousands some people suspect now, and we didn't. Alizée gave me the ammunition, I had it in my hands, and I allowed myself to be silenced." She closed her eyes and pressed a finger to the spot between her eyebrows. "I will tell you that this is the greatest regret of my life."

Dr. Benoit was silent for a long moment, then said, "So many regrets. They change nothing."

Eleanor accepted his rebuke, but when she opened her eyes, she saw it wasn't a rebuke at all. It was an acknowledgment of shared regrets, of shared guilt, of a shared future that was to be lived no matter what had come before.

He held out his card. "I cannot thank you for your many kindnesses to both me and to my sister."

Eleanor gripped the back of a chair to steady herself, unsettled by her confession, relieved to have put it into words, sickened by the truth of it. She took the card. "What will you do next?"

"I have seen and experienced many difficult things, and I believe it is now time to put this all behind me. That is why we left France. Why we will never go back. There is no more past. My wife has heard Connecticut is a nice place. I will start a medical practice there, and we will start a family and have many children who will not be burdened by any of these difficulties."

Eleanor touched his arm. "Godspeed." It was all there was left to say.

52
DANIELLE, 2015

When I discovered the next bus wasn't due
for another hour, I continued to wander
around Drancy. I had to keep moving. It
was the opposite of my stroll through Paris:
nothing of architectural interest, no history
except for the ugly apartment complex
behind me, no stylish shoes. I passed an art
school, the École d'arts decoratifs, and a
few stores with dusty window displays.

I noticed a small art gallery on a corner
and glanced in. There were some engaging
pieces. Mostly conceptual: a large metal
sculpture made of paperclips and yellow
stickies, a floor-to-ceiling woven spiderweb
that took up an entire corner, an assemblage
of hats. Presumably the work of students at
the school down the block. A series of paintings along the back wall caught my eye and
I went inside.

A balding middle-aged man barely raised
his eyes from his computer when I entered.

"Please do look around," he said in English. "I can give you more information on the art if you would like to hear it."

"Thank you," I told him in my best-accented French. "I will certainly ask."

He nodded, unimpressed.

The paintings that drew me in were the only oils on canvas in the gallery. Actually they were the only paintings in the gallery, abstract but with a sprinkling of realism, jewel tones. As I approached, I saw they were two triptychs or maybe a sextych, if there was such a thing. The shapes and colors undulated from one canvas to the next, somehow flowing both forward and backward, pushing and pulling each other, throbbing with movement. Clearly influenced by the Abstract Expressionists. By Hans Hofmann.

I leaned closer, scrutinized the signature. The first initial was either *J* or *G,* the last something with lots of syllables that started with *V.* No one I recognized. I sighed, weighted down by the many sadnesses of the last two days, by my many disappointments — Alizée, my marriage, my art, the stagnation of my life — by a sudden and powerful longing for Grand-mère, for home. By grief, I suppose.

The proprietor walked over. "I see you are

admiring the work of our own Madame Villeneuves."

I straightened. "Yes," I said. "Yes I am."

"It is good, no?"

"Very good."

"She was the matriarch of a large local
family, Josephine Villeneuves. The mother
of three sons who had many sons, daughters
also. Great-grandchildren now."

"Did she study here? In Paris, I mean."

"No. She did not study art. She worked in
a bakery." He let his eyes glide from one
painting to another. "A pity."

At the bottom of the third painting an
abstracted stand of trees appeared to rise
from nothingness, magical and comforting.
Flickers of *Lily Pads*. "She's not alive anymore?"

"She's been dead for, oh, at least five
years. I like her work very much. It is always
saying something new to me."

"Are there more?" I asked. "More of her
paintings?"

"The family must have others." He perked
up. "Would you like me to inquire for you?
And these are for sale also. Alone or together."

I checked the price and saw it was more
than reasonable. A hundred euros apiece.

He sized me up as a possible client and

held out his hand. "Tristan Bazin."

"Danielle Abrams. Dani." I shook his hand. "You said she was a baker?"

Tristan smiled. No more sidelong glances. "The Villeneuves own three bakeries in Drancy. The family business for generations. Josephine, like everyone else in the family, worked there her whole life."

"She was from here?"

"She was already an old woman when I first remember her. Behind the counter, sneaking me cookies I thought my mother did not know of." He chuckled. "She was maybe fifty then, Madame Villeneuves, only ten years older than I am now. But yes, she must have been born here. Not many people came to Drancy from the outside in those days."

I figured this was probably true in those days, too.

"I can call Nicolas if you wish," Tristan offered. "Nicolas Villeneuve. Her eldest son. Perhaps he will know if she has others."

I shrugged. "Why not?" I had the time.

While Tristan made the call, I looked at the paintings more carefully. The way the elements shifted from one canvas to the next — growing, changing, sometimes almost leaping — bore a resemblance to *Turned*. Josephine had died only recently, so she must have had access to books on abstract art. Maybe found the time to slip off to the museums in Paris between baking bread and cookies.

Tristan returned and told me Nicolas was at the bakery down the street and was happy to speak to me about his mother's art. "Please come back anytime," he said, pressing a business card in my hand. "And if you have interest in any of these, I am sure we can come to a price that is mutually agreeable."

I thanked him, feeling a little guilty about his misapprehension, but I'd never actually said anything about purchasing a painting.

It was easy to find Boulangerie de Villeneuves, the scent of almonds — *pain d'amande,* I hoped — was like a leash pulling me straight to the front door. If I'd been ten miles away, it still would have drawn me: irresistible, thick and sweet and warm. Stirring almonds and butter with Grandmère, flour in my hair, crystals of golden sugar under my fingernails, how she laughed at my impatience for the dough to rise.

The shop was smaller than I'd assumed, given Tristan's description of a large family enterprise, but it was full of every luscious bread, tart, croissant, and cake one would expect from a French bakery. And yes, *pain d'amande.*

A handsome older man with a full head of curly white hair stepped from behind the counter. "You are the American asking about the art of my mother? I am Nicolas Villeneuves."

I introduced myself and explained that I'd seen the paintings through the gallery window and had to go in. "I'm an artist, too," I said, feeling as if I was an impostor, pretending to be something I wasn't. "Which is why I was so taken with her work. It's amazing that she did this without any training. She must have been a remarkable talent."

Nicolas beamed at me. "A remarkable woman."

"I was curious if she had any other paintings," I said, at a loss as to what exactly I was doing here, what it was I wanted from this man or his mother's paintings.

"There are others. Not many. And they are small. Up until the very end she is always caring for the grandchildren and the bakeries. She does not have extra hours for painting. She is strong, but she is also, how do you say? Shaky?"

"Fragile?" I suggested.

"Yes, yes, both at the same time. It is not a good thing to push her to do more. She pushes herself too much." Nicolas's eyes clouded. "She once tells me if she had another life she would be an artist, but she is not sorry. This life is for her children."

So many reasons not to paint. "Your mother's paintings remind me of another artist. Someone whose work I admire."

"I am sorry to tell you I know nothing about art." He tilted his head to the side. "Is this artist why you are asking about my mother's paintings?"

Was this why I was asking about her paintings? Hell if I knew. "My aunt, great-aunt actually, is the other artist, also very good, probably around your mother's age. I've been looking for her."

"You believe she is still alive?" Nicolas asked gently.

"No, no, I don't think she's alive. I just want to know what happened to her. She was Jewish. Here during the war."

"You come from the museum." It wasn't a question.

"Yes."

"And there is nothing there to help you?"

I shook my head and tried to keep the tears at bay.

"I am sorry for that," Nicolas said, then perked up a bit. "We are Catholics, but my

476

family is in the resistance. We are proud of this."

"As you should be." I'd heard many more people claimed to have been in the French resistance than the actual numbers supported and hoped the Villeneuves were the real thing.

"My father speaks of this only now. The war and before is not a discussion. It is only recently that we know what he and my grandfather did."

Sounded familiar. The things you needed to do to keep on living after you had seen the depths of man's inhumanity. "Your father's still alive?"

"He does not move much, but he is, how do you say?" Nicolas smiled shyly. "Sharp as a nail?"

"As a tack." There was something very appealing about this man. "That must be nice for you."

"Sometime is nice. Other time it is not. Ninety-six years and he is too much with his nose in my business."

"My mother's like that, too. Drives me crazy."

We smiled at each other, bonding over our annoying, but well-loved, parents.

"My father," Nicolas said. "He is Matthieu. Maman's paintings are in his house.

477

He would like to show them to you."

I checked my watch. The next bus was in fifteen minutes, and I'd wasted too much of Nicolas's time already. Mine also. Still, I was reluctant to go. "I've got to catch the train back to Paris, but thank you."

Nicolas looked crestfallen. "This is too bad. He likes very much to talk about my mother. We children do not listen enough."

I hesitated. It wasn't as if I had anything pressing in Paris. And looking at these paintings made me happy. Or at least happier. It was clear I could use more of that. I was also curious about an untrained artist this talented. What she might have been able to accomplish had she lived in a different place, in a later time.

"You don't think he'd mind?"

Matthieu Villeneuves appeared to have what used to be called a clubfoot. Or was it still called that? But that probably wasn't it anyway. More likely a war injury. Even though he was pulled into himself, more the shape of an apostrophe than a man, I saw immediately that he was, indeed, as sharp as a nail.

"You are the American artist," he said, speaking better English than his son. "Welcome."

I wanted to correct him, tell him I wasn't an artist at all, just a cataloguer of art, but there seemed no point. "Thank you. You're kind to let me come over and see your wife's work."

"Not kind," Mr. Villeneuves said with a sparkle in his pale blue eyes. "I am an old man and no one listens to me. Especially my children. You like to hear me talk, I let you come over."

Nicolas gave me a meaningful look and left to return to the bakery. A caretaker was knitting in the corner.

"Nicolas tells me you like my Josephine's paintings." Mr. Villeneuves's smile was melancholy. "She is a fine painter."

"Very fine. Nicolas said she never studied art. She must have been an amazing talent to do this kind of work without any training. It's incredible."

Mr. Villeneuves beamed at me just as Nicolas had, and the resemblance was strong. "You wish to see her other paintings?"

"I'd love to." I eyed his wheelchair. "If it's not too much for you."

"Renée," he called to the caretaker. *"S'il vous plaît?"*

Renée stood and pushed his wheelchair from the parlor into a wide hallway that led to the back of the house. On the wall were five paintings, which I immediately recognized as Josephine's. As Nicolas had said, they were small and appeared unrelated to each other, unlike the six at the gallery. But they were powerful, more powerful than the others. Color and emotion and light pulsed from the canvases, and the more I looked at them, the more I saw. The more I felt. Complex. Compelling. Masterful. Beguiling.

"In the beginning I told her to paint more," Mr. Villeneuves was saying. "But she said she would not."

"How could someone who paints like this not want to do it all the time? If I had a fraction of this talent I'd never do anything but."

"My Josephine was not always well. She had been through much and could make things bigger in her head. Especially about anything that reminded her of before the war. Which was when she had painted. I admired her work very much, but it was best not to upset her. She was complicated."

I nodded. One of the paintings, a study in blues and yellows, intrigued me. I walked closer, and tears pricked at the backs of my eyes. I saw, felt, my last two days mirrored in its center. But there was more than just the sadness, although there was much of that. I stepped back to get a broader perspective, and astoundingly, I was taken over by the opposite of sadness. Optimism? It was as if Josephine had painted her way out of that darkness or, more precisely, painted herself into a place where the darkness wasn't complete.

"She was also a very good baker," he added. "A very good mother. And a very good wife."

I studied the other paintings and realized that although they weren't pieces of one work like those in the gallery, they were still very much related. But the relationship wasn't physical, it was thematic. Everywhere I looked, I saw transformation. Abstracted transformation. Light into dark. In the blue and yellow one, dark into light, or at least lighter. A smaller thing into a larger thing. A tree, perhaps, returned into a seedling. A Milky Way–like spiral moving and changing, evolving, coming apart. I could almost taste the colors.

"I wish she had done more," I finally said, not taking my eyes from the paintings. "They're completely magnetic." I paused. "Life."

"She did do more."

I turned to Mr. Villeneuves. "Do you have

them? Are they here?"

"Not pictures," he said with a smile. "A family. Josephine devoted her life to us. Once there was nothing and now there is everything."

An ordinary life, well lived. I rested my hand on the old man's shoulder, grateful that I'd stumbled into these paintings, this family, at this particular moment. "Her work reminds me of another French artist. Alizée Benoit. They were probably about the same age. Josephine didn't know her, did she? Ever mention her to you?"

Mr. Villeneuves blinked, looked perplexed. I'd clearly startled him, bumped him out of thoughts of his beloved Josephine. He shook his head slowly. "No. I do not believe so."

"I came here today, to Drancy, to try to find out what happened to Alizée. She was my great-aunt. Except for my grandfather, the rest of her — my — family were all killed. The other names are listed at the Paris Holocaust Memorial, but hers isn't."

He was silent for a long moment, and I could see that my visit had tired him. "It was a terrible time," he finally said.

There wasn't much more to add, so I explained that I had to get back to Paris to make arrangements to go to New York. "I'd planned to stay longer," I surprised myself by telling him. "But the last couple of days have been difficult and, well, after my meeting tomorrow I think I'd just like to go home."

"Then I am even more sorry," he said. "If Paris cannot make an artist happy, then your days must indeed have been very difficult."

Somehow I didn't feel like an impostor this time, didn't feel the need to correct him. Seeing these paintings, hearing Josephine's story, being with this gentle man, made me feel more like I was an artist. Or maybe that I could be. "I'm staying at a hotel near the Louvre. Maybe I should stay another day or so . . ."

"What is the name of the hotel?" he asked.

"The Tonic Hotel on rue du Roule. Do you know it?"

"The Tonic Hotel," he repeated. "It is a very long time since I have been to Paris. My Josephine did not like to travel. Even such short a distance."

So much for her being influenced by Parisian museums. I took his gnarled hands in mine. "I can't tell you how much this has meant to me. I'm not completely sure why, but seeing Josephine's paintings, talking to you, well, well, it's eased the pain. A little."

"I am glad to hear this." Mr. Villeneuves

squeezed my fingers. "It has also meant much to me."

53
ALIZÉE, 1940

After she'd slept for almost forty-eight hours and wolfed down a huge breakfast, Alizée found Mrs. Delahanty and told her she wanted to sign herself out.

"I know it's not easy to be here," the nurse protested, "but with your symptoms, your exhaustion, it really isn't a good idea to leave so soon."

But Alizée was adamant. She felt much better. Mark had exaggerated her symptoms. She'd just needed a bit of rest. She would be fine. Ultimately, there was nothing Mrs. Delahanty could do. Alizée was a voluntary admission, which meant she could request release at any time. When the nurse saw there was no persuading her, she returned Alizée's things and even called for a taxi to take her to the train station. Alizée was a little sorry to say good-bye to her.

She had the key to the ERC apartment in her pocketbook, and as the train bumped toward the city, she decided she would go directly there. It had only been three days since she'd left to meet Mark, although it seemed much longer, so the paint can was probably still there. And this way she'd avoid having to go to the office and talk to Mr. Fleishman, who was sure to be full of both questions and admonitions, neither of which she was anxious to hear. Although she was still being cautious, watching the taxi driver closely, staying in the shadows in the train station, scrutinizing the passengers in the car for police or anyone who looked suspicious, she wasn't weighed down by fear. Her route had been too circuitous over the past few days. No one could be following her.

They would have had to trail her the entire time, from her flat to the Haven, to the ERC office, to the apartment, back to her flat, to Lee's, and then to Bloom. Even given Nathan's arrest, it didn't seem likely; he wasn't the type to point fingers. Even if the police had found out about the ANL connection or that Long had been interviewed by a *Sun* reporter named Babette Pierre right before he was shot. How would they ever put it together? Connect it to her? And who knew, maybe the fire had just been a fire, a faulty furnace or electrical wire as

Mark had suggested.

But most tellingly, she didn't feel the eyes. She felt free, loose, unencumbered. She was going to France. She was going to meet Varian Fry. She was going to talk to Gaston Begnaud, Oncle's friend from university, and find Tante and Alain. Go to Drancy for Oncle. Antwerp, if necessary, for Babette and her family. Bring them all back here.

The apartment was exactly as she'd left it. Her suitcase, the paint can, the blanket she'd huddled under in the living room corner. Her ship was scheduled to leave at 6:00 p.m. that evening. She took a quick bath, folded the blanket back in the closet, slipped the ticket and money and papers into her pocketbook, left the key on the kitchen table, and headed for the pier, suitcase in hand.

It was brutally cold with an icy wind whipping off the river, but Alizée didn't feel it. It was as if there was a furnace inside her, warming her, pressing her forward. Christmas lights flickered down the long avenue, and shoppers bustled by, distracted but happier than in years past. Alizée raised a hand to hail a taxi, filled with a lightness she hadn't experienced since she'd received the letter about Oncle's arrest.

But when she looked down the wide street

and saw nested mirrors within nested mirrors, infinity leading into infinity, the lightness vanished. All the storefronts and windows were mirrors. The cars. The streetlights. Reflective surfaces all, her image at the center of every one. Likenesses. Replications. Reproductions. But all different. All distorted. She was distorted. In black-and-white. Her arm raised. Her back turned. Walking. Running. She was Maman in one, Babette in another. Mark. Mr. Fleishman. A cop. They were coming after her.

A cab pulled up, and she jumped in, dropped low in the back seat so none of the reflections could see her. They would think she was going to the port, but she'd outsmart them. "Times Square," she said. Times Square was good. Busy. Lots of taxis. She'd hop out of this one, zigzag a few blocks, grab another to the ship. If they were still with her, she'd lose them in the crowd. She could do this. She would do this. They were not going to stop her.

And they didn't. When the ship steamed out of New York Harbor, exhilaration flooded through her, and she laughed out loud. She was watched over, protected, she saw that now. It was her parents. She could go anywhere she wanted, and they would make sure she would be safe. And once she found the family, they would be safe, too. *Thank you, Maman. Thank you, Papa.*

Alizée didn't laugh for long. She'd booked a steerage ticket in order to save her money for bribes and quickly found that it was nothing like the second-class crossings she'd enjoyed before. She was on the lowest deck, below the waterline, and a storm hit early on, the hatches battened down. No access to the upper decks, no ventilation, no light and lots of seasickness, a condition to which she was prone.

She had no sense of time passing, only of retching and retching again until there was nothing more to retch, but still the spasms came. She slipped into sleep whenever she could, rolling and dropping with the heaving waves, sliding her way apathetically through endless days, indifferent to her own survival.

A tiny woman force-fed her gruel. Not that Alizée cared. At first she wondered why the woman was so intent on keeping her alive, but soon she stopped wondering. As she stopped wondering about everything. She ate when the woman brought her food, drank when she brought water, used the bucket when necessary and slept the rest of the time. It was cold, then hot, then cold again, but she couldn't feel her body anymore, so the temperature didn't matter. She floated above herself, mindless and mute, a ghost.

She was in France. She recognized the landscape, the trees, the smell and the angle of the sun. Southern France. She thought this was where she wanted to be, but wasn't sure why. The tiny woman had helped her buy a ticket. To Arles, but wasn't she supposed to stay in Marseilles? Meet someone there? She pulled herself into a fetal position and rocked herself to sleep.

"Passport and papers!" a deep voice boomed.

She jerked awake. The train had stopped.

"Now!" A German soldier in full uniform. A swastika on his sleeve.

Disoriented, she blinked, tried to clear her head. She was in France. German-occupied France. She fumbled with her pocketbook, and he jabbed her in the arm. She glared at him. "I'm an American." She was, wasn't she?

He spat on the floor. "I do not give a shit who you are," he said in heavily accented French. "Passport!"

How dare he treat her like this? She was an American. She remembered now. She glanced upward to get her parents' attention and handed him her passport.

"Benoit?" he said. "A Jew?"

"An American," she repeated. She was protected.

"A Jew."

And then she was on a different train. Not really a train, although the noise and the hypnotic rocking were the same. A train with no seats, people standing so close it was impossible to sit down. She saw the tops of many heads crushed together, heard crying and vomiting and moaning, but none of it made any sense, and it wasn't worth the bother to try to work it out. She would just sleep.

She stumbled forward. Bright lights, very bright, on poles, but very dark where the light didn't reach. She thought she was still in France, but why were there so many German words in the air? She was being led, along with a bedraggled throng, from an apartment building, down a slope to another train. Where had the other trains gone? Who were all these people?

There were many angry men. With guns pointed at the people, some of whom were old, some children. Barbed wire. The angry men yelled in German and French. If only she understood the languages she would know what was happening. But the only language she knew was English. That's how it was in America.

Floating above, she could see into the cars, there weren't any roofs. Maybe it was the same train as before. Everyone standing. More and more coming until there was no room but still more and more coming and climbing into the same car. She watched herself moving closer and closer. No. She couldn't go in there. She had to sleep and there was nowhere to lie down.

A pocket of darkness to her right. A break in the barbed wire. She ran.

She was on a street. She could feel the rough sidewalk under her feet. She had no shoes, and it was hard and cold. She liked floating better. There had been a train and an apartment building, but this was somewhere else. She needed to sleep, but she couldn't sleep in the street. All the shops were closed. It was dark. She needed to sleep.

The aroma of almonds, *pain d'amande,* like a hand reaching out to her. Maman's hand. Holding the spoon above her small one, teaching her how to stir the bubbling sugar. Home. She was nearly home. She would take her mother's hand, go home with Maman, and she would sleep with the *pain d'amande.* And the challah. On the challah. It would make such a soft pillow.

54
DANIELLE, 2015

I met Jordan at the Café Mollien at the Louvre. We'd planned to eat in one of the outdoor restaurants, but it was raining and we were forced inside. Not that it was a problem to eat within view of the Carrousel garden or under Charles-Louis Müller's painted ceiling. Still, my mood matched the rain. The pleasure I'd felt at meeting Mr. Villeneuves and seeing Josephine's paintings had receded, and I was back in a funk.

But it was difficult to stay gloomy around Jordan, who greeted me with a large hug and steered me to a table near the garden. "Only the best for the friend of a long-lost friend coming across the ocean to ask me a favor," he declared.

"I already asked you the favor," I reminded him.

"You," he said with a grin, "and I are going to get along just fine."

We shared a bottle of wine — he'd acquired the habit of lunchtime wine within a few months of moving to Paris, and I was all for getting a buzz — talked about art and gossiped about the industry. It turned out that he, too, had given up studio painting. But he'd done it due to circumstance rather than a failure of will: he and his wife had three-year-old twins.

"The boys are the best thing that's ever happened to me, but sometimes I wonder how it might have gone if things had been otherwise." He cocked his head. "What about you?"

Obviously, I'd wondered often. According to a few of my professors and art buddies, I was pretty good. Won lots of contests as a kid, a number in college, had pieces in gallery shows. Some sales. I could tell Jordan I'd quit after I lost my working-spouse-with-benefits to get a laugh, but it wasn't true. My lifestyle didn't preclude a return to painting. I was stopped by the fear of putting myself out there again, living for the break that never came, hope as the enemy.

Coward that I was, I changed the subject. "How's the show coming? Still a lot of paintings outstanding?"

Jordan rolled his eyes. "Almost all the museum pieces are here. Like I mentioned on the phone, it's the small collectors we're having a tough time with. Now that they realize the value of what they have, they're getting cold feet."

I nodded glumly.

"Their paintings are the only ones that might have one of your squares, right?"

Another glum nod. A long pull on my wine.

"You haven't found any more?" he asked.

"Just another of my wild French goose chases, I guess."

"You've got more than one?"

Another long pull on my wine. When I'd told Jordan the story of the squares, I'd omitted the part about my missing crazy great-aunt being the artist. I wanted him to take me seriously and figured it was best not to appear to be a total wacko. "Let's stick with one failure at a time."

He looked at me shrewdly but didn't press the point. "There's a possibility my boss may be leaving — she's taking the fall for all the screwups. If I get her job, even just temporarily, I'll have access to the incoming paintings. I'm sure some from the small collectors will start trickling in, and I should be able to take a first crack at their derrieres for you."

"That would be great." I tried to convince myself that it would be great, that it was a real possibility. "Thanks," I added with as much enthusiasm as I could muster. "And your possible promotion. That would be great, too."

Jordan waved for the check. "Got a meeting in five. Are you going to be here long? Want to come over for dinner one night? Meet the boys and Robin? She'd love some American company."

I hesitated. Staying in Paris had seemed like the thing to do after talking to Mr. Villeneuves, but now that I was back in the city I found I just didn't have the energy. "I'm leaving tomorrow," I said. "But thanks. Maybe the next time I'm in town."

Jordan refused my offer to split the check, claiming he got a large discount, and left me to explore the museum. I halfheartedly wandered through the magnificent Cour Marly, past sculptures by Coysevox and Coustou commissioned by Louis XIV. I went to the Richelieu Wing; Le Bon, Quarton, Poussin, and Lorrain all left me cold. Rubens Hall, the Denon Wing, standing behind all the tourists ogling the *Mona Lisa*. Nothing. I went back to the hotel, called the airline, and booked my trip back to New York.

55
JOSEPHINE, 1946

"The Nazis were an aberration, *chérie,*" Matthieu said. "The entire world is horrified. No one will let them gain power again. You do not need to do this."

How could she explain? Make him understand? The beatings, the hunger, the roofless trains. Emerging from the fog, fractured and broken. Oncle, Tante, and Alain killed at Auschwitz, Babette and her family at Breendonk in Belgium. Henri escaped from the Drancy camp and never heard of again. She was alive, but she was also dead.

She'd searched for Henri everywhere she could think of: listened religiously to radio broadcasts of camp survivors, checked newspapers listings of those looking for family members, had Matthieu contact the UN Central Tracking Bureau, poured over concentration camp rolls of the dead. Henri had written that he was headed for Portugal, then maybe on to Argentina or the Dominican Republic or Palestine, so she tried to follow his trail to those places. Nothing. Finally she was forced to admit that he, too, was gone.

This would be with her always, a part of her. The privilege of keeping them alive in her memory, the grief that this was the only place they now lived. She knew she must move beyond it, wanted to, but she needed to do this at her own pace, in a way that felt safe. Or safe enough.

"I'm Josephine Villeneuves," she told him. "I have been for almost five years, and that's who I'm going to stay."

"But we don't need to keep secrets anymore." Matthieu looked at her with such sadness that she could have wept.

Except she couldn't weep anymore. Her tears had dried up. And that was good because otherwise she might have cried for the rest of her life. Breckinridge Long, recently retired after a "successful" career at the State Department, was raising Thoroughbred horses and collecting antiques in Laurel, Maryland.

"Josephine, please," Matthieu said. "Alizée . . ."

"That girl isn't here anymore," Josephine told him. "She can't answer you." *You must remember that our family is within you,* Tante had written so many years ago, lifetimes ago, with such ghastly prescience. *You will be able to carry all of us into the future.*

"This is a sacrifice you do not have to make."

But she did. She was the sole survivor, a single seed where there had once been an entire tree, the hope of renewal within her. And this was everything. More than her name. More than her art. Homage.

She walked to the window. Little Nicolas was in the backyard, crouched close to the ground, gently poking a stick into an anthill, mesmerized by the fleeing insects, careful not to destroy their home. He was Henri, Oncle, Tante, Alain, Babette, Pierre, Sophie, and Gabrielle. Maman and Papa. She placed a hand to her swelling belly. This one, too. She would protect them all in every way she could. Carry them into the future.

"Don't you see," Josephine said, turning to face Matthieu, "it's not a sacrifice, it's a choice. I'm choosing the future in the only way I can right now." She touched his shoulder, her kind husband. "I haven't given up on Alizée or on humanity. We'll let the children know the truth, teach them to be proud of their heritage. But not until I'm sure it's safe."

56
DANIELLE, 2015

The phone rang as I was packing up the last of my things.

"This is Nicolas Villeneuves," he said in a rush. "I am happy you are not in America."

I couldn't have been more surprised. "You are?"

"My father wants to talk to you."

"I don't understand."

"It is important."

"About your mother's paintings?"

"No," Nicolas said, then corrected himself. "Yes. Yes, it is about the paintings."

"Why would —"

"I come to Paris and bring you to him." His voice was high-pitched, excited.

"Today?"

"I leave now."

A stirring. A flicker of hope. "What exactly is this about?"

"My father says not to say. He will tell it to you. But I think you will like to hear."

And then I knew. "Alizée?" I asked, and it came out as a whisper.

Nicolas didn't answer, which was an answer.

"I'm at the Tonic Hotel on —"

He laughed. "I know you are there. I meet you in front of the hotel in thirty minutes."

"It has been so many years since I have heard the name Alizée," Mr. Villeneuves began.

We were alone at the dining room table, a spread of baked goods that could feed dozens before us, *pain d'amande*. I couldn't eat a thing and didn't want to pick up my coffee cup, afraid I'd drop it and break the fragile china. The air was thick with expectation. And, I sensed, more than a little trepidation on both sides.

"It was such a shock," he continued. "We believed no one was left. But after you said it, I can see the resemblance."

"Tell me." Words somehow found their way around the lump in my throat. "Please."

He hesitated.

"Just say it fast."

"My Josephine is your aunt Alizée."

Although I hadn't been able to get this idea out of my mind on the ride to Drancy, Nicolas's silence and sidelong smiles fostering my hopes, I could only gawk at Mr. Villeneuves. I hadn't allowed myself to believe it. I wanted it too badly.

"It is true," he said gently. "This is a shock to you as it is a shock to me. I only wish she was alive to see this day. She searched for many years. So hard. For Henri especially, your . . ." His voice faltered. "Your grandfather. She finally had to accept that everyone was dead. This made her very sad. A sadness she did not ever lose."

"She survived?" I finally managed to whisper. "She lived to be old?"

The old man's smile was mischievous. "And now you must call me Oncle Matthieu."

I burst into tears.

"I told my children and grandchildren last night," my new uncle said when I finally pulled myself together. "They want very much to meet you, but I said this should wait."

Wait was good. Alizée lived. Alizée painted. Alizée had a family. How could this be happening? A random stroll to fill the time before the next bus? But then I realized there was nothing random about it. I'd followed the footsteps left by my family, by Alizée. And they had brought me here.

"Of course they know of their mother's

background," he continued. "She told them all when she believed it was safe for them to hear." He chuckled. "Our second son immediately had a bar mitzvah, and our youngest ended up marrying a Jewish girl. Many of our grandchildren and great-grandchildren are Jewish, which was a special joy to my Josephine. And to me."

I had a slew of new cousins. Wait until Liz, Adam, and Zach heard. I had to call my mother. But first I had to understand. "Please tell me how this happened," I begged, then added, "Oncle Matthieu."

He settled into his wheelchair. "It was 1941. A very bad time, but people still need bread, and my father and I worked hard in the bakery. I was twenty-two, but I was not in the army because of my bad foot, and my father was too old. Early one morning, I came out of the back door of the bakery and found what I thought was a child asleep in the alley.

"But it is not a child. It is your aunt Alizée, and she is also twenty-two years old, but I do not think she weighs more than a ten-year-old. She is skinny and fragile and sick. I know she must be Jewish, escaped from the camp across the street, and I know if I do not turn her in, I will soon be in the camp also . . ."

504

"But you didn't."

"We hid her in a supply closet and nursed her back to health. My mother did most. But it took a long time. My Josephine was horribly sick, both in her body and in her mind, but we saw she was a good person, a kind person. And very strong inside. Very brave." He pressed his hands together. "We all grew to love her, but me the most."

"So she was in hiding for the whole war?" I asked. While Grand-père was looking all over the world for her, writing her letters she never read, she'd been here, in a tiny supply closet in Drancy, harbored by strangers who put her life on par with theirs. Righteous Christians, they're now called.

My new uncle shook his head. "We told the people in Drancy she is a cousin from outside Paris come to help in the bakery. She speaks very good French and has blonde hair. No one questions this, and a few months after she 'arrives,' we get married."

I didn't want to cry again, but it was hard not to. "Thank you," I whispered. "Thank you for . . . for . . . for all you did for her. The risks and . . ."

He put his hand over mine. "You do not need to thank me. Your aunt Alizée made me a truly happy man for many, many years." He points to the photographs of the family that sit on every flat surface in the room. "Still makes me a happy man." Again the shy smile. "And I know that even with all her sadness, I made her happy, too."

57
DANIELLE, 2016

It's been over a year since I returned from France. Some things have changed and some haven't. I was mostly right about the paintings in the carton: a Rothko, a Krasner, and one of the Pollocks were authenticated. The three with the envelopes on the back. But unfortunately for Christie's, it turned out the works all belong to the federal government not the Farrell family, and the government won't be making any decisions about selling any time soon. The squares are being litigated as we speak, and the last few rulings have gone in the Farrells' favor, so Christie's is happy about that. But the biggest change is that I'm painting again, an impostor no longer.

I asked Oncle Matthieu if he knew anything about the squares, and he told me about *Montage,* explained how Josephine had always hoped the squares would somehow survive. She'd never been able to trace them but did — through a fluke — find out about the destruction of *Light in America.* She was devastated by the loss of her oeuvre and mourned her work along with her family, ultimately relinquishing her art as she'd relinquished her past in order to create another life, another family.

So I took it as my mission to resurrect both *Montage* and Alizée Benoit. Jordan Washor found another square behind a Rothko sent to the Louvre, and when I told George the whole story and showed him a photo of Jordan's square, he was forced to admit there might be more here than he'd assumed.

With his approval, the public relations people at Christie's went to work. As I suspected, no squares were found behind paintings in museums or major collections, but two more did show up. One from a New York gallery owner who pulled it off the back of an obscure painting that turned out to be an early Krasner. The other came from a tiny museum in Deadwood, South Dakota — of all places — where a Pollock had hung in a back room, misattributed to an unknown artist named Louise Bothwell. Jordan discovered yet another behind a last-minute entry, and the four were sent to us on loan. The authenticators rendered their decision, and even George and Anatoly couldn't deny the truth. Pardon me for gloating.

Oncle couldn't remember how many squares there were, wasn't sure he'd ever known, but he thought he remembered Josephine telling him the mural was made up of four separate canvases. This didn't help much. Then I had the brilliant idea of going to the New York Public Library, where *Light in America* was supposed to have been hung, where now another WPA mural — about bridge repair, of all things — was in its place. Four canvases, four feet by four feet each. Sixteen two-foot squares.

A committee was appointed, and we worked the way I suppose paleontologists and archeologists do, piecing together the squares as if they were fossilized bones or shards of clay, trying to reimagine the whole from its few parts. We devised dozens of ways the mural might have been configured, but there was no consensus on which way was the right way. I had my personal favorite, but even though I'd been responsible for creating the project, I was still low woman on the totem pole, so my theory didn't count for much.

That's when I decided to repaint *Montage.* When I fully recognized how much of Alizée's life had been shaped by the whims of her historical moment, how she'd been forced into impossible choices that rendered her unable to reach her artistic potential and unraveled her mind — and that I, on the other hand, had no such impediments.

I'd given away all my art supplies, so I blew a week's salary on canvases, paints, and brushes, then started in as if I'd never stopped. I used what I knew about Alizée's style and incorporated that with the themes and subject matter Oncle had described. I imagined myself as Alizée, gathered her inside me, her toughness and drive to survive, envisaged her painting in her studio late at night. Mark, Lee, Jack, and Bill, too. The five of them working and laughing and arguing, bringing her vision to life, creating a new vision all their own.

I worked like this for weeks, pushing Alizée's talent, her passion, her desperation, into my fingers, into the brush and onto the canvas. And then, one day, I wasn't painting as Alizée anymore. I was painting as me. I was back within the smell of turpentine, the disappearing hours, the aching shoulders, and most wondrous of all, the space in the back of my brain was brimming with ideas, empty no longer.

Now I stand in Christie's Gallery 2, a

510

public space at the front of the house where badges and security checks aren't necessary. I reread the written supplement, which describes Alizée, her time at the WPA with Pollock and Krasner and Rothko, and most important, how her work provides the missing link — particularly in terms of "the big canvas," as Krasner had referred to it, and the transformation from abstraction to realism rather than just the other way around — filling a hole in the evolution of the school of Abstract Expressionism.

This is followed by a discussion of her political escapades, about *Turned* and *Montage,* Eleanor Roosevelt, the Breckinridge Long memo, the destruction of her work, and as verified by Oncle Matthieu, the assassination attempt. Nathan Heme received ten years for the shooting and always claimed he'd worked alone. Although no judgments are rendered, it's noted that while Long and his cronies controlled immigration policy, 90 percent of the visas allocated for refugees from German-occupied countries were never approved. It concludes with the estimate that had Long granted the visas, 190,000 people would have escaped the Nazi massacre.

To the side are a couple of short paragraphs explaining how the squares were found and the mural re-created, the part both Christie's and I played in the discovery, more accolades to Christie's than to me. Still, I look proudly around the gallery.

On one wall, photographs detail some of the possible permutations of the sixteen squares, most leave space for the missing ones, but two craft the seven squares into a single whole. The actual squares, including the one Lee gave to Grand-père, stretched but unframed, are lined up, one by one, on another wall.

Turned, Lily Pads, Alizée's two triptychs, and the five paintings from Oncle's house hang on the third wall. My reinterpretation of *Montage,* sixteen feet by four feet, comprising four canvases, is on the fourth. It's abstract, representational, and surrealistic all at once, colors and images and textures leaping from one canvas to the next, fusing the styles in way that was far ahead of its time.

The mural depicts the horrors of war on humans, plants, and animals as well as the greater horror of the indifference of each species to the destruction of its own. The details may be specific to 1940 — Alizée's cry to wake Americans to the fate of the European refugees — but the emotions, the themes, speak to the human condition, to the now and to the future, transcending time and place. Which is its brilliance. Her brilliance. And I now understood in a way I hadn't before, the power of great art.

Is it exactly what Alizée painted? Of course not. Does it get to the emotion she wanted to elicit? I hope so. Will this show create a place for her in the art world, give her the credit she deserves for her work, her influence, her bravery? I hope that, too.

I glance at my watch. My mother should be here any minute. Tomorrow the French cousins arrive, eight of them, for the official opening. I debate whether to throw one of my mother's I-told-you-sos back at her, this being a perfect situation for it, the grand culmination of my efforts despite her un-wavering conviction of my foolishness. Obviously, this isn't necessary, as the show says it far better than I ever could. But still. Sometimes a girl's got to say what a girl's got to say.

AUTHOR'S NOTE

A historical novel is a work of long fiction set in a previous time period. To me, the most important word in this definition is *fiction.* The life, art, and politics of pre–World War II New York City form the setting for *The Muralist,* but Alizée Benoit and Dani Abrams, whose stories are the heart of the novel, are completely imagined.

Obviously, Eleanor Roosevelt held no conversations with Alizée, nor did Mark Rothko, Lee Krasner, or Jackson Pollock. And while Joe Kennedy and Charles Lindbergh did write op-ed pieces and give speeches pushing an isolationist agenda — I used some of their exact words — they, of course, never mentioned *Turned.*

This mix of history and invention continues throughout the novel. While it's alleged that Franklin Roosevelt claimed the United States was a Protestant country and that the Jews (and Catholics) were here under sufferance, it wasn't in reference to Long's memorandum. But the memorandum Alizée carries to Eleanor Roosevelt is an exact facsimile of the actual memo Breckinridge Long sent to his lieutenants. Today he is most famous, or infamous, for this particular communiqué, although no attempt on his life ever took place.

Alizée's story begins in 1939, and because of that I had to change the timing of certain historical elements, but the details related to these elements remain factual. For example, the Emergency Rescue Committee was established in 1940 rather than in 1939, but the organization and Varian Fry did help over two thousand refugees escape from Europe. Similarly, although the America First Committee didn't hold its first meeting until 1940, it was the largest and most powerful isolationist group working to keep the United States out of World War II.

Breckinridge Long didn't become assistant secretary of state until early 1940, although his nefarious activities, unfortunately, are all too true. And while Hiram Bingham IV had nothing to do with the infamous Long memo, as vice counsel in France, he worked with Varian Fry to help hundreds of refugees avoid the camps and escape Europe, going as far as hiding Jews in his own home.

The Drancy interment camp didn't open until after the Nazis occupied France in 1940, but it was the primary site for the deportation of French "undesirables" to extermination camps; over sixty-seven thousand Jews were sent to Auschwitz from there, including six thousand children. The Drancy Shoah Memorial evolved in stages: in 1973 the sculpture was installed, in 1988 the railroad car was added, and in 2012 a more traditional glass-fronted museum was built. Although Dani was there in 2015, she visited the site as it was in 2011.

Lee Krasner, Jackson Pollock, and Mark Rothko worked for the WPA, hung out at the Jumble Shop, and along with other artists mentioned in the book, created the first true American school of art, Abstract Expressionism, although there is no hypothesized missing link in its evolution. Mark Rothko didn't begin work on his color-block paintings until the mid-1940s, but these are considered by some to be his greatest artistic contribution. Picasso's *Guernica* was shown at the Valentine Dudensing Gallery in May 1939, not July.

On the other hand, there are events in *The Muralist* that, while accurate, may not appear so to a contemporary reader. For example, it's hard to believe that up until the attack on Pearl Harbor in December of 1941, a majority of Americans opposed the United States entering the war. And many of us still have the misapprehension that the Nazis didn't begin their persecution of Jews and others until later in the war. Kristallnacht occurred in 1938, and by 1940 Austria, Czechoslovakia, Poland, Denmark, Norway, Holland, Belgium, Luxembourg, and France were occupied and under German control. We now understand the impact of this in ways impossible for Americans at that time.

The degree of anti-Semitism in this country in the 1930s and '40s is also commonly underestimated: it is indeed true that restaurants placed signs in their windows barring Jews and blacks, and nobody objected. It's also difficult for us to imagine a world in which communication could take weeks, in which there was no instant access to information about the past, in which it was possible for the First Lady to casually meet a train.

My hope is that *The Muralist,* through its particular mixture of fact and fiction, will bring this unique moment in American history to life.

ACKNOWLEDGMENTS

I love writing acknowledgments because it means the book is finally finished — and it means I get to thank all the people who helped me reach this moment. First and foremost, as always, is Jan Brogan: I love you, I hate you, I love you. For their close reading, critiques and expertise, many thanks to Jamie Chambliss, Dan Fleishman, Scott Fleishman, Ronnie Fuchs, Ilana Katz, Michael Konover, Vicki Konover, Judy Lyons, Anastasia Maronani, Cathal Nolan, Maryanne O'Hara, Melisse Shapiro, Sandra Shapiro, Becca Starr, Alice Stone, Linda Thompson, and Dawn Tripp.

Much appreciation to my fabulous agent, Ann Collette, who always believed I could do it — even when I wasn't so sure. And to my amazing editor, Amy Gash, who stuck with me and *The Muralist* through too many rewrites to count; this book would not be if it weren't for your patience, persistence, and brilliance.

ABOUT THE AUTHOR

B. A. Shapiro is the author of the award-winning *New York Times* bestseller *The Art Forger.* She has taught sociology at Tufts University and creative writing at Northeastern University and lives in Boston with her husband, Dan, and their dog, Sagan. Her website is www.bashapirobooks.com.